ELI'S
REDEMPTION

"Golf is the closest game to the game we call life. You get bad breaks from good shots; you get good breaks from bad shots—but you have to play the ball where it lies."

BOBBY JONES

A story of broken dreams
and second chances

ELI'S REDEMPTION

PAUL ATTAWAY

Published by Linksland Publishing

Library of Congress Control Number: 2022903995

Paperback ISBN: 978-1-7354016-8-3

Hardback ISBN: 978-1-7354016-7-6

Ebook ISBN: 978-1-7354016-6-9

EPUB ISBN: 978-1-7354016-9-0

Audiobook Retail ISBN: 979-8-9858404-0-7

Audiobook Library ISBN: 979-8-9858404-1-4

Book Design: Authorsupport.com

Printed in the United States of America

This book is dedicated to my father, a man I love very much, who was taken from us too early and whom I miss every day.

He told me once that a man can strive to be a good husband, a good father, a good provider, and good at golf, and that in life you could be good at three of these at any point in time but never at all four at the same time. My dad wasn't a very good golfer.

Contents

Part One: Escape

Part Two: Finding My Way

Part Three: Friend or Foe

Part Four: The Plot Thickens

Part Five: Family Reunion

Part Six: Reconciliation

Part Seven: Rescue

PART ONE

The Escape

Chapter 1

She's Alive

Charleston County Hospital, Charleston, South Carolina, Saturday evening, October 7th, 1978

"She's alive! She's alive! We found her."

The waiting room erupted as word came in over an officer's radio. "She's alive!"

The gathered crowd surrounded Monty and the boys, Walker and Eli, hugging and celebrating. The members of the press, elated, put aside their rivalries, high-fived, and hugged, sharing in the joy of the moment. For the last twenty-four hours, officers and agents from the FBI, the local Charleston police, and the State Wildlife Fish and Game Department had conducted an exhaustive search of the swamps and Lowcountry along the Santee River for Rose Atkins, Monty's wife and mother to Walker and Eli.

Amid the celebration, Eli quietly took a step back and walked down the corridor, away from the crowd, and stared out a window into the distance. Monty, sensing Eli's absence, searched for his son in the crowd and caught his profile. Eli turned and locked eyes with his father, who saw in his son's face a look of utter confusion.

Monty clumsily backed up in his wheelchair and started down the hallway toward Eli. Still suffering under the pain of a bashed-in knee, Monty was taking painkillers and was not that sharp with the wheelchair. Mrs. Babcock hurried alongside him, placed a hand on his shoulder, and leaned in to whisper to Monty.

"Monty, will you allow me to have a private word with your son, just the two of us?" she asked.

Monty had heard only part of the story that unfolded over the last twenty-four hours, but he had learned this much: he owed Mrs. Babcock a huge debt of gratitude for Eli's return. So, he consented and did so knowing he had much more to learn.

"Yes," he said. "And Mrs. Babcock?"

"Yes, dear," she replied.

"Thank you."

She smiled, patted him on the shoulder, and set off down the hall to speak with Eli.

Monty wheeled himself back toward the waiting room and pulled up alongside his youngest son Walker and Walker's girlfriend, Isabelle.

As Mrs. Babcock waddled down the hallway, Eli turned his gaze toward her, his eyes a cold reflection of a hardened heart. She slowed her pace and Eli nodded for her to approach. Standing before her was not the scared young boy abandoned to the world five years ago but a twenty-three-year-old man, broad-shouldered and weathered by the Bahamian sun.

"Everyone is saying she's a hero," said Eli.

Mrs. Babcock was standing up straight to her full five-foot-five inches, Eli's hands in hers and holding his gaze.

"I know, child."

"Everyone wants to know why I ran if I was innocent."

"There will be time for that later," she said.

"But what am I going to do?" asked Eli. "Other than you, no one knows the truth."

"Like I said, there'll be plenty of time for that later. Right now, you're going to honor your parents."

"Honor *her*?" said Eli with a vindictiveness that could cut a diamond. "I wish Rath had killed her."

Chapter 2

Betrayal

Five years earlier—James Island, South Carolina, Wednesday, May 30th, 1973

Eli came downstairs and tiptoed into the living room, where his mother was watching the Boston Pops on PBS and needlepointing. The La-Z-Boy where Eli's father, Monty, sat was stacked full of trade journals and old, unread issues of *Golf Digest*.

"Mom?"

"Yes, Eli?"

"Where's Walker?"

"He's spending the night at Toby's house."

"Mom?"

"Yes, Eli?" said Rose in a tone of mild exasperation and impatience.

"I had a good meeting with Mr. Baslin today."

"That's nice. I'm glad you think so."

Rose Atkins, a former beauty pageant winner from Muscle Shoals, Alabama, had never stopped running from her past, one mired in abject poverty, pain, and humiliation, and was determined to prove to all that she was better than her upbringing.

"Mom, I didn't do it. You believe me, don't you?"

Rose didn't look up from her needlepoint but kept stitching and hesitated before answering.

"Of course I do. I'm your mother."

"I talked with Mr. Baslin all about where I was when Kimberly was murdered, and he believes that when we tell the jury I was home, there's no way they will believe I killed her. I told him you saw me come home early that night, and even though you're my mom and the jury might think you'd say anything to help your son, Mr. Baslin thinks people will have a hard time not believing you."

This time, Rose put her needlepoint down, raised her eyes to meet Eli's, and spoke in a condescending voice of ultimate power.

"But, Eli, I didn't see you come home that night. Remember? I told the police Saturday night when they came to the house that I hadn't seen you come home Friday night."

Eli trembled with fear, not fear of the trial or of a guilty verdict, but of the woman who sat before him. He knew she'd seen him come home that night because their eyes had met as he started up the stairs. They both knew!

Rose continued. "Now how is it going to look to folks if I'm caught in a lie on the stand? Surely Officer Pearlman will testify that I had told him I went to bed early that night and didn't hear you come home. I'm not going to let anyone show me to be a liar, and certainly not that uppity nigger."

Rose's voice grew louder and louder with each word. She began to shake, her anger pouring forth from a deep-seated fear, her fear of folks learning the truth about her. She got ahold of herself, casually picked up her needlepoint, and resumed her sewing.

"But I'm not concerned about me. Goodness no. A mother's first job is always her children. I'm just so worried about how all this is affecting Walker. Eli, have you thought for one minute how all this is affecting our son, Walker?"

Eli had never felt so alone, so isolated as when she uttered those words, "our son, Walker." Wasn't he their son too?

"Eli, if you love Walker, if you love your father and me, then you'll make all this go away. Only you can make it go away. You heard Mr. Baslin say the trial may not take place till late this year. Now how can you let this hang over this family for that long? Don't you feel selfish? Doesn't it make you feel awful knowing what you are doing to Walker? What you're doing to this family? What you're doing to me? To my family?"

Silence filled the room, and it felt as if time had stopped. Eli stood there, and tears streamed down his face. Emotions he'd tried so hard to bury poured out of him. Eli was alone and scared. But worse, he felt unloved; he felt unlovable.

"Eli, in the closet in your father's office, you'll find a safe where he keeps emergency money. The combination is our wedding anniversary. Now I'm going to bed. I feel a migraine coming on."

Rose stood from the sofa, bent over to pick up her needlepoint, and headed toward her bedroom. She stopped at the bottom of the stairs, and with one hand on the railing and her left foot on the first step, she turned and stared at Eli. "I'm hopeful that tomorrow when I wake, my pain will be gone."

And with that, she strode slowly and purposefully up the stairs, her posture perfect.

* * *

Eli was frantic, his breathing labored. He looked about his room wondering what to take. Where would he go? How long would he be gone? Would he ever return? Fifteen minutes later he was backing out of his driveway, a backpack in the passenger seat and the back of his truck loaded with gear. He had packed for a hiking trip. But to where? The mountains? The Lowcountry? Would he ever see his father again? His brother, Walker? He fought back the tears. No time for that. He had to get a grip. He had to run. He had to run for his life.

* * *

Monty pulled into the driveway a little past 10:00 pm. All the lights were out, and Eli's car was gone. After another long day at the office, Monty was too tired to worry as he entered his home and walked up the stairs. He stepped into his office just long enough to drop off his leather briefcase, a gift from his parents when he graduated law school.

After getting undressed and placing his Timex watch on the bedstand, Monty quietly climbed into bed so as not to wake Rose. But she was awake and came to him and pressed her body against his, and she slid her hand across his body, gently grazing his nipples, and down into his boxers. Unexpected to say the least, but welcome, and he was too tired to question this gift from her.

Chapter 3

On the Run

Wednesday night, May 30TH, 1973,
shortly after midnight

Eli was hiding in his truck about one hundred yards off the state highway down a service road and trying to figure out what to do and where to go. The chances of anyone discovering him at such an hour along this stretch of road were slim, but were he seen, it would look awfully suspicious. Knowing it was only a matter of time before his absence was noticed, he decided not to hide where someone would look but to hide where they wouldn't—in plain sight.

So, he drove back toward the main road and headed east, crossed the Ashley River Bridge, and parked his truck in the city marina alongside the other vehicles routinely left overnight at the marina. Having worked from time to time as a deckhand, he knew his way around. He crept to the pier and saw his target, a dinghy suspended on the back of a yacht that had pulled into dock earlier that week. He lowered the dinghy into the water and set off up the Wappoo Creek passing the Wappoo Country Club on his left.

He pulled up to the dock at the end of the Morgans' place. They had already headed north for the summer and would take their time driving up the coast visiting family, friends, and landmarks before arriving in Maine, where they would stay through September. Eli pulled the dinghy up on the riverbank and hid it in their boathouse, swapping it for one of their canoes. He figured that once the police started looking for him someone would find his truck in the marina parking lot, discover the dinghy missing, and assume he'd taken it, possibly headed out to sea intent upon hugging the coastline. It was a long shot, but he hoped it bought him time. He set off in the canoe, loaded with gear, up the Wappoo Creek.

Eli wondered: *Did anyone know he was missing yet?* He knew his mother wouldn't tell anyone. She wanted him to get away. *But what about Dad?* Eli thought to himself. *Did he know yet? And what would he do? Would he call the police? Or maybe Dad would call Mr. Baslin, his lawyer. Mr. Baslin would probably have to call the police.*

Eli was struggling to think clearly. Ideas, questions, and fears careened through his brain like pinballs.

Should I try to get as far away as possible tonight? But how far could I get before sunup? The tide's heading out, so paddling upriver is going to be slow-going, tedious, and tiring. But maybe doing so will throw them off track—everyone would expect me to go with the tide to cover more ground. Hide, maybe that's what I should do. I could hide in the swamps for a few weeks until they stop looking for me and then run.

And so it went. Questions and options but no clear plan, leaving Eli to do what it was his nature to do—go his own way, against the tide, upriver.

Chapter 4

Inspiration

At the Atkins' house, Thursday night, May 31st, 1973

Monty was at a loss. No one had seen Eli all day. Monty had overslept a bit that morning, a rare event, so he couldn't be sure whether Eli had left early that morning or even come home the night since his car was gone the previous night when Monty pulled into the driveway.

"I knew we shouldn't have let him have his car," professed Rose, Monty's wife, as she slowly cut a slice of the rump roast on her plate, never raising her eyes.

The police had arrested Eli just over a week ago for the murder of his girlfriend, Kimberly Prestwick, but owing to his youthful age, he was a senior in high school, as well as to his family's standing in the community, the judge released him on bail. The prosecutor had argued that his car should remain impounded. Originally the police impounded it so they could search it for evidence, but having concluded their work, they had no reason to hold the car other than to prevent Eli from using it to jump bail.

Eli's attorney, Chester Baslin, argued effectively that whether Eli would or would not skip town hardly depended upon whether he used his own car or simply took one of his parents' cars. The judge agreed and Eli got his car back.

But now, Eli was gone. He hadn't shown up at school or at Chester's office that afternoon to prep for his defense, and now his place at the family dinner table sat empty. Monty shot a glance at Rose knowing she blamed him for this new twist in the "demise of her good name," as she liked to say.

"Walker, are you sure you haven't heard anything?"

"No, Dad. Honest. I don't know where he is," answered Walker.

Walker, Monty and Rose's first and only child together, was five years younger than Eli and quite simply idolized him. So, it would have come as no surprise if Walker were covering for him.

Eli was Rose's firstborn, but the product of a failed marriage, a marriage Rose had desperately tried to wipe from her family's memory. But the memory of her first husband lived on for Rose, for she saw her ex-husband every time she saw Eli.

* * *

Eli was able to relax now that the sun had set. Not knowing yet whether anyone was looking for him, he hid throughout most the day. He hadn't heard any breaking news on his transistor radio, but he turned it on sparingly since he wanted to preserve the batteries for the days ahead.

Eli built a fire and cooked the fish he caught. He could feed himself in the wild—that wasn't his worry. Water was. Clean water. He boiled water and refilled his canteens, wanting to preserve his limited supply of iodine pills. *How long can I live outdoors?* Eli wondered. *It doesn't matter. Eventually I'll have to surface and enter a store.*

Eli ate his meal in silence. Under normal conditions, he would enjoy the silence. Or more typically, he'd be camping with a few buddies, or Kimberly. Oh, Kimberly. He'd kept her memory at bay throughout the day, fearful that dwelling on her would tear him apart—and he needed his wits about him. But now, alone and sitting in the dark along a creek they had canoed together, Eli's defenses crumbled, and he wept. He cried for Kimberly, a girl he loved and a girl who had been brutally murdered. And now, somehow, he was on the run, charged with her murder. How had his life reached this point? Eighteen years old and with absolutely nothing. No family. Nothing.

He ached, lying on the ground with his arms hugging his legs, rocking back and forth.

Eli suddenly missed his dad. He wanted to talk to him and rest in his arms. He needed a father. He needed a father so very badly and feared he would never see his father, Monty, again. No, Monty wasn't his real dad, but he was his father in every other sense of the word. His real father had left his mother, Rose, before he'd been born. He hated the man. But how could you hate a man you'd never met? Because the man's presence loomed over his mother and his own life in ways Eli didn't understand—couldn't understand.

"Oh, Dad," cried Eli softly. "I need you, Father. I need you."

And then, a sense of calm came over Eli. He felt something. He knew not what, but it was good.

And then a moment later, an idea popped into his head. He sat up. *That just might work,* he thought. *Yep, I need help and I need it from someone I can trust. Yep, that just might work.*

Eli finished his meal, put out the fire, packed his things in the canoe, and began to paddle toward the Wadmalaw River.

"I should be able to make it there by morning," he said to the emptiness about him, but he had a strange sense that he was not alone.

Chapter 5

Turmoil

Dinner that night at the Atkins household was quiet, awkward, and over quickly. Monty knew he should call the police or at least Eli's attorney, Chester Baslin. Chester had called Monty late that afternoon when Eli failed to show for their appointment. Monty was shaken by the news and promised to call Chester back that night. But Monty wanted to give Eli the benefit of the doubt. He knew he'd show up. So, Monty sought distraction while he waited, and hoped for Eli to show up.

"Hey, Walker, how's school going? Do you need any help with your homework?"

"No, Dad. I've already done it."

"You're starting word problems in math, aren't you? Those can be pretty hard. You sure you don't need any help?" asked Monty.

Walker sighed and figured it would be easier to just let his dad help rather than keep resisting.

Walker was tall for his age and despite his immense appetite, matched only by his father's, he was lanky. His hair was light brown and his eyes blue. He had a habit of cocking his head to one side whether he was listening, thinking, or talking. What set him apart from the crowd was his intensity. It practically radiated off him at times.

"You can take a look if you want," said Walker.

"Sure. Love to."

Walker took off for his bedroom and returned with a textbook. He opened the book to a page of problems and passed it to his dad.

"The teacher said we had to complete the first three by tomorrow, but I went ahead and did all ten. I figured she'll be asking for those by the end of the week," said Walker.

"Makes sense," said Monty as he took the textbook from Walker and began to read. "So, let's see what we have here."

Walker was standing next to his father, seated in his La-Z-Boy, and watched as his father stared at the textbook. Monty confidently read the first question aloud, paused, and stared at the page, his eyes pinched closer together in deep concentration, willing the answer off the page. He shifted in his chair and repeated the question, this time more to himself and in a bit of a mumble.

Breaking the awkward silence, Monty pointed to the worksheet in the textbook and asked, "Is that your answer there?"

"Yes."

"So, let's see your work," said Monty.

"I don't have any work to show. I just did it in my head," answered Walker.

"In your head!" exclaimed Monty. "Well, what happens if you're wrong? In my day, if we were wrong, we at least got partial credit by showing our work."

"Dad, I'm never wrong." Walker, looking bored, extended his hand in a silent request for the return of the textbook.

Rose, sitting on the sofa and busy needlepointing something, smirked as Monty handed the textbook back to Walker. Walker turned and started down the hallway. Rose rested her hands in her lap and leaned outward in a silent command that Walker give her a kiss good night on the cheek. Walker dutifully obeyed and then solemnly returned to his bedroom.

Monty picked up a contract on the lamp table next to him and resumed reviewing the document. After a few minutes, and unable to focus, Monty turned to Rose.

"Rose, I guess it's time to call Chester."

"Why don't you just wait until tomorrow morning?" said Rose. "I'm sure he'll turn up. Besides, suppose Eli has taken off; what do you expect anyone to do about it tonight? No, it's best to just wait till morning," said Rose.

"I don't know. Maybe you're right. Well, I'm going to head to my office for a bit before turning in. Do you want me to turn off the TV or change the channel?"

"Could you put it on the PBS channel?" asked Rose. "There's a program coming on soon I want to watch."

"Sure."

Monty flipped the leg rest down and rose from his chair. After changing the channel, he gave Rose a little peck on the forehead and headed up the stairs toward his office. He had already made up his mind to call Chester, and that was what he intended to do, but he was hoping Rose would support him. That wasn't to be.

So, Monty took a seat at his desk and reached for the phone. He pulled it toward the end of the desk and removed the handset from the cradle as he prepared to dial the number, and that was when he noticed it; someone had moved the recliner in the corner of his office. He replaced the handset and approached the recliner and saw the damage to the closet door.

The screams from upstairs startled Rose but didn't surprise her. It was only a matter of time. That morning, after Walker had gone to school and Monty had left for work, she had ventured into Monty's office to confirm what she suspected. Yep, Eli had taken the money. She thought about trying to hide what Eli had done by closing the safe and concealing the damage to the closet door but then thought better of it. No, in her mind, the sooner the public saw Eli as a thief, the sooner they would see him as Kimberly Prestwick's killer.

But the screams sent Walker bolting up the stairs. Rose, figuring she needed to show the same concern, followed him into Monty's office.

Monty was perched on the edge of the recliner outside the closet with his head in his hands wailing. "Oh, Eli. NO!"

Walker saw a look of unadulterated fear on his father's tear-stained face.

"Dad," cried Walker, "what's wrong?"

Monty stared past Walker, saying nothing, his breathing uncontrollable.

"Monty, dear, what is it? You're scaring Walker," exclaimed Rose.

"He's gone," said Monty.

"What do you mean, gone?" asked Walker.

Monty composed himself the best he could and sat up a bit. "Eli. He's gone. It looks like he ran," said Monty.

"No. He wouldn't," said Walker. "He *wanted* to stand trial. He's innocent."

Rose took a step toward Walker and tried to pull him in, but he pushed her away and ran out of the room.

"The money," said Rose, "did he take it?"

Monty said nothing.

"Monty, did he take the money?"

"Yes, Rose. He did."

"How much?" asked Rose.

"All of it."

"I said 'how much?'"

"Ten thousand dollars," said Monty.

Rose's eyes narrowed as she turned and walked out of his office.

* * *

Monty raised himself up from his recliner and headed for Eli's room. He had stepped into Eli's room shortly before dinner after his knocks on the door went unanswered. A quick glance inside had confirmed what he knew but didn't want to believe. Eli had run. But now, he looked about Eli's bedroom for a clue, anything that might tell Monty where his son Eli had run to.

The only clues came in the form of what Monty couldn't find: Eli's fishing gear, backpack, hiking shoes, hunting knife, some clothes, and his guns. Monty could no longer deny it. Eli had taken off, intent on escaping the law. Intent on not standing trial. But why? Eli was innocent. Monty knew it. But then why did he run? Maybe Chester told him something about the possible outcome at trial that had scared him. Who was the last person to see Eli? If he could talk to that person, maybe Monty could understand what had spooked Eli.

But now Monty had to decide what to do. Should he tell the police? Did he want Eli captured or did he want Eli to succeed in his escape? Could he live with himself if he turned in his son? Would he be disbarred if he withheld this information? Who could he talk to?

"Oh, Lord, help me," said Monty.

Monty sat on the floor next to Eli's bed and wept for him.

* * *

Monty waited until after midnight before calling Chester. He figured that if he waited long enough, he could aid Eli in his escape while not running afoul of the police. And maybe Chester wouldn't answer.

He answered.

"Chester Baslin here. Can I help you?"

"Chester, it's me, Monty. Good grief, do you always answer the phone in the middle of the night like you were at the office?"

"For criminal defense attorneys, office hours are always 24/7. Now, Monty, I presume you're calling about Eli."

"Yes, I'm afraid he's made a run for it. ... Chester, I'm so afraid."

Chapter 6

Armed and Dangerous

Early Friday morning, June 1st, 1973

Mrs. Annabelle Babcock lived alone in a single-story house along the western bank of the Wadmalaw River just shy of the bend as it turned south and then eastward before flowing into the Atlantic Ocean. Her husband Rufus had built the home for the two of them, but Mrs. Babcock lived alone now due to her husband's failing health. Rufus Babcock currently resided at the Dignity Nursing Home. Mrs. Babcock, however, despite her seventy-six years of age, could take care of herself.

She hadn't set the alarm clock in years but was still up and out of bed before sunrise. She put on her housecoat hanging on the hook on the back of her bedroom door and headed down the hallway past the guest room and into the living room and turned her Emerson radio to a station that played big band music. She set the volume low, playing it more as background music, because she was more interested in what she might hear on the police radio she kept on her kitchen counter. She developed the habit of turning on the police radio each morning in her early days with the police department.

She turned on the police radio and set about making a pot of coffee when an announcement caught her attention.

"*Repeat, Eli Atkins is believed to be armed and dangerous. Wanted for the rape and murder of Kimberly Prestwick, Eli Atkins, age 18, is believed to be on the run. Six-foot-three, 210 pounds, brown hair, brown eyes. If spotted, call for backup. Repeat, believed to be armed and dangerous.*"

Mrs. Babcock sat down and pondered all that she'd heard.

"No, Lord, it just can't be," she said.

* * *

The previous day, Eli had paddled his canoe from the Wappoo Creek to the Stono River. Throughout the night, he continued heading west and then turned north at the bend in the river where it became the Wadmalaw River. He stayed close to the shore whenever he could to avoid discovery. The new moon was both a curse and a blessing.

He pulled up to the dock leading from the river's edge to her back porch shortly after the sun had risen. Mrs. Babcock was sitting on the porch with a cup of coffee and her Bible opened to the book of Exodus.

Knowing Mrs. Babcock's sight was failing and that she always kept a shotgun at close reach when at home, Eli called out to her. "Mrs. Babcock, it's me, Eli."

"Eli?"

She placed the Bible and her coffee mug on the table beside her rocking chair and, pushing herself up, stood and took a few steps forward. Eli tied the canoe to the dock and started walking toward her, not sure what to say.

"Eli? It is you," she said. "Well, don't I feel like the Pharaoh's daughter."

* * *

"I reckon they know by now," said Eli.

She was working on a second batch of pancakes. *It was nice to have a man to cook for*, she thought.

"I reckon so, but don't you fret—I'll learn all there is to learn."

Eli stood from the table and walked over to the coffeepot and refilled his mug.

"Are you sure you want to do this?" asked Eli. He was barefoot, leaning against the kitchen counter dressed in blue jeans and a white T-shirt.

She moved the griddle off the direct heat of the eye and wiped her hands on her apron. Turning, she walked over to Eli, took his hands in hers, and looked up at him.

"Eli, don't think for a moment that you landed on my doorstep by accident. The Lord laid it on your heart to come here for a reason. Yes, I know what I'm doing. Now, remember what we talked about," she said. "You lay low. Do not leave this house. There's plenty of food in the fridge. I got books on the shelves and if you tilt the antennae just right, you can get a picture on the TV."

"I'll remember," said Eli.

Yes, Mrs. Babcock thought it was nice to have a man to cook for. Even if he was young enough to be her grandson and wanted for murder.

* * *

CHARLESTON POLICE DEPARTMENT, FRIDAY MORNING, JUNE 1ST

Mrs. Babcock didn't want to be late. She knew the office would be abuzz. Eli had told her what his mother had said and done. She grasped the situation quickly and, after feeding Eli breakfast, she told him that they would talk more that night and that she would go to work as usual and find out what everyone knew. She told him that under no circumstances was he to leave her house.

Mrs. Babcock was a fixture in the Charleston police department. She had been working for the department for fifty-five years. Her first husband, Randall Cunningham, a police officer with the department, was killed in action apprehending an armed bank robber. They had only been married a little over a year at the time. The police department rallied around the young Mrs. Cunningham and had all but guaranteed her lifetime employment. She married again, to Rufus Babcock, and they raised a large family. Her usefulness around the office, however, waned with each passing year. But what were you going to do? No one had the heart to fire her.

When Mrs. Babcock arrived for work that morning, Officers Pearlman and Tyrell were standing in Chief Riddle's office. Officers Pearlman and Tyrell, by all appearances, were exact opposites. Officer Pearlman was a white man with the complexion of chalk and was as thin as a string bean, and Officer Tyrell was short and squat with skin as black as coal. They had been partners for going on four years, and away from the office, they were the best of friends.

Mrs. Babcock, the chief of police's secretary, hurried into his office.

"Sorry I'm late, boss," said Mrs. Babcock.

"You're not late; we're just getting an early start," said Chief Riddle, clearly not happy with the state of the world.

"Mrs. Babcock, things are going to be a bit crazy around here the next few days and I'm going to need you to run interference for me and make sure no one gets through to me on the phone without you letting me know who it is first. Do you think you can handle that?" asked Chief Riddle.

"No problem, Chief. But tell me, what's all the commotion about?" she asked.

"Eli Atkins is what all the commotion is about. He skipped," answered Chief Riddle.

* * *

Mrs. Babcock was indeed busy that day. She was either patching calls through or taking down phone numbers of folks the chief wanted nothing to do with. Early that morning, Chief Riddle called in every available officer in the department. Spread out before them in the conference room was a large map of the area and the officers were gathered in groups of two or three, everyone having an opinion as to where Eli was hiding.

"All right, all right now," boomed Chief Riddle as he held up his left hand to silence the room while holding his third cup of coffee of the morning in his right hand. "I need everyone to pay attention."

The room grew quieter, and each officer stepped back a bit from the group they had been speaking with and directed their eyes toward the front of the room.

"I want to thank everyone for coming in. I know some of you had the day off, but we have a situation on our hands. Early this morning, shortly after midnight, Chester Baslin called the station and reported that Eli Atkins' whereabouts were unknown. He said that his duty to the court commanded that he tell us."

There was a grumbling from the officers around the room, most of them believing that Chester Baslin had probably known for some time.

"Pipe down, everyone, pipe down," said Chief Riddle. "We don't have time to finger-point right now. Maybe later, but right now we need to find Eli. That's our number one job. I know some of you in the room know Eli and his family and questioned his guilt when we brought him in. Well,

I'm hoping that his flight has put to rest any doubts you had and that y'all will act professionally. Everyone in this room saw the pictures of Kimberly Prestwick's body. Whoever did it, and it sure looks like it was Eli Atkins, is a monster, a monster capable of anything. So, I repeat, finding Eli is our number one job."

Chief Riddle's gaze canvassed the room, stopping to lock eyes with a few of the officers whom he knew sympathized with Eli, thinking he'd been unjustifiably charged with Kimberly Prestwick's rape and murder. Chief Riddle held their gaze until he had received acknowledgment, whether by nod or verbal agreement, that they were onboard.

"Okay. I'm now going to bring you up to speed on the steps we've taken since we got the call from Chester Baslin and then we'll hand out assignments. The call went out shortly after Baslin phoned the police department, so we have some officers in place, but as of now we're sorely understaffed. From what we know about Eli Atkins, he's comfortable in the wild. We'll be fanning out across the region looking for any trace of him. This morning and throughout the rest of the day, I'll be speaking with every sheriff and chief of police in the neighboring counties and in cities as for north as Wilmington, as far south as St. Augustine, Florida, and as far west as Atlanta. I'm in contact with the FBI, and an All-Points Bulletin has been released. Finally, later this morning, we'll be holding a press conference and taking to the local radio and TV stations announcing a reward for anyone who sees Eli and alerts us. If he surfaces, we'll find him."

"Now, don't leave this room until you've met with Officer Reynolds in the back. He'll give you your assignment. We're going to fan out and scour every inch of Charleston and the surrounding area."

As the chief was about to leave, he stopped and asked: "Are there any questions?"

A veteran officer from the back of the room raised his hand.

"Let's have it," said the chief.

"And if we find him, and he doesn't come peacefully, then what?" asked the officer.

"Shoot to kill," answered Chief Riddle.

The officers in the room lined up to receive their assignments and the adrenaline began to flow—they were anxious to get going. Mrs. Babcock, having volunteered, made detailed notes of where every officer in the department would be stationed.

Chapter 7

The Planning

FRIDAY NIGHT, AT MRS. BABCOCK'S HOUSE

Eli followed Mrs. Babcock's strict orders to lay low, for the most part. He did venture down to the river to catch dinner. When Mrs. Babcock returned home that night, a bit later than usual, Eli had cleaned, fileted, and prepared three fish for their dinner.

"Somethin' sure smells good," said Mrs. Babcock as she walked through the side door leading in from the carport. "Hush puppies! Well, bless your heart. You didn't have to go to all this trouble," she said as she leaned over the counter and spied the fish. "I 'spect those two are redfish, but what's this third fish, and are we havin' company or are you just famished?" asked Mrs. Babcock.

"Famished," said Eli, smiling slightly. "And that one's a speckled trout."

"This time of year? This far up the river? I figured it was warm enough, they'd all be back in big water by now and not this far upriver. And if you don't mind me asking, where'd you come by the bait? I know my live-well is empty. Francesco is supposed to bring me a fresh batch of shrimp on Sunday."

"I packed a cast net in my canoe. Didn't know where my next meal would be coming from. Well anyway, didn't take long to gather some mullet and shrimp. I refilled your bait tank too with some fresh shrimp and filled it with water from the bottom of the river. The water in your tank was a bit warm due to the constant circulation of top water. You get more oxygen from the colder water," said Eli.

"Now Eli, I believe it was me that taught you that."

"Yes, Mrs. B," said Eli with a big grin this time, "I believe you did. Now what do you say we finish makin' dinner?"

* * *

Eli learned to fish from his dad, Monty, but it wasn't long before Eli was teaching Monty a thing or two. Mrs. B's husband, Rufus, ran a couple of bait and tackle shops in the area and Eli, a regular at their shops, had come to know them over the years. Rufus's reputation as an angler was well known, and having taken Eli under his wing, Rufus taught him how to read the water and catch just about anything. When Rufus fell ill and was admitted to the Dignity Nursing Home, Eli began helping around the shop and the Babcocks' home. So, when Eli showed up at her back door, she welcomed him with open arms, never once believing he could have harmed Kimberly.

Eli and Mrs. B had their dinner on the back porch overlooking the river. Once the sun set, the temperature was quite nice and the sage and mint leaves burning in the small firepit kept the bugs away. After cleaning up the kitchen, the two of them returned to the back porch to talk. Mrs. B told Eli to help himself to a cold beer from the fridge.

"I always have some on hand for when my son-in-law Francesco visits," she said.

"Thank you. Can I get you one?" asked Eli.

"No, but if you don't mind pouring me a little wine, I'd appreciate it. You'll find a bottle of Madeira in the pantry on the shelf to the right as you walk in," she said.

Eli walked outside and handed Mrs. B her glass of Madeira and took a seat.

"You have more than a bottle of that wine stored in your pantry," said Eli. "Now that ain't homemade, is it?" joked Eli.

Mrs. B rocked in her chair and laughed softly.

"No, Madeira wine's not from these parts. Not at all. Comes from an island off the coast of Portugal. A hundred years ago or so, it was the favored drink amongst the South's wealthiest, but it's just about disappeared. Yep, hard to find. So, no, it's not homemade, but there's a good story behind that case of Madeira you spied in my pantry. Maybe I'll tell it to you someday. But, tonight, let's talk about you and where we go from here."

Eli had told Mrs. B early that morning when he arrived that his mother had threatened to withhold his alibi and deny seeing him come home early the night Kimberly was murdered. Mrs. Babcock knew a bit about Eli's upbringing because Eli had confided in her over the years and, being a devout and charismatic attendee of a Pentecostal church, she was no stranger to spiritual warfare.

"Eli," she said, "I been thinkin' about what your mama threatened you with. It sounds like Satan has a perch on her soul. Don't blame her, though, for the wickedness you've witnessed isn't her. But you should go," said Mrs. Babcock.

Eli leaned forward in his chair and rested his forearms across his knees with the half-empty beer between his hands and his head bowed. "But where?" he asked in desperation.

"Well, I been thinking about that too," said Mrs. B.

* * *

SATURDAY, JUNE 2ND

Mrs. Babcock set out early the next morning for the Mt. Bethel Church of Prophesy. She'd attended the small Pentecostal church since it had first opened its doors in the spring of 1936. As a founding member of the church, she had sat on or chaired every committee the church ever had. She pulled into the parking lot ostensibly to offer her services to the Church Planting Committee that was looking at a site further south in Beaufort, South Carolina. She knew three things about their congregation's efforts to plant new churches. First, the committee met on the first Saturday of each month and met early in the morning to accommodate those church members who attended the 10:00 a.m. Saturday service, believing that the Sabbath was properly observed on Saturdays and not Sundays. Second, breakfast would be involved, and finally, you needed money to build a new church. As she pulled into the parking lot alongside the church office, she spied his pickup truck and smiled.

"I was hopin' you'd be here," she said to herself as she ratcheted the gear shift on her steering column up into park. Mrs. Babcock grabbed her gargantuan purse from the passenger side and made her way into the tabernacle on the back side of the parking lot. She was wearing a loose fitting, amber colored dress that fell several inches past her knees. Her half-frame, rectangular shaped glasses were attached to a chain made by one of her grandchildren at summer camp years ago and rested on her chest just above a small cross at the end of a thin gold necklace.

As the church had grown, the chapel, while still the focal point for Sunday worship, could not accommodate all the congregation's needs. They built a more general-purpose building ten years prior, and folks just took to calling it "the tabernacle." Inside, at any point in time, one could find kids kicking a ball around, worship services in session, large meals being cooked or eaten, or meetings taking place in one of the small rooms in the back. As Mrs. Babcock entered, she saw Quaid Dawson flipping pancakes and his wife, Mirabelle, chatting up the next person in line.

Quaid had light to olive colored skin that had darkened over the years due to all the hours he spent outdoors. He had chestnut brown hair and hazel eyes. He stood six feet tall and had wide, angular, almost sharp shoulders made to look all the wider due to his narrow waist. In fact, he was all angles. His face was long and creviced. If not for a bright, joyful smile, the effect would have been to make him appear old. He often stood with his hands in his back pockets. He was dressed for a day of fishing, but then he always dressed this way.

Quaid was the sole heir to a fortune of undetermined size, a fortune with its roots firmly planted in the ground and the nation's failed experiment with Prohibition. His father, Bartholomew Dawson, was one-half of the famous South Carolina bootlegging brothers, Bartholomew and Nathaniel Dawson. In the early 1900s, Bartholomew and Nathaniel made moonshine, as did most folks raised in Hell Hole Swamp, a stretch of land running from Jamestown to Moncks Corner between the Santee River and the Cooper River.

For years, inhabitants of Hell Hole Swamp made corn whiskey for their personal consumption. However, Prohibition sired an unquenchable demand for their product in the cities of Charleston, Savannah, Memphis, Chicago, New York, and all points in between. The Dawson brothers sold the equipment moonshiners needed to build stills in the swamps and then purchased the moonshine and sold it to distributors like the notorious Chicago gangster Al Capone.

When the Twenty-First Amendment ending Prohibition passed in 1933, the Dawsons went straight and acquired several profitable liquor distributorships. These distributorships funded a lavish lifestyle for the Dawson brothers and would do so for generations to come. However, try as they might, neither Bartholomew nor Nathaniel could shake their reputations as bootleggers. They were shunned by polite society and excluded from the best clubs and homes in Charleston's toniest neighborhood, South of Broad. Nathaniel retreated to the swamps and drank himself to death while Bartholomew tried in vain to shake the poor, white-trash label off his back long associated with anyone from the swamps.

Quaid Dawson witnessed his father, Bartholomew, grow old and bitter despite his financial success because he never could buy the respectability he so craved. Quaid was thus determined to live life not caring what others thought, and that is precisely what he did. The quick temper of his father, a first-generation Irish immigrant, did not haunt Quaid's doorstep. He married Mirabelle, an Italian beauty, and they sired seven boys and a girl.

Quaid did not run from his family heritage but embraced it and made no apologies. He was extremely likable and charmed his critics with his aw-shucks humility. However, Quaid was not to be underestimated and proved to be an excellent businessman. The liquor distributorships he inherited grew in size and profitability under his guidance. Furthermore, over the years, Quaid quietly involved himself in several other business ventures. You would never know it, though, from how he lived. Quaid and Mirabelle were content to live simple lives, organized around their children and their faith in the Lord's love for them.

Quaid knew why the church's pastor, Reverend Malachi Jones, asked him to chair the committee. The Rev figured, or so Quaid assumed, that if he was involved from the beginning, he'd be more likely to step up and lead the fundraising effort for a new church. Try as he may to downplay his wealth, it followed him. He dealt with it by embracing whatever task was required around the church regardless of how menial or manual it may be. Many folks, but not all, ceased seeing him differently when he got his hands dirty.

"Good mornin', Mal," said Quaid as he placed an extra-large helping of blueberry pancakes on the reverend's plate.

"Whoa now. I'll be napping by noon if I eat all that."

"And what's wrong with that? You work hard, and besides, the junior pastor covers the Saturday services, makin' today your day of rest."

"Well, when you put it that way ... why sure, I do believe I'll have an extra helping," said Mal with a slight chuckle.

"Say, Quaid. I certainly appreciate you giving up your Saturday morning to help out."

"My pleasure, but if you ask me, all the help we'll ever need is coming this way," said Quaid as he waved to Mrs. Babcock.

The reverend turned and grinned as he saw her coming. "Annabelle, I didn't know you had volunteered to help us," said Rev Mal.

"Well, I hadn't but when I woke this morning I felt pushed in this direction. So here I am," said Mrs. Babcock.

* * *

Like any proper church committee meeting, it ran thirty minutes later than scheduled and forty minutes past the time any meaningful decisions were made. But on this morning, delays were to be expected, since most everyone had seen Eli's picture on the Friday evening local news or had heard about the search for Eli on the radio and wanted to talk about it. Mrs. Babcock was pressed for any gossip since everyone knew she worked directly for the chief of police.

"Now you know I can't be tongue-waggin' about such things," she said. She noticed that Quaid remained quiet throughout the talk about Eli and seemed uncomfortable with the whole topic of conversation, thus confirming Mrs. Babcock's hunch. So, as the meeting broke, she set out to have a one-on-one conversation with Quaid. But she was having a devil of a time because Floyd Druthers had cornered him with another one of his harebrained business propositions and looked like he wasn't going to let Quaid out of his sight until Quaid agreed to take a look at his new deal.

Growing impatient, Mrs. Babcock walked up and placed herself between Floyd and Quaid with her back to Floyd and, being nearly a foot shorter than the two men, peered up at Quaid.

"Quaid, dear, can I have a word with you?"

"Why sure, Annabelle," he said as he looked over Annabelle's head at Floyd. "Annabelle, can you give me a minute, though, while I finish talkin' to Floyd here?"

"It's just that my husband, Rufus, has taken to walking the halls of the

Dignity Nursing Home buck naked and the folks there want me to sign a bunch of papers and I was wondering if you would take a look at them for me."

Silenced by her question, Quaid and Floyd shared a bemused look and agreed to get together for breakfast sometime next week.

"That sounds good, Quaid. I'll call you Monday at your office and we'll arrange it."

"You do that," said Quaid as he placed one hand on Mrs. Babcock's shoulder and turned her toward a table where they could have a seat and talk.

"You're welcome," said Annabelle.

"For what?" asked Quaid.

"For getting you out of his clutches, that's for what. You know none of his fool ideas have amounted to anything," said Annabelle.

Quaid laughed and shook his head. "So, Rufus isn't running through the halls buck naked?"

"Heavens to Betsy, no. But I do have something to talk to you about," said Annabelle.

"Well, all right. What's on your mind?"

"Not here," said Annabelle.

* * *

Five minutes later, Quaid and Annabelle Babcock were standing in the church parking lot next to her pickup looking as nonchalant as possible.

"I'm the last person anyone will suspect, and you know that," said Annabelle.

Quaid stood quietly, his left arm crossed under his ribcage supporting his other arm as he massaged his chin with his right hand.

"Quaid? Quaid? Are you listening?" she asked.

"I'm listenin', but I'm thinkin' too," he said.

"Well, I don't need to know what you're thinkin' just yet. I just need to know if you're with me."

"I'm with you. You knew the answer to that question before you drove out here this morning. The question is ... well, what do we do *now*?" said Quaid.

"That is the question, and now that I know you're with me, I'd like to know what you're thinkin'," she said.

"Okay, but not here."

* * *

At Quaid's suggestion, they didn't leave the church together. Quaid went back inside the tabernacle and helped fold and store the chairs that had been set out for that morning's breakfast. He then drove home and busied himself for a few minutes before heading over to Mrs. Babcock's house. Forty-five minutes later, Quaid Dawson and Mrs. Annabelle Babcock were sitting around her kitchen table with fugitive Eli Atkins plotting how they could help him safely escape.

When Quaid knocked on Annabelle's side door, she had been studying a map of the area with Eli, pointing out where the local police and FBI were patrolling. She quickly brought Quaid up to speed and they had been chewing on Eli's best route out of the area ever since.

Eli had made a fresh pot of coffee and Annabelle rose to refill Quaid's cup as she continued on with her thoughts.

"Like I was sayin', nobody will suspect me."

"Annabelle, that's true. But they'll have bloodhounds at the checkpoints. You said so yourself. Hiding Eli in the trunk of your car won't do any good," said Quaid. "The dogs will sniff him out."

After twenty minutes or so of plotting and speculating, Quaid stood up from the table he'd been leaning over to straighten his back and sighed loudly.

"Go on," said Annabelle. "That sigh's tellin' me there's something more you want to say."

"Well, it seems we're focused on only half the problem—that is how we can help Eli get out of the area undetected," said Quaid. "That's all well and good, but, Eli, the bigger question is where you go from here. That's what we need to focus on. Have you given any thought to that?" asked Quaid.

"Mr. Dawson, I've lived here since the time I was three years old. I've been to Kiawah Island with my family, and to Atlanta twice to watch the Braves play. I don't mean to sound disrespectful, but how would I know where to go?"

Quaid looked at Eli and wondered how the young man was holding it together. All alone and no place to go. Quaid had known Eli through his friendship with a couple of his boys. Quaid had seven boys of his own and one beautiful daughter, Isabelle. He understood the fear gripping the community among those who believed Eli had killed Kimberly Prestwick. *My God,* he thought, *if anyone harmed a hair on the head of my daughter, I'd hunt the guilty party down myself.* In Quaid's mind, "vengeance be mine, sayeth the Lord" was all well and good except when it came to your own family.

But like Mrs. Babcock, Quaid knew Eli wasn't the killer. Eli was big for his size, physically mature beyond his years, but Quaid knew the gentle side in him as well. He'd seen it. Quaid stood up for the underdog and wouldn't stand for bullying. Quaid knew Eli's father, too, and had great respect for the man. Monty was hard-working, confident, a bit of David vs. Goliath in him but humble at the same time. Quaid hoped that if one of his boys were in trouble, someone would come to his aid. So, Quaid made the decision, right then, silently, that he'd do all he could to help the young man. Yep, a young man is what he was now. His childhood was over. He was no longer a boy.

Mrs. Babcock broke the silence.

"Quaid, I'm suspecting you have connections in the Bahamas. Connections beyond simply knowing who the best fishin' charters are."

"Go on," said Quaid, neither confirming nor denying her statement.

"Well, I have family there, sort of, and if we can get Eli to the Bahamas, between my family and your connections, we just may be able to stow our boy away until this mess blows over."

"You say you have family there?" asked Quaid.

"My son-in-law, Francesco. He's from the Bahamas. He met my daughter, Amy, when she was there on a mission trip. He was working with the hurricane relief agency our church was helpin' out. Well, he's got quite an extended family down there. Good folk. Church folk. We can trust them."

"Annabelle," said Quaid with a big grin sweeping across his face, "that is an inspired idea."

"So, do you think we can get him to the Bahamas?"

"I believe we can."

"By boat or plane?" asked Annabelle.

"Not sure right now—probably boat, though."

"So, we'll have to get him to the coast," she said.

Quaid nodded.

"And you do have connections down there, don't you?" asked Annabelle.

"Yes, yes I do," answered Quaid.

Eli sat quietly watching Quaid Dawson and Mrs. Babcock discuss his escape, his future, his life. He was torn. Part of him was thankful for their help. But another part, a growing, festering part of him, resented being talked about as if he were a child, not even there, helpless and without a voice. Angry that he needed help. Angry that he was in this mess, a fugitive from the law, unable to walk about freely, wanted for a murder he did not commit. As the reality of his life, of his situation, had begun to sink in over the past few days, anger and resentment seeped into his pores. He hadn't done anything to deserve this. But here he was. Wanted for murder and plotting his escape and others telling him where he would go, where he would live.

"So, Eli, how would you like to go to the Bahamas?" asked Quaid.

"What choice do I have?"

* * *

THE NEXT MORNING, SUNDAY, JUNE 3RD

Quaid and Annabelle had agreed to meet at church for Sunday services. After the morning worship service, they met on the patio for coffee and donuts and took a walk back toward the cemetery. They stopped and sat on the bench in front of the headstones over the graves of Annabelle's parents.

"Folks should leave us alone here," said Annabelle. "So, how are your plans coming?"

"Good. I spoke to a fishing captain I've known and worked with for years. He can be here in a few days and then take Eli back to Nassau. But he may raise suspicions if he comes into port. He's never docked in Charleston before. We have to assume that the police are taking extra precautions and monitoring who's coming and going from the ports."

"I believe you're right. The police found Eli's truck in the marina parkin' lot after the owner of that big boat reported his dinghy missing. Everyone 'spects Eli's taken to the water."

"That may be true, but I'm still leary of Eli traveling by car on account of the roadblocks," said Quaid.

The two of them sat silently on the bench, both thinking, neither speaking.

"Well, what if your captain's boat never docks?"

"I'm not sure if I'm following you," said Quaid.

"My son-in-law, Francesco, he could drop Eli off at sea. Maybe three miles out. No one would ever know your captain friend had been in these waters," said Annabelle.

"Now, that's an idea. But I'd still feel more comfortable if we could make the drop someplace other than Charleston."

"How much time till we have to tell your captain where to pick up Eli?"

"Not much," said Quaid. "We'll have to give him the general idea of the destination by tonight. He's planning on embarking early tomorrow morning, around 4:00 a.m. Once he gets close to our shore, we'll be able to make radio contact. But, again, we'll have to be careful and assume the police and the Coast Guard are listening for any word of Eli."

Annabelle sat quietly and waited. She'd been here before and knew to wait.

After a couple of minutes, she spoke.

"Beaufort."

"What?" asked Quaid.

"Beaufort. We need to get Eli to Beaufort. Tell your captain to head to Beaufort, South Carolina. We'll make radio contact with him when he gets close to shore. Francesco will motor out and drop Eli off. Now, when can your captain be here?"

"The weather forecast looks good, so I'd say sometime after midnight, Wednesday. That'd be very early Thursday morning," answered Quaid.

"So how do we get Eli to Beaufort?" asked Quaid.

Annabelle was sitting with her hands folded in her lap and her gargantuan purse at her feet and staring straight ahead.

"Quaid, have you ever driven a hearse?" asked Annabelle.

* * *

POTLUCK DINNER AT THE MT. BETHEL CHURCH OF PROPHECY SUNDAY NIGHT, JUNE 3RD

Mrs. Babcock was seated with Reverend Malachi Jones and his family. Mal was used to doing most of the talking at church functions and he grew weary of it. Too many people, including many in his congregation, believed that every word from his mouth was ordained, dripping in wisdom or some prophetic truth. His grandchildren, running about, talking up a storm, gave him a welcome break from being the center of attention.

And then there was Mrs. Babcock. She treated him no differently than anyone else. When it came to church politics and gossip, she'd seen it all.

"So, Mal, I heard Beaulah Banks is about ready to go home," said Annabelle.

"Well, Annabelle, I guess I can tell you. The Lord took her home this afternoon. That's why I was late. Just came from the hospital. I was meeting with her family."

"Oh, dear. And how's Ralph holding up?"

"'Bout well as can be expected. Her passin' didn't come as a surprise. More like a blessing. The cancer ate her up and she was sufferin'. It was her time," said Rev Mal.

"And I suppose the services will be here?" asked Annabelle.

"That's right. Wednesday mornin'. It's supposed to rain Wednesday afternoon something fierce, so we'll have to get her in the ground before the storm hits."

"That shouldn't be a problem. She'll be buried out back, won't she?" asked Annabelle.

"No, wants to be buried close to her parents, up in McClellanville. That reminds me, I need to tell our new Jr. Pastor, Wayne, that one of his duties is drivin the hearse," said Rev Mal.

"Pumpkin?" said Rev Mal turning to speak to his wife.

"Yes, dear?" she said.

"Remind me to speak to Pastor Wayne before we leave today about takin' the hearse out for a spin tomorrow, make sure she's running well and maybe wash her."

"Honey, Monday is his day off and he's got a wife and two youngins that look forward to Mondays. Can't it wait till Tuesday," his wife asked.

"Guess, it'll have to," he said.

Annabelle stood to excuse herself.

"Well, it was right nice visiting with you two and your family. But I see Quaid Dawson who I need to talk with 'bout a thing or two," said Annabelle.

"Always a pleasure visiting with you, too, Annabelle. And we hope Quaid can help you out with your, um, situation over at the Dignity Care home," said Rev Mal, his wife nodding along with him.

Annabelle looked on, a bit confused.

"We heard about Rufus. Ya know, runnin' up and down the halls naked. We'll be prayin' for you two."

"Oh, yeah, right. Well, I appreciate that," said Annabelle as she rose from the picnic table and took her plate over to the trashcan. Mumbling to herself, "Lord, that was providential, that meetin, wasn't it?" And she set off to conspire with Quaid.

* * *

"It has to be tonight," said Annabelle. "The church will need the hearse for a funeral Wednesday, and they'll be lookin to get it ready Tuesday."

"Who'll be ridin' in it?" asked Quaid.

"You and Eli, who'd you think," said Annabelle.

"No, not tonight, Wednesday?"

"Oh, sorry. Beaulah Banks. The cancer won out."

"I'm sorry to hear that. You two were close, weren't you?"

"Yes, we were. But her mind left her some time ago and I said my good-byes then. So, I've been missin' her for a while. 'Fraid that's the case with more and more of my kind. Maybe that's why I'm so determined to help Eli. Time is running out for me too and the Lord's handed me an opportunity to make amends."

"Make amends?" said Quaid. "Make amends for what, Annabelle?"

Annabelle didn't answer right away but just bowed her head, holding her gargantuan purse by the strap with both hands.

"Quaid, let's just leave it at that for now. I'm going to ask you to trust me. Can you do that?"

"Yes, of course. These last few days, I've felt a calming presence when I'm with you, a presence that gives me plenty of reason to trust you. Can't explain it."

Annabelle just smiled to herself and nodded her head knowing the reason.

"Okay, then let's stick to the plan," said Annabelle.

Chapter 8

Plan Execution

Sunday night, June 3rd, shortly after 10:00pm

The plan, such as it was, called for Quaid to meet Mrs. Babcock, on foot, behind the maintenance shed on the back end of the church property as close to 10:00 pm as possible. Quaid parked his pickup truck about a mile away on property he owned and walked the rest of the way, keeping to the woods and off the main road. He headed to the back of the church property and saw Annabelle's pickup parked in the back and behind the maintenance shed, as far away from sight as possible. He began to walk towards her truck when his attention was drawn towards the maintenance shed.

"Psst. Quaid. In here," whispered Annabelle.

Over the years, since she'd helped out the church in every conceivable way, the church decided she should have her own set of keys.

Quaid saw Annabelle poking her head out the door to the shed. She was dressed in blue jeans, boots, and a dark blue sweatshirt at least three sizes too large.

"Annabelle, that shirt's about to swallow you up," said Quaid.

"Well, I didn't have anything to wear for a breaking and entering," she said, laughing quietly. "Borrowed this sweatshirt from the closet at the house where Francesco leaves a few things."

"You look great. Now let's get movin'," said Quaid.

Annabelle led Quaid into the shed, slowly swinging a flashlight on the ground to guide their steps. Quaid's eyes adjusted to the small bit of light coming in from the windows on the side of the shed. The caretaker, Jethro, clearly took pride in his work. A place for everything and for everything a place. And Annabelle, knew right where to go. She walked over to a small metal desk in a corner of the shed and opened the bottom right drawer, pulled out an envelope, and removed the key to the hearse. She held it up head-high and dangled it like a blue ribbon, smiling at Quaid.

"How'd you know where he kept the key?" he asked.

"Jethro took over as caretaker from his pappy before him. They were like two peas from the same pod, like father, like son. When I was a young girl, we'd break in and take the hearse for a joyride. Nothin' gets folks more spooked than seein' a hearse speedin' down the road."

Quaid couldn't help but laugh.

"And you never got caught?"

"Nope," she said proudly. "We always suspected Jethro's dad knew, but since we'd return the hearse with a full tank of gas, he never said a thing. Anyway, not too long ago, out of curiosity, I was back here looking for some gardening shears and thought I'd check and see if the key was in the same place. And sure 'nuf, it was. Like I said, like father, like son. The church has got itself a new hearse since them days, but the keys are kept in the same spot!"

Annabelle walked up to Quaid and handed him the keys.

"Jethro takes Mondays off, as does everyone who works and volunteers here, so you got some time, but it's best if you put the hearse back in the shed before sunup," said Annabelle. "Just put the keys back in the desk and lock the shed. You can return the shed keys to me next week at Sunday services."

"Now, do you have your special clothes in that bag you're holding?" she asked.

"Annabelle, do you really think changing into a suit is necessary? The car windows are tinted. No one will see me."

"In case you get stopped, you have to look the part. No mortician or hearse chauffer ever wore blue jeans and a flannel shirt while driving the recently deceased to their final resting home," she said.

So, Quaid excused himself and walked over to a corner and changed clothes while Mrs. Babcock turned the other way. He called out to her as he was changing. "So, what are my chances of getting stopped?" he asked.

"I'd put it at fifty-fifty. According to my latest information from the police station, there's officers manning the southbound side of the Savannah Highway this side of the town of Ravenel. I doubt they'll stop a hearse, but you never know. Now, if they do stop you, remember to tell them you're on your way to the Marine Base in Beaufort to pick up a body. If pressed for details, have the officer call the base and ask for General Walsh.

"Is there such a general? What if they do stop us? What if they call and ask for General Walsh?" Quaid asked.

"Don't you worry about that. I've already taken care of it. The General and I go way back. He owes me."

Quaid laughed as he walked back from around the corner dressed like a mortician and his other clothes balled up in the small knapsack he was carrying. "James Bond's got nothing on you." Then Quaid raised the overhead door and walked to the driver's side as he prepared to leave. Annabelle met him at the side of the hearse and took his hands in hers. They bowed their heads and kept silent for a moment before Annabelle spoke up.

"Lord, go with Quaid. ... Now go," she said. "Eli will be waiting for you."

And with that, Quaid got inside, started the engine, and pulled the hearse into the quiet of the night and headed for the Savannah Highway. Annabelle held back a few minutes in the parking lot and then climbed into her truck and drove home. She kept the windows down and enjoyed the night air. She felt at peace knowing that the Lord would overlook this tiny indiscretion.

"And besides, good Lord, as long as we bring the hearse back with a full tank of gas, where's the harm?" She laughed like a schoolgirl and turned the radio dial to the big band station.

* * *

Earlier that day

Eli, Quaid, and Annabelle were together again, standing around Annabelle's dining room table. There was an energy in the room as they prepared for Eli's departure, all trying to ignore one simple fact: they didn't know when they would ever see each other again.

Eli and Quaid reviewed his gear together, paring it down to the bare minimum. The plan was simple. Eli would paddle his canoe inland through a winding creek along the north side of the ACE Basin until it connected to the South Edisto River. From there, he'd continue paddling upriver past Willtown Bluff toward Jacksonboro.

"Now, when you get to Jacksonboro, just before you cross under the Savannah Highway, you'll see a Baptist Church on the riverbank to your left," said Annabelle. "There's a boat landing the pastor used 'cause he lived on the river and didn't have a car, but the congregation also used it to walk folks into the water for baptisms. Right handy, actually. Anyways, the church is abandoned. The pastor disappeared and they've had a dickens of a time replacing him."

"Eli, whoever gets there first just needs to wait for the other," said Quaid. "If all goes well, I should be there by 10:45 or so. You'll need to sink your canoe. Can't leave any trail of suspicion."

Over the last hour, Eli had studied the map and gone through his personal belongings, jettisoning the fishing and hiking gear along with some clothes. He was left with a backpack and the clothes inside. Annabelle said she'd drop his spare clothes in the Salvation Army bin in town and slip the gear he was leaving behind into the monthly church swap meet.

"No trail, no suspicion—right, Quaid?" said Annabelle. She was doing her best to keep the mood light.

"Now, Eli, when you get to Nassau, before you go through customs, you'll be met by Mr. Nigel Pinder. He's a private banker in the Bahamas and an old family friend. Don't worry about finding him; he'll find you. He's made certain arrangements that he's better off telling you about than me. But know this, you can trust him," said Quaid.

"And you'll be staying with my son-in-law's family until you get settled in," said Mrs. Babcock.

And here's some cash until you find a job. Mr. Pinder will open a checking account for you, and I'll be able to wire money to it if you need any help," said Quaid.

"But isn't it dangerous to wire money to an account in my name?" asked Eli. "I mean, won't someone figure out who I am if we use my real name?"

"Good question," said Quaid. "Well, the account will not be set up in the name of Eli Atkins but in a new name. Eli, you'll have to come up with a new name soon. We'll get back to that."

"Okay. But Mr. Dawson, please, keep your cash. You've done enough already. Besides, I have enough," said Eli.

"Eli, I know you took money from your dad's safe," said Quaid.

Eli winced noticeably and looked away.

Quaid placed his hands on Eli's shoulders. "Eli, look at me."

Eli turned and looked Quaid straight in the eyes.

"Eli, it's okay. I'm not judging you. Neither is Mrs. Babcock, here. You know that. You've done nothing wrong."

Annabelle nodded her head and smiled like only a mother can.

"Eli, I mean it, son. Please, take this money. I won't miss it. It's my hope that one day you'll be able to return the money to your dad."

Eli fought back the tears and nodded his head.

"Yes, sir. Thank you."

Eli stood alone, in the middle of the living room, his backpack at his feet. Quaid and Mrs. Babcock, side by side a few feet way. No one knew quite what to say. Mrs. Babcock crossed the room to a bookshelf where she had earlier in the day placed a small Bible.

"Eli, right now I know none of this makes sense. But do you remember what I told you when you washed up on my doorstep a few days ago?" asked Mrs. Babcock.

"Yes, ma'am. You told me that it was no accident that the Lord had sent me to you."

"That's right. And you know I believe that. Don't you?"

"Yes, ma'am, I do," said Eli.

"Then know this. The Lord loves you and will protect you. I know this like I know He'll raise the sun. I'm giving you this Bible 'cause you're going to have some tough times. Trust me when I tell you this—you'll find all the comfort, encouragement, and courage you'll ever need in this little book. The Lord gave us his words in this Bible because He loves us, and if you want to know the truth and the truth about Him, well, you got several ways of learning it. You can ask Him, you can read the Bible, and then there's the third way, which is what you're going through now, and that's just livin'."

Eli took the Bible and Mrs. Babcock hugged him tightly.

Breaking the hug, Mrs. Babcock looked up at Eli and smiled. "You best be on your way."

Eli kissed her on the cheek and shook Quaid's hand. He then picked up his backpack and walked out the back door and down the dock toward the waiting canoe, never once looking back.

* * *

Eli had been on the water for two hours paddling at a quick, steady pace. He figured he had three more hours or so until he would his reach destination. The water was calm, and the sun was setting directly ahead of him, blanketing the sky in a patchwork of reds and oranges. Quite simply, it was a beautiful evening. He didn't see another living soul on the water, and it occurred to him that, given the pleasant evening, the absence of others was unusual. He felt the need to be thankful for his solitude, knowing that most everyone in these parts was on the lookout for him.

Eli had taken the Bible from Mrs. Babcock more for her sake than his. He knew it was important to her. He'd grown up in the church but hadn't had much use for it. His mother was a churchgoer and look at her. Eli felt a seething anger tinged with fear whenever he thought of his mother. A lot of good Jesus had done for her.

But then there was Monty, his adoptive father. Monty went to church, but it was different with his dad. Eli knew believing in God was real for his dad. *So, maybe there is something to it,* thought Eli. So, yes, he felt thankful for the solitude this night and because he knew what his dad would do: pray. He prayed too, the best he knew how.

"God, thank you."

* * *

Quaid was driving five miles over the speed limit. He figured that Annabelle was right and that the officers at the roadblock would waive the hearse right through, but just the same, as he approached the town of Ravenel, he grew anxious. The hearse was empty, so his only fear was whether one of the officers would recognize him and start asking questions. As the traffic slowed, he counted a dozen vehicles ahead of him and four officers at the roadblock, two state troopers and two local police officers wearing the uniform of the Charleston Police Department. As the cars edged forward, his theoretical fears became very real. The patrolman manning the roadblock and checking the cars was Billy Haskell, a close friend of Quaid's third son, Quint.

"Oh, good Lord. What now?" muttered Quaid.

* * *

"Heh, boss," said Billy.

"Yeah, what's up?"

"I'm about to piss in my pants. Been drinking too much coffee out here. Can you cover for me while I take a leak?" asked Billy.

"Yeah, but make it fast."

Quaid slowed down to leave more space between him and the car in front as he pulled close to the roadblock, not knowing what he would say if Billy recognized him, which he most certainly would. With only two cars ahead of him he watched as Billy waved over to his boss.

"Dammit, he must see me."

Quaid gripped the steering wheel and could feel sweat trickling down the back of his neck.

"Wait. Wait a minute. What's goin' on?" said Quaid. "Hold on now. Is what I think is happening actually happening?" continued Quaid. "Yep ... he's gotta go. Well, how about that!"

Quaid began to will the cars ahead of him to go faster as he saw Billy trot off to the woods along the side of the highway.

"Let's go. Let's go."

As he pulled up to the roadblock, the officer motioned for him to lower his window. The officer poked his head in, and without saying a word, motioned for him to move along.

Quaid pulled through, barely able to contain his joy and excitement when he saw Billy in his rearview mirror jog back up the hill and resume his spot, checking cars. Quaid laughed so hard he thought he was going to cry.

"Hallelujah!" he screamed at the top of his lungs as he banged his hands on the steering wheel in time with the song on the radio.

* * *

Eli knew he had to be getting close to the pickup point when he saw a church steeple peering out over the river. Sure enough, just as she had said, there was boat ramp leading up to the church parking lot. He paddled up to the riverbank, hopped out, and pulled the canoe up onto the grass. He removed his backpack and set it on dry ground. He knew he needed to sink his canoe but was reluctant to do so until he was sure Quaid was going to make it.

He was winded, having paddled for the last five hours, taking only a few breaks. He walked up to the edge of the forest, sat down, leaned against a tree, and waited. He stared up at the sky and took in the stars and thought not about what had placed him here but about what lay ahead. But there'd be more time for that, he thought, as he saw a black hearse pull into the parking lot.

Eli rose and walked down to the water. He slid the canoe into the water and turned it over, forcing it into the water at an angle so air pockets wouldn't form. It took a few minutes but before long the canoe was submerged. He maneuvered it out into the middle of the river and watched it as it sunk. He then made his way back to the bank, retrieved his backpack, and walked up the hill to the waiting hearse. Quaid was standing next to the driver's side.

"We good?" asked Quaid.

Eli said nothing but changed into dry clothes and then opened the passenger side door.

"Yeah, we're good. Let's go."

Chapter 9

No Looking Back Now

Heading south on Savannah Highway, Early Monday Morning, June 4th

"Have you given much thought to a name?" asked Quaid.

Quaid had explained to Eli the night before when they were sitting on Mrs. Babcock's back porch that he couldn't go by Eli anymore. He'd need a name and a story. He couldn't be from the Bahamas. There'd be no way to fool folks into thinking he was. No, he had to be from someplace stateside.

"Yeah. I was thinking of calling myself Aaron Westfield," said Eli.

"Aaron Westfield," repeated Quaid. "And where is Aaron Westfield from?"

"Mobile, Alabama. I figure being from someplace on the water will explain why I'm comfortable around it," explained Eli.

"Makes sense. And how'd you come up with that name?"

"Baseball. Aaron for Hank Aaron, and Westfield for Westfield, Alabama which is where Willie Mays is from. Actually, they're both from Alabama."

Quaid smiled. He relaxed now, knowing the risk of discovery was slim. There'd be no more roadblocks between here and their destination, a bait and tackle shop the Babcocks owned in Beaufort, South Carolina. Francesco left the day before to stock the refrigerator and make the place ready for Eli. Eli would spend the next two nights sleeping on a cot in a room in the back of the shop while he waited for a fishing boat captain, another friend of Quaid, to pick him up and take him to the Bahamas.

"You do love the game, don't you?" asked Quaid.

"Yes, more than anything," answered Eli, wearing one of the first smiles Quaid had seen on his face in several days. "I figure that's one thing she couldn't take away from me. Baseball. When I get settled in, well, wherever I'm headed, I'll look for a way to play baseball. I know they play it in the Bahamas. There's a Bahamian player in the Atlanta Braves farm system named Wenty Ford. He's a pitcher, right-handed."

When Quaid didn't say anything, Eli looked over and it seemed there was something Quaid didn't want to say but needed to.

"What?" asked Eli.

"Well, I was thinking. You're pretty good. Hell. You're more than pretty good. You're the best natural baseball player I've ever seen at this age and, as you know, I'm a fan of the game."

"Yeah, I am good. So what's the problem?"

"You're too good. That's the problem. You'll attract attention. You don't think pro scouts aren't always on the look for the next hot player? Eli, I'm afraid you'd attract attention. The kind of attention that could land you right back in jail."

Quaid looked over at Eli. Eli was peering out the window into the stillness of the night.

"So, you're saying that if I play, folks will talk, a scout may spot me, and before you know it, they'll figure out I ain't Aaron Westfield but am actually Eli Atkins, wanted for murder."

"I'm afraid so," said Quaid.

"Well, I'll be damned. I guess she took baseball away from me too."

Eli and Quaid rode in silence the rest of the way.

* * *

Beaufort, SC, Wednesday, June 6th, sometime after midnight

"Eli, it's time," said Francesco as he shook the small cot Eli was sleeping on.

The last few days had passed slowly but without event. The manhunt for

Eli continued, but as each day passed and the net was cast wider, there were more holes in the net for slip-through. It was a simple matter of manpower. There were just too many places for someone to hide, especially someone at ease in the wild. The authorities figured that eventually Eli would surface. He'd need food, maybe medical attention. Or maybe he'd just get sloppy or horny and go looking for a bar where he could meet a girl. What they didn't count on was Eli having friends that could secure safe hiding and transit to the Bahamas on a private fishing charter.

Eli sat up and looked around. He had slept soundly. In fact, it was the best sleep in a few days. But now it was time to move.

"Okay. Let's go," said Francesco.

Francesco cracked open the back door to the shop, looked about, and assured himself that no one was around. Eli climbed into the bed of Francesco's pickup truck and pulled a blanket up over him and his backpack.

"Very good," said Francesco. "We're just a short ride from the water. I anchored our boat in a small cove where no one will see us. Don't you worry."

Francesco was right. The ride was short but traveling over the dirt road to the hidden cove seemed like an eternity to Eli. He felt every rock and bump along the way. Francesco pulled the truck off the road and parked it out of the way. Eli climbed out of the truck, grabbed his backpack, and the two of them set off for the water. Both pros, they boarded the boat, started the engine, and set off for the open sea, neither one saying a word. After a few minutes, Francesco picked up the radio and made contact.

Three miles later, Francesco saw the charter boat, a fifty-three-foot Hatteras Classic. He pulled up alongside and placed the throttle in neutral. Eli threw his backpack to the captain of the charter, and then turned back to Francesco. They hardly knew each other, and they didn't have much time, but Eli felt a connection with him. Maybe it was because Francesco was Eli's last connection with his old life. Regardless, they embraced. Then Eli gracefully made his way from Francesco's boat to the Hatteras. Francesco slipped back into forward and was off, headed back to shore.

Once Francesco was clear, the captain began to raise the anchor.

"My name is Captain Bootle, and this is my boat. I don't know what you're runnin' from, but you're a friend of Mr. Dawson and that's good enough for me. And I don't think I want to know your name, but I need somethin' to call you. So, what should I call?"

"You can call me Aaron."

* * *

NASSAU, BAHAMAS, FRIDAY, JUNE 8TH, 1973

They were motoring east, and the sun was over their shoulders as they approached the harbor. The city's light twinkled more brightly as each minute passed and the setting sun receded. Eli was standing in the bow pulpit with his hands placed firmly on the railing. His old life was three days and 450 nautical miles behind him, but it already seemed like another lifetime.

Just over a month ago, Eli was with Kimberly, making love to her on his sleeping bag in a hidden-away corner of a beach only they knew about. She was headed to college, and he dreamt of playing center field in the majors. And now she was dead. The question that remained was whether Eli Atkins was too.

The End of Part One

PART TWO

Finding My Way

Chapter 10

My Story

My name is Eli Atkins, but I changed it to Aaron Westfield. I'm from Charleston, South Carolina, but the folks in Nassau, my home for the last five years, think I'm from Mobile, Alabama. I'm wanted in Charleston for raping and murdering my girlfriend, Kimberly Prestwick, but I'm innocent. I skipped town when my mother told me she was going to send me to the electric chair with her testimony.

This is my story, and the best place to begin is with my arrival in the Bahamas.

Chapter 11

Captain Bootle

Friday, June 8th, 1973, Nassau, Bahamas

During our time together motoring from the coast of South Carolina to Nassau Harbor, Captain Bootle and I fell into an easy rhythm. It didn't take him long to figure out I was comfortable both on the water and with silence. We took turns at the helm, sleeping below deck, and preparing food. But three days is a long time to work side by side without learning a little about the other. Since my story was off limits, we stuck to his.

It was early on our second day together—Thursday, I believe. I was coming up from the galley with a pot of coffee in my right hand using my left hand for balance. I refilled his cup and Captain Bootle nodded a thank you.

"So, Captain, do you live on New Providence?" I asked. "Do you have a family?"

"Nassau, mon. No one says New Providence. You heading to Nassau. And yes, I have a family, a beautiful family."

"Are you from Nassau? I mean, is Nassau where you were born?"

"No, mon. Jamaica. I was born in Kingston, Jamaica."

"Is that why you're wearing that T-Shirt with a picture of Bob Marley on it?"

"Sure, I guess. But Bob is loved the world over, not just in Jamaica, mon."

"If you're Jamaican, why don't you have hair like Bob Marley?"

"Used to. Then one day, I was workin' a charter and a friend got his dreadlocks caught in the reel when we had a big fish on. Pretty gruesome. I cut my hair that night. Been wearing this short afro ever since," he said as he dragged his hand across his head. "Besides, dreads are for the young. I'm old now and I got the belly to prove it," he said as he laughed and patted his gut.

"So why did you leave Jamaica?" I asked.

"For the work. Better jobs in the Bahamas."

"Are a lot of people in the Bahamas from someplace else?"

"We're all from someplace else, mon, even Bahamians."

"What about your wife? Is she from Jamaica too?"

"You ask a lot of questions."

I kept silent, sipped my coffee, and surveyed the horizon as I tried to think of what to say.

"I know you don't want to know anything about me, but know this, I'm going to be pulling into Nassau later tomorrow and I won't know anyone or anything about where I'm livin'. I ain't bein' nosy; just tryin' to figure things out."

I looked at Captain, waiting for something. Got nothing.

"Thought maybe I could know you," I said.

"You know Mr. Pinder and Mr. Dawson. That'll be good enough," he said.

I looked at Captain hoping for a crack, for something more, but he just stared straight ahead, so I did too.

After a minute of silence, he spoke again.

"And you'll know Captain Bootle."

I turned to acknowledge what he said. He never diverted his eyes from the horizon, but I saw a smile crease his face and I returned my gaze to the distant horizon and smiled as well.

Chapter 12

My New Home

Lyford Cay Marina, Nassau, Friday, June 8TH, 1973

We were three miles out and Captain Bootle told me to go down below and to stay there until he motioned for me to come up.

"What's the problem?" I asked.

"Customs, mon. If you're on board then you must be someone and we don't know yet who you are."

"Is this going to be a problem? I can't be sent back."

"No problem, mon. Like I said, you have Pinder and Dawson on your side."

I was starting to wonder about who this Mr. Pinder was and what the deal was with Mr. Dawson. How could he help me down here?

From a cabin below, I peered out the portal as we approached the harbor. I had never seen so many huge boats all in one place. These weren't boats; these were yachts. Yachts came through Charleston every year as folks were heading south from the Northeast toward the Bahamas for the winter and then returning in early summer before hurricane season returned. But that was just a few yachts here and there. This was something else altogether.

We pulled up to the dock and a young man expertly received the line cast down by Mr. Bootle and tied us off on the port side. Captain came down below and picked up a small satchel and he told me the harbor captain would be here soon to check our papers.

"You stay out of sight, mon, and there'll be no trouble."

I heard a few voices but couldn't understand a word being said.

Ten minutes later, I heard Captain Bootle step back onto the boat.

"Aaron, all is clear. Time to be on your way."

That morning, wearing shorts and a T-Shirt, flip flops, and an Atlanta Braves baseball hat, I packed everything else I owned into my backpack and duffle bag. I tossed my bags up through the hatch and went topside. As I looked around, the sight was even more impressive. Everywhere I looked was one enormous yacht or fishing boat after another. And everything was so clean, made to look more so in the reflection off the blue water. And not a cloud in the sky.

Standing on the dock alongside the boat was a man I believe was waiting on me and doing so impatiently. Glancing at his watch, he appeared to be in a hurry. Frankly, he looked like someone who was always in a hurry. He was of medium height, but everything else about him made him appear taller than he was. He was thin but not in an unhealthy manner, and he was rolling back and forth on his feet, popping up onto his toes and then back again. His eyebrows were dark and bushy and looked as if they'd been cut from the same cloth as his mustache.

"Thank you, Captain Bootle. I'll take it from here," the strange little man said.

Everything was moving so fast, and I wanted to slow it down. When I stepped off this boat, I would be in the Bahamas—more specifically, the city of Nassau. People, lots of people, had helped me escape, beginning with Mrs. Babcock. Then there was Mr. Dawson, Mrs. Babcock's son-in-law Francesco, Captain Bootle, and now apparently this nervous-looking man standing on the dock. Excuse my French, but what the hell was going on?

I turned to look at Captain Bootle. He must have sensed my apprehension.

"It's going to be all right, mon. You're going to like it here. You're going to be just fine."

"Captain Bootle?"

"Yeah, mon."

"Thank you."

And with that, Captain Bootle grabbed my duffle bag and threw it down on the dock, nearly knocking over the nervous man as I hoisted my backpack and stepped off onto the dock. I turned back to the boat to say goodbye.

"Captain Bootle, how do I find you?"

"It's a small island, mon. You want Captain Bootle, you ask for Captain Bootle."

And with that he waved and gently powered the boat off the dock as the dock hand released the line and cast it back on deck.

* * *

"Aaron Westfield, is it?"

I turned and looked at the man talking to me. He was wearing white pants and a blue blazer with two rows of buttons over a white shirt, and he was twirling a pair of sunglasses in one hand and extending the other for me to shake. Suddenly, I remembered who I was or at least who I was supposed to be—Aaron Westfield from Mobile, Alabama.

Taking his hand in mine, he shook it vigorously as I answered, "Yes sir."

"Well, all right then. I'm Nigel Pinder, at your service. Come along, we have a bit of a drive ahead of us."

And he turned and walked briskly down the dock. I grabbed my duffel bag and with my backpack still hanging off one shoulder set off to catch up with this curious little man who knew who I was and that I would be arriving this morning.

"Wait, wait a second," I called out.

He stopped and turned back toward me as I caught up, his hands clasped in front of him.

"Okay, you're Nigel Pinder, but exactly who are you? How'd you know my name and where the hell am I?" I asked as I turned and took in the sights of the mega-yachts as far as one could see.

"Ah. You are confused. I can see that now. You are at the Lyford Cay Marina, courtesy of one Mr. Quaid Dawson, and I am, as I said, Mr. Nigel Pinder, also courtesy of Mr. Quaid Dawson. I am his private banker. Now, I hope that clears everything up. So please, if we may, lunch awaits. You are hungry, I presume."

"Starving."

"Of course you are. Now, chop-chop."

"Say, does Captain Bootle work for Mr. Dawson?"

"Yes. Of course. That's Mr. Dawson's boat you've spent the last three days on. His smallest one, mind you."

"His smallest one? You've got to be kidding me. So, Mr. Dawson has more than one boat?"

"But of course."

Eli stood on the dock with his duffle bag at his feet and his backpack slung over one shoulder and wondered: *What in tarnation is a private banker?*

* * *

Five minutes later, I was sitting in the front seat of a very cool car. The top was down, and we were speeding along a two-lane road with the ocean off to the left. The wind was warm. It felt good. In a way, it felt like home—Charleston, that is.

When we left the marina, we drove through a neighborhood of beautiful homes and wide sidewalks. I couldn't help but notice similarities between these homes and many of the homes on the southern peninsula of Charleston. The colors were the same and the shutters too, but these homes were newer, not like the hundred-year-old homes in Charleston.

As we drove on, we passed a golf course. The sign announced that it was the Lyford Cay Golf Club. The grass was as green as any I had seen. I thought of my dad and his love for the game. I had played a few times. Dad joked that it wasn't right that he had to work so hard at the game and it came so naturally for me. I'd joke that if you could hit a ball that was thrown at you from sixty feet away, then how hard could it be to hit a ball sitting on the ground, right in front of you?

"Um, Mr. Pinder?"

"Yes, Aaron."

"Help me out here. I understand that the Bahamas is British and this is how y'all drive, but as I look around I see that some of the cars have the steering wheel on the right-hand side and others on the left."

"Ah, yes, I can see how this might be confusing to someone new to the islands. We're British, as you say—that is, we're part of the Commonwealth—but as for our culture, we're less British than we used to be, and change is in the wind."

"What do you mean?"

"What I mean is that we're becoming more independent in some ways and more dependent in others."

"I still don't know what you're talking about."

"Okay. Take this car for instance. It's a 1968 Aston Martin DB6. I imported it from London. Special order, you see. It was built for the market in the UK, hence the steering column on the right-hand side. While I am a Bahamian, I strongly identify with the Crown. It's been that way with my family for some time. I am a direct descendant of a Loyalist. The first Pinders came to the islands in 1783 and they came from Charleston. We have that in common."

"Yeah, I remember studying about that in history class last year. After we won the Revolutionary War, I guess some of y'all didn't feel so welcome and you left."

"That's right. But as you call it the Revolutionary War, many considered it more of a Civil War. One of the common misconceptions is that everyone living in the Colonies at the time was in favor of leaving the protection of the king and undertaking your experiment with democracy. Not so. There were many living in the Colonies who wished to remain under the Crown. At the outbreak, the war was between the Tories and the Whigs, or the Loyalists and the Patriots, as you called them. The king sent troops to quell the rebellion, but to no avail."

"And the world was never the same—at least that's what my teacher said."

"And she's right."

"Say, you don't think democracy was a bad idea, do you?"

"No, not at all. Quite fond of it, actually. Just having a little fun, that's all. Do you enjoy history?"

"Yes, it was the one class I liked."

"Fabulous, just fabulous. We're going to get along smashingly."

"But, back to the cars," I said. "Why do some have the steering column on the left and some on the right and what about the changes you said were coming?"

"Yes, of course. Back to the cars. Well, the cars with the steering column on the left are made by American companies. This is the source of much of the change. Our culture is heavily influenced by our proximity to the States. We purchase many of our products from your country. We see movies made in Hollywood. Our kids listen to your music. As we approach town, you will see fast food restaurants from your country. And then there is tourism. Our most important industry after banking. Americans vacation here and the money you spend provides the livelihood for a great many people."

"I guess that makes sense. This is a cool car. Looks like the car James Bond drove in one of his movies."

"*Goldfinger*."

"That's right."

"In that movie, he drove a model DB5. You are sitting in the newest model, the DB6. Rest easy, though. It doesn't have an ejector seat."

"Now that would be really cool.'

"Do you like James Bond movies?"

"Yeah. Who doesn't?"

"Well, maybe Mr. Dawson will introduce you to him someday—Sean Connery, that is. They play golf together on occasion at the Lyford Cay Golf Club. Ah, here we are. Lunch."

Eli remained in the car, dumbfounded, and stared at Mr. Pinder as he casually walked on ahead.

* * *

Café Abaco, Nassau

We walked up a flight of stairs and a very pretty girl who looked to be my age greeted us holding two menus under her arm. She was maybe five and a half feet tall with short, curly black hair. She wore faded bell bottom jeans and a white blouse with a pattern of dolphins running diagonally across it. Her skin was caramel colored, and she had the brightest white teeth I think I had ever seen. I tried not to stare.

"Good day, Mr. Pinder."

"And to you, Melissa. It's been a while since I have seen you."

"True, true. During school, I only work weekends, but we let out for the summer a few days back so most days you'll find me here until school starts up again."

"Well, it's lovely to see you. Is your father here?"

"Yes. Would you like to speak with him?"

"Yes, and a table for two."

"Of course, your usual table is waiting for you and ..."

"Oh, how rude of me. Melissa, I am pleased to introduce you to Aaron Westfield. Aaron, this beautiful and intelligent young girl is Melissa Bastian. I believe you know her uncle, Francesco Bastian."

"Please to meet you. How do you know Uncle Franky?"

I was speechless. What was I supposed to say? 'Oh, your uncle helped me escape the United States so I wouldn't have to face murder charges'?

"Uh, well I don't know him that well, really. I, uh … just met him once."

I looked over at Mr. Pinder, silently pleading for a little help. About then a man strolled up alongside us and introduced himself.

"Nigel, good to see you. And you must be Aaron. I'm Javon. Javon Bastian and this is my restaurant, the Café Abaco. The best food on the island. Welcome. You are my guest today. Right this way."

Before I could say more, Mr. Bastian grabbed me by the arm and led me out onto the porch. I looked back over my shoulder and smiled and waved at Melissa, but she was already greeting the next guests.

As we followed Javon Bastian, Mr. Pinder leaned over to whisper in my ear.

"Sorry about that, old boy. We'll have to work on our backstory a bit."

* * *

As the three of us sat down for lunch, an awkward silence pulled up a chair and joined us. Mr. Pinder and Mr. Bastian exchanged glances and Mr. Pinder picked up the menu nervously.

"So, Nigel, any trouble with customs?" asked Mr. Bastian.

"No. None whatsoever."

"Excellent. Then it's official," said Mr. Bastian as he looked at me.

"What? What's official?" I asked.

Mr. Pinder leaned forward and placed his elbows on the table and laced his fingers together as if he were about to say grace and answered my question.

"You are. You are officially Aaron Westfield working in the Bahamas on a work visa."

"I don't know how he did it so fast," remarked Mr. Bastian. "He had to procure and file a medical certificate, police certificate, passport pictures, a copy of your passport, written references from previous employers, a labor certificate with a Notice of Vacancy, and the requisite documentation from the business hiring you," said Mr. Bastian as he looked at me.

I looked back and forth between the two men. "I'm sorry, but what exactly is going on?"

"Ah, to have such friends," said a chuckling Mr. Pinder. "Aaron, dear boy, and it is 'Aaron' from now on, mind you."

"Yes, sir. I know. I'm now Aaron Westfield."

"That's right," said Mr. Pinder. "You see, one can't just waltz into the Bahamas and get a job. One needs an employer to sponsor them, and the employer must demonstrate that he has a job opening and that the job could not be filled locally. Without these limitations, we'd have folks from all over flocking here for work. You see, you're living in paradise now."

"So, you're saying setting me up here to live wasn't easy."

"Easy? Not by a long shot. On top of it all, he had to create Aaron Westfield first before he could apply for the young man's visa," answered Nigel.

"And let me guess, Mr. Dawson did all this," I said.

The two men across from me exchanged another glance and I couldn't help but wonder, and not for the first time that day, how Mr. Dawson, the Mr. Quaid Dawson I knew from Charleston, could be the same man they were talking about. But I was starving, and the approaching waiter interrupted my thoughts. Mr. Bastian took over and ordered for me.

The lunch was fantastic and not much different from what I could get at home. We started with something called a conch fritter that, if it were a person, would be a cousin to the hush puppy. For lunch I ate grilled mahi mahi with green peas and dirty rice. And without even asking my age, Mr. Bastian ordered me a beer, a Kalik beer. I drank three and, when I cleaned my plate in no time, Mr. Bastian had the kitchen bring me another fish to eat.

After lunch, Mr. Pinder said he had to be getting back to his office, and he told me that we would meet in his office on Monday morning. I was told Mr. Bastian would take over for now. I had so many questions I wanted to ask, but frankly I was running out of steam. The events of the last week were piling up and about to come crashing down on me, and combined with the beer, three days in the sun on a boat, and a large meal, the only thing I wanted to do was sleep.

Mr. Bastian said he just needed a few minutes with his staff and then we'd be on our way. I wanted to ask him "On our way to where?" but I figured I'd learn soon enough.

I fell asleep in the car as Mr. Bastian drove me away from downtown Nassau toward where I would be spending my first night living in the Bahamas. As the car slowed to a stop on a gravel road, Mr. Bastian nudged me and announced that I was home.

"Ya, bey ... wake up. We're here."

I sat up in the car seat and stared out over the ocean.

"Where's here?" I asked.

"Home. Adelaide Village. My parent's village and now it is yours."

I stepped out of the car and took in my surroundings. Small, humble homes, some of them no more than thatched-roof huts. Javon pointed out mine. I grabbed my bags from the back seat and walked toward my new home, framed on each side by gently swaying palm trees, and with the bluest water I had ever seen washing up onto a bright, sandy white beach, mere steps from my door. I walked farther ahead, looked to my left, and saw a hammock seemingly suspended in time.

"Beautiful, isn't it?"

It looked so much like a cove I used to visit with Kimberly. The water at home wasn't as blue but the similarities were strong. I didn't know whether to smile or cry.

"So, is this where I'm going to live?" I asked as much as stated.

"Ya, bey."

"For free or do I owe somebody rent?"

"Dat none of my business. Between you and the owner."

"The owner, huh? Let me guess—Quaid Dawson owns this place."

"Ya, bey. Your friend lives in the tall grass. He owns some prized land on this island and throughout the family islands too."

"The family islands?"

"You have a lot to learn, but we'll teach you. Starting tonight. You'll have dinner with my family. My parents live down that road," he said.

I looked in the direction he was pointing.

"Just walk about five minutes or so in that direction and you'll come to their home. We'll all be there—my parents, my wife, and our children and my sister, her husband and their children. It will be a big time."

I hesitated, searching for the right words.

"Mr. Bastian, does everyone know?" I asked.

"Know what?"

"That I'm Aaron and not Eli. Do they know who I really am?"

"No one knows you're Eli and what sent you here but me and my wife, Mr. Quaid Dawson, and Mr. Nigel Pinder. To everyone else you are Aaron Westfield from Mobile, Alabama. Does that help you?"

"I guess. It's just strange. I've been Eli my whole life."

Javon had started toward his car but stopped and walked back toward me.

"You're still Eli," he said as he tapped me on the chest with his right index finger.

"I don't know you, but I know my brother Francesco and he tells me with his hand on the Bible that you are a good man and an innocent man. You have come across our doorstep and Jesus tells me I am to help those I come across. So, know this, your secrets are safe with me, and I am opening our home to you. But only you can walk through that door. Do you hear what I'm saying?"

"Yeah. I think so."

Javon placed his hands on my shoulders and pulled me in for a hug and then stepped away, turned, and walked back toward his car, and then cried out over his shoulder, "Don't be late or Mama will let you hear about it!"

"How will I know which home is theirs?" I asked.

"Look for my car parked alongside. You get lost, just ask anyone where Chad and Ariana Bastian live. My mother will have a fresh glass of switch waiting for you."

"What time should I get there?"

"Before sundown. Now get some rest."

* * *

I entered my new home and looked about. It was simple, but it would do. It consisted of two rooms and a bathroom. I threw my duffel and backpack on the bed in the back room and returned to the front room, where I found a round table, a small icebox, and a sofa big enough for two people. I opened the icebox and found a six-pack of Kalik beer inside along with a note from Mr. Pinder.

"*Welcome to your new home, Aaron.*"

I walked outside and sat on the hammock. As I looked out across the ocean, I thought about how far I had come and how far away my old life seemed. Little League playoffs would begin soon. This was the last year Walker was eligible to play Little League baseball and his team had an excellent chance of winning it all. I was going to help as a hitting coach whenever I could. Next week, I was set to join the Charleston Pirates, a minor league baseball team affiliated with the Pittsburgh Pirates. It was Single-A ball, but it was a start.

That was the future. At least it was three weeks ago. But three weeks ago, my future changed forever when Kimberly was raped and murdered, crimes I was arrested for and charged with.

Last week I should have graduated from high school with my friends. Instead, I took to the rivers and streams surrounding Charleston and ran. And now, here I am in a small beachside village in the Bahamas. No family.

No friends. No school. No job. No baseball. No idea of what tomorrow will bring. And no idea when I can return to Charleston.

And I am at a complete loss, not knowing what to do or feel. One minute I'm angry, the next scared, sometimes confused, and other times I am overwhelmed with feelings of gratitude. Between Mrs. Babcock, Mr. Dawson, Francesco, and now his brother Javon, I am, well ... fortunate, I guess. Let's put it this way. I owe them my life. With my mother prepared to testify against me, I was looking at the death penalty for sure.

So, yeah, there are times when I don't know what to feel. I do know one thing—I'm done with the tears. I'm all cried out. And what good would it do? None. No, no more tears. No pity. So, if pressed on the issue, as to what I'm feeling, I'd say that the one lingering feeling, the taste in my mouth I can't get rid of, the one that sticks to my tongue like a bad hangover, is this: I'm livid. I'm furious because so much has been taken from me. But I am determined to live on.

* * *

LATER THAT DAY, 6:00 PM

I fell asleep in the hammock and, if it hadn't been for a barking dog down the road, I may have slept right through dinner. I went back inside and placed my clothes in the chest of drawers and hung a few items in the closet. After putting away every earthly possession I owned, I grabbed a beer and walked outside and sat in the hammock again and stared out at the blue water. I was starting to think I'd spend a lot of time on this hammock. What else was I going to do?

Looking west, I wondered what Dad and Walker were up to. Are they worried? Do they think I'm dead or alive? Are they looking for me? And what about Mom. Did she tell Dad what she threatened to do? Doubt it. And what's everybody else thinking? Now that I've fled Charleston, does everyone think I'm guilty? How could they? How could they think I killed Kimberly? And now that I've run, unless the real killer is caught, can I ever go back? Now that I've run, will the police even bother looking for the real killer?

I've got to stop thinking like this. I'd done this earlier in the day. It's pointless. And what good are tears? I'd vowed earlier I was done with them. If I dwell on these questions, what hope is there? No, I could count on Dad.

He believes in me and so does Mr. Baslin. They'd see to it that the police kept the investigation going. This would all be over soon. A month, two at most, and I'd be back in Charleston. My baseball career would just have to wait, but I could stay in shape while I was here.

Kimberly was gone forever, and I could only hope that, over time, the pain would slip away. Nothing to be done about that. But I know she would want me to go on living my life, which is what I intended to do. So, for the next month or two, I'd be Aaron Westfield. I can do this.

So, I looked west and then at my watch, and not knowing exactly what Javon meant when he said to arrive before sunset, I stood up from the hammock and walked down the road to meet the Bastian family for dinner.

Chapter 13

The Bastian Family

Adelaide Village, Nassau, Friday, June 8th, 1973, suppertime

Javon's parents, Chad and Arianna, moved to Adelaide Village ten years ago for the slower pace. Chad was a retired hotel manager and now worked as a lay pastor. Arianna had worked in the public library system and now made crafts for sale to tourists in the local street-side markets. When they moved to Adelaide Village, they encouraged their children and grandchildren to never lose sight of where they had come from, how far they had traveled, as a people, and how good the islands had been to them.

Times had not always been good and racial issues seemed to never fully go away, but there was no denying that the Bahamas became a safe haven for enslaved Africans as the world saw its way to the end of institutional slavery. Adelaide Village was founded in the early 1830s as a place enslaved people rescued from illegal slave trading ships could reside. In 1807, Great Britain outlawed the slave trade in those regions under its control and U.S. President Thomas Jefferson signed into law the act prohibiting the importation of slaves. Slavery still existed and Britain did not outlaw the institution completely in the countries it controlled until 1834. Despite the end of the legal slave trade in 1807, slave trading persisted, fed in part by the demand for slaves in Cuba, Brazil, and the Southern colonies.

In 1831, the British Navy boarded the *Rosa*, a Portuguese slave trading ship, and seized 157 African souls, making them property of the Crown. Given their proximity to Nassau, these people were brought there, where the governor at the time, Sir James Carmichael Smyth, allowed them to live on ungranted Crown land as newly liberated Africans on the southwestern end in what became known as Adelaide Village.

An apprenticeship program started by the Bahamian government assigned free blacks rescued from slave traders to masters who were charged with teaching the Africans a trade. After a period of no more than fourteen years, the apprenticeship would end, and they would be free to earn wages. During the apprenticeship, they received food, clothing, shelter, and medical care, and their lives were very similar to those of slaves they often worked shoulder to shoulder with.

* * *

Javon was sitting on their back porch with Javon's parents, Chad and Arianna Bastian, enjoying the sun's descent signaling the end of another peaceful day. Javon's wife sat with them when she wasn't needed in the kitchen. They watched their neighbors' young children, running and playing together, and Javon and Andrea dreamed of the day when they would be grandparents. Though only in their mid-forties, their oldest, their daughter Gina, was twenty-two and in love. Everyone assumed that her young beau would propose any time now, opening the way for grandchildren for them and great-grandchildren for their parents, all four of which were still alive and living either on Nassau or one of the family islands.

In addition to Gina, Javon and Andrea had two other children: Anthony, age nineteen, and their youngest, Melissa, age sixteen, whom Aaron had met earlier in the day. Javon's sister, Kia, would be arriving soon with her clan. Andrea's family lived on Abaco, so they did not see her side of the family as much.

Javon and Andrea's second child, Anthony, was talking about attending law school in the United States. But first he had to graduate from college. In the coming Fall, Anthony would move to town and be a freshman in the inaugural class at the newly formed College of Bahamas. For the last two years, since graduating from high school, he had worked in the family's restaurant and had also become politically active in the Progressive Liberal Party. He idolized Lyndon Pindling, a member of the Party, and the Bahamas' first black prime minister. It was because of this man's influence that Anthony wanted to become a lawyer and he dreamed of attending Oxford as Lyndon Pindling had. Knowing Oxford was out of his reach, he made attending law school in the United States his goal.

Javon and Andrea worked downtown and lived in a neighborhood close by, but they enjoyed visiting Javon's parents and the restful pace of Adelaide Village. His parents' move to the Village had rekindled in them an appreciation for their roots in the Bahamas. Life was changing on the islands. Some changes were for the best, but others were less welcome.

* * *

Javon was right; his parents' house was easy to spot. I wasn't sure if I should knock on the front door or follow the voices coming from the backyard. I decided to follow the voices, and as I turned the corner, I saw an elderly woman in a rocking chair. We made eye contact and she smiled at me and leaned forward slightly to speak to Javon, who was sitting across from her. Javon turned in his chair and then stood up with great fanfare to announce my arrival as the night's guest of honor.

"Aaron, come here, bey."

I walked over and Javon threw his arm around my shoulder. He was a tall man. I know because I'm six-foot-three and he was nearly my height. He had broad shoulders too. He gave off the vibe of someone who had played ball.

"Everyone, come meet our guest of honor tonight and a new friend of the family," he said.

Javon proceeded to introduce me to the woman in the rocking chair, his mother, and then to his wife, who exited the house drying her hands on a cloth wrapped around her waist. He also introduced me to his father, who had been tending a makeshift grill built from a large metal drum, and then to his three children and finally to his sister Kia and her husband Mateo and their two children.

I was overwhelmed by the fuss they were all making and didn't know what to say. After the fanfare had calmed down, I looked about and managed a few words.

"It's nice to meet y'all. Um, I'm Aaron."

Everyone laughed, but they weren't laughing at me, and it helped cut the tension.

"Someone bring this man a beer," Javon said.

As one of the younger children ran off looking for a beer, Javon's mother, Arianna, a tall and very large-breasted woman, rose from her rocking chair and gently took each of my hands in hers.

"Aaron, we are so happy to have you in our home. You are welcome anytime."

For the second time that day, I had to fight back tears as I thought to myself, *So, this is what family is.*

* * *

The Bastian clan set up a long table outside and everyone started taking their seats. Chad and Arianna each sat at on one end of the table, and I was given the middle seat on the side of the table facing the ocean, the seat of honor according to Javon. Javon's wife, Andrea, sat across from me, and the children haphazardly scrambled for the remaining seats.

I was looking at a table filled with large dishes full of food, but before we could dig in, we held hands and Chad Bastian said grace. Everyone then picked up whatever plate was in front of them, took a serving, and passed the plate to their right. I helped myself to a grilled lobster tail, thinking it was the main course, and then to a helping of peas and rice, mac and cheese, and much to my delight, more of those conch fritters I remembered from lunch. Not wanting to be rude, when I was passed a bowl of grouper boiled with potatoes and seasoned with onion and thyme, I had to study my plate and figure out how I would fit it all on.

Andrea, to my right, snickered and said: "Big Mama, I believe we need to get our guest of honor a large mixing bowl."

Passing the bowl of fish to my right, I hesitated and looked around at a table of smiling faces.

"What? What's so funny?" I asked.

"You, mon," said Chad. "But you make my wife, Big Mama over there, very happy, so eat up."

Big Mama was beaming, and everyone returned their attention to the food in front of them. The conversation never ebbed, and I felt a sense of peace and joy flowing from these people.

"So, Aaron, is this your first time in the Bahamas?" asked Mateo.

"Yes. Frankly, it's my first time anywhere."

"And what brings you here?" asked Mateo's wife, Kia.

Javon, Kia's brother, who must have sensed my anxiety over questions like this, spoke up.

"Well, Aaron here is friends with Mr. Quaid Dawson, and through his efforts, Aaron has secured a job with a small bank here in town."

Everyone at the table reacted with whistles, more laughter, and ribbing in universal acknowledgement of who Quaid Dawson was.

"Oh, mon, I feel sorry for you. Having to struggle so in this life," said Chad, making no effort to hide his good-natured sarcasm.

"Big Mama, I know why he's eating so much," said a young boy across the table. "He doesn't know where his next meal is coming from."

The boy's sister, laughing, covered her mouth full of food with a napkin.

I wasn't sure what to make of all this and I sure as hell didn't know what to make of Quaid Dawson, a man I thought I knew. I grabbed my beer and took a swig, hoping the conversation would end.

Andrea, Javon's wife, sitting to my left, patted my left hand.

"Aaron, you are among friends and Quaid Dawson has been a friend to our family and to the people of these Islands, a good friend. We're happy for you. You have much and that's okay. The Lord has blessed us all, just in different ways."

"I sure could use more of the blessings that the good Lord bestowed upon Quaid Dawson," said Mateo.

"No more of that kind of talk, now," said Big Mama. "Aaron, you no-never-mind them. They have no manners, and if they weren't all so full grown, their pappy here would take a switch to them."

Everyone laughed and I relaxed.

"Look," I said, "I'm not rich."

"What do you mean, you're not rich?" asked Javon's son, Anthony. "You're white and living and working in the Bahamas.

"Just because I'm white doesn't mean I'm rich," answered Aaron.

"It does in the Bahamas," said Chad as he laughed and took another swig of his beer. "But as my daughter-in-law Andrea said, it's all okay. We've all been blessed. Remember, you are indeed among friends."

I took a longer swig of my beer and smiled at the table.

Kia spoke up and broke the silence that had descended on the evening. "Aaron, since this is your first time in the Bahamas, you must have questions for us. What can we tell you about the islands and about life here?"

"I don't know where to start. I guess I'd like to know what it means to be from the Bahamas. I mean, the Bahamas are a bunch of Islands."

"Over seven hundred," said Anthony.

"Okay. So where is everyone from, not just your family, but everyone in the Bahamas?" I asked.

"Good questions and we can answer the question as to who Bahamians are by telling you where we are all from," said Javon. "Dad, why don't you go first?"

"Ya, mon," he said as if that answered the question. "Jamaican, through and through. Both of my parents were born in Kingston, as was I. But my family moved to Andros in 1931."

"Andros?" I asked.

"It's one of the islands in the Bahamas," said Javon.

"Why did you move?" I asked.

"For the work. I was twenty-three, mon, and restless. Life was changing in Jamaica. My family, we'd been sugar farmers for generations, but that life was growing harder. Prices kept falling. The wealthy kept buying up the land and they drove the prices down. Us smaller farms, family-owned farms, we banded together, but there's no stopping the power of cheap goods. Bananas were moving in too. More and more folks were growing bananas, which should have meant fewer people growing sugarcane, but it didn't work out that way." Chad looked at his wife, who smiled and patted him on the shoulder.

Chad continued. "I had an older brother, Winston. He got wrapped up in politics, mon. Marcus Garvey was organizing and raising trouble. He formed a trade union and one of Jamaica's first political parties. My brother thought Marcus Garvey was a god. Well, Marcus got himself arrested by your government," said Chad as he nodded at me. "My parents were no fans of Garvey. Garvey kept preaching how we all needed to return to Africa, but we liked living in Jamaica and we never had no problem with living under British rule. But Garvey's arrest? That was all lies, mon. He may have been guilty of something—we all are—but he was arrested for mail fraud. Can you believe that? If that ain't a white man's made-up crime, I don't know what is. Anyway, when he was arrested, there was trouble in the streets. My brother, he was killed. Our family home was burnt to the ground. It was time to leave. So, we up and left Jamaica. And here we are."

The silence was broken by Chad's daughter, Kia. "And we're glad you are."

"So when did you move to Andros?" I asked.

"Ah, that would have been in 1923. And times were good. My papa and I were busy diving for sponges."

"Diving for sponges?" I asked.

"Yeah, mon. Big business. Most sponges found in the bottom of the ocean come from Greece. I get it—you think sponges come in a box that you buy at a store." Chuckling, Chad shouted out to his grandchildren: "Someone fetch this young man a sponge from inside."

Kia's daughter, Jessica, scooted her chair back from the table, ran inside, and returned quickly with a sponge, which she handed me.

"Okay, I know what these are. I studied them in biology class last year."

"Well, for fifteen years, my father and I dove for them, dried them in the sun, and sold them. We did well. Most divers didn't. Even the best, those that could stay down for three minutes at a time and do it again and again. Hard work, I tell you. But my papa, he was the smart one. He knew the money was in the selling and not the diving. So, we did both. We dove and we sold. He scrimped and saved and was able to buy a boat, and then another, and then another one, until we had our own fleet. Six boats in all."

"Is that how you got this sponge?" I asked as I turned it over in my hand.

"No, mon. We bought that one from a shop in town. I bet it comes from Greece. No one really knows what happened, but in one year, sponges were wiped out in our waters," said Chad.

"The year was 1938," said Mateo. "Some sort of fungus infected and killed the sponges. Papa is right—no one really knows how it happened."

"And that's how we ended up here," said Javon. "Looking for work, my parents moved to Nassau."

"So, what did you do next?" asked Chad.

"Ah, enough about me. I thought you wanted to know where Bahamians come from. Hey, Big Mama, your turn," said Chad. Turning to me, Chad winked and said, "Now, she has a story."

"Yeah, Mama, tell Aaron here where you come from," said Kia.

"Oh, go on now. Someone else tell the story. Ya know I don't much like talkin' about myself."

"Well, I'd be honored," said Andrea, Javon's wife. Turning in her seat toward me, Andrea told a story that each of the grandchildren could have told themselves.

"Well, her story begins in Sierra Leone, takes us to your country, and then back here. Big Mama is a descendant of a woman named Ruth. Ruth's mother was born in Sierra Leone in West Africa. Ruth's mother was captured by a Muslim tribe that was waging war in Sierra Leone at the time and was shipped to the West Indies and sold as a slave. Well, while on the ship, she gave birth to Ruth. Ruth and her family, her parents and two siblings by then, were later sold to a slave trader that operated out of the Bahamas. The family lived for a short time in the Bahamas but were later shipped to Charleston, South Carolina and sold again to a rice-growing family named the Carmichaels. At the time, South Carolina was a British colony. Ruth's family worked in the rice fields. It was a brutal existence, but at least they were still together as a family."

"Would someone else like to pick up the story?" asked Andrea.

"I will," said Melissa.

"Well, by now, times were changing in the British colonies. The folks living in the colonies were growing tired of British rule and began to talk about forming their own country."

"Okay, now this is something I know about. You're talking about the American Revolutionary War," I said.

"That's right. But do you know who fought in the battles in the Carolinas?" asked Melissa.

"Sure, the American Patriots fought the British Redcoats."

"Hmmm, well yes, but not entirely correct. In the Northern colonies, yes, most of the battles were between the Patriots and the British. But in the Southern colonies, and the Carolinas in particular, many battles were fought between colonists alone, those that identified as Patriots and those that identified as Loyalists."

"Okay, I remember something about this, but most people that lived in America wanted their own country," I said.

"Hmm. Again, I don't know what you mean by most, but in South Carolina the population was fairly well split between those that wanted to remain loyal to the king of England, the Loyalists or the Tories, and those that wanted their independence, the Patriots or the Whig Party."

"How do you know so much about my country's history?" I asked.

"Because you can't understand ours without understanding yours," answered Mateo. Mateo turned to Melissa. "Go on," he said.

Well, the Carmichaels had a daughter who caught the attention of a British merchant living in Charleston named James Bristol. The two of them were married and Mr. Bristol found himself the owner of a rice plantation and quite a few slaves. Mr. and Mrs. Bristol were both Loyalists, but only Mr. Bristol stood opposed to slavery. By the time the hostilities between the colonists and Great Britain turned to full-scale war, their marriage was struggling, and when James Bristol offered his slaves their freedom if they would fight for Britain, the marriage ended. No surprise, they took him up on his offer. Ruth couldn't fight, but she could cook, and persuaded James that troops needed nourishment, so he freed her too. In actuality, he didn't take much persuading; they'd been carrying on a secret romance, another reason why the marriage between James Bristol and the Carmichael daughter was doomed."

"I've been going on for a while, now," said Melissa. "Does someone else want to bring it home? Papa, how about you?"

Javon smiled and began.

"The Brits occupied Charleston from May 1780 through the end of 1782, and during that time James Bristol felt somewhat safe even though the Carmichaels wanted him dead. He moved into town and was no longer living with their daughter, and though not openly living with Ruth, there were rumors. Quite a scandal, you can imagine. Well, there came a point when the war was turning, and it appeared the Patriots might win. Many Loyalists, fearing not only for their life but for their way of life, fled Charleston. James Bristol, as did others, headed to Florida, also a colony at the time but one not caught up in the war. Many of those who moved to Florida thought the move was temporary and that either Britain would win the war or, even if the Colonies won, their experiment with democracy would fail and Britain would be back in charge. Well, all that changed in 1783 with the signing of the Treaty of Paris."

"The treaty that ended the Revolutionary War," I said.

"That's right," said Javon.

"Yes, but it didn't just end the Revolutionary War because France and Spain also signed it. The treaty ended a bunch of wars. And Spain got Florida when it was signed." I thought to myself that my American History teacher, Helen Smith, would be very proud of me.

"That's right, which meant that James Bristol and many of his former slaves that had traveled with him, including Ruth, no longer felt at home in Florida. So they moved again, and this time they moved to the Bahamas."

"I'll take it from here," said Big Mama.

"That's right, that's how we ended up here. When James Bristol moved here, Ruth and many of the other formerly enslaved from the Carmichael plantation came to the Bahamas. They took the last name of Bristol. Ruth and James were never officially married. Such relations still would not have been acceptable at the time, but Mr. Bristol was good to Ruth and her family, and they prospered as we have all these years. Yes, some years better or worse than others, but at every turn, there was family."

"Now, I want my mom to tell Aaron about the pirates in her family."

"Hush, child. Enough about us."

"Pirates?" I asked.

"Lies and rumors, I tell you," Andrea said as she stood, laughing, and began to clear the table. "Children, help me now. It's time to go soon. Help me clean up."

"Let me help," I said.

"There be none of that," said Andrea. "You're our guest."

"Besides, working in a bank for this Mr. Pinder. Ooohwee, that's got to be some hard work," said Chad. "You be needing to rest up for your first day of work."

I laughed along with them and sat back and listened to the men talk while the girls tended to the kitchen, and I felt farther away from home than I could imagine, and in more ways than one.

Chapter 14

Reality Sets In

Café Abaco, three weeks after Aaron landed in Nassau, Sunday, June 24th, 1973

I was sitting at a table at the restaurant Javon owned and the spot I had my first meal when arriving here three weeks ago and I was waiting for Quaid Dawson to arrive. In my time here, I'd learned a fair amount about the islands and the people. I remember a teacher once telling me that traveling was the best education possible, and I was beginning to understand why. It helped that I woke each day with the mindset of one on a working vacation.

This attitude was the one I had adopted to keep my worst fears at bay. I didn't live here, not really. I was just on a grand adventure, as a fugitive from the law. One day, when looking back on this period of my life, I would regale folks with stories of how I'd evaded capture and spent six weeks working and playing in the Bahamas. I'd been here three weeks, so six weeks felt about right.

I was waiting for Quaid Dawson because, two days ago, Mr. Pinder told me Quaid would be in town and he wanted to see me. I was anxious and excited to see Mr. Dawson, hopeful for good news from home, and that possibly there had been a break in the case. I was also prepared to repay him money he'd loaned me upon my arrival.

Since arriving, I'd begin each week meeting Mr. Pinder at his office. Nigel Pinder's family business, the Pinder Bank and Trust Company, was my employer. He would hire me out to clients who had odd jobs for me to complete. His clients were primarily Brits, Canadians, and Americans. It was apparent early on that I knew my way around boats, was an accomplished fisherman, and was generally handy and able to repair and assemble any number of items. I was in great demand.

At my first meeting with Mr. Pinder, I learned he had opened a checking account for me, and that Quaid made the opening deposit. This was the money I intended to repay from wages Mr. Pinder paid me the Friday before. At my first meeting with Mr. Pinder was also when I deposited the ten thousand dollars I had stolen from my dad when I fled Charleston. Mr. Pinder joked that I was likely the first person in my high school class with an offshore bank account protected by the world's strictest privacy laws. I had no idea what he was talking about, but he thought it was a pretty funny thing to say.

Right on time, Quaid pulled up in a small Alpha Romeo convertible. A young boy appeared out of nowhere and took his keys and offered to park the car for him. I watched Quaid hand the young boy some money, and then his keys, then shake the boy's hand and walk inside. A minute later, Quaid arrived at the top of the stairs and spoke a minute with Javon before glancing in my direction. He looked nervous, or maybe it was just that I was nervous.

He finished his conversation with Javon, turned, and walked out onto the patio. I stood to shake Quaid's hand, but when we did, he wouldn't let go and pulled me in for a hug. I let him, and it relaxed me a bit. But neither of us knew what to say and it's hard to know how long the silence would have carried on if the waiter hadn't interrupted us with two beers, compliments of the house. We took our seats and clinked our beer bottles in a toast.

"It's good to see you, Aaron. It is Aaron, right?"

"Yes, sir. I'm Aaron."

"And how is that going?"

I took a swig of my beer and stared across the street, thinking about how to answer the question. I didn't want to answer it. I didn't want to think about it. So, I asked one of my own.

"What I want to know is: When can I go back to being Eli?"

* * *

Charleston Police Department, two days ago, Friday, June 22nd, 1973

Chief Riddle was sitting at his desk looking out his window at Monty and Rose Atkins and their attorney, Chester Baslin. He was sure they knew where Eli was. Just sure of it. What parent wouldn't do anything for their kids? He knew he would. He was certain Monty would stop at nothing to protect Eli, even if it meant breaking the law. He wasn't so sure about the mom, Rose. She was a cold one.

And then there was Chester Baslin. The attorney. A defense attorney, no less. Oh, he knew that some of the boys in the department had good things to say about the man, but in the mind of Chief Riddle, all defense attorneys were the same; they were snakes and not to be trusted.

Well, anyway, here he was looking at what some would call an unsolved murder. But there was no way he was going to have this blemish on his excellent record of solving major crimes in Charleston just because the perp had run. No, it was time to shut things down.

"Mrs. Babcock, can you step in here, please?" he shouted from his desk.

"Yes, Chief Riddle." Mrs. Babcock scooted into his office with a pen and pad in her hand, ready to be useful. She stood barely five-foot-five. Her employment file, opened fifty-five years earlier, listed her at five-foot-eight.

"Did the report come back from the hospital yet?" asked Chief Riddle.

"Yes, Officer Tyrell has it. Would you like me to get him for you?"

Chief Riddle could have rung him from his desk phone, but he got a kick out of Mrs. Babcock's always helpful attitude. "Yes, would you, please?"

"Right away, Chief," said Mrs. Babcock with a quick salute as she scooted back out the door and down the hallway, choosing not to call him from the phone on her desk.

Five minutes later, a distraught Officer Tyrell was leaning against the door frame of the chief's office with a yellow evidence folder under his arm.

"Well, Officer Tyrell, what's the verdict?" asked Chief Riddle.

Officer Tyrell waddled into the office and sat in the chair across the desk from the chief. "The hospital reported that the blood sample is human and not from an animal," answered Officer Tyrell as he leaned across the desk to pass the file folder to the chief.

"Anything else? Is the blood A negative? O positive? Anything like that?

If we knew that, then we could subpoena Eli's medical records and see if we got a match," said the chief as he thumbed through the file.

"No, sir. The blood sample was dry. The hospital only has equipment for running those types of tests on wet samples. The technician I spoke with said there are new test methods under development that allow more extensive testing on dry samples. She suggested we contact the FBI for further help."

"I don't think that will be necessary," said the chief. "We have a hot-headed boyfriend seen fighting with his girlfriend in a bar right before the girlfriend storms out, leaving him alone, embarrassed, and angry. That girl turns up dead a few hours later with injuries caused by a serrated hunting knife. The boyfriend runs from the police to avoid arrest. His family hires a high-powered attorney, but he skips bail anyway, and now we learn that the hunting knife with the serrated edge found in the bed of his truck has dried human blood on the blade. Seems open and shut to me. Wouldn't you agree, Officer Tyrell?"

Officer Tyrell shifted his large frame in the chair before answering. "Chief Riddle, with all due respect, I do not. Anyone could have put the knife in his truck," said Officer Tyrell.

"Now that's a stretch," replied Chief Riddle. "Eli had motive. Your mystery killer, what's his motive? You can only guess. Your theory is just that, a theory and a theory that rests on nothing more than your desire for Eli to be innocent. You're too close to this. I'm aware that your son, Leroy, and Eli were friends. But sometimes, the most obvious answer is the answer. Most of the time, in fact."

"Then why were fingerprints wiped from the knife handle, but the bloodstain wasn't?" asked Officer Tyrell.

Chief Riddle stared curiously at the officer in front of him, not searching for an answer to the question but wondering how he was going to put this matter to rest.

"Well, we would have found out on cross-examination if the defendant hadn't run. Officer Tyrell, the case is closed. Please box up the contents and place the evidence box in storage. Mark it for disposal in seven years. If Eli doesn't show up in seven years, we'll presume him dead."

* * *

Sunday, June 24th, late afternoon at the Mt. Bethel Church of Prophesy

Annabelle Babcock and the other ladies, a small group of four women, all leaning slightly forward in their chairs, in a tight circle, were holding hands with their heads bowed. These four women, with a combined age of over 320 years, no one knowing the correct number since the one lie none of them carried any guilt over was the one about their age, had convened with a single purpose in mind, to pray for Eli.

They were part of a larger prayer group that met every other Sunday night at church. The church bulletin made mention of their group, and folks each Sunday wrote down prayer requests on slips of paper and passed the small notes through the slot on top of a box sitting on a folding table out front. The ladies in the prayer group would pull the slips from the box and pray about whatever was written down. The requests usually fell into one of several categories: someone was sick, someone had died and their family was in mourning, someone's husband was out of work and looking for a job, someone had strayed, someone was drinking too much and wanted to stop, someone was gossiping and hurting others.

But tonight, Mrs. Babcock and the other three women, all carefully selected by Mrs. Babcock, were here to pray for Eli Atkins and no one would, or could, know. If Mrs. Babcock had been asked why she selected these three women to confide in, she would have said that each had seen and experienced injustice and knew that matters were not always as they seemed. Mrs. Babcock confided in these women and told them that Eli was alive and in need of their prayers.

They raised their heads. Annabelle had just asked Irene to lead them in a brief prayer inviting Jesus to sit with them as they discussed Eli.

"So, he made it to the Bahamas safely and he has a permanent place to stay?" Irene asked.

"Yes, Quaid came through for us."

"Praise the Lord."

"And he's all right?" asked Evelyn. "I mean, how's he doing?"

"Well, I don't know. But I'm expecting a report from Quaid. He went to the Bahamas yesterday and will be meeting with Eli. Hopes to have dinner with him tonight. And from what I learned Friday, Eli and Quaid need our prayers."

"Oh, dear," said Maybelle. "What have you learned?"

"Friday, at the Police Department, I overheard Chief Riddle talking to Officer Tyrell, and he told him the case was closed. The police chief assumes Eli did it and he's not going to look anymore for who really killed that poor girl, Kimberly," explained Annabelle. "I called Quaid last night in the Bahamas and told him what I learned, and he was going to break the news to Eli."

"You called long-distance?" asked Evelyn.

"Quaid accepted the charges," said Annabelle.

"He's such a sweetheart."

"Yes, he is. But he wasn't looking forward to telling Eli."

"Oh, that poor boy," said Irene.

"I know he was hoping he'd only be gone for a short while and that once the real killer was caught, he'd be able to come home," said Annabelle.

"But, if the real killer is never found, will Eli ever be able to come home?" asked Maybelle.

"No, and that's what Quaid has to tell Eli and he's telling him tonight. That's why I called you here. Eli needs our prayers now more than ever," said Annabelle.

And the four women leaned forward, clasped hands, and prayed.

* * *

CAFÉ ABACO: THE WAITER HAS TAKEN THEIR ORDERS

"What do you mean, the case is closed!"

Quaid looked around to see if anyone had overheard them. He looked nervous and uncomfortable. I took a deep breath and leaned across the table, and in a lowered voice I asked the question again.

"What do you mean, the case is closed?"

"I spoke with Mrs. Babcock late yesterday. She'd been in the office and overheard Chief Riddle tell Officer Tyrell that the case was closed."

"But why?" I pleaded.

Quaid was uncomfortable. That was clear to me.

"Because you ran," he answered.

I said nothing. Slumped in my chair, I stared off into the distance, avoiding eye contact.

Quaid sat there, visibly upset. The waiter appeared and he waved him off.

"Aaron, I'm sorry."

"For what?" I asked

"Well, I helped you run and if you hadn't run ..."

I looked at Quaid.

"If I hadn't run, I'd have stood trial and my own mother would have testified against me, and I would have gone to jail for life or been strapped to an electric chair. So, what choice did I have?"

Quaid held my gaze and was about to say something.

"No, don't. Don't say a word. Mr. Dawson, I don't blame you and I don't blame Mrs. Babcock."

I picked up my fork and resumed eating dinner, and so did Quaid.

After a moment, I broke the painful silence.

"Story of my life. What choice did I have?"

* * *

Nassau, the Bahamas, July 4th, 1973

And so began my demise. My worst fears were coming true. When I arrived a month ago, I kept these fears at bay with a combination of wishful thinking and full days, days spent working for Mr. Pinder's clients or fishing and learning about the island from Javon's son, Anthony, and his friends. During busy times at the Bastian family restaurant, the Café Abaco, I worked as an extra hand in the kitchen. Frankly, I enjoyed this work as much as any other. I started out washing dishes and then, one night when one of the chefs called in sick, I volunteered to man the grill. Mr. Bastian was skeptical but had no choice; someone had to cook. He handed me five orders and told me not to mash it up. I didn't, and I've been working the grill from time to time ever since.

The other positive about working the café is that it gives me something to do at night. Nights are the worst. My other odd jobs keep me busy during the day, but at night, time drags unless I'm hanging out with Anthony and his friends. At first, I was a regular visitor at the Bastian's house in Adelaide Village. But I'm pulling back. Their hospitality is great, but it's also a stark reminder of something I miss, or better yet, something I've never really had—a genuinely happy home life.

Hearing me say that, you might scratch your head and ask, "What do you mean you've never had a happy home life?" Let's just say it's complicated. Times with Dad were great, and I love and miss Walker, but there was an ever-present cloud in our home. I didn't know the cloud had a name until recently.

When you're young, your idea of normal is the life you have. It's only as you grow older and encounter others your age and other families that you realize life can be different. I didn't know it at the time, but the name of the cloud in our household was fear. And when I'm afraid, I lash out.

What did I fear? That's easy. I feared her, my mother, Rose Atkins. But now, what I fear is a lifetime of anonymity. A lifetime wondering what could have been.

And, despite the pleadings of the well-intentioned to embrace the island life and just fit in, I can't. Take the current festivities as an example. In three days, the Bahamas will celebrate gaining their independence from Great Britain. They will no longer be a colony but instead will be a member of the Commonwealth. Lynden Pindling became the colony's first black premier in 1967 and then the first prime minister in 1969. I don't understand the difference between premier and prime minister, and I don't understand the difference between being a colony as opposed to a member of the Commonwealth. But it must all be very important.

But frankly, I don't care. It's July 4th and I should be at home celebrating my country's Independence Day with my family and friends. Instead, I'm expected to be happy about the impending independence here. I don't begrudge them their happiness, but the happier they are, the more miserable I am. I take no joy from their celebration. In fact, it makes me feel more like an outsider and thus more alone.

When I arrived here on June 8th, just shy of a month ago, I wondered what was to become of Eli Atkins. But no more. Now I know. Eli Atkins is dead.

Chapter 15

Not in Our Backyard

Café Abaco, Saturday night, July 7th, 1973

After 325 years of British rule, the Bahamas were finally becoming an independent, self-ruled country and the good people of the Bahamas were in a mood to celebrate. Parties and celebrations had been going on for a week and there was no end in sight. Dignitaries from over fifty nations were in town to participate and recognize the world's newest nation and to celebrate the Bahamas leaving its status as a colony behind and becoming the newest member of the Commonwealth.

As a result, business was good for Javon and his family. Café Abaco sits on the northwest corner of Bay Street and Charlotte Street, a block from the Prince George Wharf, ground zero for all the festivities. From the view of the patio on the second floor, one could see revelers dancing in the streets beneath clear skies filled with firework displays going off all over the island as people were spilling out of parties taking place at every restaurant and bar in town, in private homes, and in every government ministerial building.

And sitting in a corner of the patio, leaning back in his chair enjoying a beer and a cigar, was Quaid Dawson and a friend.

"Did you ever think this would happen?" asked Quaid.

"Actually, yes," said Nash. "And ... it's good," he added with a bit of hesitation.

"But ...?"

"What do you mean 'But'?" asked Nash.

"Well, you're here, for one, and I don't think you're here for the fishing—not this time."

"You're right, I'm not here for the fishing. I'd be lying if I didn't admit we aren't watching the situation carefully and with a bit of concern."

"What are you worried about? This is a peaceful handoff. Prince Charles arrived earlier this week as the Queen's representative. We're going to have a peaceful transfer of power. In fact, from the beginning, Britain's rule all these years has been relatively peaceful."

"Yep, I agree. I saw the prince arrive on the HMS *Minerva*, walk down the gangplank, and shake hands with the governor as well as Lyndon Pindling, the Bahamas' new prime minister. Wonderful pomp and ceremony, if you go in for that sort of thing. No, the change is welcome by most everyone. There's no opposition to what's happening at all."

"Well, there's opposition to leaving Crown rule, but those that stand in opposition are displaying their displeasure by simply sitting out one hell of a party," said Quaid as he raised his mug and cheered the throngs in the streets.

"So, I'll ask you again," said Quaid. "Why are you here?"

"Because of what's happening in Central America. Because of what happened in Cuba. If the Bahamas fail as a nation, if the economy goes in the tank, you could see the people take to the streets for altogether different reasons."

"You're worried about the Bahamas becoming a communist nation?"

"We're not so much worried about the Bahamas, per se, as we are about any nation fifty miles off our coast. We didn't see what happened in Cuba coming and we're not going to make that mistake again. When these islands were under Crown rule, we knew what to expect. Now, not so much," explained Nash.

"But they're still part of the Commonwealth. Shouldn't that count for something?"

"We hope so, but ultimately, the capital markets may decide that for us."

"I'm not following you."

"Look, I don't like saying this, but it's a reality. There are some who believe that this place is headed for trouble because it's going to be ruled by black people that have never ruled a nation before. When the Bay Street Boys ruled these islands, Wall Street and other investors were happy to invest here, in the hotels, ports, tourism, and in local industry. But there's already some grumbling on the street that investment capital is going to dry up. If the Bahamas lose their allure as a tourist destination or are overtaken by other destinations, then this economy will suffer big time."

"I think you're exaggerating the risk," said Quaid.

"Do you? I get it. Race relations here are good for the most part. The country is 80 percent black and was ruled by the minority white population, and yet times were still good. Well, if a black man is ruling the country and things head south, what do you think will happen?"

Quaid just shrugged his shoulders.

"I'll tell you. There will be voices screaming that the changes taking place tonight were just the beginning, only a first step, and that the country needs to move faster toward an egalitarian society."

Nash could tell Quaid still wasn't buying it, so he continued.

"Take the system of land ownership on the islands. It's a mess. Most privately owned land is owned by wealthy, white people or by Canadian, American, and British companies. Much of the Indigenous population lives on land they have no title to and therefore can't borrow against and raise cash to start a business or pay for college. And anyone can challenge the title to land here under what they call the Quieting Titles Act."

"I'll give you that. Intentions were good when the General Assembly passed the law, but when they made it easier for people to establish title to land they had been living on, they also made it easier for crooks to file fraudulent claims. There's more risk now for legitimate landowners than ever before."

"Exactly," said Nash. "Who wants to risk an expensive development only to be drug into court by someone claiming they owned the land all along? And that's just part of the problem. Lyndon Pindling, the new PM, has his work cut out for him. I've never met the man, but I did my homework before heading down here, and our research speaks highly of him. However, he is facing institutional and cultural barriers and challenges that will not be easy to overcome which could be his undoing. The problem with great hope and great expectations arises when you can't meet them."

"And so, you're here and you're worried," said Quaid.

"Only fifty miles off our coast. We can't handle another Cuba."

* * *

It was a busy night here at the café. Hell, it was busy all over town. Everyone thought I was crazy offering to work tonight, what with all the great parties everywhere. But what did I care? Bahamian independence meant nothing to me.

I saw Quaid walk in a while ago with some guy. I haven't seen him since we had dinner here a couple of weeks ago, the night he told me I couldn't go home, ever. The night I *truly* became Aaron Westfield. It's not his fault, I know. So, I really should go say hello. Things were finally slowing down, and Javon said I could knock off as soon as I finished with the dishes in the sink.

After drying and putting away the last of the dinner plates, I dried my hands, poured myself a beer, and walked over to Quaid's table.

"Hi, Mr. Dawson."

"Aaron, how are you? Join us?"

"Yes, thank you."

"Aaron, I'd like you to meet a good friend of mine, Nash Hawthorne."

"Pleased to meet you, Mr. Hawthorne."

Mr. Hawthorne stood up and we shook hands.

Chapter 16

Nash

Georgetown, Washington, D.C., July 22nd, 1973, 5:00 a.m.

William Nash Hawthorne, or Nash as he preferred, was a legend around the Office—a great man, nicknamed "The Hawk." Whether this nickname was to be attributed to his narrow, beak-shaped nose or his prowess on the court was a subject of debate. Tall and lanky, he possessed strong, calloused hands and sinewy, rope-like arms developed over a lifetime of sailing. His skin was tan—not in the style of the idle rich but weathered. He was handsome but lacked movie-star looks. His deep-set eyes, grey and piercing, made him appear older than he was. His hair was short and dark and greying at the corners.

The Hawthorne family money was so old that many believed they not only crossed over on the *Mayflower* but built and financed it too. It was said Nash was born wearing a white dinner jacket. Even at prep school, surrounded by others of similar ilk, he was mocked good-naturedly for his family's patrician ways. In his senior year, someone highjacked the yearbook on the way to the printer and so for all eternity the name beneath his picture read "William Nash Radcliffe Hawthorne Jr., the 4th."

Despite growing up in the tony neighborhood of Old Greenwich, Connecticut, one underestimated Nash at his own peril. Nash rose quickly through the ranks and more than earned his reputation as a covert operative in Southeast Asia. His greatest weapon, second only to his lethal marksmanship, was his intellect.

Nash's driver dropped him off on the curb on Wisconsin Avenue outside *Au Pied de Cochon*, then pulled around the corner to park and wait for his boss to return. When he entered the restaurant, he saw his friend at his usual table in the corner with a stack of newspapers and a cup of coffee.

"Fresh off the press, I presume," said Nash.

To Nash, privately, his friend was simply the "Old Man," but to other close friends, Cyril James Atley was Cy or CJ. But to all, he was a man of routine. He kept a home in the vicinity of 34th Street and R Street, and when he was in DC, every Sunday morning, rain or shine, wind, snow, or extreme humidity, he would leave his house at 4:30 a.m. by foot and arrive at his favorite all-night diner as the delivery trucks were dropping off the morning's newspapers around town. Spread on the table before him were copies of the *New York Times*, the *Washington Post*, and the *Baltimore Sun*.

"You look tired, my friend," the Old Man said.

Nash was indeed. He had just landed ninety minutes earlier at a remote air strip in Maryland on a private jet owned and operated by a mutual friend who also owned the surrounding 3,200 acres.

The waiter appeared and placed a cup of coffee in front of Nash as he took a seat.

"Thank you, and can you bring me an order of the Crepes a la Reine?" Nash asked the waiter. The waiter nodded and quietly disappeared, leaving the two gentlemen to their business.

"Yes, tired but holding up. You're looking good, Cy, as always."

Cy was seventy-five-years old, but you wouldn't know it from looking at or talking with him. He kept fit by sailing and by walking when he played golf. "I'll take a cart when I'm dead," he was fond of saying. He was wearing grey slacks, topsiders, and a crisp white golf shirt from Pine Valley Golf Club.

"Are you in town long?" asked Nash.

"No, just for a few days, then heading west until this blasted heat passes."

Nash could have asked where he was heading specifically but knew that if Cy Atley wanted him to know, he would have told him, which meant Cy could have been on his way to any number of properties the Atley family owned, from Pebble Beach to Idaho, and others. Cy subscribed to the same philosophy every generation of Atleys subscribed to. Never sell.

The Atley clan came from Great Britain to America's shores in 1630 as part of the great migration. The family made its first fortune in lumber and quickly added mining to its portfolio. They had remained fiercely private and, again, they never sold. Consequently, their balance sheet, something only privy to a handful of people, was impressive to say the least.

"But we're not here to discuss the weather, are we, Nash?"

"No, sir."

"Tell me about your trip and what you learned."

After witnessing the Bahamas' birth as a nation and visiting Quaid Dawson two weeks ago, Nash had been on a tour of the hot spots throughout Central America and, for the next half-hour, reported what he had learned.

"It's hard to know where trouble will bubble over first—Nicaragua, Honduras, Guatemala, or El Salvador—but I fear it's only a matter of time. We haven't lost the leadership of any country yet, but the Soviets are intent on stirring up trouble among the masses," said Nash.

"And what is the position of the Office?" asked Cy.

"The same. Nothing changes. They'll support any strongmen as long as they aren't socialists."

"Even if they're murderers?" asked Cy.

"Afraid so. You see, the Office hasn't had much success with regime change. Guatemala has been stuck in permanent civil war since we ousted Jacobo Arbenz in 1954. We don't get to choose our partners sometimes."

"And do we have anything to be concerned about in the Bahamas?"

"Yes and no," said Nash. "As an island chain, they're isolated, and so troubles can't easily spill over from neighboring countries like they can in Central and South America."

"We said that about Cuba in 1959."

"True, but the Bahamas government will have Great Britain's backing," explained Nash.

"As Batista's Cuban government had ours in 1959," answered Cy.

"True. But Lynden Pindling is no Batista. He represents the country's majority as opposed to the wealthy, minority ruling class that supported Batista, as is often the case in developing countries. So, if we support Pindling, we're aligned with the majority and thus better positioned to head off efforts by the Soviets to sow discord amongst the general population."

The two men said nothing and sat back in the chairs as the waiter placed their meals in front of them. They each ate in silence.

"You don't seem satisfied," said Nash after a few minutes. "Does the Family have a concern?"

"Do you?" asked Cy.

"Yes, of course. I imagine we share the same concerns."

"Good. We'd hate it if our man in Washington had gone wonky on us."

"No reason for that," said a smiling Nash. "I may work at the Office, but I'm still Family."

Yes, Nash was still Family and Cy Atley was the Family's point man. The Family, or the Ancestors as some within their small, close-knit group called themselves, were five families that could trace their roots in America to the seventeenth century. They all shared a common goal: preserving, protecting, and spreading the ideals and virtues of individual liberty. They believed they were ancestors of this country's freedom-loving traditions.

Each of the five families comprising the Family was represented by one man. Since changes within this inner circle could be a challenge if subsequent generations didn't share the same worldview, great care was taken when picking a replacement when one of the five in the inner circle died. The other four men would select the replacement from a list of candidates put forth by the family in need of a representative.

Each of the men in the inner circle was fabulously wealthy, with assets around the world, and was largely untouchable by any single government. They recognized the need for government but also saw it as freedom's greatest threat. They had no illusions about the heart of man, understanding it to be dark, all believing that we live in a fallen world. They were vehemently opposed to crony capitalism even though it was a game that, if they chose to play, could bring them even more power and money. On the contrary, to the extent that they were selfish in their motivations, they saw a free and growing world economy, one that improved the lot of all, as the ticket to even greater wealth.

So, what did the Family do? They provided a worldwide, intelligence-gathering, and operational support apparatus to the United States government and, on occasion, other friendly governments. Beyond the considerable resources of the five families, they had recruited helpers or associates carefully placed around the globe and in positions to quickly provide needed assistance. They were loyal to the precepts of freedom, to man's God given rights, before loyalty to any nation. They supported and worked with the USA but not blindly. They often worked on their own.

The representatives of the five families selected their point man, and this leader met with friends within the CIA and the White House. Relations with the CIA and the Office of the President were not formalized. The group never interfered with domestic politics or elections, and if the occupant of the White House or the top brass in the intelligence agencies were not allies, it would make no overtures. Typically, with each administration, there was a new CIA director, and the handoff could be tricky. Operations improved greatly when Nash joined the CIA and moved up the ranks because Nash was one of them; he was a member of one of the five families.

"So, you're saying we have reason to be concerned about the Bahamas," said Cy.

"My fear that is that Pindling, or those around him, will succumb to the trappings of power and his government will turn into a kleptocracy, thus ending the hope of a middle class ever developing. Absent a middle class, the gap between the rich and the poor will grow, and his tenure could be viewed as a failure, providing an entre and a voice to the communists."

"Do you have reason to fear Pindling is susceptible to these temptations?" asked Cy.

"No more than the next man. But trouble may come from those he has surrounded himself with."

"So, what can we do? How can we help?" asked Cy.

"Right now, we need eyes and ears on the man, and we need to know who he consorts with, who has access to him, who may be gathering undue influence," explained Nash.

"And the Office won't give you the support you need," said Cy.

"That's right. They're too focused on Central America, and the Mideast is heating up again. I'm afraid by the time they notice the Bahamas, it will be when trouble has taken root."

"And you think it's best if we keep trouble from taking root?" asked Cy.

"Yes, sir."

"Then you have the Family's support. Let me know what you need."

"Will do."

Chapter 17

Chivalry

The Ocean Club, January 7th, 1977, a Friday night

Time passed slowly on the island. Have you ever been on a trip, and you didn't know where you were going and since you have never made the trip before, it seemed like you would never get there? And then the next time you make the exact same trip, it takes no time at all? Well, imagine if all of life was like that first trip. That's how life was for me now. I had no idea how long I would be here. No idea how long I would be Aaron Westfield. No idea what my future held. And so, every day was an eternity.

I was encouraged to just relax. "You're on island time, now. Just relax," I was told. "What's your hurry?" they'd ask. I tried to adopt the same attitude of those around me, folks who were born on the islands, but it didn't take. They knew what tomorrow held and they were fine with it. I too knew what tomorrow held, but I wasn't fine with it because I didn't know how many more such tomorrows there would be. So tonight, when I showed up to work behind the bar at the Ocean Club, it was just another night.

I hated the uniform they made me wear, but the tips were good, and being a Friday night, the bar would soon be filled with beautiful women. Sunset was forty minutes away and the crowd was picking up. I was working the bar along with Ritchie. Ritchie was one of the resort's first hires and he'd been working behind the bar for sixteen years. He seemed content, but the idea of serving bar in the same place for that long depressed the hell out of me. No, tending bar was just one more thing I could do to make a few bucks, so I did it.

I was mixing a couple of Tom Collins drinks for an elderly gentleman and his much younger companion, his niece no doubt, when my attention was drawn to a single woman taking a seat at the far end of the bar. I finished pouring the drinks and asked him if he wanted to open a tab for the evening. He nodded yes and handed me a Barclaycard. I placed the card inside the cash register and made my way down the bar.

"Would you like to wait for your date to arrive before ordering?" I asked.

She glanced up from the book she was reading and smiled.

"Do you think I'm incapable of ordering my own drink or are you just trying to determine if I am with anyone tonight?" she asked.

I returned the smile. It wasn't hard to do. I was looking at a stunningly beautiful woman. Her skin was fair, flawless but for freckles beneath each of her eyes. And her eyes! Large, round, and a deep blue, almost hypnotic color. Flowing red hair framed her face and spilled over her shoulders. I don't know much about women's clothing, but what she was wearing worked. The kind of dress that looked expensive and made her look sexy but elegant.

"You look quite capable. Will you allow me to make you a drink?"

"Make it a good one," she said, and returned to her book.

A minute later, I placed a martini glass on the bar in front of her, took a step back, and bowed slightly. "Compliments of the house." I then turned back toward the middle of the bar and tended to other patrons. As I was popping the cork on a bottle of champagne, ordered by the elderly gentleman who said he was celebrating his niece's twenty-fifth birthday, I happened a glance to gauge her reaction to my drink. She took a sip, smiled as if suddenly made aware of an inside joke, placed the drink back on the bar, and resumed reading.

Fifteen minutes later, we were locked in a standoff of sorts—me standing before her, she sensing my presence but never veering from her book. I blinked first.

"Did you like your drink?"

"Three measures of Gordon's, one of vodka, half a measure of Kina Lillet, shaken, not stirred, with a thin slice of lemon peel. Really? A bit cliché, don't you think? A little advice. Shake it if you must but once, twice at most, though I prefer it stirred. You see, you overdid it—the shaking, that is. Part of the show, I know. But when you do, you dilute the drink, and it loses its texture. Finally, martinis were never intended to have ice shards floating on top. Amateur hour if you ask me, but this drink is an ode to one of the island's more infamous nocturnal animals, so we are stuck with it, I presume."

I was stunned and, for the first time in memory, speechless around a girl.

"So, is that a 'no'?" I managed.

"Yes, it's a 'no.' But now you know what I like. Let's see if you were listening." And she returned to her book.

I stood motionless, my feet cemented to the floor.

She glanced up. "Hurry along now."

I retreated to the other end of the bar, ignoring the efforts of two overly tanned young men, new arrivals who looked familiar, waving in vain to get my attention. A few minutes later, I placed a martini, stirred, not shaken, in front of the mysterious and beguiling woman. I placed both hands on the bar and waited patiently.

She let me wait. But then, looking up from her book, she took an inventory of me before taking a sip of the drink.

"Now that's more like it," she said as she extended her right hand. "Rachel Fleming. And you are?"

I removed the white towel draped over my left shoulder, washed my hands, and then gently took the fingers of her delicate, beautiful hand in my palm. "Aaron. Aaron Westfield."

I didn't shake her hand but instead held it suspended in the air.

She held my gaze and then asked if she could have her hand back.

"Besides, I believe you have some impatient guests needing a drink," she said as she nodded toward the same two men who had been trying to get my attention and a drink since they sat down.

"Let me know if there is anything else I can get for you."

"Oh, I will," she said.

I walked over to the two impatient young men, just a few years older than me by my estimation, wiped down the bar top, and asked them what I could get them.

"Well, it's about time. Make it two Jack and Cokes."

"Make 'em doubles," remarked the other man. "You seem a bit slow—don't know when we'll see you again," he said, laughing to his buddy.

I bit my tongue. "Coming right up and sorry for the wait."

As I turned to mix their drinks, I overheard them laughing and saying something about how I seemed slow in more ways than one. And then it struck me where I had seen them. Earlier in the week, I was cutting the grass at the home of one of Mr. Pinder's clients and these two arrogant jerks were sitting by the pool giving off the vibe of those who felt entitled, though not having earned a dime of their parents' money.

I did my best to ignore them and I waited on other patrons, but after twenty minutes, I decided to check in on her.

"What are you reading?" I asked.

She turned the paperback over and placed it pages down on the bar.

"A book by John le Carre. It's about a Soviet double-agent working in the British Intelligence forces. It appears to be based on the Cambridge Five."

"The Cambridge Five?" I asked.

"The Cambridge Five were a group of men working throughout the British government who were Soviet spies. They were supposedly recruited by the Soviet Union in the 1930s while attending Cambridge University. You might have heard of Kim Philby. He was the most famous of the group."

I leaned over the bar and turned my head to read the title. "*Tinker Taylor Soldier Spy*. Never heard of it. Most folks around here are reading *Jaws*."

"No doubt."

"So, it's a spy novel."

"Yes," she said. "A real spy novel. No automobile ejector seats, I'm afraid. More of an espionage book."

I watched her smile as she said this and wasn't entirely sure, but she might have been having a little fun at my expense. I couldn't have cared less. I was mesmerized by this woman. Her voice was lilting, and it drew me in as each sentence seemingly finished in the form of a question. The spell was broken by the two trust-fund babies.

"Hey, barkeep. Can we get another round? Really, we're dying over here."

"Yeah, I'm as dry as the Sahara," said the smaller of the two.

I heard them laughing again and talking between themselves, though loud enough for others to hear.

"Hey," the taller one said. "Give the guy a break—he doesn't know what the Sahara is."

The shorter one thought that was hysterical.

"Would you like to order dinner?" I asked her. "The kitchen is going to get pretty busy soon."

"Yes, thank you. Please bring me the lobster and conch salad"

"Another drink?"

"Yes, but how about a Chardonnay? Do you still have the '66 Romanée-Conti?" she asked.

"I believe we still have a few bottles. Shall I open one for you?"

"Please."

"Coming right up."

I returned to wait on Tweedle-Dee and Tweedle-Dum, doing my best to ignore their remarks.

* * *

AN HOUR LATER, SAME BAR

"You're crazy," said the taller one. "Lynn Swann is the best ever. No way Biletnikoff is the best."

"Which one is playin' in the Super Bowl?" asked the shorter one. "Biletnikoff. That's who."

I'd been listening to those two idiots go on for half an hour about football and the upcoming Super Bowl. I'd served each of them three more drinks and a couple of beers during that time and they hadn't eaten a thing. They were well on their way and becoming louder and more belligerent with each sip. I'd tried to ignore them but when they moved down toward Rachel, I paid more attention.

"I'm sure whatever you two boys are talking about is of no interest to me," she said as she was finishing her desert.

"Sure, it is. The Super Bowl is in two days. The Oakland Raiders against the Minnesota Vikings. Who you pullin' for?" asked the taller one.

"Me, I think the Raiders are gonna win," slurred the shorter one.

As drunk and as loud as they were, I was going to have to do something. Others were starting to stare.

"I'm asking you two to lower your voices. Other folks are trying to enjoy the evening."

I turned to Rachel. "The Super Bowl is the final game of our football season, and the winner is the champion."

"Oh, I see. And this is a big deal?" she asked.

"Yes, ma'am," I answered. "In my country, America that is, it's a very big deal."

"Heh, doll face, don't they play football in England?" asked the tall one.

"Scotland. I'm from Edinburgh, Scotland. We play football, in Scotland and England, but not the type you're used to."

"Well, then I won't be headin' to Scotland or England any time soon," said the tall one, laughing, as if that was the brightest comment ever made.

"Pity," she said.

I laughed, a bit too loudly, and reached for Rachel's dessert plate to move it away.

"Hey, moron?"

I stopped, turned, and looked him straight in the eye.

"Yeah, I'm talkin to you. Leave us alone down here and go back to waitin' on people. 'Bout the only thing you're good for."

And then, placing his arm around Rachel's shoulder and leering down the front of her dress, he suggested she leave with him and his buddy so she could experience what a real American man was all about. Rachel threw her drink in his face, and he responded by slapping her with the back of his hand.

The others in the vicinity would have a good story to tell by the pool the next day, a story about the bartender who beat two men senseless. But I inflicted far more damage than was necessary to either stop their boorish behavior or defend Rachel's honor. The smaller one was nothing. I quickly rendered him unconscious, and if the three police officers hadn't arrived when they did, I might have killed the other one. This is not something I'm proud of, but when I snap, I snap. His broken nose will be no big deal, but the shattered zygomatic bone forming the outer wall of his left eye socket, his crushed larynx, and cracked ribs will take months to heal.

* * *

NASSAU CITY JAIL, THE NEXT AFTERNOON

"You made bail, again," said the duty cop. "Hurry along. I got better things to do than care for your lazy bones."

This was not a shock, but frankly, I was expecting the news a little earlier in the day. This was not my first trip to the jailhouse, but I can't remember this much cell time.

"Tell Pinder that if he's gonna make me waste a whole day here then he can wait a few."

I had my back to the cell door and was relieving myself in an empty Folgers coffee can while the duty cop, Felix, waited for me.

"Not Pinder."

"Not Pinder? Then who?"

"Don't know. Not my job. Now get outta here before the judge changes his mind and books ya for attempted murder."

"That bad, huh?"

"Ya, bey. Bad. Very bad."

I tried to act tough and like I didn't care, but I did care, and not just for the poor sop that I beat silly, but for me as well. The judge warned me the last time I was thrown in jail for fighting that there'd be no further lenience. Yea, that's right, this wasn't my first trip to the city jail. Another beat down and I'd do time, the judge said; he didn't care who I knew.

I zipped up and walked out the cell door and down the hall wondering who had bailed me out and why Nigel hadn't. As I entered the front office and signed for my personal belongings—a pair of shoes, a belt, and my wallet—I looked about the room for my savior. Sitting in a chair by himself reading the paper was a man I recognized from Lyford Cay Golf Club.

I collected my things and walked over to the man in the chair. As I approached, he folded the paper and stood, placing the folded paper under his arm.

"Aaron Westfield, is it?"

"Yes, sir."

"Let me see your hands."

"Excuse me?" I replied.

"Your hands. Let me see your hands," he insisted.

I held out my hands and he grabbed each one by my wrist, turning them this way and that. They were bruised from the beating I'd handed out the night before and calloused from manual labor.

"Very well, then. Now come along," he said as he turned and walked out the door with a slight limp.

I started down the hall after him. As we exited the building and stepped into the bright, burning sun, I caught up.

"Sir, who are you?"

"My name is Lachlan McGregor. You can call me Lach, or coach."

"Coach? Why Coach?"

"Because I am your coach."

"Coach? Coach at what?"

"Golf, my dear boy. Golf. What else is there?"

Chapter 18

Taking Inventory

It's been three and a half years since I landed in the Bahamas. A lifetime ago, but a lifetime in which both nothing has changed, and everything has. Nothing has changed in that each day is like the one before. But everything has changed because I'm no longer a young man with a future, just one running from his past.

I haven't completely given up hope, though. I can't. Hope is all I have. My father, Monty, liked to say that you made your own future and that your future was brighter with interesting people in your orbit. That sounds all well and good, but for that to happen, these people he's talking about, ... well, you gotta be able to trust them and count on them, and in my life, who has that been?

But I recently met this man named Lach, and he's been teaching me the game of golf. Good grief does he have some crazy teaching methods. And then there's his niece, Rachel. Don't get me started. I can hardly complete a sentence when she's around.

So maybe things are looking up. Maybe this guy, Lach, is one of those people Dad was talking about. I have a feeling he could be. In fact, I think my life is about to become very interesting because of people like Lach and others I am destined to meet. Yes, I have hope. It's all I've got right now.

End of Part Two

PART THREE

Friend or Foe

Chapter 19

Lach McGregor

Gullane Golf Club, Gullane, East Lothian, Scotland, July 1913

"You must be proud," said one member of the small gallery standing behind the green on the 18th hole of the oldest of the three courses at Gullane Golf Club.

Indeed, they were. Taylor and Emily McGregor were the parents of Lachlan McGregor, who was standing on the tee, nearly 350 meters away, preparing to hit his tee shot. The 18th hole is considered one of the easier holes on the championship course, giving hope to the young man standing to the side and waiting his turn to swing away.

Having birdied the 17th hole to take a one-stroke lead, young Lachlan had honors. He was standing behind his ball, looking down the fairway, gently swinging his play club back and forth. The wind had been fierce all day, no less so on the home hole. It blew hard from behind and over his left shoulder. Any ball in flight would be pushed from the left side of the fairway to the right side and would likely carry farther. The ideal shot for the slight dogleg left would be to the right side of the fairway, especially since the hole was cut in the back left corner of the green. But that was where two treacherous pot bunkers laid, providing an ideal defense against a well-played shot. No, it was best to lay up short of the bunkers or trust that you could drive the ball past them.

Lachlan chose to play well short, knowing that if he didn't the wind could drive his ball into one of the bunkers. As his father had taught him, "Son, why use a long club when a short one will do?" Lach, as he was called by family and friends, stepped into the shot and hit the ball down the left side of the fairway. The wind caught it, pushed it rightward, and when it hit the ground, it bounced and rolled to the right side of the fairway, but shy of the bunkers, leaving him a straightaway shot into the green. The scattering of applause acknowledged a well-played shot.

Knowing he had few options and that he needed a birdie to tie the match, Aiken Aldridge, the defending champion of the Gullane Junior Amateur Championship, walked up to the teeing ground, and not taking much time at all, unleashed a mighty swing. The ball started out down the left side but sailed too high and, caught up in the wind, flew left toward the bunkers. Urging the ball forward, Aiken was visibly pained as the ball carried the bunker but hit on the back side and bounced furiously to the right, only to disappear into the gorse. An audible grown from the crowd signaled "advantage Lach."

The players walked silently up the fairway. Lach arrived at his ball first and sized up his shot to a green 150 meters away. Since there were not any bunkers to contend with and only a depression to the left of the green poising any problems, and with the wind behind him, Lach knew the wise shot was one played principally along the ground. Taking his long spoon, he closed the clubface oh so slightly and, using a shorter backswing, propelled the ball on a low trajectory, ensuring it would bounce forward unaffected by the wind. Having judged the distance beautifully, the ball bounced and rolled up to the front middle of the green. Now a mere two-putt stood between Lach and victory. Only a masterful shot by his competitor could overcome what was clear for all to see. The gallery acknowledged his chess move with firm applause.

Aiken's ball was sitting down in the gorse, but it was playable. He'd been in worse lies. Nevertheless, given the hacking swing needed to free the ball from the gorse, it would be a matter of luck for his ball to land on and hold the green. He took his position and with a vicious downward motion he excavated the ball from its lie and sent it flying toward the green. But the gorse had grabbed the clubhead, turning it to an overly closed position, and the ball carried hard to the left of the fairway into the gorse on the other side. The outcome was a formality by this point, but Master Aldridge soldiered on. He played one more shot, this time flying the green and landing on the road to the right of the course, at which point he removed his hat and walked up and shook Lach's hand. The match was over. Lach McGregor, age fifteen, was the champion.

A brief ceremony was held outside the clubhouse. Lachlan gathered his trophy and a small purse of ten pounds that the members of Gullane Golf Club had collected. Neither Lach nor his parents were allowed in the clubhouse, however. The McGregors were not members of the club, but that detail could have been easily overlooked had it not been for the fact that the McGregors were clearly working folk and not of the landed gentry that populated many private club memberships. Taking no offense and pleased with the warm reception, the McGregor family retired to a local pub in town to celebrate.

At dinner, Emily listened to her husband and son relive every shot made that day. Though she at times feigned boredom with the tedium of every remembered swing, she was thrilled with their camaraderie, knowing it was a blessing.

The town of Gullane sits on the southern shore of the Firth of Forth, the tidal mouth where several Scottish rivers meet the North Sea. Players from as far west as Glasgow and as far south as the fishing port of Eyemouth, Scotland had gathered for the matches. Word of Lach's victory would spread. Lach and his father, Taylor, talked of his future in golf. It was bright. With this victory, he would have his pick of jobs in the burgeoning golf industry in the UK. He was learning club-making, and any private club would be proud to hire the reigning Gullane Junior Amateur champion as an assistant pro while he grew into the job of a head pro.

But Lach also had dreams of earning a living playing golf as a professional. The idea of playing golf as anything other than an amateur was gaining ground. Their talks went on late into the evening, and it was too late to begin their journey back to Edinburgh, where they lived. One of the members of the Gullane Golf Club had an extra room for rent, which he let go for the night at no charge, so they spent the night in Gullane and returned home the next day, and young Lach went to bed secure in the knowledge that regardless of whether he took a job as a club pro or played golf as a professional, his future was bright.

* * *

How many lives of young men and women unfold in the anticipated manner? It's safe to say, very few. Whether that is a blessing or a burden depends upon where you start, where you end, how you get there, and the attitude you carry with you on your journey. This was true for Lach, a young man whose life in 1913, at the age of fifteen, seemed full of promise. The first hurdle he could not have imagined and one that would forever alter the course of his life was World War I.

After his victory at Gullane in the summer of 1913, Lach won two more tournaments before the North Berwick New Golf Club hired him as an assistant pro. He moved to North Berwick in late August to begin his career. North Berwick is a seaside town a little over thirty kilometers east of St. Andrews and home of a true links championship quality course. The game had grown in popularity since the North Berwick Golf Club opened in 1832. Bowing to the need for capital to build a proper clubhouse, a new club had been incorporated in the early 1880s. The membership grew until it made sense for the original club and the new club to merge into one club, the North Berwick New Golf Club, or simply the New Club, as it was known in the surrounding area.

Life was good for Lach. He was supporting himself financially and even able to send a little money home to help his parents, his father having fallen from a ladder and thus was out of work. At times he couldn't believe his good fortune—he was paid to play a game he loved.

All that changed on May 23rd, 1915. Lach was enjoying a pint with friends in a local pub at the end of the day when word reached the town that a horrible train wreck had occurred at a switching station the day before in Dumfriesshire, Scotland. The news was sketchy at this point, but it was believed that the accident involved several trains at a station due to the negligent behavior of one or more signalmen. One of the trains involved was a troop train headed for Liverpool, England. From there, the troops were to be deployed to Gallipoli, Turkey. Over two hundred young men, men Lach's age, died in the trainwreck on their way to serving their country.

Lach was devastated—all of Scotland was. The next day, a Monday and thus a slow workday, Lach and the other employees were allowed to play the course. So, it was with a heavy heart that Lach and a few friends took to the links. His golf was uninspired. The game seemed silly. Men his age, boys really, had died and more would as the world went to war. He was standing on the 15th hole, a long par-three, to a well-defended green built at a near forty-five-degree angle from the tee box alignment and sloping in a downward trajectory from right to left, making it one of the most difficult pars on the course. Since he'd first played the course, he'd struggled to master a tee shot that would hold the green. The challenge was complicated by a regularly shifting wind, meaning one day a high fade was required, and the next a draw would better serve your purposes.

But as he stood on the tee box this morning, he realized he just didn't care. He placed his golf ball in the hand of one of his playing partners and set off toward the clubhouse.

"Lach ... LACH," one of the other lads called out. "Where are you going?"

"I don't know, but our country has gone to war, so I must too."

And with that, Lach strode off toward town. Before enlisting, he went home to visit his parents. They had come to rely upon the extra few pounds he sent each month, so it was important they knew what was on his mind. Lach's father assured him he was getting along well and would be back to work soon enough, and though he was afraid for his son, he was proud, nonetheless.

* * *

Owing to his father's legacy as an accomplished Scottish footballer, Lach was accepted into the 16th Battalion of the Royal Scots, affectionately known as McCrae's Battalion, and the battalion best known for its large contingency of Scottish footballers and other athletes giving up their careers to fight for their country. Lach joined the battalion in France and fought in the Battle of the Somme at Delville Wood, where the British Expeditionary Force achieved a costly success over the Germans along this section of the Western Front.

This battle would be the only action Lach would see. A German hand grenade separated Lach's right leg below his knee from the rest of his body, and he returned to Edinburgh a hero, but a hero whose promising golf career had been cut short, or so it seemed.

Lach was determined to stay connected to the game and wasn't convinced his career as a golfer was over. After four months of recovery, and walking with a crutch, he returned to work in North Berwick, where the New Club hired him back in a gesture of national patriotism. The head professional at the club doubted what use a one-legged man could be on a golf course, but he liked Lach and was determined to do all he could to help the young lad.

Lach was a skilled club maker, but the future of the local club maker was dismal. The craft of making clubs was changing rapidly. Fading were the days of hickory-shafted clubs made one at a time. Improvements in iron making made iron clubheads lighter and easier to play, and Lach mastered these new techniques. But the real threat to individual club making came with the growth of the game. The demand for clubs was simply too strong, and with the improvement in the quality of factory-produced clubs coupled with falling prices, fewer and fewer golf club memberships could justify the expense of a dedicated club maker.

Lach's parents fretted. They sympathized with their son and appreciated his love of the game, but they believed there would come a time when his utility around a golf course would vanish, leaving him unemployed and without a trade to fall back on. They encouraged their son to take classes and learn accounting or become a teacher. One night, when he was back in Edinburgh for holiday, he had a particularly heated argument with his father about his future. Lach was convinced he could still play the game, even on one leg, and was willing to wager his future on it. He made a deal with his father: If he could score par or better at the Old Course within the month, he'd pursue his dreams and his parents would let the matter drop. If he couldn't, he'd enter university and study to become an accountant. The two men shook on it.

The next day, in his first round at a local course, he shot a 93, a far cry from 72, but he did so with a 41 on the returning nine. Lacking the ability to drive the ball with the lower half of his body, he had to modify his swing and rely upon his upper body. But how to do so without losing your balance and falling over? He caught a glimpse of the answer to this question on an unremarkable hole, on a long-forgotten course, playing alone with only the help of a friend who caddied for him since he couldn't carry his bag and walk the course with his crutch.

"Look, mate, you fall one more time and I'm headin' in and then you'll have to as well," deplored his friend.

"I can do it. I know I can."

"Yeah, you can hit it but to get any length you have to swing so hard you fall down."

Lach was trying to get up by himself as his friend walked over and reached out a hand to him. Back on his feet and with a crutch under his right arm, Lach trudged along to where he had hit his ball. His caddie, Troy, reluctantly followed along.

"If only you could swing the club without swinging your body, you'd have a chance," said Troy as he stared down the fairway.

"What did you say?"

"I said, 'If only you could swing the club without having to swing your body, you'd have a chance.'"

Lach continued to stare at his friend as if he were Edison discovering the carbon filament.

"Or maybe if I were to swing the club first instead of moving my body first ..." replied Lach as his voice trailed off. "Hand me my mashie," said Lach.

Troy handed Lach the club in exchange for the crutch. Balanced on his left leg, Lach began to gently swing the clubhead by breaking his wrist until he felt the weight of the clubhead in his hands. The weight of the clubhead in a swinging motion pulled his body's center of mass slowly left to right and then back to the right again and then left again, instead of starting the swing with his body and then pulling the club along. Gently, he found the rhythm, speeding up a bit and doing it so that his swing was slowest at each end but accelerating through the bottom of the swing.

After swinging the clubhead in this manner a full minute or two, Lach settled in over the ball. He cocked his wrists and pulled the clubhead back with his arms close to his sides, his body following along, and then gently reversed the swing at its apex and started down and back through, letting gravity have its way, accelerating at the bottom and completing the motion on the other side. The result was the farthest, straightest, and purest shot of the day.

In his excitement, Lach asked Troy for another ball. Troy tossed a ball to the ground and Lach stepped into his swing and hit another beautiful shot, this one a little farther. He did so again and again until Troy announced that they were out of balls. But collecting the balls wouldn't be difficult, for they all lay within five meters of each other, 120 meters down the middle of the fairway.

And that's how one of the most momentous developments of the modern game unfolded—with the swinging of the clubhead.

Three weeks later, Lach shot a 71 on the Old Course at St. Andrews to the delight of his father and the small gallery that had heard about their wager. St. Andrews was so enamored with the display that they offered Lach a job, which he happily took. To be an assistant pro at the home of golf! Could life get any better?

Lach's game continued to improve, as did his technique and fascination with his new ideas about the golf swing. On any given day, Lach could compete with the finest golfers in the area, which meant he could compete with the finest golfers in the world. However, despite his poetic swing, the rigors of walking a golf course four days in a row with a crutch were too great and he was never able to seriously threaten to win any four-day tournament. So, it was at this point in the year 1918 that Lach McGregor dedicated himself to becoming a teaching pro.

* * *

The Criterion, a pub in St. Andrews, Scotland, Sunday, June 19th, 1921

Lach had been asked to meet his boss for a pint at the end of the day and he was worried. The rumor was that if the boss was happy with you, he'd invite you inside the clubhouse for a pint, a rare treat for a golf professional, whose status in the world was still considered second class to the gentlemen making up the club's membership. The rumor continued that if he asked to meet you at a neighboring pub, then, well, the news wasn't good.

Lach's teaching assignments had suffered. His teaching sessions were down, and he wasn't attracting new pupils. Lach attributed it to nasty rumors started by his fellow teachers jealous of his success. If you want to hit the ball like a lady, they'd say, then take lessons from Lach McGregor, but if you want to hit the ball a country mile like Ted Ray, the previous year's U.S. Open champion, then you need a powerful, full-bodied, leg-driven swing like what they'll teach you.

Lach had put up with negative reactions and naysayers since he began teaching his methods. Always the same too:

"You make the game seem too easy."

"The game demands a full body motion and the concentration and athleticism that goes with it."

"If you're handicapped, he's your man."

Lach remained undeterred. He was convinced that his "Swing the Clubhead" method was the key to consistent and enjoyable golf, and nothing would deter him. But he had to eat, and fees from teaching were falling. So, with these thoughts rambling around in his head, Lach entered the pub, and when he entered, he saw his boss, Brodie, sitting in the corner halfway through a pint.

"Hello, Lach. Thank you for coming. Can I get you a pint?"

"Sure."

"What'll you have?"

Lach, observing what Brodie was drinking, nodded and answered: "I'll have one of those."

Turning to the bar, Brodie shouted loudly enough to be heard, "Two Guinness, please."

"Well, the Irish got this much right," he said as he took a swig of his beer.

"You wanted to see me, sir?" said Lach.

"Yes. I'm afraid so," he said as he bowed his head slightly to avoid looking him in the eyes. But then, raising his head, he responded. "It's about your continued utility here at the club."

Brodie grew silent and Lach feared where this was heading but said nothing.

"It's your damn teaching methods, son."

"But sir, they work. I'm living proof as are my pupils."

"That you can play the game as well as you do is a miracle and one I'm proud to have witnessed, but it is the membership's opinion that the game is changing. It's length that all anybody wants these days. Every young golfer wants to hit as far as Ted Ray. And the new equipment! It's extraordinary. Good God, man, even I'm hitting it farther with these new steel shafts and I'm getting on in my years. No, Lach, I'm afraid the game has changed and is leaving us old-timers behind."

The two men sat silently. Lach still had not touched his Guinness and was staring across the room.

"But Lach, the club is grateful, and not only for your time here but for your service in the war. So, we're offering you a job in the office and tending bar if you like. But as for teaching, I'm afraid we can't let you do that anymore."

Lach wasn't entirely surprised by the bad news, but he wasn't expecting the offer of a desk job. He had to admit, it softened the blow. But he knew what people would say, or at least what people would think, and the last thing he wanted was pity.

"Sir, you are misreading the game. My methods will produce long-ball hitters as easily as any swing Ted Ray can muster, but I've heard your say and I won't argue. As for the offer of a job inside, it is most gracious, but I'm afraid I will have to pass. I believe with all my heart there is a place for me teaching the game and I intend to find it."

"Very well, then. I must say, I admire your moxie. But can we handle this situation quietly? The Open Championship is this week, and the tournament is drawing more attention than ever given that the Americans sent a contingency of twelve of their top professionals and a few amateurs as well. I hear this young fellow Bobby Jones made the trip. There's a lot of talk about him."

"Yes, I'm anxious to see his swing."

"As am I, but so far, as to his future success in tournament play, it's a lot of talk, I hear. Seems he has a temper to match his talent, a temper that is his undoing. Well, anyway, your help will be needed through the weekend and there's no reason for any distractions. Will you stay on until the end of the month?"

"Yes, sir. Happily so, and thank you."

* * *

As Lach walked back to his flat that evening, he thought about his future and whether he'd have one in golf. He disagreed with his boss and the higher-ups who had termed his teaching methods unsound, but was he being too stubborn? What would become of him? No doubt, word would spread as to the real reason he'd been let go. Could he get work in the area? He would of course have to tell his parents. Fortunately, his father had returned to work, and they were no longer dependent upon him for financial help. He was single and without the burden of a family. He had his life ahead of him. Despite his near terminal optimism, these thoughts weighed heavily on Lach, but he wasn't ready to give up hope. And, to put himself in a better mood, he focused on the Open Championship. The greatest golfers in the world had descended on St. Andrews, and with qualifying rounds to begin in the morning, Lach looked forward to a wonderful week. He'd think about his future tomorrow or maybe at the end of the week.

* * *

THE CRITERION, ST. ANDREWS, SCOTLAND, SATURDAY NIGHT, JUNE 25TH, 1921

"A Scotsman is a Scotsman, I don't care where ye live," said a patron leaning against the bar.

"Damn traitor, if ye ask me," said another.

"Thir be noon of that kinda talk in my pub," said the bartender. "Jock is a friend of mine. Born right here in St. Andrews. He's as Scottish as you or me."

John "Jock" Hutchison had indeed been born in St. Andrews but the year before he became a naturalized American citizen. That was all well and good, but because he had just won the Open Championship in an eighteen-hole playoff, many questioned whether he was another Scotsman to have won the Claret Jug or the first American to have won it. The debate raged on, but one thing was clear—the Americans, whether born and bred or adopted, were coming. In another year, there would be no dispute as to whether an American had ever won across the pond, for Walter Hagen would win the Open in 1922 at Royal St. George's in England.

Lach walked into the pub at half-past eight that evening intent on having dinner with friends, but when he entered, he saw none other than the talented young American Bobby Jones sitting in the corner with, as luck would have it, a golf instructor from Lach's youth. Lach approached their table tentatively, hoping to attract their attention without disturbing them too much.

"Mr. Stewart?"

"Yes, can I help you?"

"I don't expect you to remember me, but you gave me lessons when I was barely seven years old at Carnoustie. My name is Lach. Lach McGregor."

Mr. Maiden had taught many young lads over the years and couldn't say whether he remembered him or not, but he surmised that he must be the same one-legged golfer he'd been hearing about, so it made sense to feign recognition.

"But of course. Lach McGregor. My, my. Yes, it has been some time."

Stewart Maiden noticed Lach stealing glances at Bobby. "Where are my manners? Lach McGregor, may I introduce my good friend here, Bobby Jones."

"Oh, I know who he is."

Bobby Jones stood and reached out his hand. "The pleasure is all mine. Care to join us?"

Lach forgot all about meeting his friends. There was so much he wanted to ask these two men. Stewart Maiden had been born in the neighboring town of Carnoustie and followed in his older brother's footsteps as the head golf pro at East Lake Golf Club in Atlanta, Georgia. It was widely known, at least among the Scots of the world, that Maiden taught Bobby how to swing the club. Though he had moved on to be the head pro at a club in St. Louis, Missouri, they had remained good friends. As they were both in St. Andrews for the Open Championship, they'd arranged to dine together.

"Why, yes. Thank you. Mr. Jones ..."

"Please, call me Bobby. I should be calling you Mr. ..."

After an awkward moment, Lach leaned his crutch against the wall and took a seat.

"Bobby, I had the pleasure of watching you play Monday in a qualifying round, and I was so enamored with your swing, I followed you all day Tuesday as well."

"Good thing you didn't follow me yesterday. Dismal performance. On the course and off, I'm afraid. I understand that this infernal game calls St. Andrews its home, but to be frank, I consider the Old Course among the very worst courses I have ever played."

"You might want to keep that opinion to yourself," said Stewart.

"Take that bunker on the 11th hole. Took me four shots to get out. Four shots! I was done. Shouldn't have quit like that, though. Please accept my apologies. I wish I could apologize to all of Scotland. What's that bunker's name, anyway?" he asked.

"That bunker is called the 'Hill' bunker," answered Lach.

"Well, it should be renamed 'Hell' bunker, if you ask me," replied Bobby.

"Then they'd have to rename the bunker on the 14th hole," remarked Stewart.

Bobby laughed and took a bite of his meal.

Breaking the silence, Lach tried to return the conversation to Bobby's swing. "And you had been swinging the club so well."

"And therein lies the problem," said Bobby. "I started thinking I had this course licked. Just goes to show there's no bigger fool than the man who thinks he's got this game figured out."

And then Bobby, true to his reputation as a gentleman, making no mention of the man's handicap, made Lach feel part of the game, its past and present.

"So, Lach, tell me about your game, and why I should want to return to play the Old Course?"

If Lach had died that night, he would have died a happy man. He spent the rest of the evening telling Bobby Jones and his instructor, a fellow Scotsman, his theories on the golf swing. The conversation was hardy. It was rigorous. They challenged him at times, but in the end, they agreed with him in many respects. There was more than just a place for his methods! Why, Bobby Jones himself said so.

"Oh, I just knew it. I just knew it," exclaimed Lach.

"Knew what?" asked Bobby.

"From the first time I saw you swing the club. The effortless way you take the club back and how you accelerate through the ball, and with your hands. You let the clubhead do the work. It looked as if you were barely swinging, but then, at the bottom of the swing ... Oh my, it was poetry."

"You sound like a friend of mine back home," said Bobby, chuckling to himself.

"Oh? Who would that be?" asked Lach.

"A sportswriter. Doubt you've heard of him over here. Goes by the name O. B. Keeler. He was sitting with us earlier tonight but had to leave. Something about a deadline he had to meet. You just missed him."

"Lach, it's been a pleasure meeting you and hearing your passion for the game," said Bobby. "From the sounds of it, you have a decision to make."

"Sir?"

"Don't know what the big decision is, though. You love the game. You love teaching. Why wouldn't you continue on?" asked Bobby.

"Well, as I said, my methods here are considered 'unsound' by some."

"Then come to America. Stewart here did it. His replacement as head pro at East Lake used to make clubs right here in St. Andrews. Willie Ogg. He's an excellent golfer. I expect he will have a fine golf career in America."

"But where would I live?"

"Come to Atlanta. If we can't find work for you there, I'm certain Walter Hagen could help you find work in New York. Oh, you should see some of the courses they have on Long Island."

The gentlemen talked a while longer and then called it a day, but that fateful evening marked a turning point for Lach. You see, he took Bobby Jones' advice and moved to America. A year later he was working on Long Island. Two years later, he was married, and they were expecting a child and living the American dream.

* * *

Forty-four years later, Lach McGregor was still looking for his first job as a head pro at a private country club. He had achieved national acclaim as a teacher, even if only in a small circle. He taught several championship-quality players over the years but had never gained the broader, universal acclaim he felt he deserved. He remained friends with Bobby Jones, who promoted him whenever he could, but Bobby was such a star in his own right, despite his intentions, his kind and encouraging words appeared as crumbs from the table.

Lach was growing weary. He had a running feud with the PGA of America over his teaching methods. He complained bitterly that the teaching pros the PGA turned out were like cookies from a mold, all emphasizing mechanics over feel. The president of the PGA responded that one can teach mechanics, but you can't teach feel, so how in the hell was the PGA to promote the game and its teachers without teaching the game's mechanics? To which Lach would reply, and loudly, "I can teach feel!"

And so it went. Absent the PGA's endorsement, Lach would never attain the position of head pro at a preeminent golf club. His wife would remind him that he loved teaching and that his income had provided them with a wonderful, though modest, living. They were happy as were their three children. What more did he want or expect? He'd come a long way from his humble beginnings. Lach knew she was right, but he still felt cheated. There was also the nagging feeling that his missing leg had something to do with his lack of advancement. Though he had been fitted with a prosthetic, he feared his leg still turned heads.

So the phone call he received in the fall of 1955 from a friend in the industry, Dick Wilson, came as a complete surprise. Dick was an accomplished golf course designer, and the two of them had enjoyed many a spirited conversation over their preferred drinks whenever they found themselves together at tournaments, PGA meetings, and industry tradeshows and conferences.

"Still designing those cookie-cut courses, are you?" asked Lach good-naturedly.

"Let's see *you* design an interesting course in Florida, on the world's flattest terrain."

"Yes, but those elevated greens. All so overly engineered. Not like a links course that is merely lying there waiting to be discovered, now, is it?"

"I've heard it all before, but Ben Hogan likes my latest work at Pine Tree Golf Club and that's good enough for me."

"Touché. But I do like your bunkers. They provide an excellent defense."

"We call 'em sand traps over here. After forty years, I figured you would have learned that."

"Ah, I do miss our banter. But I doubt you called to give me a good ribbing. Are you in town?"

"No, but I have a proposition for you. How would you like to be the head pro at a brand new, swanky private club?"

Lach hesitated. Was his friend serious or just pulling his leg?

"Sure, Dick. I suppose you're calling on behalf of Augusta National. Let me guess, they commissioned you to fix that mess of a course Bobby and Dr. MacKenzie designed down there?"

"I'm serious. I'm about to wrap up a project in the Bahamas. You wouldn't believe this place. Absolutely beautiful. And the membership ... oh, good grief. The dough these folks are rolling in! It's like nothing you've ever seen. They're still looking for a head pro. It seems every candidate they've interviewed is reluctant to move their family down here. I've put in a good word for you, and I'll bet Bobby would do the same if you were to ask him. What do you say? Will you at least consider it?"

Lach could hardly contain himself. Would he consider it? Of course he would, and if not for the need to speak with his wife Laurel about it, he would have said yes on the phone and been on the first flight to Nassau before Doug could hang up. But his wife's opinion was too important. She'd be home soon from a trip to the city with girlfriends, so he asked Doug if he could have some time to talk to Laurel about it. He answered yes, and they agreed to speak early the next week.

As it turns out, Laurel had been thinking about a move as well. The kids had left home, and it was just the two of them. The hard winters in New York had grown tiresome and she knew of her husband's long, unfulfilled dreams to be a head pro. So, it was decided, the McGregors were moving to the Bahamas.

* * *

Thirteen years later, Nassau International Airport, Wednesday, December 11th, 1968

Lach was waiting at the airport to pick up his wife, Laurel. The children and grandchildren would be flying in late Friday afternoon. Laurel had traveled to Miami the previous week to do the kind of Christmas shopping she claimed you couldn't do on the islands. Lach and Laurel were preparing for an extra special Christmas and New Year celebration this year. The last day of school for the grandkids was this Friday, so the kids would spend three weeks with Grandpa and Grandma. Their parents would return to the States for a few days after the Big Shindig this Saturday night before returning for Christmas.

Ah, yes, the Big Shindig this Saturday night. They'd been talking about it and referring to it as the "Big Shindig" for some time. At the age of seventy, Lach was retiring and the Country Club of Lyford Cay where he had proudly served for the last twelve years as head golf pro was throwing him a retirement party for the ages. Many of golf's luminaries of the time would be in attendance, and the club had scheduled a small tournament for anyone interested. An invitation had been extended to Bobby, but his health had declined precipitously, and confined to a wheelchair as he was, he declined. Dick Wilson, the course architect, and the man who brought Lach to Lyford Cay, passed away three years earlier.

Yes, many from Lach's era had passed, and while he was in good health, he knew it was time to pass the mantle to a younger pro. Besides, he had such plans with Laurel. They were intent on traveling and spending more time with the grandchildren. Their three children all lived in the South, two in Miami and their youngest in Atlanta, making visiting them convenient. Finally, Lach hadn't been back to Scotland in some time, and with the Open Championship returning to St. Andrews in 1970, they planned to attend.

Life was good. Lach sat in the airport terminal with a newspaper folded in his lap and happily reminisced about his life with Laurel. Drawing a line from the major and minor events of his life, connecting the dots so to speak, had placed him right here. What if he hadn't walked into The Criterion pub that night in 1921 and met Bobby Jones? Would he have ended up in America? If he hadn't made it to America, would he have ever met Laurel? Or Dick Wilson for that matter, the man who set their feet on a path toward his first and only job as a head pro, here in the Bahamas. No, it was funny, scary at times, but ultimately wonderful how life can turn out.

Lach's optimism had served him well. Never one to over plan, he took life as it came, and even when times looked dark, and there had been dark times—what marriage isn't tested?—he'd seen it through. They'd seen it through. Lach was in wonderful spirits. Life was good.

The announcement came over the loudspeaker: "The Pan American Airways flight from Miami is on approach and will be landing soon."

Many in the terminal walked up to the large windows to watch the plane land, but Lach remained seated. He had a clear view where he was sitting and would watch Laurel descend the stairs to the runway. A few minutes later, the plane landed and taxied to the terminal. A set of large rolling stairs was wheeled into position and the door was finally opened. Lach stood knowing his wife would soon be walking down the steps. He would greet her with a hug and a kiss when she walked through the door.

Ten minutes later, and no sign of Laurel. Lach was staring out the window, checking his watch and questioning whether he had the day and flight information right. They'd spoken on Sunday night when she called from their son's house. The flight attendants and pilots were now coming down the stairs. He greeted them as they entered the terminal and he asked about his wife. One of the flight attendants checked her passenger manifest and confirmed that a Laurel McGregor had been booked on the flight but had never made the flight.

Five minutes later, he was standing at a payphone placing a call to his son, Condon.

"Yes, I'll accept the charges," Condon said.

"Okay, I'm putting you through, Mr. McGregor."

"Thank you," said Lach.

"Hey, Dad. What's up?"

"Your mother missed the flight. Has she called you?"

"She missed her flight? That's impossible. You know how she is about air travel, always getting to the airport two hours early."

"I know. I know. Son, I'm at the airport. I'm going to see if there's another flight coming in today and if not, I'll head home. See if you can find out anything and we'll talk tonight."

"Okay, Dad. Will do. I'm sure everything is fine."

* * *

There were no other flights that day and everything was not fine. As Lach sat at home waiting for a call from his son or his wife, he imagined the worst. *Something has happened to my dear Laurel,* he feared. And then, as if on cue, a knock came at the door. He slowly stood up from his La-Z-Boy chair and walked to the front door. He opened it and, seeing two uniformed police officers, he broke down and cried.

* * *

The Big Shindig never happened. Instead, the next day, Lach McGregor boarded a Pan American flight for Miami, where he was met by his two daughters and his son. Later that week they buried his wife, their mother, and the grandmother of nine adorable grandchildren. Laurel McGregor never made it to the airport that day. A driver running a red light crashed into the taxi carrying her to the airport. He survived, but just barely, as did the taxi driver. The coroner surmised that Laurel had died instantly. No pain. Small consolation.

This time, when Lach thought about lines connecting dots, he wondered about all the things, big and small, that had placed Laurel and the other driver at that intersection at that point in time. What if the redlight runner had been just a little sooner or a little later? What if he'd answered the ringing phone on his desk instead of hurrying out the door to make it to wherever he was going? What if he'd stopped to fill up with gas? Would Laurel still be alive? What if…? What if?

* * *

After his wife's death, Lach fell off the map, literally, disappearing without a trace. Funeral services were held in Nassau, and the club held a reception afterward. The funeral home said there was no way they could accommodate the expected crowds. Lach and Laurel had been immensely popular not just in the club but on the island. They were generous with their time and money, and since the club paid Lach well, and due to some fortunate and well-timed stock tips thrown his way by the membership and others, they had plenty of money with which to be generous. The club rulers had embraced Lach's teaching methods, and Lach joked about all the golfers he'd birthed the way an obstetrician in a small town does about the children they've brought into the world.

The outpouring of support Lach received in the week between the accident and the reception on the island made Lach's disappearance all the more unusual. There was no reason for him to leave. He was among friends. Lach, the eternal optimist. Yes, losing your spouse so unexpectedly is devastating, but Lach would recover. That was the consensus. But whether Lach recovered was a mystery because his whereabouts were a mystery. As the reception following his wife's funeral was winding down, Lach said his goodbyes and excused himself, explaining that he felt rest was in order. He was seen driving toward his home and that was it. He was gone.

His children did what they could to find him but to no avail. Lach emptied his bank account the Friday before the funeral and had arranged for an attorney to sell his home and wire him the money. The attorney stood behind the attorney-client privilege and refused to tell the children anything. Sharing with them where he wired the money would have brought them no closer to finding their father, however, because he kept moving the money. Lach did not trust the lawyer to keep his mouth shut for the simple reason that he didn't trust lawyers at all. But he did trust bankers to keep theirs shut. Besides, with the help of a banker in Nassau, his money was wired from one bank to another and another such that not even the first banker knew where Lach had sent it. Lach had gone off the grid before there even was a grid.

And then one spring day four years later, he walked into the clubhouse at the Lyford Cay Golf Club and walked back to his locker as if nothing had changed. When he retired, the club gave him a membership and it seemed that all along he had continued to pay his club dues. He laced up his spikes, walked out to the driving range, and began hitting balls. Word quickly spread that a man on the driving range was hitting beautiful, high irons and doing so on one leg. It couldn't have been anyone else. Lach McGregor was back.

Before arriving in Nassau, he'd stopped in Atlanta and Miami to see his children and grandchildren and to beg their forgiveness. For the last four years, the only communication any of them had received were birthday cards and Christmas cards and always from different locations sure to discourage them from looking for him. The grandchildren were quick to forgive and showered him with hugs and kisses. It would take longer with his children, but his visit was a start, and they all promised to visit him when school was out.

It was good to have Lach back, but he wasn't the same. Old friends tried to bring him back into their orbit, but he kept them at arm's length. When asked where he'd been all these years, he'd laugh and make an offhand remark intent upon shutting down further inquiry, and he never explained his four-year absence, at least not to anyone at the club. The head pro said he could teach lessons if he wanted, and he declined. Lach was invited to play golf, and he declined. He didn't enter tournaments and only played golf by himself either early in the morning or late in the day when others were not around. He was often seen dining in the clubhouse, alone. He wasn't rude, not at all. He would just politely wave a book he was reading as if that explained why he preferred or needed to be alone.

Quite simply, he'd invested everything in this life, and it had been taken from him. He didn't want to risk the pain of losing anyone again. The overtures to his children and grandchildren were the only risks he was willing to take. As for getting close to others, he preferred the distance. It was safer.

* * *

When Lach wasn't hitting balls on the range, he would sit in a rocking chair on the veranda, sip tea, or if late enough in the day, a single malt Scotch whisky, and watch the other players on the range. One afternoon, as the sun was beginning its descent, he watched a young man in a golf cart drive up the 18th fairway toward a maintenance shed. He parked the cart, hopped off, and began walking toward the pro shop with an iron in his hand, and then with a flip of his wrist he effortlessly picked a golf ball up off the ground. The ball floated up over his head and he caught it on the face of the club, which he was then holding hip high on his right side. Still walking and with the ball resting in place on the face of the iron, he flipped it back into the air and bounced it on the face of the club, never breaking stride and only looking at the ball occasionally. Lach had never seen anything like it. And then, as if that were not enough, he switched the club to his left hand all the while continuing to bounce the ball, still never breaking stride.

As he approached the pro shop, he walked up along one side of the driving range, at which point he lobbed the ball a bit higher into the air and with the swing of a baseball player launched the ball to the far end of the range. He then grabbed the club mid-shaft and jogged gracefully up to the pro shop. He'd been sent out to the 17th hole where one of the members had left a club next to a green-side bunker. After he returned the club to the pro shop, he walked back out of the pro shop and toward the parking lot as if what he had just done was the most natural thing in the world. Lach was amazed.

Lach kept his eye out for the young man. He learned that he worked as a caddie sometimes and other times he worked maintenance and picked the driving range. No one knew much about him. He was a loner and from the States. Most folks figured he was hiding from something. He had powerful friends, though, which only fueled the mystery. Lach's patience was rewarded two weeks later when he saw the young man picking up golf balls on the range. Lach watched as he stopped the cart, pulled an old iron from the back of the truck, and began hitting balls. This was not an uncommon sight. Many on the maintenance staff did this late in the day when there weren't any members on the driving range. But what Lach witnessed gave him goosebumps.

* * *

IN THE PARKING LOT BEHIND THE NASSAU CITY JAIL, SATURDAY, JANUARY 8TH, 1977

Aaron walked out into the bright sun of a new day struggling to understand what had just happened and who this man Lach was.

"Excuse me, sir. I don't mean to be disrespectful, but can you tell me what's going on and who you are besides claiming to be my coach? Did Nigel Pinder or Quaid Dawson send you?" Aaron asked.

Lach walked to his side of the car, opened the door, and maneuvered himself into the front seat. He then reached over to the passenger side and unlocked the door. Aaron was still standing next to the car, wondering what was expected of him. Lach opened his door and poked his head out and said something about not having all day and if Aaron wanted a ride, he'd best get in. So, Aaron got in.

"It seems you made quite an impression on my niece last night," he said as he pulled out of the jail parking lot. "She phoned from the bar and alerted me to your situation. I want to thank you for defending her honor. For that I am grateful and was more than willing to bail you out."

"You're Rachel's uncle?"

"I am indeed," he said as he started the car. "Now is that enough of an explanation for you?"

"Sort of. But what do you mean about being my golf coach? I've never even had a lesson."

Putting the car into gear and looking back over his shoulder as he pulled into traffic, he answered. "And if you had, I wouldn't waste my time with you."

* * *

And so began their relationship together. Teacher and student. Aaron still worked at the Lyford Cay Golf Club, but due to Lach's status at the club, Aaron was allowed time on the driving range late in the day when most of the other members had adjourned for drinks and gin rummy.

Lach was a tireless teacher, never missing an opportunity to impart his years of wisdom. His methods were simple—strip away everything Aaron thought he knew about hitting the golf ball. And the first thing to go was that very thought, the idea that Aaron knew anything at all about striking a ball.

"You're not here to hit the golf ball. You're here to strike it and you do that by swinging the clubhead."

For the first week together, Aaron never even picked up a club. Instead, he would swing a weight on the end of a handkerchief until he found the rhythm and could swing a weight without ever looking at his hands or like a pendulum, all the while carrying on a conversation.

After day five of this seemingly pointless exercise, Aaron voiced his extreme frustration. "Okay, I'm about done with this. Can we move on?"

"Absolutely. Next week we'll do the same thing but with the left hand. Have a good weekend."

* * *

It was not until week three that Aaron held a club. In this drill, he held the club, but he also held the same handkerchief with the weighted end between his right thumb and forefinger. He now had to swing the club as he imagined one would swing a club and do so such that the handkerchief moved parallel to the shaft of the club and remained taut with the weighted end, always swinging in tandem with the club.

For the first five or so minutes, at the top of the swing, as he changed directions, the weight at the end of the handkerchief would fall toward the ground before he could change the direction of the clubhead. For the next five, Aaron changed the club's direction so quickly that the weighted end of the handkerchief fell behind in the swing and came swinging through furiously in a herky-jerky manner.

Aaron lost his cool and threw the club, end over end, fifty yards down the driving range.

"This is ridiculous. I already know how to hit a golf ball," said Aaron as he paced about on the driving range.

"Oh, you do, do you?" asked Lach.

"Yeah. I played with my dad a bit growin' up. Never had lessons. Never needed 'em. I hit the ball a country mile."

"Hit it indeed, I'm sure. Very well. See that green flag down the driving range, two hundred yards out?"

"Yeah."

"I'll give you five shots at it to my one. If I'm closer, we carry on. If any one of your shots is closer, then you can be on your way."

"You're on."

Aaron grabbed a club out of the bag and stepped up to the ball and looking back over his shoulder announced: "Six-iron. All I'm gonna need."

Lach nodded as Aaron waggled the clubhead. He then wrapped his arms around him on his takeaway and pulled the club through with an audible noise as the ball was launched. It flew high and was online but then veered violently to the left, missing the target by a good forty yards.

He pulled another ball over from the pile and set up right of the target. He tried to replicate the same swing but this time it went farther left and fell short. Frustrated but trying not to show it, Aaron walked over to his bag and grabbed the five-iron and remarked that there must be some wind up there.

This time, trying to fix his hook, Aaron shoved his hands out in front before snapping them through. His machinations sent the ball flying high but fading from the onset, and while he had the distance, he missed the target by forty yards again, this time to the right. He repeated his efforts but with greater wrist pronation, as he snapped his wrists even harder in order to start the ball out to the right and draw it back to the left; he hit the ball fat and it fell weakly to the ground thirty yards down the fairway. Barely able to control his temper at this point, his final swing, the fastest of the five, was the worst yet. Shank. Dead right.

"My turn," said Lach.

Aaron could hardly watch; he knew what was coming. But then Lach added insult to injury when he removed his prosthetic right leg and hopped on one foot over to the bag and took out a five-wood. He managed to place the ball on a tee and then took a few smooth swings before assuming his stance. With one fluid swing, Lach launched the ball on a gentle, high, right-to-left draw. It settled within ten feet of the target.

Without saying a word, Lach hopped back to the bench, reattached his leg, stood, tipped his hat at Aaron, and walked off.

"See you tomorrow?" Lach asked over his shoulder.

"Son-of-a-biscuit," Aaron muttered to himself. "Yeah, yeah, yeah. I'll see you tomorrow."

Lach smiled as he entered the clubhouse thinking he'd buy a friend or two a drink, maybe stay for dinner.

* * *

The change in Lach was immediate and obvious to all. He was in his element, teaching again, and oh, what a talent he had in young Aaron Westfield! By the end of their first month together, small galleries would appear on the driving range to watch the two of them work together. The pro shop began placing a row of rocking chairs for members to sit in, and the bar served the group of regulars who appeared at the end of each day to observe. The time Lach and Aaron spent together became a clinic of sorts for anyone who wanted to watch and learn.

"Control. Balance. Timing. This is all one needs to swing the clubhead. "And Aaron, how do we achieve control?" Lach would ask.

"By moving the club with a swinging action," Aaron would answer.

"Correct."

"And balance. How do we achieve balance?"

"We don't. It happens when we swing the clubhead. If we think about it, we lose it, but if we swing the clubhead, we maintain balance without even trying, without even thinking about it."

"Correct. And timing. What, dear boy, is timing?"

"It, too, occurs naturally from swinging the clubhead in a smooth, rhythmic manner. You feel it; you don't produce it."

"And where do you feel it?"

"In your hands. Everything begins with your hands," Aaron would answer.

"True. And what will this timing produce?" Lach would ask.

"Consistency and maximum clubhead speed at the instant of impact against the ball," Aaron would answer.

Lach began and ended each session reciting these mantras with Aaron. With most students, Lach spent countless hours unteaching them what they thought they knew about playing golf. Most teachers break the golf swing down into a laborious list of steps or components, one built upon the other, until your average golfer spent more time thinking about what they were doing wrong at each step instead of focusing on what to do right. The only aspects of a swing Lach taught as essential to a good swing were the grip and the stance. He preached a simple, overlap grip where pressure was felt in the thumb and forefinger of each hand and a stance that was comfortable, putting the player into position to swing the clubhead naturally. Beyond that, he taught players how to feel.

"When you listen to a beautiful symphony, you hear the whole, not the parts, and that's how it is with golf. You learn the whole swing, as a swing, and not the parts, for there are no parts," he would repeat to anyone who would listen. And as word of Aaron's talent spread, more people were listening.

Lach knew he was a good teacher, but he also knew that Aaron had that *something* that could not be taught. He was a natural, and when he could ignore the inner voices telling him to swing hard, his swing was as graceful as a waltz. No prolonged setup, no complicated club waggle, no gimmicks, just the swing of a clubhead, propelled by two powerful hands, perfectly timed, traveling rhythmically back and forth on a long, beautiful arc.

As God's supreme creation, it is the hands that separate man more from other primates than any other aspect of his physical nature. If all the muscles that power the hands and make it possible to scale rock walls were in the hands, then they would lack the dexterity to perform intricate surgeries. But the muscles are not in the hands; they are in the forearms and connect to the finger bones along tendons passing through flexible, rotating wrists. The same hands that work mines and perform manual labor, whether outdoors or over a stove, or mangled from arthritis induced by a lifetime of pushing a broom, are also capable of a gentle caress.

There are twenty-seven bones in each hand, fifty-four bones in total gripping clubs of varying length and acting in concert with the human body to propel a ball 1.68 inches in diameter through the air towards a hole 4.25 inches in diameter several hundred yards away. And it was Aaron's hands that won Lach over the day he bailed him out of jail, that and a rare combination of eye-hand coordination, rhythm, calm, and strength—a combination he'd only seen in one other man.

* * *

After six weeks on the range, Aaron was itching to take his game to the course. There was only one problem—Aaron was not a member of the club but was an employee.

"Okay, so I quit and then I can play as a guest," suggested Aaron one Friday afternoon after a practice session. Aaron and Lach were standing in the parking lot and Aaron was straddling his motorcycle, putting on his helmet. For Lach, his home was just a short walk and one he enjoyed taking.

"A temporary solution at best. As a guest, you're only allowed six rounds a year. I'd like to see you playing half that many rounds each week. No, I'm afraid we have a bit of sticky wicket here," said Lach.

"Maybe I should just turn pro," joked Aaron. "Then I can play wherever I want."

"What was that, lad?"

"I said maybe I should just turn pro and then I can play wherever I want."

"Well, Bob's your uncle!" exclaimed Lach as he beamed ear to ear and set off for home.

"Who's Bob?" asked Aaron.

"Never you mind that, but you might be on to something. Now stay out of trouble and I'll see you in a day or two."

* * *

The next morning, Lach was in the office of the club general manager, Mr. Bradford Bishop, imploring him to reconsider.

"I'm telling you he could be a champion golfer. He has the talent," said Lach.

"Yes, you said that, but you're asking us to give a non-member playing privileges here and at no charge as your permanent guest. There's simply no precedent for it."

"Then let's set a precedent. Wouldn't you want to support the game by giving an amateur the chance to play and develop his game? Just think of the notoriety it would bring our club were he to win on the professional tour?"

"Lach, dear boy, you seemed to have forgotten where you are. The last thing our members want is notoriety. And this boy—and let's be clear, he is a boy—this boy you are putting up for, I don't know what you call it, but this special brand of membership is not exactly the breed of person we seek here as a member."

"Aw, bollocks," said Lach. "And neither am I, if truth be told. I was born poor. Kept out of the best clubs in Scotland, and here I am. Do you want to kick me out too?"

"Now, Lach. Nothing of the sort. Come now, it's just that we have our standards."

The two went back and forth but to no avail. The club wouldn't budge. He hated having to break the news to Aaron, but for the moment, Lach was out of ideas.

Chapter 20

Bernard Lasko

Café Abaco, March 12th, 1977, two weeks later

"Aaron, could you bring us two more beers?" asked Quaid.

Aaron nodded and returned to the kitchen without so much as a word.

"What's he doing back here at the Café Abaco? You told me he was spending his time at the club," said Nash.

"He still works there most days, but they can always use an extra hand here. I'm not really involved in the day-to-day with him. That's Nigel's job. I just see him when I'm in town."

"Well, he seems miserable. I went to a lot of trouble and on short notice a few years back helping you with the kid's papers. I guess I'd like to think there was a reason for it all."

"And I appreciate it. You know that," said Quaid, and the two men clinked their beer bottles. "Look, he's just a kid. You know how moody they can be."

"Yeah, but this one had to grow up and become an adult overnight if

I remember correctly. No time anymore to be moody. He fled Charleston because his mom was going to testify against him in a murder trial. Am I right?"

"Yep. He's had it tough. At first, when he got here, he did okay, but once it became clear that he may never be able to go home, well, it's been rough on him since then. Things had been looking up, though. The ex-club pro at Lyford Cay took him under his arm and was teaching him the game. From what I hear, he's a hell of a golfer."

"Yeah, you told me about that. What changed?" asked Nash.

"His teacher, an old Scotsman named Lach McGregor, asked the club if Aaron could play golf on a special exemption at their club. Seems this guy McGregor believes Aaron could turn pro one day and he was hoping the club would support Aaron and let him play the course as an amateur. Gave the club the whole song and dance about carrying on the beauty of the amateur game in the spirit of Bobby Jones."

"And the club wasn't buying it," said Nash.

"Nope. Not at all. According to Nigel, Aaron boycotted the place for a week, but a few members for whom he regularly caddied tracked him down and convinced him to return. He did, but he's still angry about it. Can't say I blame him. The kid just can't get a break."

"But if he's still wanted for murder in Charleston, turning pro wasn't really in the cards, was it? I mean, someone was bound to recognize him," said Nash.

"Yeah, you're right. Probably better the kid never gets his hopes up. But it still ain't right."

"Speaking of golf, when are you and I going to play?" asked Nash.

"You know I'm not a golfer."

"You belong to this swanky club, and you hardly ever play. I don't get it. At least have me as a guest?"

"Fine, you're on. I'll set something up for later this week. But, Nash, I doubt you came all this way to finagle a round of golf out of me. Is trouble brewing?"

"You might say that. A cancer has landed on your peaceful little corner of paradise, and he has our attention, or at least mine."

"Really? Who are you talkin' about?" asked Quaid.

And as fate would have it, as Nash finished taking the last swig of his beer, a throng of men exited the bank across the street. Nash put his empty bottle down on the table, sat up straighter, and nodded toward the gathering outside the bank waiting for the doors to several limos to open. "I'm talkin' about *him*," Nash said.

"Lynden Pindling?" asked Quaid. "The prime minister?"

"No. The man he's shaking hands with," answered Nash.

"You mean Bernard Lasko," said Aaron as he placed two fresh beers on the table.

"You know him?" asked Nash.

"Sure, I caddie for him all the time," said Aaron.

* * *

Bernard Lasko was born in 1915 in Manitowoc, Wisconsin, eighty miles north of Milwaukee and a few miles from the shores of Lake Michigan. For his first ten years, his parents shared a home with his mother's parents. The wind off the lake defined their existence, and in the winter, it would sweep under the house and rattle the windows, rendering futile all attempts to stay warm. The home lacked indoor plumbing, and their only modes of transportation in the early years were bicycles, horse-drawn buggies, and their feet. Bernard had no formal education, and if it wasn't for his grandmother teaching him, he would have never learned to read.

For the next eight years, he bounced back and forth between homes his parents tried in vain to rent and his grandparents' house. Bernard's father, Cilas, was forever pursuing one get-rich plan after another but in every instance ended up losing everything he invested and, with hat in hand, would crawl back to his father-in-law and ask if they could move back in. Every time, he received the same lecture.

"You have a good job delivering milk for Old Man Jorgensen. Why can't that be enough?"

Or ...

"Stop chasing after these foolish ideas of yours and learn to take care of your family."

And every time, Cilas would nod his head in agreement and recommit himself to life as a milkman. The day Bernard turned six years old was the first day he rode with his father in the cab of the milk delivery truck.

For the next twelve years, Bernard witnessed his father rise before sunup and travel to the Jorgensen Dairy Farm, where he would be handed the keys to a milk truck. In the early days, Cilas pedalled his bike to the Jorgensen farm, but over time he managed to save enough so the family could afford a used Model-T. The milk trucks Cilas drove over the years changed as well, and by the 1920s, Old Man Jorgensen could afford top-of-the-line Oshkosh milk trucks.

Cilas drove his routes religiously, and because he was done by early afternoon, he used the second half of his days doing odd jobs for folks in the area to earn extra cash or to pursue his latest business idea. In the summer, owing to the lack of refrigeration, Cilas never had a day off because not a day passed that folks didn't drink milk. During the winter months, however, folks used their back porch as a refrigerator, and took to ordering enough milk, butter, and eggs needed for two or more days, allowing Cilas time off to chase his dreams.

Cash was always in short supply. Bernard was an only child, and years later he would wonder whether he had grown up without siblings because his parents knew they could barely care for one let alone two or more children—or because they shared a loveless marriage. But Cilas was determined to work his way to prosperity like Mr. Jorgensen of Jorgensen Dairy had. One day, Cilas worked out a deal with Mr. Jorgensen whereby he would no longer be an employee of Jorgensen Dairy but instead would buy his own trucks and deliver the milk for the dairy. Mr. Jorgensen was getting on in years and concluded that letting someone else manage the routes would ease both the financial and physical burden of running the business.

Business for Cilas started out well enough. His small savings and a bank loan, cosigned by Mr. Jorgensen, allowed Cilas to buy one truck, and then another, and then another, and after five years, he had a fleet of ten trucks and was managing every route previously managed by Jorgensen Dairy. But Cilas had taken on more than he could handle, for he had debt on all ten trucks and was working harder than ever. While hard work has been known to beget good luck for some, such wasn't the case for Cilas Lasko. The trucks were in constant need of repair, and the growing threat of unions put many workers in a hostile mindset toward him before he'd paid them a day's wages. The final straw came when one of his drivers fell asleep at the wheel and drove his delivery truck off the road, across the drainage ditch that paralleled the state highway, and through a barbed-wire fence, striking and killing a cow—a Holstein, prized in these parts more than your firstborn.

Cilas fought with the insurance company to recover the cost to repair the truck, but the financial damage was done. His margins were thin to begin with and he was now paying interest on ten trucks but only driving nine. Cilas stood to lose his trucks as well as the home he'd purchased the summer before. Mr. Jorgensen helped him out how he could, but he had his own responsibilities and business to take care of. But being Christian minded, he wasn't going to cancel his contract with Cilas and leave him out in the cold. No, he made his mind up to both offer Cilas his old job back and to take over the bank payments on the ten trucks—he'd be needing them anyway.

Mr. Jorgensen never got the chance to talk with Cilas, though, because while he was studying the matter on his back porch, Cilas Lasko was blowing his brains out with the Colt revolver he'd brought home with him from his service in France during WWI. Two days later, Bernard, who had moved out the summer before, found his father on the floor and two notes on the kitchen table, one from his mother addressed to his father explaining she couldn't keep on this way and was leaving him, and the other note from his father addressed to him simply saying, "I'm sorry."

Thirty minutes later, eighteen-year-old Bernard Lasko had loaded his meager possessions into his father's beat-up old Model T and was heading south on State Highway 42, never to return to Manitowoc, Wisconsin again.

* * *

Bernard Lasko appeared on the scene in Nassau like a clap of thunder. When he first arrived in 1976, he lived on his yacht until he found a suitable home. He located his target—a twenty thousand square foot mansion on the westernmost tip of the island at the end of E. P. Taylor Drive overlooking Clifton Bay and the Atlantic Ocean. There was only one problem: It wasn't for sale, and its owner, a retired fashion industry mogul, made it clear he would never sell. "I'll be buried in my private Shangri-La before I ever sell," he was fond of saying.

But then rumors of the mogul's proclivity for young children surfaced, and the man was fighting extradition to the United States on charges of child pornography and pedophilia filed in New York City, where he maintained a condo. As the noose was tightening, a strange turn of events unfolded: charges were dropped, the man was allowed to board a private plane for Thailand, and the sale of his Lyford Cay estate to Nassau's newest celebrity, Bernard Lasko, was recorded. For anyone paying attention and wondering if dots could be connected, they would have observed that the week before all this happened, Lasko attended a fundraiser in New York City for an ambitious young lawyer in the Attorney General's office who was leaving his post as director of the Crimes Against Children Division so he could run for governor.

Lasko was rumored to have made his first fortune as a manager of other people's money, but quickly moved up in the world and made his next fortune managing his own. He was considered a financial genius, or at least so by the trade journals in which he purchased expensive ads. At least one daily regularly referred to him as a "money manager's money manager." His investment funds were closed, he would say, and he was not letting in any more investors. "I prefer the company of a trusted few" was his standard answer when asked if he would ever allow in new money. "I'll let others chase dreams of large management fees. I'm content with things as they are."

Eventually, the drumbeat grew too loud and Lasko consented and opened a series of funds for others to invest in. It was as if the dam at Niagara Falls had broken. Investors lined up, drooling at the prospects of double-digit returns, year-in and year-out.

In Nassau, very quickly Lasko was everywhere. Making generous donations to build a new wing at a hospital. Buying textbooks for the public school system. Hosting charity balls for ecology groups. Lasko looked good in a tuxedo but was equally at home on the water, marlin fishing. He was renowned as a big tipper, and quickly became known as a man of the people.

And he liked to gamble.

Chapter 21

Travis McCoy

The Lyford Cay Golf Club, Tuesday, March 15th, 1977

"Aaron, you're up," said Tony Rolle, the caddie master, and the only caddie master the club ever had. Tony was a big man, and it was rumored he had a promising boxing career ahead of him but lost sight in one eye when the referee failed to stop a fight that should have been stopped. He'd put on some pounds since leaving the ring, but he still possessed the quick reflexes of a boxer and reigned over the other caddies with a mixture of fear and respect. And he always had a cigar in his mouth. His years in the sun had darkened his skin and tuned his hair white.

Tony was from the island of Exuma and could trace his lineage back to slaves owned by Denys Rolle, a British Loyalist and slave owner who was granted land on Exuma by the king of England. That came after Spain seized Rolle's substantial land holdings in Florida when Florida came under Spanish control as a result of the 1783 Treaty of Paris. Like many of the slaves owned by the Rolle family, when they were freed in 1838, they took the surname Rolle.

Tony didn't care much for the history surrounding the Rolle name, and when asked about which Rolles he was really related to and which he was not, he'd piss and moan about it all and tell you what he thought. "It don't make a hill of beans who you are. If you want a good caddie at Lyford Cay, you gots to come to me."

"Aaron, you're carrying for Lasko again. Seems he's taken a real shine to you, boy," said Tony.

"And who else?" asked Aaron.

"Dr. Rawlings. And Mateo, you'll be on the bag for the Colonel and his guest, some Texan named Travis McCoy. The word is he's quite a stick; played some golf in college back in the States. You two be on your game today. They's likely to be playin' for big dollars. Willy and Kevon, I got you two going out in the foursome ahead of Lasko and the Colonel. You're carrying for Quaid Dawson and his guest and the Dinkins brothers. Dawson ain't any good so keep them movin'. You got that? I don't want anything holdin' up this high-stakes game we got here."

And high stakes it was. Aaron and Mateo stood off to the side of the 1st tee and listened as the four players negotiated the bets, each team trying to decide if the other was carrying an honest handicap. Lasko said he was a ten handicap and his playing partner, Dr. Rawlings, and the Colonel both carried six handicaps. Though Lasko was new to the club, he'd played enough golf to establish a reputation.

The real mystery was the Colonel's guest, Travis McCoy. Travis said he was a plus-two at his home course in Dallas, the Brook Hollow Golf Club, but with a guest, one never really knew. Did he turn in all his scores? Was he carrying an ego handicap, or could he really play to a plus-two? Lasko's partner was suspicious and figured Travis was better than a plus-two because why would the Colonel have brought in a partner who everyone else would get strokes from if, in fact, he wasn't even better than he claimed to be? But Lasko didn't share Dr. Rawlings' suspicions. Lasko dealt with facts. He'd set the match up a few days earlier and had done his homework by calling associates in Dallas, who confirmed that Travis McCoy was the real deal.

Travis was a third-generation Texan from Dallas. Tall and lanky, he was pure Texan and he looked at home on a horse as much as he did on a golf course. His granddad had first struck oil in the Permian Basin of Western Texas in the 1920s. He rode the wave of boom-and-bust cycles with an uncanny talent for entering and leaving on the right end of the cycle. Today, while the family's roots were still firmly planted in the oil fields of Texas, the foundation his grandfather and father laid had allowed the family to expand. The McCoy family now owned extensive real estate holdings around the country, a chain of seventy-five gas stations, a majority interest in numerous businesses (including a nationwide chain of roadside diners specializing in comfort food), a machine tool and parts manufacturer, and several amusement parks. It was rumored the family wished to enter the world of professional sports and was shopping for an NFL franchise.

Yes, the holdings were impressive, and the money allowed Travis to pursue his passions—scotch, women, and golf. Travis played college golf for the University of Texas and was coached by the great Harvey Penick. Wonderful things were expected of Travis when in his freshmen year he took down Jack Nicklaus in a match play format at an invitational tournament sponsored by alumni from the Big Ten and Southwestern Conferences. Jack had placed second at the U.S. Open the previous summer and was unbeatable by anyone in the college ranks.

Travis never lived up to the expectations placed upon him but was no worse for the wear. He took a shot at the pro tour but couldn't handle the rigors of tour life. Over the course of four days, he would lose his concentration. But in an eighteen-hole, match play format, Travis was known as one of the best golfers of his day. He didn't need the money, so there was nothing keeping him on the tour other than a want for something to do with his life.

The answer to that question came to him one afternoon when he was packing his car after missing another cut at a tournament outside of Houston. A man pulled up next to him in the parking lot driving a 1965 Shelby Cobra and introduced himself.

"My name is Shane Banks. I watched you play today. You have your moments. How would you like to play me tomorrow at the BraeBurn Country Club for $10,000 a side?"

Travis McCoy found his calling that day. He lost that match, and the loss left a mark. That day was the first day in his education, an education that became a lifelong pursuit to become the greatest hustler of his day. Travis' greatest asset was that everyone liked him. He was spoiled but not a spoiled brat. He knew he'd been born with a silver spoon in his mouth and neither apologized nor took any credit for it. He wasn't stupid or lazy. He simply had no ambition to grow the family business. His older brother did, so why get in the way? And he left little room for his parents to complain.

So, while he would not be active in the family business, he would not be an embarrassment either. He was no slave to alcohol, he knew how to hold it, and as for the women, discretion was his middle name. His grandfather harbored dreams of Travis becoming governor of the great state of Texas, and then who knew from there? Yes, everyone loved Travis. But beneath the handsome veneer swam a predator. On the golf course, he was relentless. He'd rip your heart out and wait patiently while you paid him and then shake your hand and tell you what a pleasure it was to meet you.

When it was all said and done, they'd agreed to play a $5,000 Nassau, best-ball format—$5,000 on the front, $5,000 on the back, $10,000 on the eighteen with automatic presses if you were two down. Lasko was getting twelve strokes, and his partner and the Colonel would be getting eight. Travis would play straight up. Aaron and Mateo just smiled, figuring there'd be a big tip at the end of the round and more than a few stories to share with the other caddies.

Three and a half hours later, the foursome was standing on the 18th tee. Travis McCoy and his partner had been two-up going into the 9th hole, but Lasko sunk a critical putt to win the hole and the press, leaving them one-and-one on the front side with McCoy's team one-up on the eighteen-hole match. At one-and-one on the front, the money match was all square.

Lasko lived up to his reputation both by playing better than his handicap and by moving about or making noise during an opponent's backswing. Travis was annoyed by the man's antics, but he'd seen it all before. Standing on the 18th tee, the match stood as follows: If Travis' team won the 18th hole, he'd win $15k—$5k for winning the back and $10k for winning the eighteen; if they tied the hole, no one would win any money on the back but he'd still win the eighteen-hole match and $10k; but, if he lost the hole, they would tie the eighteen-hole match and Travis would lose $5k on the day by losing the back nine. Travis didn't expect to lose the hole outright, but Lasko had a stroke on the last hole, so Travis would likely need a birdie just to tie the other team's best ball.

The 18th hole was a long par-five, dogleg right. It was virtually impossible to get on the green in two because of the difficulty of the drive. If you took a driver, unless you hit a perfect fade, you ran the risk of running through the fairway and into the rough, where you would find your approach to the green blocked by strategically placed trees and bushes. Your only option would then be to pitch the ball back into the fairway, leaving you with a long approach to the green. If you tried to cut the right corner, you risked not hitting it high enough, in which case you were clipped by the trees and your shot would fall short into the woods. But if you hit the ball high enough to clear the trees, you likely couldn't carry the right-side rough or the deep fairway bunker guarding the inside of the dogleg.

Then there was the green—tiny, bowl-shaped, elevated, and narrow as it ran downhill from the front left corner of the fairway back to the right, protected by sand bunkers on the left and right sides. The only reliable way to hit and hold the green on the third shot was if you could place your second shot short of the green and on the left side of the fairway. In a nutshell, for a par-five, one had very little room for error.

Lasko's team had honors and both Lasko and Dr. Rawlings teed off safely, hitting their drives down the left side of the fairway, short drives but in play. Travis now had a choice to make. Because of his length off the tee, if he used a driver, he ran the risk of hitting through the dogleg and into the thick rough on the left side of the fairway. If he played his three-wood well and his second shot short and left of the green, he would leave himself with a wedge to the green. Complicating the decision was the fact that the Colonel, his playing partner, had just hit his tee shot right into the woods. He'd be lucky if he got on in four. The match was on Travis' shoulders. He pulled his three-wood from the bag and stepped up to the tee. He'd play for a tie on 18 and be happy winning the overall match and $10k.

As he walked up to the tee, he overheard Lasko's caddie say something under his breath to the other caddie.

"What did you say?" asked Travis.

Aaron stood there as quietly as possible, knowing he had screwed up. When Aaron said nothing, Travis settled in for his shot.

"I believe he called you a loser," said Lasko.

Aaron hung his head, wishing he could just disappear.

"Hey, caddie, what's your name?" asked Travis. "Yeah, you. You know I'm talking to you. What's your name?"

"Aaron."

"Aaron what?"

"Aaron Westfield, sir."

"So, you think I should hit driver here. Is that right?" asked Travis.

"No, sir," said Aaron sheepishly.

"Now, who's the loser?" said Travis, laughing at Aaron.

Aaron fumed. "I mean yes. Yes, you should hit driver, get on in two, and win the match."

"You hear that, Travis? My caddie thinks you should hit driver," said Lasko.

"Stupid shot. Low percentage," said Travis as he settled back into his preshot routine. "That's why he's just a caddie and always will be."

"I can make it," said Aaron.

Travis stepped away from the ball and shot Aaron a look that could kill.

"Whoa! Sounds like we have the makings of a bet. Travis, you hit your three-wood. We'll finish out our match, but I want to see if the kid here can hit the shot. I'll bet you five thousand bucks he can cut the corner and end up in the fairway. What do ya say?"

Travis hated these sorts of side bets. He was a purist and only liked betting on a full eighteen-hole match. Anyone could get lucky with one shot, but he couldn't back down now.

"Fine. You're on, but first let me hit my shot."

Which he did: a fine, predictable low fade down the left side of the fairway, setting up a straightforward approach shot to the front, left side of the green.

And now it was Aaron's turn. Travis flipped him a golf ball and offered him his glove, which he declined.

"May I," asked Aaron as he stood before Travis' bag with his hand on his driver.

"Be my guest," said Travis.

Aaron pulled the driver and took a few practice swings, getting a feel for the club. It was a McGregor driver, the same club he'd been practicing with for the last two months. Aaron teed up his golf ball, took a few practice swings, and without further fanfare, addressed the ball. He pulled the clubhead back on a long, smooth arc, and then at the top of the swing his wrists cocked naturally. After a barely discernable hesitation, he began his downswing, accelerating beautifully through the bottom of the swing, his hands, arms, lower body, and head following through in one connected, athletic move. The ball cleared the trees easily and landed right in the middle of the fairway.

His shot was followed by silence and then Lasko's uproarious shouts and laughter. Aaron handed Travis his club back, picked up the bags he was carrying, and started down the fairway. The proceedings so rattled Travis that he pulled his second shot into the thick rough. His third shot was on the green but a good twenty feet from the hole. He two-putted for par but lost the hole to Lasko, who also parred the hole but had a stroke for a net four. The eighteen-hole match was tied, but Lasko won the back side and $5k plus an additional $5k on the shot Aaron made. Lasko gave Aaron $1,000 for his trouble and entered the bar announcing to all that drinks were on him.

* * *

Aaron and Mateo were busy cleaning their players' clubs, and Aaron was trying to act like nothing had happened, but he knew differently. Word of this would travel.

"Damn, Aaron. That was awesome, but what were you thinking? You're gonna get yourself fired pulling stunts like that," said Mateo.

"I don't care. I really don't. I can beat anyone in this club, and they know it. That's why they won't let me play. Let 'em fire me."

But Aaron needed the job and he liked working outdoors and caddying, even if the club wouldn't let him play. About that time, Travis McCoy exited the clubhouse and came their way. Aaron decided he'd eat crow and try to make amends.

"Here comes trouble," said Mateo.

"Aaron, can I have a word with you?" asked Travis.

Aaron finished putting the last clubhead cover on Travis's clubs and walked his way.

"Mr. McCoy, I'm sorry," said Aaron. "I was out of line, and ..."

"Hold on right there," said Travis. "You don't owe me an apology. I owe you one. I'm sorry, and not for doubting you could hit the shot, but for how I treated you. I was raised better. I hope you'll forgive me."

"Forgive you? Uh, sure, I guess," said Aaron.

"And that was one hell of a shot. Here's my card. I'd love to play you in a match. We'll keep it simple—a $5 Nassau. How does that sound?"

"That sounds great, but I can afford more now," Aaron said, smiling, laughing, and holding up the money Lasko gave him.

"You better hold on to that money," said Travis, returning the smile. "The Colonel's pretty ticked off at you. After today, I'm not sure you'll be keeping your job here."

And with that, Travis walked his clubs over to his car and placed them in the trunk.

"Good luck, Aaron Westfield. I have a feeling our paths will cross again."

* * *

Back in the clubhouse, Lasko was surrounded by an audience at the bar as he regaled them with the story of Aaron's monstrous tee shot on 18, and he told the story well. Everyone was having a grand time, everyone except the Colonel, that is, who had cornered the club general manager demanding that the club immediately fire Aaron.

In the corner of the bar, settling up their $5 bet, Quaid and Nash took it all in.

Chapter 22

Friends in High Places

Georgetown, Washington, DC, Saturday, March 19th, 1977, 7:00 p.m.

It was a beautiful DC spring evening. The last vestiges of winter had released their hold on the city in late February, and the cherry blossom trees were beginning to bloom. Nash was dressed in khaki pants, a white oxford button-down shirt, topsiders, and a blue sport coat. Standard uniform around town. No one noticed him as he walked out of his townhome on O Street for his meeting with the Old Man. Today they were meeting at Cy Atley's home on 34th Street.

Ten minutes later, he was crossing over R Street and saw a young couple leave their home in formal wear and hop into a limousine. Cy met him at the door before he had a chance to knock. Cy was dressed in his customary grey slacks and white shirt combo, but tonight he was also wearing a Princeton sweater. He stepped outside and waved to the young couple.

"Relations with your neighbors are better this year, I see," said Nash.

"You could say that. Got together with the other neighbors and had those hooligan Georgetown students kicked out."

"How'd you manage that?" asked Nash.

"Well, the chairman of the Senate Foreign Relations Committee lives two doors down. You'd be surprised how quickly the police arrive when he calls in a complaint. Last spring, the boys living there threw a party for the ages, as they put it. Well, it was their last party in that house. Once we let the owner of the house know we'd fight any tenant he put in there, he decided to sell."

"And that couple bought it?" asked Nash.

"No. I did. I'm their landlord."

"Of course you are."

The two men laughed at the absurdity of it all and then headed into the library and poured themselves a drink from Cy's well-provisioned bar.

"I've been looking forward to our time together, Nash. I'm anxious to hear about what's happening in the Bahamas."

The two men took seats opposite each other in high leather-backed chairs. Nash was about to place his drink on the small table to his right when he noticed a book on the table.

"I see you found it, Edgar Allan Poe's *Tamerlane*," said Nash.

"Yes. One of our associates, a rare-book collector in Charleston, had his eye out for it on my behalf. It's a birthday present for my wife. She's visiting some of our grandchildren in Phoenix. Gets home Friday. Think she'll be surprised?"

"Are you kidding me? Who wouldn't be? Is this the only copy?" asked Nash.

"My friend believes there are only twelve copies in the world."

"She'll be surprised."

"Excellent. Now let me freshen up your drink and let's get down to business."

"It's as I feared," said Nash. "Pindling is a magnet for bad guys. One in particular—Bernard Lasko."

"The Double-Digit Man."

"I haven't heard that one."

"That's what a few of us call him. He somehow manages to deliver double-digit returns on his investment funds regardless of the state of the economy. Frankly, we're doubtful."

"Whose 'we'?"

"Me, the Family, and a few others in the investment world. It can't be done. It's like this. If someone told you that they shot exactly 82 every time they played golf, would you believe them?"

"I'm not much of a golfer, but I doubt it. Not even pro golfers are that consistent."

"Exactly. We'd been hearing about his fantastic returns, so we did a little digging. We're always looking for good managers. Well, one of my associates got his hands on a list of every score he recorded at St. Andrews Golf Club up in New York last year. He recorded an 82 every single round. The man cheats at golf. That was enough for me. I stay away from him."

"So, what do you think he's doing with his investment funds?" asked Nash.

"He's got to be running a Ponzi scheme. It's the only explanation."

"And how would that work?"

"It's like this. Someone will invest a million dollars in one of his funds and is entitled to their share of the fund's profit. Typically, these funds distribute profits to the investors every quarter or maybe twice a year. If the fund generates a 10 percent return in a year, our investor will make $100,000 on his $1 million investment and will receive a check for $25,000 every three months. Well, I'm telling you, it's impossible to make that kind of return year in and year out. So, this is what we suspect he does. He's always raising money for his fund. So, the next guy who invests a million dollars, not all of his money will be invested because Lasko needs some of it to make the quarterly distributions to the current investors. As long as Lasko continues to raise money, he'll have enough to make the quarterly payments. But if he can't keep raising money, the merry-go-round stops, he won't be able to make his payments, and he'll be exposed."

"And has he been raising money?" asked Nash.

"Hand over fist. The '72 recession was actually good for him. Because he kept paying his investors those ridiculous returns, even during a recession, everyone thought he was this mad genius, able to walk on water. He opened a new fund to new investors and the money just poured in."

"Who else knows this?"

"No one knows this. There's just a handful of us, the old-school guys, who suspect he's a fraud. But his success will be his undoing," said Cy.

"How's that?"

"Well, he had so much success bringing in new investors during and after the '72 recession that, to keep the scheme going, he'll have to raise an astronomical sum of money. There's no way he can close his fund to new investors or else he won't have enough money to make the quarterly payments.

Basically, he's on a fast track to implosion. So, has Pindling invested with Lasko?"

"We have reason to believe he has."

"Well, look, I think Lasko is a crook, but I'm not sure I'd fear that his relationship with Pindling is going to cause the Bahamas to fall to the Commies."

"If securities fraud was all Lasko was involved in, I'd agree with you," said Nash.

"But there's more, you're telling me."

"Oh yeah," said Nash.

"Such as?"

"Money laundering for drug traffickers, weapons trading with rebel forces in Central America, kidnapping, and the sex trade, to name a few. But he's also money laundering for communist guerrillas in Central America, so he is in effect helping fund their operations. This is my primary concern. We need to shut him down."

"And he has his claws in Pindling?"

"Yes, and others."

"So, what's your plan?"

"I need to get a man close to him. Someone who will report on who Lasko consorts with, banks with, etc. ..."

"Do you have someone in mind?"

"Yes. And he's perfect because Lasko will never suspect him."

"How can I help?"

"Do you still belong to Lyford Cay Golf Club?"

* * *

LYFORD CAY GOLF CLUB, A WEEK LATER, MARCH 25TH, 1977

"I see Lach has a few lessons this morning," said Bradford Bishop, the general manager to the head pro.

Peter Gentry, the head pro who replaced Lach when he retired, was unboxing some new logoed shirts for the pro shop when the GM walked in.

"That's right. He's busy till lunch."

"Would you ask that he see me in my office before the day is out?"

"Absolutely. Is everything okay?" Peter asked.

"Just have him see me."

"Of course, sir."

* * *

Shortly after lunch that day

Bradford Bishop was seated behind a large mahogany desk when he heard the rap on his door. The door was open, and he waved for Lach to enter.

"Have a seat if you like. This won't take long," Bradford said.

Lach remained standing, his hands behind his back holding on to his hat.

"The Board has had a change of heart. Seems they are all fired up about your man Aaron taking a run at the tour. He's free to practice and play as much as he'd like."

"Thank you, Bradford. Thank you," said Lach.

Clearly not happy with the decision, Bradford held up his hand and interrupted Lach.

"He's to sign your account for any food or drinks while he's here and he's not allowed in the bar. Is that clear?"

"Crystal. What about a greens fee? Will he owe one?" asked Lach.

"No. Those are being taken care of."

"By whom, may I ask?"

"I don't know," said Bradford. "I really don't know, but this kid must have some well-connected friends."

End of Part Three

PART FOUR

The Plot Thickens

Chapter 23

High Stakes

Lyford Cay Golf Club, April 29th, 1977

Since Lach shared the good news with me, that I could play the course, I'd been caddying less and less. My days were full as it were, practicing and playing. But I couldn't swing the club all day, and besides, I liked caddying and the extra cash I earned. And since word had spread about my shot on the 18th hole, I was in high demand. It seemed everyone wanted me as their caddie. So, this morning, as I pulled into the parking lot, I was looking forward to time on the driving range followed by lunch and then caddying that afternoon for a couple of members.

I parked my motorcycle and headed for the course, but before I got there I was stopped by Mateo.

"Tony be lookin' for you, bey," said Mateo.

"Oh yeah? What about?"

"He don't tell me notin' but who I be loopin' for. You know dat."

I thanked Mateo and set off toward the caddie shack. As I approached,

I saw Tony Rolle smoking a big cigar and holding court with some of the newer caddies about his importance at the club.

"You see, this fine Cuban cigar is a gift from one of our esteemed members. You take care of them, and they'll take care of you. Let that be a lesson to you," said Tony.

Tony saw me coming and shooed the young caddies away. He was furious when he heard about my shot on the 18th and was happy when I left, but when a few influential members wanted me back, Tony concluded it was better to cozy up rather than relegate me to the bottom rung of the caddie ladder.

"Aaron, old friend, you're here," he said.

"In the flesh. Mateo said you're looking for me."

"That's right. It's about Mr. Lasko. He came looking for you this morning."

"Okay, tell him I can carry for him this afternoon or anytime tomorrow."

"He doesn't want you on his bag; he wants you as his partner this afternoon," said Tony.

"His partner?"

"Ya, bey. The word is that you two are going to take on the Colonel and that fellow you bested a few weeks ago, Travis McCoy, in a big stakes match."

"You gotta be kidding. I don't have that kind of money."

"No, but Lasko does. You're his horse. He's backing you. He places the bets and if you win, he'll keep most of the money and throw you a nice piece for your efforts."

"But what if we lose?" I asked.

"That's the beauty of it, bey. If you lose, he covers all the losses."

Tony laughed and walked away, shouting back over his shoulder. "You're in the tall grass now, bey."

* * *

THAT AFTERNOON

My time on the driving range that morning didn't go well. All I could think about was the match that was starting in about ten minutes. If it was anything like the match I caddied for a few weeks ago, then we'd be playing for up to $20,000. Granted, it wasn't my money, but it was somebody's! I was sitting at a table by myself outside the snack bar trying to eat a hot dog, but

I could hardly keep down my first bite. I threw it in the trash can and set off for the 1st tee.

As I approached the tee box, I saw the Colonel, Travis McCoy, and Mr. Lasko in conversation, like they were negotiating the bet. Off to the side, Mateo and Graham, the oldest and most experienced caddie at the club, were on our bags. Oh, good Lord. It just got worse. How could I work with these guys again after today?

"There you are," said Travis. "I was beginning to think you wouldn't show."

"Nonsense. Aaron here wouldn't miss this opportunity. Would you?" Lasko asked as he stared at me.

"Uh, no, sir," I managed to stammer out.

Everyone seemed to be in a good mood except for the Colonel. No surprise there. I'd heard he wanted me gone.

"I got no problem with the stakes. It's this boy's handicap I'm concerned about," said the Colonel. "He doesn't have one."

"Let's see what we can do about that. Aaron, can you tell us how you scored in your last few rounds?" asked Lasko.

"Uh, yes, sir. I shot a 70 and two 67s. Oh, and last Friday I shot a 65. That's my best round ever. But the next day, I shot a 76."

"So, what do you think? Play him scratch?" asked Lasko.

"He's a hell of a lot better than scratch if he can put up a 65," demanded the Colonel.

"Aaron, ever play for big stakes?" asked Travis.

"No, sir."

"Hm, well this is a bit tricky, but I'm comfortable with him carrying a zero handicap," said Travis.

And that was that. The Colonel reluctantly agreed to the game, and we were all set to play for $5,000 a side and $10,000 for the eighteen-hole match. Owing to me being an unknown quantity, it was agreed that presses would not be automatic.

Four hours later, it was clear to all that the time spent dickering over my handicap on the 1st tee was a comical waste of time. I would have needed four or five shots a side to have been relevant. Travis was on fire. He never wavered under the pressure. Lasko played better than was expected, but every time it looked like we might win a hole, Travis would respond with a long putt, or an approach shot within a few feet of the pin. It was uncanny. And whenever I had an opportunity to put two good shots together and help the team, I floundered. Had it not been for my chip in from forty feet on the 18th, we would have lost the back side too. As it stood, we lost the front and the eighteen. Lasko calmly reached into his golf bag at the end of the round and peeled off $15,000 for both Travis and the Colonel. The Colonel's grin was sickening. I wanted to hide. Actually, I wanted to strangle him and then hide.

"Same time next week, boys?" asked Lasko.

They all looked at him in a state of shock but then agreed quickly before Lasko came to his senses. Travis and the Colonel were off to the bar and in a fine mood and I just stood there trying to think of what to say.

"I know you're trying to think of what to say, but don't bother," Lasko told me. "You stunk it up pretty bad today, but I saw enough. Meet me here tomorrow morning and be ready to go at 8 a.m. sharp and then again in the afternoon."

"What?! You're kidding me, right?" I asked.

He walked right up to me and got in my face. "I never kid about money. Two matches tomorrow."

I visibly swallowed and Lasko just smiled.

"Relax, kid. You're gonna make me a fortune." And then he walked away like a man without a care in the world.

"No partying tonight, Aaron. Got that?"

"Yes, sir," I managed.

* * *

I was awake early, and a bundle of nerves. I had to do something. I thought about going for a run, but I wasn't a fan; that was Walker's thing. I went for a swim in the ocean instead and it helped refresh me and calm me down a bit. I couldn't believe I was expected to play two money matches today. What had I gotten myself into? I made a bowl of grits for breakfast and threw in some shrimp, and then took off for the club.

When I arrived at 7 a.m., I had the driving range to myself. The day before, every shot had been an adventure. I had no idea where any shot would end up. After twenty minutes on the range of nothing but the same, I saw Lach exit the clubhouse and head my way.

"Are you trying to get me fired?" he asked.

"Fired? What do you mean?"

"If anyone sees you thrashing away like this and they hear I'm your coach, I'll never get another student."

"Very funny."

"I heard about yesterday."

"Super. Just super."

"This Lasko character. He's no good. He's no good for your game. He's no good for you."

"What makes you say that?"

"Just a feeling, Laddy. I've been around this game a long time and around men like him. He'll use you and throw you away."

"Well, I'm not sure what choice I have today. He's got us booked for two rounds and I'd better show up on the course or else he's gonna lose big again."

"That's his problem."

What did this guy expect from me? How would it look if I lost big and just quit?

"Look, can't you just look at my swing? I'm lost. I don't understand. My swing just vanished."

"All right, all right. First, you're not swinging; you're hitting. Anyone can hit a ball. My God, it's just sitting there. Now, what have we gone over, and over?"

"Swing the clubhead," I answered with a heavy sigh.

"That's right. So that's what you're going to do for the next ten minutes. Don't even place a ball on the ground. Just swing the clubhead and the timing and rhythm will return."

For the next ten minutes, I followed his instructions, and a sense of calm and confidence returned. Then I started working my way through my bag, hitting balls, and my game was back. I thanked Lach and headed for the first tee.

As with the day before, Lasko was already there and negotiating the bets. When I walked up to shake hands with the group, our opponents were smiling. Yep, word was out that I had collapsed the day before and these men were licking their chops.

Four hours later, as we walked off the course, those same two men were hardly talking to each other. While I played better, Lasko carried us to victory. The other two had been so focused on my anticipated bad play that they underestimated Lasko's game. As I stood off to the side, I saw each of them reach into their bag, pull out wads of cash, and hand a stack of bills to Lasko. He shook their hands, slipped the money into his back pocket, and caught up with me.

"Shall we have lunch? It's on me," he said.

* * *

I still wasn't allowed in the clubhouse, so Lasko bought us each a hamburger at the snack bar. We were waiting for our food, and I decided now was as good a time as any to ask him what my cut would be.

"Mr. Lasko, I'm not sure how to bring this up, but it was my understanding that when we won, I'd get part of the winnings."

"That's right. This is how I see it. I'll give you 10 percent. How does that sound?"

"Uh, I'm not sure. How much did we just win?"

"Those guys are small-time. We played $2,500 on the front, back, and eighteen. We pushed the front and won the back and the eighteen, so we won $5,000. We should have won the front but you skulled your wedge shot on the 9th hole across the back of the green."

"Yeah, sorry about that."

"Look, Aaron. Don't be sorry. Sorry is for losers. Just play better. Understand?"

"Uh, yeah."

"And quit this 'uh, yeah' crap. You sound like a damn kid. If you're going to play for big stakes, you need to instill a little fear in the other guy, and that you don't. This ain't no damn charity. Got it?"

This guy was starting to piss me off.

"Yes, sir," I said, but with an attitude.

He just nodded at me. "Now let's finish up," he said. "We have another match."

Lasko stood, told me to take care of his trash, and he started walking toward the course.

"Hey, Lasko! You owe me $500."

He turned and stared at me with lifeless eyes, like those of a shark, and then slowly a grin spread across his face.

"Now, that's more like it. We'll settle up at the end of the day. Now you hold back and let me set the bet, then I want you walking up onto the tee with confidence. Can you do that?"

"No problem. And Lasko, if it will help you negotiate bigger stakes, I'll play to a plus-one handicap."

He smiled and headed to the 1st tee.

* * *

Sometimes there's nothing better than the taste of a cold beer. I ordered two Kaliks from the snack bar and was halfway through mine when Lasko caught up and joined me.

"So, what was our take this afternoon?" I asked.

"Ten grand. They were reluctant to play auto presses, but they leaped at it when I gave them each an extra stroke a side."

"Well, you're welcome."

"What's that supposed to mean?" Lasko asked.

"I carried you on the front nine. All three of you had strokes on holes two and three and you were out of both holes off the tee. We were two holes down after three holes. I brought us back."

"Yeah, well, sometimes the fastest way to get a press on is to lose two holes yourself," Lasko said.

"What? Are you telling me you tanked the holes on purpose?"

"Look, kid. You've got a lot to learn. Yeah, so what. With the press on early, we had time to come back and win the front and the front side press. That rattled them, they got tight, and we won the back side up 3 and 1. So don't go thinkin' you're the reason we won. I wanted them to have that stroke on the 3rd hole. It set up the rest of the match. We won our money today on the 1st tee before you even showed up."

I was stunned.

"And that's legal?"

"Legal's got nothing to do with it. It's gambling. So, you just show up and play your magnificent game and leave the rest to me. Capeesh? Now, I'm heading into the bar. Sorry you can't join me. I'll be in touch once I set up some more matches."

"Hey, you owe me $1,500."

"How do you figure?"

"You said I'd make 10 percent of what we won. Well, we won $15k today. You owe me $1,500."

"I don't owe you a thing, yet. You lost me $30k in our match against the Colonel and his pal, Travis. Now $15,000 of that belongs to you. I covered it but you owe it, so I'll hold back your winnings until you've made me that $15k back and then I'll owe you if we keep winning. Got it?"

"That wasn't the deal," I said.

Lasko moved in my direction so fast that out of instinct, I was on my feet, coiled, and ready to pounce.

"Go ahead," he whispered as he leaned in close. "I know all about your temper and I've seen what you can do. I was in the bar that night when you wrecked those two punks hittin' on old McGregor's niece. Rachel, I believe. You don't like the deal? Fine. Once you've won back the rest of the $15k, you can walk. But let me make myself clear—if you ever threaten me, you'll never walk again."

Lasko turned and headed for the bar.

"Say hello to Rachel for me," he said over his shoulder. "You'd hate to lose a girl like her."

I had only been this scared of one other person, on one other occasion.

Chapter 24

Rachel

Now you know how my life became entangled with Lasko's. Over the next three weeks, we played fifteen matches and I won back some of the money I owed Lasko. But we didn't win every match, and sometimes we didn't win much, so my debt to him still stood at $8,000. And the reason why we sometimes lost the bet or won so little? Me. I quickly developed a reputation around the club as a player and no one would wager big stakes against us unless we gave them more and more strokes, which simply made winning harder. But Lasko was willing to do exactly that because personally he was winning big: He kept 90 percent of what I should have been winning when we did win plus what he was winning. When we lost, my share of the losses was added to my debt to him. He owned me.

Because of my growing reputation at the club, Lasko had to bring in folks for us to play. He found plenty of marks at the Paradise Island Casino where he spent most evenings. Since he was a regular at the casino, management took care of him. He was introduced to the other high-stake gamblers coming to town and hungry for action. It was in the back room reserved for Texas Hold 'Em, where he met more than a handful of golfers who had heard about my game and wanted a shot at me.

My circle of friends shrank considerably. The members all looked at me as a second-class citizen and they were ticked off about losing money to Lasko. The other caddies kept their distance. It was hard to work as a caddie one day and play golf with one of the loopers on my bag the next. They all assumed I was getting rich and wanted nothing to do with me. Somehow, in their eyes, I was a traitor. Even Lach lost interest in working with me. I was playing so much, I had little time to practice. On those few occasions when we worked together, he was distant and uninterested.

I finally lost my cool late one afternoon and laid into him.

"Dammit, Lach. What's your problem? You don't want to be here. That's obvious. Why don't you just leave? I'll figure it all out on my own."

"Oh, you will, will you? Ha. You'll be dead within the year and me too at this rate."

"What are you talking about? You're a crazy old man."

"I'm old all right, and I must be crazy to spend time with you. How does it look? Hum? How does it look for me to be giving lessons to a man that's swindling other members out of large chunks of money?"

"I ain't swindling anybody and who cares anyway? They all have plenty."

"That they do, but it's not the point. It's wrong what you're doing and you're disrespecting the game."

"Look. It ain't my doing. I don't have a choice here. I just play. Lasko sets up the bets."

"No. You have a choice. You don't have to play."

"Yeah, I do," I said as I hung my head and looked away.

"He's makin' you earn back your losses, isn't he?"

I was too pissed to answer.

"Thought so. Your silence tells me everything I need to know. I can help. I'll loan you what you need to get out from under him and you can take all the time you need to pay me back and do so with honest wages."

"Lach, I'm close. I can do this. I can win back what I owe him and then walk away. I appreciate your offer and I'm sorry I lost my cool. But I need this. If I take money from you, I'll feel defeated. I need to win it back and then I'll walk away. I promise."

"It's not just you I'm worried about. It's my dear niece, Rachel. She's quite taken with you, but she doesn't like what she's seeing in you. You've changed, Aaron. He's changed you. I don't want Rachel hurt in all of this. Do you hear me?"

Rachel. What was I going to do? He was right.

"Aaron, I'm talking to you."

"No, Lach. I hear you. I understand, I don't want her to get hurt either. I'm going to end this but I'm going to do it my way."

"If you say so."

* * *

Rachel and I had been seeing each other since shortly after her uncle began giving me lessons. If you remember, when we first began working together, our lessons drew quite a crowd. Once the crowds became a distraction, he had the benches and chairs folks were occupying removed from our end of the driving range. Members still watched but did so from under the veranda outside the clubhouse bar.

There was one distraction, though, that Lach had a harder time removing. His niece. One day early on when Lach and I were working together, she came down to the range and took up a spot three bays over. She started off with a few simple stretches and then began working her way through her bag beginning with the wedge. Lach had his back to her and hadn't noticed when she arrived, but I certainly did. I hadn't seen her since that first time in the bar when I laid into those idiots hitting on her.

"What's the matter with you, boy? Where's your head? I'm talkin' to you," he said.

He then turned and saw his niece swinging the club gracefully.

"Oh, Lordy. Rachel, my dear, we're workin' here. Could you be a luv and move as far away as possible? How do you expect this young man to concentrate with that waggle of yours?"

Lach turned back and took one look at me. "You look as flushed as a red robin. Get a grip on yourself, laddy."

"I'm almost done, Uncle Lach," she said. "Just a few drivers and I'll be on my way."

She reached into her bag and found a tee and then pulled her driver out. In a very ladylike manner, she bent both knees and lowered herself in a curtsey-like motion and worked the tee into the soil, carefully placed a ball on the tee, rose back up, and stepped behind the ball as she focused on her shot. She walked up to the ball and stepped into position, preparing to swing the clubhead. And then she waggled, pulled the clubhead back on plane, and hit a lovely little draw. She admired her shot and began all over again. I was mesmerized.

"That's it. That's it. Lesson over for the day. Be off with you, laddy."

* * *

I took my bag and headed for the bag stand next to the parking lot, taking my time in the hopes of seeing her again. I methodically checked my bag for tees, gloves, golf balls, ball markers, and surgical tape for the tender spot on the inside of my forefinger on my left hand. I removed my golf shoes and, using a tee, cleaned every speck of grass from the spikes. I cleaned each clubhead, twice. My patience was rewarded. I saw Rachel leave the clubhouse and walk toward the parking lot.

"Excuse me," I called out as I abandoned my bag and headed in her direction. "Rachel?"

She stopped and turned in the direction of my voice. She made no effort to close the distance between us but waited instead for me to approach.

"Hi."

"Hello. It's Aaron, isn't it?"

"Yes. Um, I wanted to thank you. Your uncle told me you called him that night we met at the bar. He bailed me out of jail."

"I know. I called him."

"Um, yeah. So, thanks."

"You're welcome, Aaron. But it's I that should be thanking you."

She took two steps closer to me, reached up with both hands, and buttoned the lower of the two buttons on my golf shirt.

"You were my knight in shining armor."

She patted my chest. "There, that's better."

"Why did you do that?" I asked.

"Because you need to look your best if you're going to ask me out."

She was standing so close. She cocked her head slightly to the side and removed her sunglasses and I stared into her beautiful, emerald-green eyes. Time stopped. I couldn't breathe. I stood motionless. So did she.

I removed my hat. "Rachel, would you go out with me?"

"I would be delighted."

* * *

When I first arrived in the Bahamas, I thought my stay would be short. The Charleston police would find the real killer and then I would go home. But when Quaid visited and I learned the police had shut down the investigation because they simply assumed I was guilty, I knew then that I'd likely never go home again. I fell into a deep funk and the only emotion I could muster was anger. My anger morphed into self-pity, but even I was able to recognize what a waste of time that was. After a while, it simply became easier to keep my distance from people. I didn't need a psychology degree to understand that I was afraid of getting hurt and that the best defense against future emotional pain was to remain aloof. If I don't get close to anyone then I can't get hurt. No problem. I could live this way. Plenty of people do.

The trick was forgetting about Kimberly. When I was alone, memories of her crept back in and reminded me of what I had lost. But when I was with people, thoughts of Kimberly would fade. So, how do you surround yourself with friends and associates and remain aloof, a loner, at the same time? Turns out, it's not as hard as you'd think. The key is not caring about others. You can be friends and spend time together, but when you start caring about their happiness and well-being ahead of your own, that's a sign to pull back and find new friends.

I'd become adept at the art of the quick friendship, be it with guys or gals. I still hung out with Anthony and the rest of the Bastian clan from time to time, but they were so engrained in Bahamian culture and their family and friends that I was never going to fit in. They likely would have allowed me to stick around, but when I distanced myself and moved on, I bet they saw it as a sign I was building a life in the Bahamas, and they never expressed concern.

I hung out with the other caddies and had developed a crew around the docks. Most captains knew I was a reliable mate, whether sailing or charter fishing. In the restaurant world, fellow bartenders and cooks were always up for late-night drinks. I fit in well with these crowds and, as an American with a hazy backstory, I was always a novelty.

Now, the girls, that was an altogether different story. Never fished the local ponds. Nope, no need to. The island was crawling with women on vacation looking for a fling, and I was happy to make their time on the island memorable. We'd spend days and nights together and they'd leave after a week or so. It was perfect. I was local but American. Dangerous but safe. They left with stories to tell their girlfriends back home and, as for me, I never had to get close to anyone.

Rachel threatened to change all of that. We started seeing each other regularly. When I asked her out the first time, I didn't know what to do for a first date. Clearly, she was more sophisticated than me. I suspected there was money in her background by the way she carried herself. No, she wasn't haughty or arrogant. On the contrary, she was elegant and graceful. Frankly,

I had no idea what she saw in me. I know I'm good-looking enough for women to show interest in, but I haven't seen the world. I don't drive a fancy car and the nicest clothes in my closet are the golf shirts with the Lyford Cay logo that Lasko bought me. He added their cost to my debt to him. What an asshole.

But she must have enjoyed my company because the first date turned into a second date, which turned into a third date, and now it's just a given that we see each other. So, you may be wondering what I did for our first date. Well, I went with my strengths and asked Quaid if I could borrow one of his boats—his small one, the one I came over on with Captain Bootle. I loaded it up with food and wine and we motored out to a quiet cove. I opened the wine and poured her a drink and she watched as I prepared dinner and manned the barbeque grill affixed to the stern. After we watched the sunset, we enjoyed a meal of grouper, fresh grilled vegetables, and rice under a starlit sky. Not bad, huh?

"Aaron, where did you learn to cook like this?" she asked.

"At home, but since arriving here I've picked up a thing or two."

"Yes, you have. Everything is wonderful. You have a flair for it."

"It's not that hard, really."

"That's what makes it so scrumptious—it comes easily for you. I was watching. You weren't struggling with measurements or constantly looking at a recipe. You were perfectly at home with the ingredients."

What she said resonated with me. It did come easily for me—cooking, that is. As for as feeling at home, that was a foreign concept for me, but I knew what she meant.

"Tell me about yourself, Aaron Westfield," she said.

"There's not much to tell, really."

"Well, you're here but you're not from here, so there must be a story there?"

I stood up and walked down into the galley and came back up with another bottle of wine, hoping my departure and return would kill this particular conversation.

"Aaron, did I say something to upset you?"

"No, it's just that I find you more interesting than talking about me," I said as I leaned over to refill her glass.

"Then maybe you'll find this interesting," she said as she took the bottle out of my hand and pulled me down to kiss her.

Chapter 25

A Game Plan

January 1st, 1978

I lay in bed, flat on my stomach, as still as possible, head throbbing and my right arm hanging off the edge, searching for my watch. It had to be after twelve. Found it, on the floor along with my wallet and clothes. So, I'd managed to undress the night before. Must have, not that I remember. Looking at my watch, I confirmed that it was a little past noon. Well, as the man said, to ensure you never wake up in the morning hungover, sleep past twelve. Mission accomplished.

I sat up and slowly placed my feet on the floor and my head in my hands. I could hear the surf beckoning. I pulled on shorts and walked outside and into the ocean. I swam about, trying to exorcise the demons and clear my head. I felt better but now desperately needed something cool to drink. I found a single can of Coke in my refrigerator, and I don't believe I have ever felt more thankful for small miracles. But within half an hour, as I ran out of steam, the hammock beckoned. The new year could wait.

Tomorrow, tomorrow I'll get on with my life. The same promise I'd been making for some time now.

* * *

JANUARY 2ND

I started the day with a swim, a more meaningful one this time, followed by breakfast, and then a walk around Adelaide Village. I needed time to think. My situation with Lasko had not improved. When we won, Lasko kept 90 percent of what I won but those winnings were not credited against what I owed him. I had to pay down that debt out of my own winnings. The only way I'd ever be able to repay him was if we never lost, we raised the stakes, or if I could keep more than 10 percent of my winnings. I entered the new year intent on getting out from under his foot. I had to if I wanted any future with Rachel.

Rachel's objections to my lifestyle grew louder with each passing week. When I hooked up with Lasko, I never imagined the hold he would have over my life. But he does. I have little time for anything other than the golf matches he sets up, and no idea how to free myself from his grip.

When Rachel and I started dating, I did not expect to fall for her or her for me. Sure, she's beautiful. What guy wouldn't want to go out with her? But it's more than that. I began thinking about a future, and when I did, I wanted her to be part of it. I want to spend every minute with her. She's funny and smart, and she makes me feel good about myself, something no one has done in a long time.

But any future with me is haunted by my past. Rachel knows me as Aaron Westfield, but I am in fact Eli Atkins. Should I tell her? Yes. But if I do, will that end it? Possibly. No, more like "yes." She talks of returning to Britain or moving to the States and had begun hinting that I go with her. When I try to move us off these conversations, she becomes annoyed and questions my ambition, which bring us to another problem, Lasko. Am I going to spend the rest of my life as a golf hustler living under his thumb? I swear to her I'm not, but right now, I'm stuck.

So, yes, I have problems on the Rachel front. It's why I began the new year hungover. Actually, I began the new year hungover because I drank too much. But I drank too much because I spent the night before with a bunch of buddies from the docks. A surly group. I spent New Year's Eve with them instead of Rachel because we had fought the day after Christmas when she told me something needed to change in 1978 or she saw no future for us.

So, yes, something has to change. I need a plan. Walking around the village, one begins to form.

* * *

THAT SAME DAY, AT LASKO'S HOME

Bernard Lasko stood on his balcony looking out over the Atlantic, thinking about how far he had traveled. From a life lived in perpetual poverty, as the boy with a father, mocked by others, always barely scraping by while chasing one foolish idea after another, to where he stood today, as a man feared and revered, he had indeed traveled far. And there was no going back.

Wall Street hailed him as a "money manager's money manager." He knew others derisively called him the Double-Digit Man. Whatever. The funds were a goldmine, or at least they had been. Yes, he was an excellent money manager and he'd had his share of success picking stocks, but you can't rely on that to deliver double-digit returns every quarter. It's impossible. But he was in too deep. No, he had to keep the money flowing, in and out. He needed new investors, constantly, and he needed to keep paying 10 to 12 percent returns, constantly. And solving the second problem took care of the first.

When it came to solving the second problem, he'd become quite adept. There were plenty of ways to make a buck, especially when out from under the glare of government oversight. Offshore banking allowed him to take money he made illegally and commingle that money with money legitimately made managing his fund. He could draw on the commingled funds to make the quarterly payments to his investors.

If only the Dow Jones Industrial Average would help out! The stock markets had been dropping steadily since 1972, meaning he needed to make more and more money illegally because he wasn't making much money legally. His insatiable need for cash had driven him into several new cash-only businesses and with a very demanding clientele.

He now laundered money for Mexican drug cartels. He set up limited liability corporations for them in the Bahamas and other tax shelter and offshore banking havens. He identified compliant lawyers in these locales who served as the registered agents for the corporations, and they would take actions on the corporation's behalf at his direction. Drug dealers delivered large bags of cash, which he deposited into bank accounts owned by the newly formed corporations. He took a 30 percent fee right off the top and then directed the corporation to invest the balance of the cash in his own funds. The drug lords were quite happy with double-digit returns, tax free of course, and the money came back clean and freshly laundered.

As his reputation in the underworld grew, so did his appetite for more of everything. Using a similar money laundering scheme, he now worked with Russian and Middle Eastern weapons traders and a particularly nasty group that trafficked in young girls. In the sex trade, he also acted as a middleman, brokering transactions between those who kidnapped young girls and those who desired them. The two women passed out in his bed, twenty years in age, girls really, were gifts from a happy client. He was told by the client to "return them within the week, slightly used but unharmed."

He couldn't have cared less about the legalities of his activities, but he cared greatly about getting caught and going to jail. He was walking a fine line. His double-digit returns were drawing unwanted attention by U.S. authorities as people were growing suspicious of his success, given the poor overall stock market performance. He knew that, as long as he never missed a quarterly payment, no real scrutiny would ever arrive. But if he missed even a single quarterly payment, the U.S. authorities were the least of his concerns. His new fund investors cared about one thing and one thing only, money, and they would kill Lasko if he didn't deliver.

If matters ever came to that, he might need the federal government to save his ass. If it took turning state's evidence, he would. He could go into the Federal Witness Protection Program and start all over. How then to ensure that the Feds would want to protect him? That was simple. Be a man of the people. Build hospitals. Speak up for the poor and downtrodden. And always, always, do it for the children.

* * *

LYFORD CAY GOLF CLUB, JANUARY 10TH, 1978

"It's wonderful to see so many members of the press here today. We can use your help spreading the word," said Bradford Bishop, the club general manager. "About what you may ask? Well, to answer that question, I'd like to bring up on stage one of our newer members, but one who has made quite a splash here in the Bahamas, Mr. Bernard Lasko."

The applause was polite but not overwhelming. Lasko walked to the front of the room and shook hands with Bradford and then stood before the microphone and raised his hands to signal to all for quiet. He was about to speak.

"I want to extend my thanks to all in attendance today. Let me get right to the point. I'm fortunate. I'm well fed, well clothed, and as I look around, I see a room full of people who can boast the same. But for far too many children, that's not the case, and that's why we're here today. I'm launching a foundation to raise money for underprivileged children here in the Bahamas. I'll seed this foundation with $1,000,000 and hire the staff to run it, and I'll pay their salaries out of my pocket, ensuring that all contributions to the foundation go to those in need."

This time, the applause was hardier.

"But there's more. We're not just looking for donations. No, we're going to bring world-class entertainment to the islands, make money doing so, and donate the profits to the foundation."

The folks in the room looked around smiling, clearly liking what they were hearing, and clapped a little louder.

Lasko continued. "One of our big events will be a golf tournament to be held later this year in December. I know everyone in this room knows and loves our very own Lach McGregor, and this December marks the tenth year since the tragic loss of his dear wife, Laurel. I can't think of a better way to honor her memory than with a golf tournament designed to attract some of the biggest names in golf, amongst amateurs and gamblers such as myself, and maybe even a few real pros."

This time the applause was unrestrained. Lasko went on. Throughout the year, he would host smaller tournaments of four to eight players in a match play format for high stakes. Every participant would donate a portion of their winnings to the foundation. Lasko, as the promoter and the 'bookie', he said to a room full of laughter, announced he would donate his vig, the fee a bookie is paid, to the foundation. "It's for the children, for God's sake," he said to universal acclaim.

Everyone thought it was a great idea, everyone except Lach. Lach wasn't in the room that day but heard all about it and was fit to be tied by the man's presumed connection with his wife's memory. He implored the club to disassociate Lach's tournament from any mention of his wife, but the club threw up its hands.

* * *

CAFÉ ABACO, JANUARY 15TH, 1978

The plan I worked out two weeks earlier was simple. Win enough money to pay back Lasko and then cut cords with him. The problem is that, given my arrangement with him, I'll never climb out of debt. No, I need to arrange and win big money matches on my own, and to do that, I need money.

Nigel Pinder controls my money. When I arrived in Nassau, I deposited the $10,000 I'd stolen from my father in the checking account Nigel opened for me. Quaid encouraged me to hold on to that money so I could return it to my dad someday. That all sounded great back when my return to Charleston was a possibility. But now, it looks like I'll never clear my name. So, I'm here, and it only makes sense that I should be able to spend that money. But to do that, I need Nigel's cooperation. When I showed up at his office on January 3rd to draw the money, he frowned and said I had to clear it with Quaid.

As luck would have it, Quaid was due to arrive in town along with his wife and good friend Nash Hawthorne and his wife. They were taking a short vacation together. I asked Nigel if he could get a hold of Quaid and set up a meal. He did, and here I am, sitting at Quaid Dawson's usual table waiting for him to arrive.

I didn't have to wait long. I saw a car pull up and Quaid and Nash get out and the driver pull around the corner and park. Well, this was awkward. I wanted to see Quaid alone. Didn't Nigel tell Quaid why I needed to see him? Three minutes later, they walked out onto the patio each with a beer in their hands and took a seat.

"Aaron, good to see you again. You remember my friend Nash, right?"

"Yes, sir. Hi, Mr. Hawthorne."

"Aaron, good to see you."

"Aaron, Nigel tells me you wanted to see me and ask me some questions," said Quaid.

"That's right but I thought we'd be alone. I want to talk to you about a business proposition," I said.

Quaid and Nash shared a glance and Quaid continued.

"Yeah. I know a little something about that, which is why I asked Nash to join us. Nigel tells me that you are in debt to Bernard Lasko, and you believe you can make enough money in singles matches to pay him back."

"That's right. I need to sever my relationship with him, and I can't do that playing with him. I've been trying but it seems like just when I'm about to get out of debt, we lose a match and I slip back into debt."

"Sounds about right. Look, Nash knows a bit about Lasko. Nash, you want to take over?"

Nash sat up straighter in his chair and leaned over the table so he could speak quietly.

"Aaron, I'm not really a professor. Well, I am, but it's a cover. I teach European history at Georgetown University, one class a semester, and the position allows me to travel, etc. ... As for my other job, well, I work for the United States government and my job is to monitor the activities of people who could harm our country or the cause of freedom."

"You're a spy," I said.

"Something like that," Nash said.

"Aaron, you need to get away from Lasko. I don't like your plan. From what Nash tells me, this Lasko is one bad dude."

"Aaron, we have reason to believe that Lasko launders money for Mexican drug cartels and genuine bad guys selling weapons in some of the most dangerous places around the world. Lately, we've heard rumors he's into human trafficking," said Nash.

"What's human trafficking?" I asked.

"He buys and sells young girls who are held captive and used for sex."

"This is crazy," I said. "Everyone knows him as a Wall Street guy. He runs some kind of investment fund. Are you sure you have the right guy?"

"Yes. We're sure," Nash said.

"So, Aaron, you can see why I don't want you getting hooked up with this guy. I don't care how good of a golfer you are, he's dangerous," said Quaid. "I'll lend you what you need to pay him off, but I can't let you use the money in your account to pursue your plan. If something were to happen to you, I'd feel terrible."

"So, Mr. Hawthorne, you're here telling me all this so I'll take Mr. Dawson seriously?"

"Yes, but there's more. I have a vested interest in you."

I didn't know what he meant by that, and I looked at Quaid for help.

"Aaron, when you arrived here, everyone was amazed that you were able to have a new identity and working papers from the Bahamian government so quickly. Everyone thought I was a magician pulling it off. Well, all I did was call Nash and ask a favor. Nash and I go back a ways. Part of his job is maintaining a network of friends who from time to time can help him with his intelligence gathering. My father knew Nash's predecessor, and well, you could say that our interests have been aligned ever since."

"So, you're a spy too?" I asked.

"No, not at all. I'm a businessman. Nash, maybe you can explain."

"Aaron, Nash is right. I work with a network of people, very quiet people, typically very wealthy and powerful people, who can help me do things I could never get done working through our government. I run this loose organization, and Quaid, well, he's one of my associates, an asset. But he's more than an asset; he's a friend. When he reached out to me and told me about your problem just short of five years ago, I was happy to help. So, you see, I have a vested interest in you."

"Okay, I believe you. Lasko is a bad guy. If he's as bad as you say, will he even let me walk if I pay him back?"

"That's a good question and one I posed to Quaid."

"Damn. What have I gotten myself into?" I said.

"All is not lost. Aaron, how would you like to be eyes and ears for me?"

"Go on," I said.

"Quaid and I talked about this. Aaron, take Quaid's money and pay Lasko back. Quaid's got plenty of money."

Quaid nodded and took a swig of his beer.

"And maybe Lasko will let you walk. He's got plenty on his plate. If he does, your problem is solved. But if he doesn't, get word to me through Nigel and I'll contact you. I'll tell you how you can help and more importantly, I can put eyes on you and protect you if things go south."

I sat there looking into the distance, amazed at how far removed I was from playing center field for my high school baseball team.

"Aaron, what do you think?" Nash asked.

"Sure. I'll do it. What choice do I have?"

Chapter 26

The Upper Hand

After further discussion with Mr. Dawson and Mr. Hawthorne, who by the way said I should now call them Quaid and Nash, we agreed it would look suspicious if I showed up one day at Lasko's home with the money to pay him back. I needed to win this money on the golf course, something I was happy to do. If showing up at Lasko's door with the money to pay him back would look suspicious, then suddenly playing for big bucks on my own would look suspicious too. I would start small and as my winnings grew, I would make larger bets. We agreed to meet again at Café Abaco in a month.

Relations with Rachel improved, with Lach too. I met Rachel for breakfast shortly after meeting with Quaid and Nash and I told her my plan to win enough money to pay Lasko back and be free of him. I didn't tell her about Nash and his real identity. She wasn't thrilled with my plan but took it as evidence I was serious about escaping his clutches and serious about us. Lach's attitude as my coach improved as well. A month later, I met Quaid and Nash at our usual table with news, good and bad.

"Aaron, how's your game? Are you winning?"

"Yes I am, but hustling is harder than it looks. By winning constantly, it makes continually lining up bets more difficult."

"Aaron, have you had to throw any matches to keep guys coming back?" asked Nash.

The mere mention of something like that pained me and it was visible to Quaid and Nash.

Nash continued. "Throwing matches is a common practice amongst hustlers. They'll lose a small bet to set someone up for a larger bet later down the line."

"I know, but I can't. I can't make myself do it. I accomplish the same thing, though, by giving my opponent so many strokes it makes it nearly impossible for me to win."

"Okay. I guess that works," said Nash. "So, what's the problem?"

"It's taking me too long to make enough money to set up a big match I can win. I still don't have the money I owe Lasko."

"What if I were to help you stage a match with someone who will bet you high stakes and you'd be assured of winning?" asked Nash.

"I don't need help winning—that is, if I don't give them too many strokes. I just need someone who will play me for a lot of money."

"Do either of you have any idea of who we could get?" Quaid asked.

"There is one guy who I believe would, but I don't know how to reach him," I said.

"Does he live here on the island?" Quaid asked.

"No, but he visits a lot. His name is Travis McCoy. He's from Texas and played golf for the University of Texas. Terrific player. He's super rich. His family owns a lot of oil fields or something. I've played him a couple of times. He likes the action, he's an excellent golfer, and he'll play me. I just don't know how to get a hold of him or when he'll be back."

"Travis McCoy, huh? Let me see what I can do about finding him," said Nash.

* * *

A WEEK LATER

I was on the driving range, going through my bag working on different ball flights with each club, when who do you think walks up? Yep, Travis McCoy himself.

"I hear you're lookin' for a game," he said.

"You could say that."

"How about match play, $7,500 on the front and the back and another $15,000 on the eighteen. No strokes, straight up. And if you can't cover the losses, I'll carry you. You can win it from some other poor soul out here and owe me but not the way you owe Lasko. Does that work?"

"Why are you doing this?" I asked.

"Didn't I tell you I thought our paths would cross again?"

That wasn't really an answer to my question, but I took it as one and we shook on the bet. He reserved a tee time for 12:30 that day and by the time we walked up to the 1st tee, word had spread. We had a small gallery, Lasko included, following us that afternoon.

Travis played well, but he played conservatively, always choosing the safe shot, the shot best suited to earn him a par on the hole. I was on my game, firing at every pin in a quest for birdies. That's the beautiful thing about match play, it makes no difference if you shoot a five on the hole and lose to your competitor who records a four or if you shoot a seven on the hole, because all you lose is one hole in the match. Match play rewards aggressive shots where the winner is the player who wins the most holes, whereas in stroke play, the winner is determined by the total score over eighteen holes. In stroke play, typically a more conservative approach is called for because one or two blowup holes can kill your chances of winning.

What surprised me was that Travis knew this and yet he played it safe most of the day. On the one hole he took a more aggressive line at the pin, he mishit the shot badly, leading to a bogey. By the time we got to the 17th hole, I had won the back side, up three holes with two holes to go, and the eighteen-hole match. We pushed the front, so I pocketed $22,500 on the day and now had enough money to pay off Lasko and celebrate with Rachel over a nice dinner in town.

"Congrats, Aaron. You were on your game today. I'll be expecting a chance to win my money back."

"Any time, Travis. Any time."

Travis reached into his bag, pulled out a large wad of cash held together by a rubber band, and peeled off the money he owed me. I never got used to seeing these gambling types walk around with so much cash, but they all did it.

"I'd invite you in and let you buy me a drink, but I guess they still won't let you in the bar, will they?"

"Afraid not, but can I owe you?"

"Absolutely," he said.

We shook hands, and as he set off for the bar, I hurried to find Rachel. I couldn't wait to tell her.

* * *

Back at Aaron's place on the cove

I was resting in the hammock under a clear, star-filled sky, reflecting on the day. I hadn't seen Rachel this happy in a long time. Our relationship, though better since our fight after Christmas, had still been strained. Lasko's boot on my neck was the eight-hundred-pound gorilla in the room. Any talk of a future was pointless until my debt to him was paid off.

"Oh, Aaron. You know what this means, don't you? We have our future in front of us. You and me. What do you think of that?" she asked.

For a moment, I forgot that I was Eli Atkins, a fugitive, and wanted for murder in the United States. I still hadn't told her who I was. I didn't have the heart, but how long could I lead her on?

One thing at a time. Tomorrow, I'd track down Lasko and pay him off. I couldn't wait to see the look on his face when I handed him the near $20,000 I owed him. Yep, one thing at a time. Once I'd freed myself from his clutches, I'd focus on getting my name back. Maybe Nash could help.

I finished my beer and walked inside, anticipating a good night's sleep, my first in a while.

* * *

The next day

I was sitting outside the pro shop when Peter Gentry, the head pro, arrived to open for the day.

"You're here early, Aaron. Who are you going to fleece today?" he asked, none too happy to see me. Peter was wearing khaki slacks, a white belt, and a blue golf shirt with the club monogram.

"I'm not here to fleece anyone, sir. I'm looking for Mr. Lasko and I want to see if he is on the tee sheet today."

The head pro looked at me wearily and unlocked the door. "Come on in and let's see what we got," he said.

He stepped around behind the counter and pulled the tee sheet out from inside the top drawer. He dragged his index finger down the sheet, scanning the times and names.

"No. He's not signed up to play and the sheet is full, so I don't expect to see him unless he shows up for lunch or a drink late in the day."

I stood there looking perturbed.

"Is there anything else I can do for you, Aaron?"

"Can you give me his phone number?" I asked.

"You know I can't hand out a member's home phone number. Now I got things to do."

Seeing that I wasn't leaving, he told me I should try the general manager.

I walked down the hall and found him at his desk. He wouldn't give me Lasko's number either, but I was persistent, and he offered to call Lasko on my behalf. I stood there until he did.

"Mr. Lasko? Yes, it's Mr. Bishop here. I'm sorry to bother you at home, but young Aaron Westfield is standing in my office and insists on talking to you. May I put him on?"

Slight pause.

"Thank you, Mr. Lasko. Here he is."

He thrust the phone in my face as if to say, "Make it quick."

"Mr. Lasko, I need to see you, today," I said.

"Yes Mr. Lasko, I know the road."

"Thank you, sir. I'll see you in fifteen minutes."

I handed the phone back to Mr. Bishop and hurried out the door. Lasko seemed fine hearing from me. Maybe this wasn't going to be so hard after all. Maybe I'd hand him the money, he'd smile, and we'd laugh a bit and he'd wish me luck.

Twelve minutes later, I was pressing a button on a gate. No voice came over the loudspeaker at the gate, but I heard a buzz and a whir, and the gate opened. Three minutes later, I was pulling into the circular driveway of the most prized residential real estate on the entire island. My shack could fit under the second-floor portico hanging over the entryway.

My knock on the door was answered by a man who filled the entire doorway, wearing a tank top and a pistol in a shoulder harness. He stepped to the side as I entered, shut the door behind him, locked it, and told me to follow him. He said that Mr. Lasko was waiting for me on the terrace.

When I walked out onto the terrace, I saw Lasko pacing back and forth with a phone pressed to his ear connected by a long cord to the base, which rested twenty feet away on a table. The table had a pot of coffee on it, one cup, and only one chair by its side. Hardly looked like he was expecting me. His glance at me said one thing: he was annoyed. But at who? Me or whoever was on the other end of the line? I couldn't hear what he was saying, but there was no misunderstanding his body language. I wished I was somewhere else. But maybe Nash was right? Maybe this man was so busy that he might not care if I paid him back. I was about to find out. He walked back to the table and hung up the phone. He pulled a cigarette from a pack in his front breast pocket and looked at me.

"Well, you're here. What's so goddamn important that it couldn't wait until we play again?"

"Um, sir, it's about that. I'm here to pay you what I owe you." I pulled the envelope from my front pocket and handed it to him. "It's all there, $19,875."

He took the envelope from me and tossed it onto the table without counting it.

"Aren't you going to count it?" I asked.

"Do I need to?"

"Um, no. It's all there."

"Yeah, you said that. Now, in two days, we've got a match against some fat cat from Florida. He's heard about you and wants a shot. He fancies himself a real stick. We're going to start out at $10,000 on the front and back and another $20,000 on the eighteen, but this is how it's going to go down. You'll miss a few approach shots, maybe push a drive or two. We'll lose the front and I'm going to get visibly pissed at you and threaten to storm off the course at the turn. If I play it right, he'll give me odds on the back and the eighteen, but then you'll find your game miraculously on the back side and we'll clean the son-of-a-bitch out."

"Um, Mr. Lasko, I'm done."

He still hadn't lit his cigarette but decided that now was the time to do so. After one drag, he returned to the matter at hand.

"What did you say?"

"I'm done. I ... I ... I'm not your gambling partner anymore," I stammered. "I'm not doing this anymore."

"You're not?"

"No, sir. And now that I've paid you back, we're all square."

"Oh, so you think that you can just walk away?"

The doorman or bodyguard, or whoever that guy was who met me at the front door, had been standing off to the side this entire time. He now took two steps toward me. Sweat poured down the side of my head. Not knowing what to do, I stuck my hand out toward Lasko to shake his, hoping to end this meeting as quickly as possible. He just stared at it, so I turned to walk out.

"Get back here," Lasko said. "And don't you ever walk away from me again. I own your ass."

I snapped and lunged for him, but his bodyguard was faster and stronger and had me on the ground with his gun to the back of my head before I could react. I screamed uncontrollably. "No! No one owns me! No one!"

"Let him up," Lasko said nonchalantly.

The brute allowed me to my feet, and I stood there with blood pouring from my nose, my breathing short and rapid.

Lasko walked up to me and with his face mere inches from mine announced: "Oh, but I do, Eli Atkins. I do."

Chapter 27

An Answer to Prayer

CHARLESTON, EARLIER THAT MORNING

Annabelle Babcock was a sound sleeper, but she didn't need much sleep anymore, typically rising each morning by 5:30 a.m. This morning was no different. She made a pot of coffee and checked on the bait traps while the coffee was brewing. Suddenly she felt weak and took a seat on the steps of the back porch. She could hear the familiar sounds of the coffeepot bubbling and hissing, signaling it was almost ready, but she felt compelled to stay seated. The moon was still visible in the sky even as the sun's rays crept into sight over the horizon. Annabelle sat very still and quiet, knowing that it was in these moments she heard His voice.

"Watch over him, Lord. Send him an angel. He may be a man, but he will always be one of your children."

* * *

"That's right, Eli, I know who you are and that you killed your girlfriend back in Charleston, raped her too."

I started at him again but the brute's vice-like grip on my right arm and pistol to my head stopped me in my tracks.

"Does Rachel know?" he asked. Eyeing me carefully, he continued. "No, she doesn't, does she? The way I figure it, no one knows, but someone does. You're here, with a new name and papers. Pretty impressive. My bet's on Quaid Dawson being your sugar daddy."

Lasko walked inside the sliding glass door and yelled back over his shoulder. "This calls for a drink. Can I get you anything, Eli?"

I remained silent and he returned with two beers.

"You gonna make me drink alone?" he asked.

I took the beer, reluctantly thinking I could use it as a weapon, but thought better of it.

"You see, Eli, I got suspicious about you. Where you came from. How you got here. Why you ran instead of facing the charges in a courtroom. If Quaid's helping you, he must think you're innocent, but you've been here five years now so the way I figure it, the cops still make you for the killer. So, if you want to keep what's left of your miserable life, then you'd better keep me happy or else I'll report your whereabouts to the local police. In that I'm a well-respected philanthropist in town and do business with many of the judges on the island, you wouldn't stand a chance fighting extradition. Not even Quaid's money could save you."

"So, what do you say we toast our new partnership? It's a simple arrangement. I tell you what to do and you do it. Cheers!"

* * *

I don't remember the walk from Lasko's house to my car. I don't remember getting in the car or driving through his gate or back on the road or even where I was heading. But I know this much, I was carried into another state of mind, to another world. No longer was I a twenty-three-year-old man with a glimpse of a future, a future with a family and a purpose. A future with Rachel. No, that dream was dead. I'm twenty-three, wanted for murder, and so must conceal my identity even from the girl I love, a girl I believe loves me, too. If my cover is blown, I'll be sent back to Charleston to stand trial for a crime I did not commit, and if found guilty, I'll be sent to the electric chair. And the man who has the power to blow my cover is a powerful, wealthy criminal who launders drug money and buys kidnapped girls and sells them to sexual predators.

What would you do? Would you think about killing yourself? I did, but not in detail because at some level I knew that if I thought about it, I wouldn't go through with it. But it seemed like the only way out, and in a haze of clarity, it seemed logical, the perfect ending. I had no choice, so I took the one lying right in front of me. Semi-aware of where I was, I sped up and then it made sense, a car accident. No one would suspect. An accident would be the perfect cover. I pressed the gas pedal down methodically and emptied my mind, carried forward by the car toward the sharp turn ahead bordered by the steep ravine to the right, the Atlantic Ocean a hundred feet below.

From nowhere, she appeared in the corner of my eye, a young girl on a bicycle pulling a basket behind her full of homemade crafts destined for a roadside market at a turnoff a few hundred feet away. I hit the brakes and swerved to avoid hitting her and slid into thick brush up against a tree. The young girl came to a stop, hopped off her bicycle, and ran to my car.

"I'm so sorry. Didn't see you. Are you okay?"

I was dazed and it took me a minute to gather in my surroundings and what had happened.

"What's your name?" I asked.

"Aariaani."

"That's a beautiful name."

"Thank you. My mama says it means 'gift from God.'"

"She's right."

Chapter 28

Heartbreak

Three days later, at the Ocean Club

"There you are," she said. "Where have you been? I was starting to worry."

I had avoided Rachel since leaving Lasko's house. I stayed away from Lyford Cay and didn't spend much time at my place figuring she'd come looking for me. But it was only a matter of time. I stopped by Nigel's office since I needed work and he told me that the Ocean Club was looking for a bartender.

"I thought after my fight there they didn't want me back," I had commented.

"Well, that was some time ago, and some of their regulars asked about you. So, do you want the gig?"

I'd said sure, so here I was tending bar, the same bar where we had first met. I didn't have the heart to do the right thing and break it off, but there was no avoiding it now. Lasko left me no choice. She would not tolerate me hooking up with him again knowing I was no longer indebted to him, and I had decided not to tell her about my alter ego, Eli Atkins. So, I had two choices: break it off, or by my actions, so enrage her that she'd break it off. But, regardless of how it happened, I couldn't keep dating her. Knowing what I now knew Lasko was capable of, I didn't want her connected to him in any way.

"I've been laying low. Sorry, guess I should have called you somehow."

"Not having a phone in your hut is just one more reason why you should move in with me," she said, beaming from ear to ear. "But we can talk about that later. Tell me, how did it go with Lasko?"

"Look, about that. I don't know how available I'm going to be as a boyfriend. I'm gonna be workin' more for Lasko. We'll still be playing golf—gambling, you know—but he's got other jobs for me now. Just thought you needed to know."

If there's one thing I hate, one thing that causes me genuine pain, it's the look on a woman's face as she's about to cry. I was dying inside, wanting so much to tell Rachel how much I loved her. She left, tears streaming down her lovely face before I had a chance to say anything.

* * *

My shift at the bar after Rachel left was interminable. I had to get out of there. I returned to my place and tried to clear my head with a swim. No luck. I collapsed on the hammock and screamed at the night. Why? Why? My father, Monty, my real father as far as I was concerned, had told me shortly after the prosecutor decided to press charges against me for murdering Kimberly, that when times seemed darkest, that's when God shows up. I didn't see him anywhere and I couldn't imagine things getting much darker. I'd credited the girl on the bike for saving my life three days ago and chalked that one up to God, but maybe that was just His cruel sense of humor, keeping me alive a little longer so he could torment me more. My sadness was turning to anger, anger at Lasko for sure, but anger again at Rose. She's the reason I'm here, the reason I can't go home, the reason Lasko has leverage over me, the reason I can't be with Rachel.

No, things couldn't get much darker, and maybe that was for the best because as I considered my options, I found I was out of them. Only one thing left to do. I'd tell Rachel. I'd tell her everything and let the chips fall. If she abandoned me, so be it, but she'd do so knowing I loved her. And if she stuck with me ...? I'd be endangering her life, but maybe this was one of those decisions we needed to make together.

* * *

THE NEXT MORNING

"Lach, is Rachel here?"

He normally would invite me in but instead stood in the doorway. She must have told him.

"Please, Lach, it's important."

"She doesn't want to see you, and I don't blame her. I'll tell her you stopped by—now be gone."

He slammed the door in my face. With nothing else to do, I headed for the driving range. Lasko was there and he approached me as if we were old friends, the best of friends. He told me he didn't want there to be any hard feelings and that he was going to help me become a very rich man.

"I've got big plans for you and not just on the golf course. You'll see."

He told me I could start keeping 25 percent of my winnings and that, when we lost, he'd count half of what he won from my share when we did win toward my debt to him. I wanted to kill him.

He'd arranged a match for us that afternoon. I took my anger out on our opponents and we won big. My anger focused my concentration instead of derailing it. He handed me my cash and I gave half of it to Mateo and told him to share it with the other caddies. A pointless gesture but it made me feel better.

I gave Rachel her space and left her alone for a few days, but then returned intent on telling her everything.

"You're too late, laddie. She left yesterday for London."

I was stunned, and I believe for a moment Lach felt sorry for me.

"I don't know what got into your head, but I suspect Lasko has something on you 'cause why else would anyone hurt such a lovely young woman? But you did and she's done with ya and so am I."

Chapter 29

Eyes and Ears

When sadness threatens to overwhelm you and darkness closes in and the God your father believes in never shows up, but you've decided to go on living anyway, then guess what happens to your sadness? It vanishes, leaving a void to be filled by something. Anger is exhausting, but bitterness isn't. Bitterness takes root. Bitterness defines you.

But it doesn't fill your days. So how did I deal with everything? I guess you could say I threw myself into my work. I forgot all about Quaid and Nash and of course Lach and Rachel. Lasko turned me into an errand boy. We still played golf, but there was no one left at the club who would play us unless I gave them more strokes than we could overcome. Lasko began flying in folks to play.

As part of the runup to his December Charity Golf Tournament, he hosted smaller, four- and eight-man tournaments. Sometimes, we'd play a team format and other times singles matches. He'd bring in the occasional celebrity and a pro golfer from the tour, but most players were simply low-handicap gamblers who all saw themselves as better players than they were. The good ones, the good gamblers that is, understood that most bets were won on the 1st tee and by properly understanding your opponent. At this, Lasko was a genius.

He'd sell tickets to the matches and the club would host private dinners for those in attendance. Of course, it was all for charity. After the club bar shut down, some of the crowd, those from outside the Bahamas whom Lasko invited, retired to his place for a late-night party. Lasko hired me as a bartender. I was disgusted by what I saw.

Once a week, I still checked in with Nigel. There wasn't much reason to anymore, but doing so was the last reminder of my old life. He had work for me if I wanted it, which I did, needing a break from Lasko. He gave me the name of a fishing charter in need of a first mate, which explains why I was up before dawn and headed to the pier this morning.

I found my captain and inquired about the charter. He told me the man was already onboard, down below, and that we were ready to shove off. I untied us and pushed off as the captain expertly turned the boat away from the dock. We had worked before, and I knew what was expected, so I set out preparing the rods for a day of fishing. The charter was still below when we left the harbor and was missing a beautiful sunrise, but to each their own. Once we were clear of the harbor and other boats in the vicinity, he came up the stairs.

"Hello, Aaron."

"Mr. Hawthorne!"

"It's Nash, remember? We need to talk."

I knew from the tone in his voice that he knew something wasn't right. I later learned that Lach had gone to Nigel and expressed concern for my safety. He was angry at me for hurting Rachel, but he surmised I was in danger from Lasko. Nigel knew to call Nash, and here we were.

"So, he's blackmailing you."

"You could say that."

"You ready to help me nail the bastard?"

"Absolutely."

And that's how I became a spy. We spent the next hour reviewing pictures of people whom Nash wanted to know if I had seen. The answer was "yes," I had seen many of the men in the photographs at Lasko's house. Nash wanted to know when and for how long and descriptions of who else might have been there.

"Nash, what's this all about?" I asked.

"Your information confirms our suspicions. Lasko is in trouble and getting desperate. My sources tell me that because of the poor-performing stock market, some of his investors are antsy and want their money out. When they demand the return of their investment, Lasko calls them personally and tells them why they shouldn't pull out."

"That makes sense," I said. "I hear him on the phone all the time telling them not to worry because they won't lose money if they don't sell. But I thought this guy worked with drug dealers and the like. What does some investment fund for a bunch of rich guys have to do with anything and why does the CIA care? I assume it's the CIA you work for."

"Good questions. I care about phony investment funds and stock market scams but only personally. Professionally, that's the SEC's problem. But his investors are one of our pressure points. What I'm concerned with is his involvement with weapons dealers and communist groups working to topple democracies in Central and South America. We believe he's funding subversive activities and rebel outfits."

"In the Bahamas?" I asked.

"No, elsewhere, but it may come to the Bahamas if the government in place doesn't live up to billing. It's a bad sign that the prime minister keeps company with Lasko. Also, one of the men you identified in the pictures is an old friend of the prime minister who we believe handles the prime minister's personal investments, and this man is one of the men you identified in the pictures. Right now, Lasko is using the Bahamas as his base of operations. He hides behind the private banking laws, and we likely couldn't extradite him to the United States were we to try because of his friends in the Bahamian judiciary."

"By friends, you mean judges he's bribed."

"Yes, or that he has dirt on."

"So, again, what does any of this have to do with his investment funds?"

"Associates of mine invested in one or more of his funds, and at my request, they're putting the pressure on him. They're asking for their money back. One in particular is threatening to go to the SEC if he doesn't get his principal back. The pressure to deliver quarterly returns coupled with the added pressure of having to potentially return investment dollars is driving Lasko to take greater and greater risks. In other words, he's desperate for cash any way he can get it."

"So, when I help him win on the golf course, I'm helping him?"

"In a small way, yes. But he needs millions of dollars and not thousands. It's more likely he's using the golf course and the allure of playing golf for big dollars to lure potential investors for his fund. Let me ask you, do you sometimes lose matches you should win?"

"Absolutely."

"Do some of these people you lose to end up investing with him?"

"I know they do. I've seen them sit down together at Lasko's house and sign papers. Lasko will joke with the guy about how he owes him a chance to win his money back on the course."

"That's just one example of how he's keeping his empire afloat," said Nash.

"Why doesn't Lasko stop paying high quarterly returns until the market returns?" I asked.

"That's the sixty-four-dollar question, isn't it? Why do criminals do what they do? Many of them are smart enough to make a fine living playing it straight, but they just can't. I gave up a long time ago trying to understand why they do what they do. I'm just no longer surprised at what they do, at the depravity of man. Anyway, at this point, Lasko is so deep in this mess, he can't turn back. It's only a matter of time until he trips up. My goal is to track his involvement with communist guerrillas and eliminate him as a source of their funding."

"How can I help?" I asked.

"You have. Just keep watching him and paying attention to who he sees. And now that you know what I'm looking for, keep your eyes and ears open for any schemes he may be launching to make money or reel in more investors."

* * *

When I first agreed to help Nash, I was happy to do so if it would help Nash nail Lasko, but I also had the murder charge hanging over my head. At our second meeting, I asked Nash if he could help me get the police to drop those charges, and he led me to believe some of his friends in the FBI could help. At each meeting, I'd ask if he'd made any progress and at each meeting his answers became more and more vague and less and less committal. I was growing weary of the arrangement.

Over the next six weeks, Nash and I met under the same circumstances. I'd appear at Nigel's office each week, and every two weeks, I'd meet Nash on the same boat. We'd spend half the time fishing and half the time debriefing and sharing intel. To hide my tracks, I also took on bartending jobs and helped at Café Abaco.

One night while tending bar at the Ocean Club, I saw her, Rachel. She walked into the restaurant in an evening gown, she looked absolutely gorgeous. My heart jumped. She must have sensed me looking across the room because she glanced my way and we made eye contact for the briefest of moments. I know she saw me, but she expressed no recognition at all. Then she turned and allowed a man in a tuxedo entering behind her to place his hand on her hip as he spoke with the maître d' like old friends. They were escorted to a table in the corner with a fine view of the harbor and the ocean beyond. I couldn't have been in more pain if she'd thrust a spear through my heart and twisted it herself.

I found Lach the next day on the driving range giving a lesson. We'd hardly exchanged a word since he told me Rachel had returned to St. Andrews. He was obviously perturbed that I was interrupting a lesson, so I retreated and waited in a chair on the veranda. Once his lesson was over, he left quickly, no doubt hoping to avoid contact with me. I caught up with him in the parking lot.

"She's back, isn't she?" I asked.

"Yes, been back over a week now. She has a boyfriend. A man she knows from home and they're here on holiday."

"I know. I saw them last night."

"She mentioned it. Asked about you."

"She did?"

"Yes, but don't go getting ideas. Best you leave her be. It's for the best."

"Not for me."

"Look, Aaron, I 'spect you're not operatin' of your own free will doing Lasko's bidding, but what am I to do? She's my very own niece, my sister's child, her only child. I vowed to watch out for her when my sister got sick, and her deadbeat husband left and that's what I'm doin'. I'm all the family Rachel has left. I'm sorry, I truly am, but you mustn't see her again."

I had to let Nash know he was running out of time.

Two days later, we were twenty miles out looking for sailfish when I told him that unless I saw some movement on the murder charges, I was done. I had to get out from under Lasko and recover my name. Nash assured me that by helping him bust Lasko, I'd be out from under him and then he'd be in a better position to argue my case to the Charleston Police.

"Look, Aaron, Lasko knows who you are. Somehow, he found out. If he or one of his sources sees me or someone from another government agency trying to get your murder charges dropped, don't you think he'll figure out you're working with someone in DC? He's one smart cookie. You'll be putting your life on the line if he suspects you have friends in Washington. Trust me. This will work. I'm your ticket. Just keep working with me and you'll get your life back. It's your best chance. It's your only choice."

What he said made sense, but we were on two different schedules. He was patient. I wasn't. Rachel was back. I needed my freedom now. But what was I to do?

Chapter 30

Highs and Lows

Adelaide Village, Nassau, Bahamas,
Thursday, September 28th, 1978

I heard the screen door open and the sound of mail falling to the floor. Walking into the front room, I saw a large envelope, picked it up, and smiled at the familiar handwriting. I opened the envelope and read the press clippings about Walker's latest accomplishments.

"Way to go, Walkie Talkie. Way to go."

Walkie Talkie had been my nickname for Walker since he first started talking. He just wouldn't shut up, trying so hard to keep up with everyone else.

Inside the large envelope was another smaller one. I opened it and found a collection of newspaper stories on a decidedly different subject, and a short, simple handwritten note: "Eli, it's time to come home."

I placed the envelope in a drawer with the others and sat behind the small desk, staring out to sea before setting off for the club, thinking this was my chance but wondering if Charleston would ever be my home again.

* * *

For the past five years, Mrs. Babcock had been my connection to the world I left, the world I'd been forced to leave. She would fill a large manila envelope with stories from the local newspaper, the *Post & Courier*, along with a copy of the Porter-Gaud school newspaper, and hand the envelope to Quaid at church. Quaid would place the envelope in packages he mailed to Nigel Pinder. Nigel would send me the envelopes via courier.

Walker was a senior now and he wrote for the paper. Sometimes Dad would be mentioned in a story in the Post & Courier about new banking legislation, and I would read those stories. But Walker was always being mentioned, in the school newspaper and the *Post & Courier*, for his performance on the school debate and cross-country teams.

But the news clippings in the envelope I received this morning were about a renewed investigation into who killed Kimberly Prestwick, and as I drove into town, I grew more excited by the news Mrs. Babcock shared. The police recently held a press conference at which my mother, Rose, and Kimberly's mother, Stephanie Cunningham, were together at the podium. Cunningham? Huh, she must have gone back to her maiden name. At the press conference, the chief of police, a Chief Crandall, said they had new evidence that could exonerate me and pointed in the direction of someone else, someone wanted for multiple murders around the southeastern United States.

This could be it. Finally, a chance to get my name back. Charleston had a new police chief. The old chief had it out for me and shut down the investigation when I fled Charleston, but apparently the new chief was willing to look for the real killer. And if I was no longer wanted for murder, Lasko would have no hold over me. I could tell Rachel everything and we could be together again.

Things were looking up. But could I go home again? Was Mrs. Babcock right? Was it "time to come home"? Would Charleston ever be my home again? Since I was innocent all along, everyone will want to know why I ran in the first place. What would I tell folks? *Well, you see, my mom was going to testify and contradict my alibi and say that I had not come home early the night Kimberly was killed and that I was lying when I said I had.*

Hell of a homecoming that would be. But more importantly, if Rachel and I get back together, did I want to go home? But I was getting ahead of myself, way ahead of myself. First things first. What to do with Mrs. Babcock's good news?

On the drive to the club a plan came together, but I would need help, starting with Nigel. I pulled up to his office and found him at his desk.

"Ah, Aaron. I wasn't expecting you. Is everything all right?"

"Everything is great, Mr. Pinder. The envelope dropped off this morning contained good news. It seems I may be a free man soon. There's a new chief of police in Charleston and he's reopening the case about the murder of my old girlfriend. They have new evidence pointing toward someone else. So, you know the woman who gives Quaid those packages that he sends me through you? Well, she says I can go home."

"I see. Well, that is interesting news."

"Interesting? Are you kidding me? If I can clear my name, then I can get out from under Lasko's boot and get my life back. It's more than interesting, it's great. It's fantastic. It's life changing!"

"Yes, yes. Of course, how foolish of me. How can I help?" Nigel asked.

"Can you contact Captain Bootle and Quaid and see if they can take me back?"

"Consider it done. Now when would you like to leave?"

"Now, today, as soon as possible," I said.

"Well, I best get cracking. Meet me at the pier this afternoon as if you were working on a fishing charter. Between now and then, I will make the necessary arrangements."

"Thank you, Mr. Pinder. Thank you. I can't believe it. This may all be ending soon."

"Aaron, it's been my pleasure, and before you go, would you do me a favor?"

"Yes, anything."

Mr. Pinder stood and came around his desk and stood before me.

"You're not the scared boy I met five years ago. No, you're a man now. So please, call me Nigel."

"Nigel it is."

We shook hands and then he pulled me in for a hug.

"Very un-British of you, Nigel. Hugging a man, that is."

"One word to Quaid, and I'll box your ears. Now off with you," he said.

I was going to miss Nigel.

* * *

If Nigel was going to arrange Aaron's clandestine departure for this afternoon, he would have to speak with Quaid as soon as possible, but first he needed to speak with Nash. Nigel was, after all, one of the Family's associates.

Nash picked up quickly and Nigel explained the situation.

"How important is young Aaron to our operations here?" Nigel asked.

"Important but he has redemption on his mind, and he'll be of no use to us if we stop him from leaving. In fact, it might be dangerous for him to stay. If he's not properly motivated, he could screw up, and if Lasko figures out he's an asset, he'll kill him. No, best let him go."

"I couldn't agree more."

Nash offered an idea or two about how Aaron should leave the island, and then Nigel called Quaid and Captain Bootle to work out the details.

* * *

Walking toward the pier, I acted as nonchalant as possible. Just another fishing charter. Earlier in the day, I dropped off at Nigel's office all my worldly possessions packed in the same duffel bag and backpack I'd brought with me five years earlier. He said they would be onboard waiting for me.

When I arrived at the pier, Nigel was there, wearing a straw hat and dressed for a day of fishing.

"I don't believe I've ever seen you dressed quite so casually, Nigel," I said.

"All part of the cover, dear boy. Now there's one more thing."

"What?" I asked.

"The money you have in my bank account. I've brought you some cash, just in case you need it on your trip, but the balance I'm afraid is too large to carry around in your pocket."

"Good grief, in my excitement about leaving, I'd completely forgotten."

"So, this is what you do. Once you're firmly established in Charleston, free of being arrested and all that, open an account at a local bank, and I will transfer your funds into your new bank account. If you have any trouble, just contact Quaid."

"Is that all?" I asked.

"Yes, I believe so. Time for you to shove off."

"Almost. And now I have a favor to ask of you, Nigel."

"But of course. Anything."

"Can you deliver this letter to Rachel McGregor for me? You know we were dating for a while. But she never knew who I really was. She doesn't know about Eli Atkins and that I'm wanted for murder. I never told her. I was afraid she'd leave me. But it's important that she know and that she knows I'll return to the Bahamas just as soon as all this is cleared up."

Nigel stood there with the look of a concerned parent who still needed convincing.

"Nigel, this is important to me. I love her and I think she loves me."

"You don't know, do you?" he asked.

"Know what?"

"She's engaged to that chap she's been seen with around town. Why, I received a wedding announcement in the afternoon mail. They're to be married next spring in St. Andrews, Scotland. She's going home, Aaron. Rumor has it Lach is too. Oh, Aaron, I'm so sorry."

Chapter 31

A Homecoming?

Nigel tried to console me by reminding me that I was going home too. He meant well, but his words only deepened my sorrow. Fighting back tears, I shoved my letter to Rachel in my back pocket, shook his hand one last time, and boarded Captain Knowles' boat. Twenty minutes later, we had left the harbor and were heading north. Captain Knowles, the boat captain when I had been meeting secretly with Nash, explained what would happen next. Given that we were on his boat and the detailed planning involved with my departure, I assumed Nash had lent a hand. For that I was thankful.

We were headed fifty miles north to a small island called Fanny Cay, where I would be dropped off along with a kayak Captain Knowles had aboard. From Fanny Cay, I would kayak two miles north to a larger island called Great Harbor Cay, where I would spend the night.

Captain Knowles left me alone. I didn't know what he knew, and I didn't care. I didn't care about much of anything. I was on autopilot. He dropped me off with the kayak, said goodbye with a casual salute, and headed back toward Nassau as I paddled toward the island due north that he'd pointed out. The waters were calm due to their position east of the Berry Islands, a string of small islands running north to south, and I made good time.

When I arrived at Great Harbor Cay, I abandoned the kayak and hiked into town and found my way to a small, seaside bar where I met a woman named Jessica who was related to the Bastian family, one of Javon's cousins. She provided a cot in the back room for me. When I rose the next morning, there was a note waiting for me she had slid under the door.

"Make yourself at home."

Which I did. I made a pot of coffee and helped myself to some coconut bread. The food in the Bahamas was one thing I would miss.

I was standing on the beach as the sun was rising when a familiar looking 53' Hatteras came into view. I watched as the man at the helm dropped anchor and lowered a small rubber dinghy into the water. He started up the small outboard engine and set off for shore. He pulled the dinghy up onto the beach and approached, holding a mug of coffee in his hand.

"Captain Bootle at your service."

I gathered my things and boarded the boat. We delayed our departure for the States out of fear that Lasko would suspect that's where I was heading and would launch a full-scale manhunt. We headed to Abaco Island instead, where we stayed with members of the Bastian extended family, folks we could trust. Then late Monday afternoon, Captain Bootle and I headed for the coast of South Carolina.

THE FOLLOWING MORNING, TUESDAY, OCTOBER 3RD, IN THE ATLANTIC OCEAN, MOTORING WEST TOWARD THE UNITED STATES

We took turns manning the helm. We had two long days ahead of us and expected to come alongside the eastern seaboard of the United States a few miles off the coast of Beaufort, South Carolina late Wednesday night. We shared the task of preparing food, we slept from time to time, and rechecked our route, all in a silent rhythm. As with the first time we met, some five years earlier, not much was said in transit.

Captain Bootle did not know what I was running from five years ago, and unless someone had told him, he still didn't. But we had worked together several times over the years, me as his first mate, and we were friends.

"Aaron."

"Yes, Captain."

"You're going home, are you?"

"It would appear."

"Will it be safe? What drove you away five years ago, does that no longer concern you?"

I didn't know how to answer that question because I didn't know myself. If Kimberly's killer was caught, then I'd be safe from prosecution. But would I be welcome? Was I going home? This is what concerned me as my eyes scanned the horizon.

Captain Bootle waited for an answer, and none came. He tried again.

"So, my friend, are you going home?" he asked.

I still had the letter I had written to Rachel in my back pocket. At first, I was numb to the pain, but the anesthetizing effect of the shock of the news had worn off, and now, I simply hurt. Captain Bootle wanted to know if I was going home. As I tossed my letter to Rachel into the ocean, all I knew for sure was that the Bahamas was no longer my home.

"Captain Bootle, I don't know. I honestly don't know."

Chapter 32

Loves Lost

We're close now. In the distance, I can just make out the Eastern Seaboard. Now that you know more about me, it's time to wrap things up and let go of the reins of this story.

In a few hours, Captain Bootle will drop me off three miles from the coast of South Carolina, close to the town of Beaufort, where I will be met by Francesco Bastian, Mrs. Babcock's son-in-law and the man who helped me escape over five years ago.

I've lost so much, beginning with Kimberly and ending with Rachel. To have loved two such women in one life is extraordinary. To have lost them both is a tragedy. But I remain hopeful, hopeful I can piece together a life beginning with the recovery of my name, Eli Atkins.

End of Part Four

PART FIVE

Family Reunion

Chapter 33

Mysterious Ways

Mrs. Babcock's home, Charleston area,
Monday morning, October 2nd, 1978

While Eli Atkins and Captain Bootle were resting on Abaco Island preparing to take to the high seas, destination South Carolina, Mrs. Babcock was rising before the sun, as was her habit. At church the day before, Quaid told her Eli was on his way and, weather permitting, would make it to Beaufort sometime late Wednesday night. She was as excited as a schoolgirl, and nervous too.

She was nervous because she felt responsible for his decision to run. She encouraged him once Eli told her that his mother, Rose Atkins, would deny his alibi the night of the murder, testimony that would send Eli to the electric chair. Encouraged him?! Good grief, she'd done more than that. Along with Quaid's assistance, they helped him escape. At the time, it felt like the right thing to do. But once the police chief shut down the investigation, she worried she had doomed him to a life on the run, a life spent denying his own identity or risk capture.

Why had she done it? Why had she been so gosh-darn set on saving the young man? Why couldn't she just let it go? Why did it eat at her still and why did she see Eli as a chance at her own redemption?

* * *

Annabelle stood in front of the church in open defiance, her fists clasped shut by her side. It had been a year ago today since she had been inside, the day she buried her husband, Randal Cunningham, an officer in the Charleston police department. Annabelle was twenty-five years old, and the mother of a one-year-old son named after her husband who had been shot dead in the line of duty. He was in the bank bathroom when the robber entered, and hearing the commotion, came out with his gun drawn and yelling at the robber to drop his. The robber never hesitated and shot him.

Anabelle sat in the courtroom every day and watched the man who killed her husband endure the trial with the ease of one who knew his fate and could not have cared less. When the judge handed down the sentence, he said the death penalty was in order in part due to the man's total lack of empathy for the officer he had killed. The judge asked if he had anything to say in his defense, and he smiled and said, "No."

Anabelle was bitter and angry, even after witnessing the bastard's death. The prior week, against the advice of some, she attended the execution and watched as the man was shot down by the state-sanctioned firing squad. She'd hoped that watching him die would relieve her of her anger and bitterness. It had not; instead, it burned hotter. Watching him die wasn't enough. Her husband was gone forever and there was nothing that could be done about that.

All her life she'd rested in the knowledge that God was not just there but was good. She believed in heaven and hell and had no problem with her husband's killer burning in hell. But that damn priest who met with the killer in his cell before the execution! Who did he think he was? He had no business trying to forgive that man! And what was it he said to her in the parking lot?

"Mrs. Cunningham, if I may?"

"Yes? What do you want?"

"My name is Reverend Withers. I'm the chaplain for the state prison system. I know from my review of the case file that you are a Christian. I thought you might want to know that Mr. Tankersley confessed his sins and accepted Christ into his heart this morning before his execution. He's in heaven with the Lord now. I know that as a Christian this news might bring you some comfort on this dark day."

"Mister, my dear husband is in heaven right now, which means there's no room for *that* man, so you can take your *good news* and go to hell."

Mrs. Babcock also watched the trials of the other two men involved in the bank robbery, Mr. William Greenly, who drove the getaway car, and Mr. Roscoe Boylston, who stood outside as a lookout. Neither fired a gun and were both convicted of robbery but not murder and received lighter sentences. When they came up for parole, she attended. And after the wives of the men in prison, with their children in tow, pleaded for early release, Mrs. Babcock took to the stand and argued against it. She knew her position in the police department carried weight with the parole board.

Every year, Mrs. Greenly would approach Mrs. Babcock hoping to make peace and every year she received a cold shoulder in return. The other family, Mrs. Boylston and her two daughters and a son, were openly hostile to her. Seeing them every year at the hearing, Annabelle watched the children grow up and remembered reading one day that Mrs. Boylston's son had dropped out of school and ended up dead in a back alley after having fallen into a life of crime. Mrs. Babcock smiled at the mother's loss.

One year returning home from a parole hearing, Annabelle had a flat tire and had to pull off to the side of the road. As she was opening the trunk looking for a spare tire, it began to rain and Mrs. Greenly approached in her car and slowed down. Her son lowered the passenger side window and asked if she needed help. As it began to rain harder, she said she did, and the young man hopped out of the car, and she reluctantly slid into the passenger side seat with Mrs. Greenly.

"Thank you," Annabelle said meekly to the woman in the driver's seat.

"Why of course. You looked so helpless on the side of the road and what with the storm coming."

"But you didn't have to. The others didn't."

Silence.

"I saw them. The Boylston family. They slowed down but smiled in a mean way and kept driving."

Silence.

"But you stopped," said Annabelle.

"I see you always carry a Bible into the parole hearings," said the woman. "But I wonder how much of it you've read."

"The whole thing, twice."

"I see."

"What's that supposed to mean?" asked Annabelle.

"'And who is my neighbor? asked the man.' Does that sound familiar?" the woman asked.

Annabelle knew exactly what she was referring to.

"Oh! So you see yourself as the good Samaritan and I'm the man beat up by robbers and lying on the side of the road," Annabelle said indignantly. "Well, you seem to forget that your husband and the others were the robbers, so if I've been beat up and left alongside the road it's because my first born has had to grow up without his father. You have no idea what that's like."

"Oh, I don't? Is that what you think? Who do you think taught my son how to change a tire? I did. And do you know why? Because his father will likely spend another fifteen years in prison with no chance of parole."

"Well, don't expect me to apologize for that."

"I don't. Not at all. We've made the best of what we have, the three of us."

"The three of you?"

"Yes. Me, William, and our son, Ezekiel. Mrs. Babcock, I'm not asking you to apologize to me for appearing at all the parole hearings and arguing against my husband's release. I've forgiven you and so has my husband and so has our son. We're at peace. William is sorry for what he did, for the role he played, and he asked for and received the Lord's forgiveness. He's learned a craft in prison and is involved with Bible studies. He's led more men to Jesus while in prison than you can imagine. The Lord has worked in wonderful and mysterious ways in our lives."

Annabelle sat silently and said nothing.

"Mrs. Babcock, may I say something else, though it might seem presumptuous?"

Annabelle nodded for her to continue.

"I'm truly sorry that your husband was killed, but it seems to me that the person that has beat you up and left you on the side of the road is you."

Silence.

The young boy was about done changing the tire.

"Looks like the rain is stopping," said the woman.

The young boy came back to the car and tapped on the passenger-side window. Annabelle cranked the window down.

"Okay. You're all set. The spare tire looks to be in pretty good shape, but I'd drive on the slower side until you can get to a garage and buy a new tire. Would you like us to follow you to a service station?"

"No thank you, young man. You've been very kind."

Annabelle turned to the woman next to her and with tears welling up simply said, "Thank you."

A year later, Annabelle was back at the parole hearing arguing in favor of early release for the two men, but there was nothing to be done for Mrs. Boylston's boy, and it weighed on her.

* * *

Mrs. Babcock was determined that a similar fate would not befall Eli. If she could help it, Eli would neither suffer for the absence of his parents, his father in particular, nor let bitterness ravage him as it had her. But after five years, she had all but given up hope until a series of strange, unexplained things began to happen around town and in the police department.

The first such unexplained incident was part one of a two-part story that ran in the local newspaper back in July about a suspected serial killer on the loose. Mrs. Babcock was not familiar with the term "serial killer," but from what she'd learned about these depraved individuals, the presence of such a man in their midst would explain the horrible things done to Kimberly Prestwick. The next peculiarity was when that northerner, Edmond Locard, who claimed he was working with the FBI on unsolved cases, showed up in the Charleston Police Department shortly after the newspaper story ran asking all sorts of questions about Kimberly Prestwick, her murder, and the crime scene. Now Mrs. Babcock believed in the power of prayer but not coincidence, so when Eli's father, Monty Atkins, walked into the police department around the same time, Mrs. Babcock became suspicious and hopeful.

Chapter 34

A Ray of Hope

What Mrs. Babcock did not know was that Monty Atkins had also never given up hope for Eli. Shortly after Eli fled in 1973, his attorney, Chester Baslin, introduced Monty to a private detective out of New Orleans named Lazare Fontenot, Laz to his friends and a diehard LSU fan. Monty originally hired Laz to find Eli, but when Laz didn't turn up anything, he changed tactics and hired Laz to find the real killer. Monty figured that if the real killer were captured then he could broadcast the news to the world and Eli would be free to come home.

Laz surmised that if Eli wasn't the killer, then the real killer had to be an unknown madman. Laz knew just who to contact, Edmond Locard. Edmond Locard was a specialist on serial killers as well as cutting-edge forensics techniques involving the identification of dried blood samples and tying them to specific victims or assailants.

Edmond was a third generation American. His family came over from France in the late 1800s, got off the boat at Ellis Island, and never left. In fact, Edmond was the first of his clan to even leave New York. He was a dapper dresser and wore horn-rimmed glasses. A real bookish type. He graduated with degrees in psychology and journalism from Emory University and from George Washington University with a degree in criminology. He worked extensively with the FBI and first met Laz while working a case in New Orleans.

Laz added Edmond to the team and Edmond set out to prove that a serial killer and not Eli Atkins had killed Kimberly Prestwick. Edmond wrote the two articles that ran in the local Charleston newspaper, the *Post & Courier*, and the stories had the intended effect—folks began talking about a serial killer on the loose. As fears of a serial killer tormenting the southeastern United States spread, so did talk that Kimberly Prestwick was one of his victims and thus speculation that Eli had been falsely accused.

Between the time the two stories ran in the *Post & Courier* about serial killers, Edmond Locard visited the Charleston Police department and met with Officer Pearlman, who along with Officer Tyrell, had investigated Kimberly Prestwick's murder. Neither officer believed Eli had committed the crime, but early evidence did cast him in a suspicious light, and they were duty bound to investigate. When Eli fled the scene, they were torn. So, when Edmond Locard showed up five years later and began asking questions and pointing out the similarities between the Kimberly crime scene and other crime scenes in the Southeast, their faith in Eli was restored.

The Chief of Police, Chief Crandall, initially doubted Edmond Locard's theories about a serial killer roaming the countryside, as he put it, but when Monty and Officer Tyrell proved to him that a murder, very similar in style, had taken place at the same time and hundreds of miles away from where Eli was playing in the state high school baseball championship game, then even he had to acknowledge that doubts had been raised.

The next morning, Monday, August 21st, the day after the second story about a serial killer on the loose ran in the *Post & Courier*, Chief Crandall agreed to investigate matters but not officially reopen the case, and he made all concerned—Officers Tyrell and Pearlman, Edmond Locard, and Monty—swear to silence. Chief Crandall shipped the evidence taken from Kimberly Prestwick's crime scene, which had been kept in the back of the evidence locker all these years, to FBI headquarters in Quantico, Virginia where the latest forensics techniques would be employed.

The next morning, Monty, Edmond, and Laz met for breakfast and Edmond briefed them on what would happen next. The FBI would need three weeks to perform tests, and if DNA taken from Kimberly Prestwick's crime scene matched DNA taken from one of several other crime scenes, crimes that Eli could not have committed given where he lived at the time, then there would be strong evidence clearing Eli's name. At which point, Monty would push hard to have all changes against Eli dropped so that he could broadcast the news far and wide in the hope Eli would hear it and come home.

After breakfast, Monty headed to his office. He entered and walked down the hall whistling happily as he passed Abigail's office. She followed him with a stack of files and phone messages. He plopped himself down behind his desk and sighed peacefully.

"Well, aren't we in a good mood this morning?" said Abigail.

Abigail Baker had been Monty's secretary since he first opened his practice. She was fresh out of college when she answered Monty's ad in the local paper. A Charleston native, like her mother before her, Abigail had attended Ole Miss. Her folks were surprised when she took the job. They figured she'd be married by now and spitting out kids.

Abigail was single by choice and not because of any apparent shortcomings. She just didn't want to marry right away. Abigail had her share of suitors. She was bright, blessed with a quick wit, and easy on the eyes. She had long, wavy brown hair that danced across her shoulders, green eyes, and a figure that both men and women noticed.

"Yes, Abigail, we are in a good mood. So, what do ya have for me?"

"Here are your phone messages in order of importance. You'll find the corresponding file in the stack. You have a court appearance Wednesday and a meeting tomorrow afternoon with Mr. and Mrs. Hancock. They're potential new clients, so be on your game."

Monty smiled as he flipped through the phone messages.

"I see Hank called a few times."

"Yes, it's about the mining rights he claims to own in California. It seems his grandfather may have purchased a gold mine, if you believe that."

Henry "Hank" Barstow ran the local post office and delivering mail was the family business. Hank would ramble on for hours with stories of his grandfather, who rode the Pony Express, and about the fortune he made and lost during the California Gold Rush.

"Yep, I remember. Thinks he may be a millionaire," said Monty.

"Do you think he'd give up delivering the mail if he became a millionaire?" asked Abigail.

"I suspect not. He loves it, and frankly, I can't imagine Hank not delivering the mail."

"Do you think there's anything to the mining rights?" asked Abigail.

"No. Hank wants to talk to me about his daughter. The gold mine story is his cover, I imagine. His daughter gives him fits. Can you find some time on my calendar for us to meet?"

"Will do." As Abigail turned to head back to her desk, she asked, "Do you want your door open or closed?"

"Could you shut it, please? I've got some work to do."

Yes, it was good to be back at the office and Monty was ecstatic. The nightmare was almost over.

Chapter 35

Family Secrets

If only Monty could share the good news with someone. On the drive to his work that morning after leaving breakfast with Edmond and Laz, he was surprisingly calm about the upcoming three-week wait before hearing from the FBI. Yes, he wanted the results now, but he was so confident they would prove Eli's innocence that, in a small way, he was already celebrating. Should he share the good news with Rose? He knew she'd had her doubts, but given what Monty had learned, he felt guilty not telling Rose all he knew.

But as he had pulled up to his office that morning, he decided to not tempt fate but to keep the good news to himself. Whereas Monty was determined to see Eli cleared of all charges, Rose was determined that the case remain shut and that there never be a trial even if it meant Eli, her firstborn, would forever be thought of as the killer, spending the rest of his life on the run.

Why, you may ask, would any mother forsake a child like this? The answer, though unsatisfying, was that Rose feared she had more to lose were the identity of Kimberly's killer revealed than if it were to remain hidden. And again, how could that be? Because Rose knew who the killer was.

* * *

James Island, South Carolina, November 16th, 1973, six months after Kimberly was killed

It was a beautiful, fall day. The temperature was hovering in the low sixties, but the bright sun against the blue sky made it feel warmer. Rose was determined to be in a good mood if for no other reason than to prove to others that all was right in her family.

But all was not right. It had been six months since Eli had vanished and neither her husband, Monty, nor their son, Walker, would snap out of it. They were both in a deep funk, lost, adrift, incapable of mustering the energy to pursue anything with gusto. But not Rose. No, she had laid low long enough. It was back to work, proving to everyone that she belonged, that she was not white trash. She collected positions on church and school committees as a defense against all comers daring them to push back. She would not hide in the background.

Monty, on the other hand, had taken a back seat in all aspects of life and was content to do so until he could prove Eli's innocence. "*He's constantly talking to that hick, Laz, the private detective he'd hired to find Eli*" she thought. Now that was something she had to shut down. The question on everyone's lips after Eli ran had been: "If he were innocent, then why did he run?" For many, the answer was simple—he wasn't innocent. Rose was fine with that answer, for it bestowed upon her status as a victim, something she could wear well. It was harder for Monty, because Monty didn't know what was at stake if the truth came out. When the police chief shut down the investigation into Kimberly's murder, thereby practically hanging the verdict of guilty around Eli's neck, Rose breathed a huge sigh of relief.

So, here she was, six months removed from it all and with Thanksgiving the next week, she was determined to be in a good mood. Monty and Walker wanted to escape to Kiawah for the holiday and remain out of sight, but Rose prevailed and wore them down; they would enjoy their Thanksgiving meal at the Wappoo Country Club, where she could be seen by all the finest people. No, it was time to reenter high society, her rightful place, and nothing could stop her, nothing but the tentacles of her past, reaching out on this beautiful, fall day, courtesy of the US Postal Service.

Rose waved at her neighbor and remarked about the weather as she retrieved the mail. She poured herself a glass of fresh orange juice she had made earlier that day and took a seat on the patio, intent on enjoying the latest issue of *Better Home and Garden*, but first a glance at the rest of the mail. Three envelopes down, she came upon a standard business envelope with her name and address scrawled on the front. Her heart nearly stopped when she recognized the menacing penmanship. She turned it over and in the bottom right corner, he had written, *How's my little Rosebud?* She looked over her shoulder to confirm she was alone, ripped open the envelope, and as she read the note inside, she feared her entire sordid history spilling out for all to see.

> Hello, Rose. Tell me something, when you heard about all the terrible things done to that whore our son Eli was fuckin', how long did it take you to figure me for it? Not long, I bet. Yep, that was my handiwork and I'm right proud of it. The blows with the baseball bat, that's my signature move. Bruise the body something awful and break their arms and legs, but don't kill them and never hit them in the head or scar their face. I want them alive and looking beautiful for what happens next. I'm still working on my technique, but I took my time and savored every minute. I could go on with all the delish details but I'm guessing you read em' all in the police report written up on our boy Eli.
>
> Speaking of Eli, where is he? He must've got spooked and ran. Was that your handiwork, Rosebud? I bet so. Well, you keep my secrets and I'll keep yours.
>
> Rose, this is just the beginning. You'll want to check your mail regular now for updates from me. Have a blessed Thanksgiving.
>
> Your devoted husband,
>
> Rath

Rose was in a full-blown panic. If folks in town learned who her first husband was, she'd be a laughingstock. Worse, if they learned that he'd killed Kimberly, then Eli could come home, and he'd tell everyone she'd forced him to run. What would folks say? Eventually, her childhood would be dug up and everyone would know she was nothing but white trash, just like her father and her wretched brother. This could not happen. She'd worked too hard and climbed too far. Her family—Monty and Walker—were under attack. She was under attack. She would do what had to be done. Bury it. Bury her past. And since Eli was evidence of her past, then bury his memory.

Ten minutes later, after having burned the letter and flushed the ashes down the toilet, Rose was on her way to the post office with the envelope in her purse. She had to find Hank Barstow. Hank had been delivering the mail in the area for as long as anyone could remember. Although he now ran the local branch, he still liked to drive his routes and deliver the mail occasionally and Rose and Monty were on his route. Hank's wife, Ethel, was in Rose's Adult Bible Study class at church. Surely, Hank would listen.

When she drove into the post office parking lot, she saw Hank getting out of his truck, gunned it, and pulled up next to him.

"Hank, can I have a word?" she asked.

"Of course, Rose. How are you?"

"I'm just fine. And you? How is Ethel? I missed her last Sunday in class."

"Oh, I'm just fine. Ethel too. She was in Columbia fetching her mother. The poor soul can't drive anymore, and Ethel picked her up and brought her to our place. She's visiting through the holidays, and last Sunday was the only time Ethel could get away. She commented how she hated missin' your teachin'."

"Well, that is sweet of her to say. Please give her my best."

"I'll be sure to. Now, how can I help you today?"

"Hank, it's about this letter," she said, holding up the envelope for him to see.

Chapter 36

Through Thick and Through Thin

At Monty's office, Thursday, September 7th, 1978

On Thursday, Monty woke in a fine mood. Sharp and rested. A couple of uninterrupted weeks in the office relaxed him; feeling productive always did. But he was growing anxious again knowing the FBI would report the results within the week. If these new forensics tests were all Edmond Locard had said they were, then any day now he would have what he needed to call Eli home.

Monty was drafting an engagement letter to new clients when Abigail reminded him of his meeting with Mr. Hank Barstow and that Hank asked if they could meet at the post office.

"For goodness sakes, I almost forgot. What would I do without you, Abigail?"

"The wheels of progress would grind to a halt, no doubt. Will you be coming back to the office after your meeting?"

"I was thinking of sneaking off to the driving range this afternoon, maybe playing a quick nine. Would I be missed?"

"In ways I can't explain, but we'll survive."

"Thanks, Abigail."

Monty grabbed his briefcase and car keys and headed toward the front door. Sometimes he couldn't tell when Abigail was pulling his leg.

* * *

Monty entered the post office around 11:30. There were a few people in line, so when Hank Barstow saw Monty enter, he waved him around to the side. Hank bent over and spoke to a younger man sitting at the desk. The man took Hank's place at the counter, and Hank walked over to a swinging gate where Monty was waiting.

Monty stepped through the swinging gate and waited for Hank as he grabbed a stack of mail. Hank was flipping through the mail as he walked down the hall, Monty right behind him, commenting aimlessly about the weather, when he stopped and held a letter up to get a closer look.

"Well, I thought we'd seen the last of these," said Hank.

"What was that?" remarked Monty.

"The letters your wife asked me to return to sender. Just got another one."

Hank looked at Monty and Monty at Hank as each realized that Monty had no idea what Hank was talking about.

"Can I see that letter?" asked Monty.

"Sure."

Monty took the letter and opened it. The penmanship was crude and menacing. As he read the letter, Monty's world was flipped upside down.

> Rose, it's been a while. But don't think I don't know you've been thinking about me. I've been in the news, and I suspect you put two and two together and figured it was me. I told you I wasn't going to stop. Kimberly was just the first, well the first I told you about, that is. And just think—you coulda' put a stop to all of it. Many of those girls would be alive today, and who knows where I'd be ... probably strapped to old sparky by now. But I knew you was proud ... too proud to go to the police. And now you're knee-deep in pig shit. You got too much invested, don't you? And just think what people would say all these years later if you was to go to the police? Oh my. No sir, that ain't happenin', is it? Well, I'll be signing off now. Just remember—every time I rape and kill, you deserve some of the credit.

Monty didn't make it to the golf course that afternoon.

"Monty, you okay? Do you need to sit down?" asked Hank.

"Hank, when did you get the first letter?" asked Monty.

"Well, I don't remember exactly, but I'd say it was about five years ago."

"Oh, good Lord," muttered Monty. Monty did the math in his head and realized that the man who wrote the letter he was holding had first mailed his wife Rose a letter approximately six months after he had killed Kimberly Prestwick.

"And you say my wife asked you to return these letters to the sender?"

"That's right," said Hank.

"But there's no return address on this envelope. Did the others have a return address?" asked Monty.

"No. They didn't. I tried to explain that to your wife, but she was set on me not ever delivering these letters to her."

"But how would you know? How would you know if all the letters were all from the same person?"

"Well, it was rather easy to tell. The envelopes were all standard business envelopes for one, and the handwriting is somewhat identifiable. But the real tipoff was what he'd write on the back of the envelope. In the bottom of the right corner, he'd write something curious like 'Miss me?' or 'Maybe I'll pay you a visit.'"

"If you couldn't return them, Hank, what did you do with them?"

Hank looked a bit sheepish and stared at the ground in the hope his shoes held the answer.

"Monty, I know it's against the law to tamper with the mail, but I know your wife and what she's been through. My wife, Ethel, goes on about what a wonderful Sunday school teacher your wife is, and Rose was so upset when I attempted delivery of the first few letters. Well, I didn't know what to do, so I just kept them. I put them in a place where no one would find them. I call it my private 'dead-letter drawer.' I didn't feel right throwing them away."

"Hank, are you telling me you still have them?"

"Yes, sir, that's what I'm saying."

"Hank, I'd be obliged if you'd give them to me."

"Well, I don't know. They're not addressed to you."

"No, but they are addressed to the home I own."

Hank paused for a moment before commenting. "Yes, sir, they are. Would you like me to run and fetch them?"

"Yes, Hank, I would."

"All right, then. You know, I'll feel better having them out of the office. What should I do if I get more of them letters?"

"Just give them to me, Hank. Just give them to me."

Monty stared out the window as he waited for Hank to return with a stack of letters addressed to his wife by the man who had committed the crime their son Eli had been charged with.

* * *

After leaving the post office with the stack of letters, Monty walked to a corner coffee shop and read every one. Each letter was a window into the mind of a deranged killer. So focused was his hatred of women that Monty couldn't fathom what had drawn Rose to him.

When Monty met Rose, she was married to a deadbeat named Rathbone Cummings, pregnant with Eli, and trying to hide the bruise on her face from where Rath had struck her. At first, Monty provided stability and a shoulder to cry on, but before too long they fell in love. Rose divorced Rath who put up no objection. It wasn't long before Monty asked Rose to marry him. But in a bid to reject any help from a man, she said no and moved to Atlanta with Eli, who was still just an infant. Monty was patient, though, and wrote her and visited her in Atlanta. His patience paid off and they were ultimately married, and they went on to have a son of their own, Walker.

All those years ago, even after Monty rescued Rose from the depths of her depression, Rath was a fixture in their lives, lingering on the periphery, always there, as Eli's father. Rose's insistence that Rath's name never be mentioned in their house failed to banish him from their lives. Rose demanded perfection from Eli as proof that she wasn't like the white trash that had fathered her or her firstborn. But the early years in Atlanta when Rose and Eli were living in squalor and Eli was being passed from one caregiver to another, combined with Rose's unrelenting demands upon Eli as he grew older, took their toll on Eli. There was no way Eli could live up to Rose's expectations. Every cry, every lashing out on Eli's part, was proof to Rose that she'd never be free of Rath.

And now these letters. She'd read the first one, that much Monty knew. That was damning enough. *Had Rath admitted to killing Kimberly in that letter*, Monty wondered. *Probably*, he thought. In the letters Monty read, Rath admitted to killing Kimberly and boasted he had killed others. Did Rose know he continued to send letters? Many of the letters detailed the time, place, and method of other gruesome crimes. What was he to do? If he took them to the police, they'd have to reopen the case and drop all charges against Eli. But then the truth of what Rose had done would come out. Everyone would know she had allowed her son to take the fall for the crimes of rape and murder. And why? Because she was too proud? Yes. She couldn't stand people speaking ill of her. And this is the woman he'd vowed to stay married to, through thick and through thin. "*What am I supposed to do now*?" he thought.

Monty knew bits and pieces of Rose's childhood, of her upbringing. In a rare moment of complete honesty and humility early in their marriage, Rose told Monty what her brother had done, and that her father had laughed it off. She told him of the things her father had said. "Beulah, she's your daughter. I got no time for her."

Monty hadn't known what to say or do, so he had just held her, held her tight. He knew she carried baggage. To have been raped by her own brother. Horrifying. Monty was left with the distinct impression it happened more than once. And for her father to have known and done nothing? It explained so much.

And then she met Rath. Monty couldn't understand why Rose had been attracted to a man like her father, a man she hated with every fiber. Monty was no psychiatrist, but perversely, maybe it made sense. Rose wanted her father's love, so she was attracted to a man just like him, seeking his approval, his love.

No, Monty hadn't known what to say to Rose that night, but he promised himself that he'd do everything he could to love her and to make her feel loved. Rose had never known a man who simply loved her. Well, Monty would be that man.

But this newest revelation was more than he could bear. After seeking solace and advice from his good friend Chester Baslin, Monty drove home that night with a plan to draw Rath out into the open and kill him, but first he'd confront Rose with the truth.

And in an encounter that could only be described as fueled by the Holy Spirit, Monty broke through and freed Rose from the hold Satan had on her. And afterwards, sitting on the floor, exhausted and staring into each other's tear-stained faces, they took joy in the intimacy of conversation. The first conversation in some time in which each felt at ease, perfectly aware, and at peace with the other's fears, pains, hopes, and dreams. And they dreamt, and they planned, and they stood up recommitted to the other and to doing whatever they had to do to save their family.

CHAPTER 37

A Simple Plan

FRIDAY, SEPTEMBER 8TH

Monty and Rose's plan was simple and straightforward, though fraught with risk. They were going to show Rath's letters to the police and insist that they drop all charges against Eli. They would then ask that Chief Crandall announce Eli's innocence in a press conference in the hope Eli would hear it and come home. There was a real possibility the police would charge Rose with obstruction of justice, but they were content to let the chips fall where they may and trust in the Lord. They would of course hire Chester as their attorney and have him negotiate on their behalf. Chester was holding Rath's letters in his office vault. Monty gave them to him after they met the day Hank gave the letters to Monty and before Monty confronted Rose.

Monty quickly changed his mind the following morning when he arrived at work and saw that Laz had called and left a message. Monty returned the call and listened to Laz report that the FBI, based upon the lab results, believed that whoever killed Kimberly was also responsible for multiple murders around the southeast over a fifteen-year span meaning that there was no way Eli was guilty.

Monty was overjoyed and tried to convince Rose they didn't need to give the police the letters and that the FBI lab results would be enough for the Charleston Police Department to drop charges against Eli. Rose feared they were trying to control and manage the situation too much. She was ready to turn over the letters and to trust the Lord. But she consented, and Rose and Monty asked Chief Crandall to drop all charges against Eli on the strength of the FBI lab results. He was reluctant to, but when Kimberly's mother asked that he reopen the case, he agreed to that, and on September 13th, a press conference was held. And it was indeed heard far and wide.

* * *

DOTHAN, ALABAMA

The sign outside read 'Mickey's Bar and Grill' but there wasn't a grill, and the owner wasn't named Mickey, but the patrons couldn't have cared less because there was a bar, and the bar served their favorites—cheap beer, cheap liquor, free bowls of nuts, and there was a cigarette machine in the hallway you passed on the way to the single bathroom. The black-and-white TV above the bar was the only connection to the outside world, for the men inside had tuned out long ago.

Joe, the bartender, was going over the bills of lading from that morning's delivery when a man walked in he didn't recognize. New faces at Mickey's were a rare sight. The stranger moved slowly down the bar to the end farthest from the entrance and took a seat, like he'd been entering establishments such as Mickey's his whole life. Joe walked over to wipe the countertop in front of him.

"What can I get ya?"

"Bring me what ya got on tap, as long as it's cold," said the stranger.

Joe walked away and returned with a cold beer, well, as cold as one could expect at Mickey's, and then retreated to the other end of the bar and tried to look busy. Joe didn't like the look of the man. He was lean and cut and wore a dirty tank top, two sizes too small. His worn blue jeans were pulled down over unpolished, pointed-toe cowboy boots. His long, sinewy arms were covered in tattoos, and he hadn't shaved or showered in days. Unkempt greasy hair, hidden by a baseball cap, hung over his collar. But his eyes were alert, moving from side to side, taking in his surroundings, not as someone curious about the world around him, but as a predator. Yep, there was something about him that gave Joe the creeps.

"Hey, buddy, could you turn it up?"

Joe barely glanced his way.

"The TV. Turn it up!" he demanded.

"Hey, did you hear me? I said, turn up the damn TV and bring me some more nuts while you're at it."

Joe returned the mug to the shelf below, reached for the TV, and turned up the volume before walking a bowl of nuts down to the man. He then returned to the other end of the bar.

"Was that so hard?" asked the man as he plunged his grimy fingers into the bowl, licking them clean before plunging them into the bowl again, never taking his eyes off the TV.

He sat on his stool, enthralled by what he was hearing. *I'm a celebrity,* he thought as he watched the woman on the TV talk about him. *They're calling me the Louisville Slugger.* He looked around the bar to see if anyone else was paying attention. They were not. *Losers. All of them. Worthless losers,* he thought. *I'm a fucking god.*

His attention was drawn back to the television.

"And now we're going live to a press conference from the police department in Charleston, South Carolina," announced the local TV anchor.

> Standing behind me today are two courageous women, Gloria Cunningham, the mother of Kimberly Prestwick who was brutally murdered over five years ago, and Rose Atkins, the mother of Eli Atkins, the young man accused of the murder. I'm here today to announce that, in cooperation with the FBI, we are taking a fresh look at the case. New evidence has come to light that casts real doubt on whether Eli Atkins was the murderer. This new evidence also implicates a man at large who may be responsible for multiple murders in the southeastern United States. I want to thank Monty and Rose Atkins for their role in bringing this evidence to our attention and to Gloria Cunningham for her support. In my discussions with Ms. Cunningham, she was adamant that the true killer be found. Thank you for coming. That will be all.

"What the fuck!" he muttered. "New evidence? What's that bitch up to?" he said to no one. Joe registered alarm and moved further away.

He bowed his head in pain. Like nails piercing his temples, a blinding light burned the back of his sockets as he buried the heels of his hands into his shut eyelids. She wouldn't dare, he thought. No, she's too fucking proud. The letters.

He knew she'd never tell anyone. Too afraid folks would figure out she was nothing but trash. Fucked by her brother. Daddy too. So why now? After all these years?

"She thought she was too good for me. Ends up with that faggot of a husband. No one is too good for me," he pronounced to himself.

"I've let you alone long enough, Rose darlin'. I'm coming home. It's what you wanted, ain't it?"

He threw a few bills down on the bar, grabbed his jacket, and slinked out the front door like a cat, his head still pounding and only one way to ease the pain.

* * *

After the Press Conference, Mrs. Babcock asked Chief Riddle if he was ready to drop the warrant for Eli's arrest. He told her he was too busy to deal with the formality at the time and that he preferred to do so once they had identified the new suspect and issued a new warrant.

But the press conference was all she needed, and she felt it was time to tell Eli what was happening. She penned a letter to Eli and handed it to Quaid at church the following Sunday along with a collection of stories about the renewed investigation into Kimberly's murder and the hunt for a serial killer. Quaid delivered the letter to Nigel Pinder later that week inside a larger envelope of business correspondence. Two weeks after the press conference, Eli Atkins, aka Aaron Westfield, was boarding a boat for his return home.

With the press conference behind them, the final question for Rose and Monty was what to do with the letters. Monty wanted to keep them hidden and protect Rose from the inevitable backlash were it ever discovered that she had known who the killer was from the beginning. Rose, on the other hand, was resolved to her role. In the end, they reached a compromise.

Monty would mail the police department an anonymous letter identifying Rath as the killer. They would include a picture of Rath in the envelope that Rose had cut from an album from her days at the University of Alabama. Fearful that a keen detective could probably link it all back to Rose, Monty suggested they mail the letter from a neighboring town.

So, on Monday, October 2nd, 1978, when Eli and Captain Bootle were resting on Abaco Island, Monty was driving to Savannah to mail proof to the Charleston Police Department that Rathbone Cummings was Kimberly's killer.

Chapter 38

Hell Comes to Town

Monday, October 2nd, 1978

Ever since the press conference nearly three weeks ago, the police department had been abuzz with activity. It wasn't just that Kimberly's case had been reopened, the police now believed her killer was wanted for an untold number of other murders as well. Consequently, Chief Crandall was in regular communication with the FBI and other police departments in the Southeast, all taking fresh looks at their cold cases.

And with the FBI's involvement, the inevitable turf wars between the Bureau and local police departments surfaced. Chief Crandall, determined to avoid these pointless power plays, encouraged everyone to coordinate with the folks from Quantico. For him, it was simple: they had resources and expertise in forensics his department simply didn't have.

Unfortunately, Monty and Rose's goal of drawing Rath out of hiding worked too well. Police departments in the Southeast were now on alert for any evidence of a predator working their communities and were in communication with the FBI. The bodies of two young girls, recently deceased, had been found by police officers in Albany and Vidalia, Georgia. The crime scenes were gruesome and similar, and you could draw a straight line from Albany to Vidalia to Charleston. Rath was on his way.

That straight line ended at a Winn Dixie outside of Charleston. There, Rath was lying in wait for Rose and her son Walker while Monty, having returned from his trip to Savannah, was hitting golf balls on the driving range at Wappoo Country Club.

Monty finished his session on the driving range and headed home, pulling into the driveway a little before 7:00, as the sun was setting. When he walked inside, he was struck by the silence. It was quiet. Too quiet. Not the quiet of a house when no one was home, but the kind of quiet when something was wrong.

"Rose? Walker? Anybody home?"

He checked the garage. Empty. He searched the kitchen for a note. Anything. Again, nothing. And then he saw it through the kitchen window. A cat nailed with a railroad spike to the post supporting a corner of the porch. He approached the cat, a wad of paper spilling out of its mouth. Removing the wad of paper, he read the note.

"Monty, I'm looking forward to seeing you again. It's been too long. We have so much in common. For one, there's Rose. Two, she's the mother of our boys. Of course, my boy, Eli, was taken from me. And now, I've taken yours. I'll be in touch.

"Call the cops, and I return your boy and our wife, Rosebud, in little bitty pieces."

"What have I done?" said Monty to the empty porch.

* * *

ON THE ATLANTIC OCEAN, THAT SAME NIGHT

Visibility was good; there wasn't a cloud in the sky and the moon shone brightly. Eli and Captain Bootle finished dinner, double-checked their headings, and settled in for the evening. Eli would man the helm first while Captain got some rest.

"Forty-eight hours to go, mon. The weather looks good. You'll be home soon enough."

Eli nodded but didn't answer.

Forty-eight hours, he thought.

Chapter 39

A Moses Basket and Damaged Goods

Wednesday, October 4th

"Charleston Police Department, may I help you?" said Charlene.

"Good morning, Charlene. This is Amy. Is my mother available?'

"Amy, it's so nice to hear your voice. We missed you at the PTA meeting last week. Is everything all right?"

"Oh, yes. Just fine. I was a little under the weather, that's all."

"Well, bless your little heart. Good to hear you're back on your feet. And yes, your mama is here. The last I saw of her she was in the break room talking with a few of the new recruits. You know we all just love her so. I don't know what Chief Crandall would do without her. Can I put you on hold and I'll go fetch her?

"Why yes, thank you," said Amy.

Charlene rose from behind the front desk and strolled down the hall and stuck her head into the break room. "Mrs. Babcock? Your daughter Amy is on the line waiting for you. Shall I transfer the call to your desk?

"Yes, child. Tell her I'll be right there."

Mrs. Babcock turned back to the attentive, young new recruits. "So, as I was saying, if any of you boys have any questions as to how things are done around here, you just come see Mrs. Babcock."

"Yes, ma'am," they said in unison, their heads nodding respectfully.

Mrs. Babcock waddled back to her desk positioned just outside the chief's office.

"Mrs. Babcock's office. How can I help you?" she said.

"Hello, Mom."

"Amy, dear, is everything okay, sweetheart?"

"Yes, Mom. I just wanted to let you know that it would just be me and Francesco for dinner tomorrow night. The kids won't make it."

"Oh dear. I was so hoping to see them."

"I know, Mama. Maybe next time. But I think it's best."

"Oh?"

"Yes. I'll be bringing a Moses basket with me that could use a little tending to. Do you think you could help mend it?"

"But of course. I'll see y'all at supper." Mrs. Babcock beamed ear to ear as she hung up the phone. *He's back,* she thought to herself.

* * *

Monty Atkins' office

Tuesday had been a hellish eternity for Monty as he waited for word from Rath. He hadn't gone to the police, nor had he told anyone. He was exhausted from lack of sleep and couldn't eat. His waiting ended on Wednesday when he received a short letter at the office marked confidential.

Be patient now, Monty, and be on the lookout for a package.

* * *

Thursday, October 5th, back at the Charleston Police Department

Mrs. Babcock could hardly contain herself she was so excited. She was the one who had dreamed up the idea of using the phrase "Moses basket" whenever they had news about Eli to discuss. "No one will suspect anything," she'd told Quaid. Quaid chuckled when she first mentioned it and took to calling her Miss Moneypenny. Moses baskets are made from bulrush, a locally harvested marshgrass, by descendants of African slaves brought to Charleston beginning in the late sixteenth century. Though Mrs. Babcock didn't know how to repair these baskets, the message was clear—Eli was coming to dinner, and he wasn't well.

Despite the heightened tension and activity level in the office, Thursday crept by for Mrs. Babcock. Though the FBI was lending a hand, everyone was busy and working overtime, and that included Mrs. Babcock. Chief Crandall needed something for her to do that appeared important but wasn't too taxing. She was over eighty years old, for Pete's sake. What could he expect?

He was wrong. He could expect a lot. She was as committed and driven as anyone, and she stayed on top of the latest news, rumors, and developments in the case. In fact, because he could always count on her for the latest update, the chief included her in all office meetings.

But as for official duties, he let her continue to handle his mail and gave her the heightened responsibility of handling the entire department's mail. Charlene at the front desk was happy for the help. The phone hadn't stopped ringing since the press conference, and at eight months pregnant, nature would soon demand her full attention. It was best the office began delegating her duties until a replacement could be hired.

Since the press conference, the Police Department received two to three times as much mail as usual. Everyone had a theory or something to add or a citing perhaps. There was so much mail that the post office now waited until late in the day to deliver it. Well, that didn't leave Mrs. Babcock sufficient time to perform her duties. She took matters into her own hands and called Hank Barstow directly. Mrs. Babcock explained her challenge and Hank suggested they deliver the mail twice a day—once early in the morning and again right after lunch. Mrs. Babcock thought that was a fine idea.

Mrs. Babcock engineered her own method of sorting and delivering the mail. Twice a day, the mailman would leave the mail in large plastic bins on top of the rolling cart behind Charlene's desk at the front of the office. Mrs. Babcock would wheel the cart into the conference room and sort mail into stacks according to which department or person it was addressed to. If the envelope bore no specific "attention to" address, she would open it herself and determine who should get it. She would then secure each stack with a rubber band, place them back into the bins on top of the rolling cart, and then roll the cart around the office to deliver each stack.

While she was proficient at sorting the mail, when it came to delivering it, due to her propensity to engage every officer in small talk, gossip, and general chitchat, a task that could be completed in ten minutes took closer to forty-five. Given recent events, and her perceived duty to know everything about the investigation into the serial killer's identity, the morning's mail delivery sometimes occupied her until the post office dropped off the afternoon batch.

But this afternoon was different. Mrs. Babcock had a skip in her step and spent far less time tongue-waggin' with folks in the office. If anyone had noticed, they'd have seen her repeatedly check the clock on the wall. Though she routinely stayed till 5:00 or later, by 4:30, and upon successfully delivering all the day's mail, she felt it was okay if she left early.

So, she stuck her head into Chief Crandall's office, where he was busy reviewing the day's progress with Officers Pearlman and Tyrell.

"Hey, boss. My daughter Amy and her husband Francesco are coming over for supper tonight. Mind if I skedaddle a little early today?" she asked.

"No, Mrs. Babcock, not at all. Have a good night."

"Thanks, boss." And she grabbed her gargantuan purse off her desk, filled with Lord knows what, and headed for the front door.

As she was shuffling down the hall and out of earshot, Officer Tyrell commented: "I don't know what I'd do if I ever came to the office and found someone else sittin' outside your office, Chief."

Smiling, Chief Crandall answered: "I don't think you have to worry about that. I'm beginning to think she'll outlive us all."

As Mrs. Babcock quickly shuffled past the front desk, Charlene called out. "Mrs. Babcock?"

"Yes, dear."

"Here's an envelope from the afternoon mail delivery. It must have slid off the top of the bin onto the floor," said Charlene.

Mrs. Babcock returned to the front counter, took the envelope from Charlene's hand, and noticed that it was addressed generically to the "Police Department."

"Thank you, Charlene. I'll have to open it to find out who should receive it. I'll look at it first thing tomorrow morning," she said as she slipped the envelope into her purse.

"Is Amy joining you for dinner?" asked Charlene.

"Yes, and her husband, Francesco," said a proud Mrs. Babcock. *And Eli Atkins,* she thought to herself.

* * *

By the time Mrs. Babcock pulled into her garage, it was after 6:00. The stop at the supermarket took longer than she'd planned. She'd been held up in the parking lot by Mrs. Brooks, a woman notorious for going on and on about near anything. But she'd lost her husband recently to lung cancer, lifelong smoker he was, so Mrs. Babcock gave her all the time she needed. But the hitch in her plans meant there would be less time to prep for dinner.

By 6:45, Amy pulled into the driveway in the family station wagon. Amy was forty-eight and fighting her weight. She'd recently taken up jogging, it was the latest craze, and she could often be seen running around her neighborhood in pink sweatpants and matching shirt and a pair of Adidas. Tonight, she was wearing flared jeans, a dark green cotton blouse, and earth shoes.

Mrs. Babcock met her at the door and Amy, carrying a bag of groceries in her left arm, bent over to give her mom a kiss on the cheek.

"Where's Francesco? And, is ... is Eli here? Is he back in Charleston?"

"Yes, Mama. They'll be here, but we felt it best if we split up and not all travel together by car. It's been five years, but were we stopped for any reason, there's still a good chance Eli would be recognized. They'll be coming up the river after sunset."

"Good thinkin', honey. So why don't we get started on dinner?

* * *

Mrs. Babcock and her daughter, Amy, had finished prepping dinner and were sitting on the porch overlooking the river. Francesco would fire up the grill once he arrived. Amy was trying to occupy her mom with talk about the kids, but it was obvious her mother's mind was elsewhere.

"Mama, he's going to be okay."

Mrs. Babcock was rocking in her chair, a glass of Madeira clasped between her two hands. "You know, he ran because of me. It was my idea. I've worried and prayed since the day he left that I did right by him."

"Mama, you did what you thought was best. You saw a risk to him standing trial on account of his mother."

"Yes, that's true. A wickedness had overtaken her. But still, I've worried so. But you say he's going to be okay?"

"Yes. He's scared, but he won't let on to it. And Mama, he's a man now. Twenty-three years old. He's not the young boy who left us. But there's still a lot of pain about why he had to leave. About what his mother did to him. At least that's what Francesco thinks. They had some time together on the drive up here from Beaufort. Francesco believes Eli blames his mother for crushing his dreams of playin' professional baseball."

"Why, there's still time. He's only twenty-three. That's young."

About then, they both turned their heads toward the water and a small skip coming around the bend came into their vision. Francesco was manning the till, and a young man whom Mrs. Babcock wondered if she'd ever see again sat toward the bow of the boat.

* * *

That same evening, sixty miles north as the crow flies, in a shack somewhere in Hell Hole Swamp west of McClellanville, South Carolina

Rathbone Cummings, aka "Rath," a purely evil being possessing a hardened heart and lacking in any capacity for empathy for another human being, stomped around the cabin, snorting like a pig in heat. *She's supposed to fear me, but she don't,* thought Rath. *The others always did.*

"Rath, I know I should pray for you, but I can't, and I'm okay with that," said Rose.

"Pray for me? Bitch, you should be praying for yourself and your boy here," said Rath.

"You can't touch us. You can't take anything away from us because what we have has been paid for," said Rose.

"What do you have, Rosebud, that I can't take?" snarled Rath.

"Salvation and the knowledge that I'm loved, Rath."

The back of Rath's hand was a blur as it crashed into the side of her face, nearly knocking her over in the chair. Rose lifted her head high.

"You'll never get away with this," said Rose.

Rath paced the room furiously, snorting again. After a minute, his breathing slowed, he tried to regain control of the situation.

"Walker, your mama here thinks I'm gonna get caught. What do you think, boy?" asked Rath.

"Leave him alone," she demanded.

"I'm talkin' to you, boy. Do you think I'll get away with it?"

"He doesn't know what you've done," said Rose. "How do you expect him to answer? Tell him. Tell him what you've done. Kimberly wasn't the first girl you killed, was she, Rath?"

"Nope. Not by a far stretch."

"How many others were there?" asked Rose.

"Shut up, Rose. None of your goddamned business," yelled Rath.

"Yeah, I thought so. There weren't any others, were there? You're all talk, Rath," said Rose mockingly.

Rath walked over to Rose and leaned down until they were eye to eye. "You want details, Rose? Will that get you off? Fine, details it is." And then, turning back to Walker, he named every victim over the last twenty years, providing gruesome descriptions of the murders and the locations of their bodies.

"So Walker, my boy, what do you think now that you know a bit more about me? Hmm? Will I get away with it?" asked Rath.

"No," Walker answered. "You'll burn in hell."

Rath strutted around the shack like that was the funniest thing he'd ever heard.

"Well, on that, I do agree. Now say goodbye to your mama, 'cause you and I got a date with your dad."

"No, Rath, please. Take me. Leave Monty and Walker alone."

"Rose, honey, don't you worry. I'm gonna take you. But you'll have to wait 'cause Walker and I are off to rendezvous with the man you left me for."

Walker would never forget the sound of his mother screaming when Rath dragged him out of the shack, hands and feet tied behind his back.

Chapter 40

A World of Thanks

Thursday evening, October 5th,
the back porch of Mrs. Babcock's house

Francesco was tending to the grill and was drinking a beer when his wife, Amy, walked from the kitchen out onto the back porch, drying her hands on a dishrag.

"They look good," she said as she peered over the grill. "How much longer?"

"Maybe another ten minutes."

"I'm hungry and a good steak should hit the spot. Your idea?"

"No. Eli's. I asked Eli if there was anything he wanted for dinner on his first real meal back home in the States, and you know what he said?" asked Francesco.

Amy shrugged.

He said: "Who says I'm home? But since you're asking, I could go for a thick steak."

"Oh dear. This is going to be hard for him, isn't it?

"I'm afraid so. When I picked him up in our boat, he seemed okay, you know, happy to see me. But that was late Wednesday night, and he may have just been really tired from his trip. He spent the night in the back of our bait and tackle shop in Beaufort and I stayed at our house. I invited him to stay at our place, but he said it seemed right that he re-enter the country the same way he left. He laughed when he said it. The next morning when I picked him up, it was like he was a different person. He was surly and angry, and on the drive back to Charleston he seemed to get angrier with each passing mile."

Francesco picked up the tongs and flipped the steaks. Amy, standing at his side, cast her eyes in Eli's direction. He was at the bottom of the stairs at the end of the porch sitting in a chair across from Mrs. Babcock. He was hunched over, his elbows on his knees and his forehead resting in his hands. Mrs. Babcock was sitting on the end of her chair, her hands folded in her lap, fingers interlaced, gently talking to him. Occasionally he would look up at her and nod.

"What do you think they're talking about?" Amy asked.

"I don't know. She's your mom. What do you think?"

"I don't know, but it seems right."

"What does?"

"The two of them. It's like they each need the other right now."

"I'm not sure I follow you, but from the looks of these steaks, we need to eat. Do you want to call them up while I take care of these?" asked Francesco as he pointed to a plate full of thick steaks.

Amy nodded yes.

* * *

Whatever Mrs. Babcock had said to Eli before dinner must have affected him because he was relaxed and seemed at peace during dinner and not at all what Amy expected given Francesco's earlier assessment. Eli answered their questions about life in the Bahamas, and he regaled them with a few stories. It was a delightful evening, and everyone ignored the elephant in the room, meaning the reopened investigation into Kimberly's murder.

"Mama, that was wonderful. Thank you."

"Don't thank me. You and Francesco did most of the work."

"I'll clean up," said Eli. "I didn't do a thing but eat and have seconds."

"Well let me help you. It'll be quicker, and Amy and I need to get moving. I can't believe how late it got," said Francesco.

"Francesco, dear, Eli's going to stay out here for a few days," said Mrs. Babcock. "It will be safer for all concerned. I figure no one will get in trouble if it's me that breaks the news to the chief that this here known fugitive is staying at my place."

Eli smiled at her remark.

"Besides, what are the police going to do to little old me? No, it's better he stay here, just until the coast is clear."

"All right, Mama. Whatever you say."

The four of them rose and took their plates into the kitchen. As Francesco and Amy began to clear their plates, Mrs. Babcock shooed them toward the door.

"Hold on a minute, please," said Eli.

Amy had picked up her purse and Francesco was fishing his keys out of his pocket and they both turned to face Eli.

"Francesco, in the car ride yesterday, I was angry. Very angry. I still am, but I know I need to deal with it," said Eli as he glanced at Mrs. Babcock. "But I want you to know that I was not angry at you. Far from it. I owe each of you my life. I want to thank you for what you've done. When I left five years ago ... Good grief, five years ago," he said, shaking his head. "It's all such a blur. Anyway, I didn't properly thank you then. Well, I'm doing it now. I know each of you put your own safety and well-being in harm's way to help me and you didn't have to. If you hadn't, I would probably be in jail today or possibly dead. I just want you to know how much I appreciate each one of you."

Amy was crying, Francesco looked at Eli as the man he had become, and Mrs. Babcock beamed like a proud mother.

Chapter 41

A World Turned Upside Down

Friday morning, October 6th

When Mrs. Babcock rose the next morning, Eli was already up and sitting on the back porch with a cup of coffee and reading a book.

"I hope you don't mind," said Eli. "I grabbed this book off your shelf in the living room."

"Not at all. What did you pick?"

"*And Then There Were None.*"

"Agatha Christie! Oh, she's my favorite."

"She must be. You have an entire shelf in there dedicated to her."

"I believe I do."

"How many books did she write?"

"Oh goodness. I don't rightly know. Over sixty for sure."

"I'm not sure I've read that many books in my life."

"Well, you're young. Plenty of time ahead of you. And I can't think of a better way for you to spend your day than reading that book. How about tonight at dinner you tell me who you think the murderer is?"

Eli flipped through the pages, sizing up how much he had left to read. "Okay. I can do that."

"Good. Now I have to run and get to the office. I'm going to corner the chief and see what it's going to take for you to leave this house."

"Can't I just stay here?"

"No. Eli, you can't. You're going to have to face her eventually."

"I know. Maybe we can start with me seeing Walker first and then my dad."

"That sounds like a fine idea," said Mrs. Babcock. She walked over and gave him a kiss on the forehead and then quickly headed for the door. Before she made even a few steps down the walkway, she turned and scootched back into the kitchen and reached across the table for her gargantuan purse.

* * *

LATER THAT MORNING AT MONTY ATKINS' LAW OFFICES

Abigail Baker, Monty's loyal administrative assistant, was worried about Monty. Something was up, that was clear. But what? He'd looked ill on Tuesday morning, and when asked about it, he told Abigail that the dinner Rose had cooked the night before, fried oysters, hadn't sat well and that he had been up all night. Of course, Monty was lying, but he could hardly tell her the truth. *Well, Abigail, you see, a madman named Rath, Rose's first husband, kidnapped Rose and my son Walker and is holding them hostage. And to make matters worse, he's a deranged killer. In fact, he killed Kimberly Prestwick. You remember her, don't you? She was dating our other son, Eli, and he was arrested for the murder and then fled the state, never to be seen again.* No, he couldn't tell her the truth.

"Are you heading out for the day?" asked Abigail.

"Hm?"

"Monty, I asked if you are heading out for the day. You look distracted."

Monty hadn't heard a word she had said, oblivious to her presence.

"Abigail, I'm headin' to lunch early today, then dropping by the post office. I need to follow up with Hank on a few matters," said Monty. Monty needed an excuse to pick up any package deliveries as soon as possible.

"Hank Barstow? We're working for him?" asked Abigail.

"Well, yes, Abigail. I thought you knew."

"It's just that you never recorded any time after your last meeting. I noticed when I prepared the bills."

"I haven't gotten around to it. And I may not. Hank's not well off. Thinks he is. Thinks he may own a gold mine," chuckled Monty. "Right now, I'm just helpin' out a little."

"You're the boss. What time should I expect you back? You know, in case any paying clients want to know," asked Abigail.

Monty collected a few things from his desk and reached for his jacket.

"Monty? Hello, Monty. What time should I say you'll be back?"

Heading out the door, his mind clearly elsewhere, he answered, "I don't know. Today. Tomorrow. Don't know."

Abigail, holding a stack of files, watched him walk down the hall. *Something's wrong,* she thought.

* * *

"Next," announced the man behind the post office counter.

"Is Hank Barstow in?" asked Monty.

"No. But he should be back soon if you want to take a seat over there," explained the young man.

"How long until he'll be back?"

"Ten minutes, maybe?"

"Okay. I'll wait."

"He usually comes through the back door. I'll put a note on his desk. Who should I say is asking for him?"

"Monty Atkins."

"Mr. Atkins? I believe we have a package for you. Hold on a minute."

Monty rose from his chair and quickly approached the counter. The man disappeared into the back room, then returned shortly with a small package wrapped in brown kraft paper.

"If you want to sign right here," said the man as he presented Monty with a clipboard and a pen.

"Can you tell me where this package was mailed from?" asked Monty.

Leaning across the counter with his head turned, the young man examined the package and answered, "Looks like it came from the post office in Jamestown."

"Thanks," said Monty as he started toward the door.

"Hey. Ain't you gonna wait for Mr. Barstow?"

* * *

BACK AT MRS. BABCOCK'S HOME

Eli was sitting on Mrs. Babcock's back porch enjoying a spectacular fall morning, or doing the best he could. The book was frustrating. Every time he thought he knew who the killer was in *And Then There Were None*, that person would die. The morning, though, was indeed beautiful. That wasn't the problem. The problem was simply that Eli was a mess.

What was he doing here? Why had he come back? Based upon what Mrs. Babcock had told him last night after Francesco and Amy had left, the police and the FBI now believed that whoever had killed Kimberly had killed numerous other girls in the Southeast. Okay. But there was still a warrant out for his arrest, and until that was dropped, he couldn't resume a normal life. He was beginning to question why he had returned.

And what if the warrant was dropped? Could his life return to normal? What would he tell people when they asked him where he had been and why he had run? What would he say to his mother? Did Dad know? Did Monty know that Rose threatened to testify against him at trial if he didn't run away all those years ago? Did Walker know? And if they didn't know, should he tell them? What would knowing do to their family?

Eli had voiced all these concerns to Mrs. Babcock the night before. Quaid Dawson, Mrs. Babcock, Amy, and Francesco were the only ones who knew what his mother Rose had done. Eli felt at ease speaking with her. She listened and rarely told him what to think or do, which he had always appreciated. But last night, he wanted answers. He wanted her to tell him what to do.

"Eli, I can't tell you what to do," she had said. "But I know what needs to happen."

"And what needs to happen?" he'd asked.

"You'll know."

"Well, if you know, I wish you would tell me, because not knowing is driving me crazy."

"And if I told you and you weren't ready to hear it, what good would that do?"

"I really don't know what you're talkin' about."

"Eli, this is your life. It's not what you planned. It's not what you wanted to happen, but this is your life. This is where you stand. You're all eaten up inside with bitterness about what was taken from you. You keep talking about how your life was taken from you. This bitterness will kill you, Eli. There's nothing you can do about the past other than decide whether it will rule your future. So the question is—what are you going to now?"

"Mrs. Babcock, everything you say makes sense. I get it up here," said Eli, tapping the side of his head with his finger. "But in my heart, in my gut, I can't let go, I can't forget what my mom did. And you're right, it eats at me."

"I know, child, and until you learn how to let go of that bitterness, your heart and your head will never be aligned."

Eli, remembering the conversation, sat still, and turned over in his mind how he could ever forget. How could he stop being bitter about what Rose had done? Was Mrs. Babcock saying he was supposed to forgive his mom? What, and let her off the hook? No way, not a chance. She deserved to suffer for what she did. In Eli's mind if he forgave her, she'd be getting away with it and that he could not allow.

Eli stood from his chair and walked back into the kitchen to refill his coffee cup. He walked over to the counter and noticed there were a few things on the floor across the kitchen. That was where Mrs. Babcock had placed her purse. Eli remembered seeing her fetch it as she hurried out the door. He walked over to pick up the items on the floor, items that must have fallen from her purse. A hairbrush, a tube of lipstick, an Agatha Christie paperback, and an envelope.

Eli placed the items on the kitchen table where she would see them when she got home. As he placed the envelope on the table, something caught his eye. Something familiar. He picked up the envelope and stared at the handwritten address. It was his father's handwriting. He'd know it anywhere. Eli opened the envelope and pulled out a typed memo and a picture of his biological father as a younger man.

The memo was addressed to the Charleston Police Department, and it explained that the man who had killed Kimberly Prestwick was named Rathbone Cummings, aka "Rath," and that he was from Mobile, Alabama and had attended the University of Alabama in 1952-53 but likely never graduated. The memo then provided details about other women Rath had killed over the years beginning with a young woman at the University of Alabama in 1953. The enclosed picture looked like it had been cut from a school annual.

Eli knew he was adopted but hadn't known his father's last name until he was about ten years old. He had been snooping in the attic and found a box hidden in the back. Inside the box he found a few old newspaper clippings. One was a wedding announcement in the *Mobile Daily*: "*Mr. and Mrs. Cummings are proud to announce that their son, Rathbone Cummings, this Saturday will be wedded to Rose Barstol of Muscle Shoals, Alabama, the only daughter of Cleotus Barstol and Beulah Rose Barstol.*"

Eli was reeling. His father, his biological father, had killed Kimberly, and others, and his mother, Rose, and adoptive father, Monty, knew. How did they know about the others? How did they know Rath had killed Kimberly? How long had they known? Eli bolted up from his chair, grabbed his coffee mug, and hurled it at the front door.

* * *

Monty ripped open the package once he was in his car and found Rose's clothes and a note.

"What do you say we have a little family reunion? Tonight. Drive north on Highway 17 past McClellanville until you come to the turnoff for the Santee Coastal Reserve. Go to the Anglers bait and tackle shop and rent a skiff. Head upstream on the Santee River. I'll find you. Come alone. Oh, and bring the letters. If you don't bring the letters, then bring their dental records—you'll need them."

So that was it, thought Monty. He doesn't want money. He wants the letters.

Monty was sitting in his car, and he looked at his watch. Enough time to stop at Chester's office and get the letters and then run by the house for a few things.

"Okay, Rath," said Monty to the inside of his car. "You want me? You want the letters? Fine, you can have me. You can have the letters. But Lord help you if you harm Rose or Walker. I'm prepared to die, Rath. Are you?"

* * *

"Hey, boss, do you have a minute?"

"For you, Mrs. Babcock? Always," answered Chief Crandall.

"I was thinkin' yesterday as I was tidying up some of our records that now that we're all busy looking for a serial killer maybe we should pull the warrant for Eli Atkins' arrest."

"Mrs. Babcock, we'll get around to it. We're all swamped right now, and no one has seen Eli in five years, so I doubt we'll be arresting him anytime soon."

"Well, with all the publicity out there, Eli might have a mind to come home if he knew it was safe."

Chief Crandall was walking around his office gathering files and clearly looking for something he had misplaced as Mrs. Babcock made her case.

"Okay. That makes sense, though how he would hear, I have no idea. But I don't have time to deal with it now. You've been around this office long enough, I bet you can figure it out. Put together the necessary paperwork and I'll sign it."

"Will do, boss."

But first, she had to make a phone call.

* * *

"What the ... Eli, it's me, Quaid."

The coffee mug had shattered against the door frame as Quaid Dawson was about to open the screen door. Quaid walked in and saw an enraged Eli. The veins in his neck bulging, his fists clenched by his side, and he was struggling to control his breathing.

"Eli, what is it? What's wrong?"

"Did you know?" screamed Eli. "DID YOU KNOW?"

"Know what?"

Eli stormed out the back of the house onto the porch, slamming the screen door on his way.

Quaid looked out the door Eli had barged through and then back to the kitchen table, where he noticed the opened envelope and its contents. He picked up the memo and began reading. After finishing the memo, he walked outside.

"Eli, talk to me. What's going on?"

"You read the letter on the kitchen table, right?"

"Yeah, but it doesn't make much sense to me. Where did you get it?"

"I found it on the floor this morning after Mrs. Babcock had left for work. It was in an envelope that fell out of her purse."

"Okay. But it was addressed to the Charleston Police Department. Why did you open it?"

"The handwriting on the envelope ... It's my dad's."

"What? Really? Interesting."

"And the killer mentioned in the letter, Rath?"

"Yeah? What about it?" asked Quaid.

"He's my biological dad."

"Oh, good Lord."

* * *

Monty was finally on the water. "Damn that press conference," he said.

Monty feared that the man at the bait and tackle shop, Francesco he said his name was, had recognized him. Must have seen him on TV at the press conference. How else? Anyway, it had taken too long to rent the boat. The man at the counter had asked too many questions. "You goin' fishin'?" he had asked. "Crappie don't bite this time of year," he said. He suggested catfish, given the hotter water. "Do you need to rent any equipment?"

I should have brought equipment, thought Monty. *Looks suspicious, that's for sure.*

Monty sat with his left hand on the tiller and headed west on the Santee River toward Lake Marion. Despite the weight of his mission, he marveled at the beauty all around him. The sun would be setting in a few hours, bringing a kaleidoscope of colors reflecting off the water and the clumps of green algae scattered across the surface. The sky was alive with the sights and sounds of song sparrows and warblers. His skiff slipped past moss-covered trees rising up from the swamps and grass islands. Alligators slipped off the banks, eyes hovering above the water's edge.

"Lord, forgive me for taking so much of your creation for granted."

* * *

"When I told you that the handwriting on the envelope was my dad's—Monty's, that is—you said that was interesting. What did you mean?" asked Eli.

"Eli, you asked me just a minute ago if I knew. No, I did not know that your biological dad killed Kimberly, but I did know that Monty hired a private investigator to find the real killer. You see, Monty and I are business partners—this is a recent development. As we were putting together our partnership, he told me that he would need to devote energy from time to time to finding Kimberly's killer. When you ran, he hired a private detective to look for you. Well, we did a hell of a job hiding you. So, after a while, he asked his private detective to find the real killer, instead. I'm guessing that his private detective uncovered all of this."

"Why are you just now telling me?" asked Eli. "We saw each other whenever you were in the Bahamas. Why now?"

"Well, I'm just now learning it too. Eli, it tore me up to not be able to tell Monty where you were. He was dying inside. I know this. I've grown close to him. He loves you and wants nothing more than for your safe return. But I couldn't tell him where you were because he did not know Rose had betrayed you. Mrs. Babcock and I were fearful that if he found out where you were, Rose would too and then your cover could have been blown. So, I never told your dad that I knew where you were."

"That had to be tough."

"Oh, it was. But I did reassure your father that if the real killer was caught that I was confident that somehow you'd hear about it and be able to come home. And here you are."

"And here I am." A slight smile creased Eli's face. "And why are you here?" asked Eli.

"Oh, yeah, I almost forgot. Mrs. Babcock called me and asked me to come pick you up. She talked to the chief of police this morning. The warrant for your arrest has been dropped. You're a free man."

CHAPTER 42

Taking Charge

CHARLESTON POLICE DEPARTMENT, FRIDAY, OCTOBER 6TH

"So, you think this man, this killer, is here in Charleston?" asked Chief Crandall. He addressed his question to the room. Around the conference table sat Officers Pearlman and Tyrell, Edmond Locard, and FBI Special Agent Morose, who had arrived in town that morning.

"That's right," answered Morose. "There are striking similarities not just between Kimberly Prestwick's murder and others in the southeastern United States, as we have already identified, but also with the murders of the young girls in Albany and Vidalia, Georgia, which occurred over the last few weeks."

"Okay, maybe so, but it's quite a stretch to conclude he drove *here*. He could have driven anywhere," replied Chief Crandall.

"If you look at a map, it's a straight shot from Albany to Vidalia to Charleston," said Officer Tyrell.

Chief Crandall looked concerned but still not convinced.

"There's more," said Officer Pearlman. "Earlier this week, an abandoned car was called in. It had been spotted in the woods behind the Winn-Dixie. We had it towed. There was no license plate on the car, and the VIN had been scratched off. After Agent Morose briefed us this morning, we called the repo lot to check for any items found in the car."

"And?" asked Chief Crandall.

"A hotel key was found between the seats. For a Motel 6 in Albany, Georgia," explained Officer Pearlman.

"And I have more bad news," said Edmond. "I just spoke with Laz who has been in contact with Monty's secretary. It appears as if Rose and their son, Walker, are missing. Which is why I think it's time for a manhunt."

"A manhunt? You've got to be kidding," said Chief Crandall to the group in the conference room.

Chief Crandall was frustrated, worried, and hungry. Edmond's news hadn't helped. The chief continued.

"Look, I'm worried. I am. But you watch too much TV. I don't have a SWAT team on call for manhunts. Besides, I wouldn't know where to look," said Chief Crandall.

"I do," said Chester Baslin, who had just walked in and was standing in the doorway, Mrs. Babcock right behind.

When Chester entered a room, you noticed. At six-feet-six-inches and over 250 pounds, Chester was an imposing figure. He was a local football legend, having dominated both in high school and in college playing for the Gamecocks. Upon graduation, he shocked everyone by entering law school instead of the NFL.

Chester told everyone in the room about Rath, who he was, and about the note nailed to Monty's porch on Monday afternoon. Chester did not tell them about Rath's letters to Rose. Chester then asked Mrs. Babcock to tell everyone what she had learned.

"My son-in-law, Francesco, runs our family's bait and tackle stores," said Mrs. Babcock. "He's from the Bahamas. Our daughter met him on a mission trip to the Caribbean. He took over running the business when my husband got sick."

Chester urged her to skip the formalities and get on with the story.

"Right, of course," she said. "Tuesday night, I had dinner with my daughter Amy, and Francesco told me that a skiff had gone missing overnight."

"Gone missing?" remarked Chief Crandall.

"Stolen," said Mrs. Babcock.

"A few minutes ago, Chester asked me to call Francesco and see if the skiff had turned up."

"Well, has it?" asked Chief Crandall.

"No," said Mrs. Babcock, "but Monty Atkins has. He rented a boat about thirty minutes ago. My son-in-law recognized him from the press conference. Said he seemed upset."

"You know what this means, don't you?" asked Chester of the room.

"I think we're putting it together," answered Chief Crandall. "It looks like Rath kidnapped Rose and Walker, and Monty set out on a fool's mission to rescue them."

"Yep, and now we know where to conduct our manhunt," replied Chester.

"That may be true, but I'm betting Rath has them hidden in the swamps somewhere," said Officer Pearlman.

"That's right," said Officer Tyrell. "They could be anywhere. There are dozens of fishing cabins, shacks really, in those swamps. And if you don't know where you're going, you're just as likely to get lost."

"What we need is someone who fishes those waters. Someone who can guide us in. We need a man who knows the area," said Chester.

"Maybe I can help."

And then a ghost walked in.

Eli Atkins.

* * *

Officers Tyrell and Pearlman shook hands with Eli and then fell into a big group hug. Chester embraced Eli, fighting back the tears. Mrs. Babcock, Chief Crandall noticed, hung in the background, beaming from ear to ear like a proud grandmother. Chief Crandall couldn't put his finger on it, but he felt he knew less about the goings-on in the room than anyone else.

"Eli, I'm Chief Crandall. It's a pleasure to meet you."

"Are you going to arrest me, sir?" asked Eli.

"No, young man, I'm not. Now tell me how you can help."

As Monty had always said, if Eli wasn't playing ball, he was fishing or hunting. He was a natural, knew every inch of the Lowcountry, and felt at home, whether on the high seas or on the swamps of the Santee and Pee Dee rivers.

Chief Crandall said that he had access to a few powerboats that would help them catch up with Rath and Monty.

"You do that, you'll get us all killed," said Eli. "The swamps are littered with hidden tree stumps. And the duckweed will gum up the rotors of any inboard, so no boats with steering columns. You need flat-bottomed boats with tilled handles. No more than three men to a boat, one on the till, and the other two armed and at the bow. We'll need at least six boats," explained Eli.

"Excuse me, Eli. That sounds like a great plan, but if these waters are as harrowing as you say, where are we going to find more men to captain the boats who know the waters as well as you do?

"You got a phone I can use?" asked Eli.

Forty minutes later, Officers Tyrell, Pearlman, and Crandall, Edmond Locard, and Special Agent Morose, along with eight Charleston policemen and FBI agents, were standing dockside. Francesco, Eli, Quaid Dawson, and five of his seven sons were busy outfitting six skiffs to Eli's specifications.

When the boats were ready, Eli and five of Quaid's boys, ages eighteen to twenty-seven, each took command of a boat.

Chief Crandall pulled Eli and Quaid aside.

"Look, Mr. Dawson, I appreciate what you're doing here, but your boys, well, they're just boys. I can't have them leading my men into danger," said Chief Crandall. "Are you sure you know what you're doing?"

"Chief Crandall, my pappy and his brother ran moonshine in these parts during Prohibition. They supplied half the bathtub gin this nation drank. I was raised in these swamps—my boys too, hunting and fishing these waters since they could walk. I still have extended family that's never left. So you ask me if I know what I'm doing? Yes, sir, I do. Now we're wasting precious time. Are your men coming or not?" asked Quaid.

Chief Crandall turned and nodded at Agent Morose, and the police officers and FBI men, all heavily armed, took up their positions. Quaid climbed into a small skiff, and Francesco powered the boat out into the harbor where Quaid's Cessna 172 floatplane awaited. He would fly ahead and stay in radio contact with Chief Crandall, who would be in the first boat with Eli.

With Eli at the till, and Quaid in the air, the small regatta left the dock in search of Eli's family.

* * *

The search lasted a couple of hours and ended triumphantly when Eli and Chief Crandall burst through the door of a shack where Rath was holding

Monty and Walker. Walker was tied to a chair and Monty was taking a beating from Rath—but taking it, he was. His refusal to succumb to the blows had enraged Rath who, in anger, fired his gun repeatedly trying to shut Monty up. Instead, the gunshots led Eli and the others to the shack. Monty was in a bad way, his knee having suffered a wicked blow by Rath with a baseball bat. Walker was okay, all things considered, except for the emotional scars that would likely run deep. But Rose was nowhere to be found.

A manhunt was launched, and twenty-four hours later, Rose was wheeled into the emergency room of the hospital.

End of Part Five

PART SIX

Reconciliation

Chapter 43

Full Circle

Charleston County Hospital, Charleston, South Carolina, Saturday evening, October 7th, 1978

"So, you think it would have been better if Rath had killed Rose?" asked Mrs. Babcock.

"Yes, I do. Then her secrets would have died with her, and I'd be free."

"You think so, do you?" asked Mrs. Babcock. "*Honor* your parents, I said. I'm not telling you to love her. It's not my place, and besides, you got a right to what you're feeling."

"You're damn right I do."

Mrs. Babcock's eyes never moved from his, but she cocked her head slightly and Eli turned away.

"I'm sorry," said Eli. "I just don't know what you expect from me. I've been gone for over five years. You make contact and tell me I should come home, so I do. And then all hell breaks loose. I found out that my real dad killed Kimberly and is holding my family hostage. I lead the manhunt, and along with Quaid and his boys and a few cops, we kill the psychopath and rescue my brother Walker and the only man who's ever been a dad to me. And now I found out that the one person that could have prevented all this, my mother, is still alive AND SOMEHOW SHE'S THE HERO!"

"Like I said, you got a right to what you're feeling."

Eli's shoulders slumped and he looked at Mrs. Babcock. "So, how do I honor my parents?"

She smiled. "Well, for now, look at it as if you're honoring your father."

Eli gazed out the window, then, turning back to Mrs. Babcock, bowed his head slightly and nodded his consent.

* * *

When the ambulance sped into the hospital driveway, it was met by a team of nurses and EMTs standing ready with a gurney. Rose was removed from the back of the van on a stretcher and placed on a waiting gurney. As she was being rolled into the hospital emergency room, she was met in the driveway by her youngest son, Walker. Rose received his hug and spying over his shoulder saw her husband, Monty, in a wheelchair. Behind him stood her oldest son, a young man she had betrayed five years earlier. She looked at him and in a moment of clarity understood perfectly what she wanted to say to him, what she wanted him to hear, in the hopes he could forgive. And then she slipped into a state of unconsciousness.

* * *

CHARLESTON COUNTY HOSPITAL, SUNDAY MORNING, OCTOBER 8TH, THE NEXT DAY

Eli sat alone in a chair a few feet from the others. Walker and his girlfriend, Isabelle, were seated together on a bench against the wall beneath a nondescript painting of the seaside. Monty was sitting in his wheelchair on the other side of the bench but cocked at an angle so he could see the three of them. No one had spoken in over thirty minutes, but only Eli seemed comfortable with the silence. Walker and Monty would steal a glimpse at each other occasionally, the same unspoken questions floating back and forth between them. All the questions about Eli, all the questions they wanted to ask. *"Eli, where have you been? How did you get there? What have you been doing all these years? Why didn't you try to contact us? You know, to let us know you were okay? How did you get back here?"* And the big one, the one everyone was asking: *"Why did you run?"*

Eli knew what they were thinking. He caught all the glances out of the corner of their eyes, as if looking at him askew and not head-on would render their morbid curiosity any less rude. Eli wasn't talking, though. Not yet anyway. Let them wonder. What would they do with the truth anyway? How would they *use* it? You see, when you are betrayed by the woman who brought you into this world, how do you ever trust again?

The hospital halls had grown quiet since the day before. The manic activity and the buzz surrounding Eli's return and the daring rescue of Walker, Monty, and Rose had passed. Rath was dead and was now suspected in the serial killings of over two dozen young girls. Rath was unaware of Walker's near photographic memory when he bragged about all his killing and raping over the years. Rose knew, though. Rose knew her son had near perfect recall and had goaded Rath into talking about all he had done, and she had done so hoping the Lord would spare her son Walker, and then the police would learn what Rath had done.

So the four of them sat together alone in their thoughts until the painful silence was broken by the sound of a nurse's squeaking shoes.

"The doctor says you can see her now."

Walker and Isabelle stood, and Monty turned his wheelchair toward the direction of Rose's room. Eli didn't budge. Walker turned and looked at his brother and cocked his head twice quickly as if to say, "Come on." Eli stood hesitantly, and in that moment, despite his six-foot-three frame, he looked like a scared child. They set off toward her room.

* * *

Dr. Spelman was standing outside the hospital room where Rose lay with a clipboard in his hand in a conversation with another doctor and a nurse at his side, diligently taking notes. Dr. Spelman was nearing sixty years old and looked like a doctor you would see on TV. When he saw the family approach, he concluded his conversation with the other doctor, and they shook hands. The other doctor nodded at the family and then turned to walk down the hall for another consultation. The nurse stayed at Dr. Spelman's side.

Dr. Spelman took a few steps toward Monty and bent over slightly to shake the man's hand as he approached.

"Mr. Atkins, you're looking much better than you did yesterday when they brought you in. You too, Walker."

"Thanks to you," said Monty.

Dr. Spelman nodded graciously, absorbing the compliment.

"Now, Monty, I have to warn you. Rose suffered greatly. A broken collarbone, numerous broken ribs, a broken hip and ankle. She took more than one blow to the head, so she had a concussion, no doubt. Internal bleeding too. He beat her badly. And she lost a lot of blood. It's a miracle she's alive, really. If the police hadn't found her when they did, I suspect she wouldn't have lasted much longer. Those are just the visible scars. Reverend Coker and his wife will be by later today. She'll need spiritual comforting as well. There's no telling what other damage she's suffered. I'm telling you all this so you'll know what to expect."

Monty did his best to hold back the tears. He wished he could see Rath gunned down all over again.

"Walker, how are you holding up?" asked Dr. Spelman. Walker was relatively free of physical damage from the ordeal, but there was no telling how the trauma would play out in the young man's psyche.

"Just fine, sir," said Walker.

"And Eli, the man of the hour. You're quite the hero around here. It's great to see you. I remember watching you run the bases. You were inspiring. Just loved watching you play, even if you did beat us every year," said Dr. Spelman with a well-intentioned smile.

Eli's fear of the confrontation that lay behind the hospital room door over the doctor's shoulder vanished in a flash as he raised his chin from his chest and returned the doctor's kind words with a cold, blank stare.

* * *

THE WAFFLE HOUSE ON SAVANNAH HIGHWAY, THAT SAME SUNDAY MORNING, OCTOBER 8TH, 1978

Officers Bruce Pearlman and Will Tyrell parked their squad car on the front side of the Waffle House pointed at an angle so they could quickly pull back onto the road in the event of an emergency, though none was expected. It was a Sunday morning, typically a quiet time, and in a cosmic view of the world, their corner of it was due a rest after the events of the last two days. Normally, given their seniority in the department, they would have Sunday off, but Chief Crandall asked for an early meeting with a few key people. Chief Crandall promised the local press a report Sunday afternoon so they could hit the presses running in time for the Monday issue, and he wanted to meet with Officers Pearlman and Tyrell before anyone else. These two men had been responsible for the investigation into the murder of Kimberly Prestwick five years earlier. Bruce and Willie had agreed the night before to meet at the Waffle House on their way into the police station.

"Good morning. Welcome to Waffle House," was called out by more than one waitress.

Bruce and Will shuffled over to their usual table, a booth alongside the counter separating the kitchen from the dining area. Darla appeared as if on cue with two coffees.

"Good mornin', fellas. The usual?"

"That'll be fine," said Officer Tyrell.

"Me too, Darla."

Darla walked over toward the kitchen and stood on a red tile and shouted back to the chefs:

> Mark. Pull one sirloin med rare, one country ham. Drop 2 hash browns;
>
> Order scramble cheese plate smothered covered;
>
> Mark. Country ham and eggs over medium plate smothered peppers and capped. A bowl of cheese grits.

Darla returned and leaned over the counter holding her order pad between both hands.

"The way tongues are waggin' this morning nearly set the griddle ablaze all by itself. Now you two wouldn't know anything about that, would ya?"

"Darla, I'm afraid I don't know what yer talkin' about," said Officer Pearlman. The two officers shared a sly smile. They enjoyed ribbing Darla; she'd been working at the Waffle House since the beginning of time.

Darla stood up straight and placed her hands on her hips. "No, sir. That ain't gonna cut it. Word is a serial killer was on the loose and Eli Atkins appeared out of nowhere and gunned him down."

"Something like that," said Officer Tyrell.

Darla stood her ground, feet wide, looking back and forth between them as they each sipped at their coffee. "Now folks be comin' in here all day, and I'm expected to know this from that so out with it."

"Okay, Darla, Okay."

Then Officers Pearlman and Tyrell shared with Darla what they knew to be true, knowing it would have a hard time surviving amongst the weeds of half-truths and lies that were sure to sprout.

"So, you're tellin' me that the man that killed that girl Kimberly five years ago showed up here and kidnapped Rose Atkins and her boy, Walker?"

"Yep."

"And this Rose Atkins was at one time married to the killer?"

"Yep."

"And this man is Eli's real dad?"

"That's right."

"And Eli is back in town and you're saying he helped track down and kill the bastard?"

"That's right."

"Well, that's the damndest thing I ever heard. So, Eli was innocent the whole time."

"Sure looks that way."

"Then why did he run?"

This conversation, or a variant of it, was taking place all over Charleston and the surrounding area.

* * *

Walker pressed the door open and held it so Monty could wheel his chair in. Isabelle said she'd wait outside in the hallway. Walker looked at Eli, and then he entered the room with Eli following behind. The doctor left the family alone with Rose and said they could stay for thirty minutes at most. Rose needed her rest.

Monty wheeled up beside the bed and looked at Rose. He reached out and took her left hand. An IV was attached to her right arm and connected to a bag hanging off a metal contraption that reminded Monty of a rolling coat rack. When he took her hand, she turned her head and opened her eyes and saw her husband and her two boys. Her family. At a complete loss for words, she smiled, and she cried, not heavily, but the tears were real. As were Monty's and Walker's.

Walker had moved to the end of the bed, where he now sat, but before doing so he lowered the metal frame running alongside the bed so Monty could more easily hold Mom's hand. Eli stood.

"We did it, Rose. We did it," said Monty.

Rose smiled and squeezed his hand, silently acknowledging their victory.

Monty turned to look at his two boys and then back at Rose, beaming. "Our family. We're back together. Praise the Lord. I admit, there were days I thought I'd never see us all together again."

And then Eli spoke.

"And what about you, Mom? Were there times when you wondered if we'd ever be together again? You know, like the good old days?"

Rose looked away. Monty's head slumped and he squeezed his eyes shut, and again, he was torn. How was he to stand by his wife and be a good father when doing either seemingly made the other impossible? He knew Eli was lost and needed his support. That was clear. He'd hardly said a word since the EMTs wheeled Rose into the hospital the day before, but good grief, Monty wondered, why couldn't whatever was eating at Eli wait a day or two?

"Eli, son, I know this must all be very confusing, but can't we just enjoy the moment?"

And then there was Walker. He had learned a great deal over the last few days. He now knew that the man who had killed Kimberly, the man who had kidnapped him, Rath, was his mother's first husband and Eli's dad. But now he feared that he no longer knew the man standing next to him, his brother, a brother he had grown up idolizing.

Rose raised her head and collected herself. "Monty. Walker. Could you give me and Eli some time alone?"

* * *

It was just the two of them in the hospital room separated by a few feet and an unimaginable chasm of pain.

"So, Rose, what should I tell them?"

"Oh, Eli, I'm so sorry."

"Shut up. I don't want to hear it. Now answer the question: What should I tell folks when they ask me why I ran?"

"Can you at least call me Mother or Mom?"

"I don't have a mother or a father. I killed my father yesterday and my mother died years ago."

Rose wept. Eli stood dispassionately at the end of the bed.

"Oh, by the way, Eli's dead too. I'm now Aaron Westfield and I live in the Bahamas, and for all practical purposes, I'm an orphan."

Rose's shoulders shook. She couldn't look at him, so she stared into her hands. There was a part of her that knew she deserved this.

"So, *Mom*, you got your wish—you never had me. I don't exist. Now you can resume your lofty position in society."

"Eli, please. I've changed."

"It's too late," Eli stated with a quiet intensity. "It's. Too. Late. You robbed me of everything. My life. My dreams of playing baseball. My brother, Walker. You took from me the one man that ever loved me, my other dad, my *real* dad, Monty."

Eli slowly approached Rose and leaned over the bed, his gaze pressing down on her.

"You took everything."

And then he walked out of the room.

Chapter 44

Time to Mend

Monty, Walker, and Isabelle were sitting in the cafeteria when they saw Eli hurry by.

"Eli, wait," said Monty as he wheeled his chair away from the table and toward the hallway.

"Hey, Eli. Where are you going?"

Eli stopped and looked at his father and then back toward the table where Walker and Isabelle were still seated. If he knew the answer to the question, he would have told them. But he didn't know where he was going, and anger was the only emotion he was comfortable with. It filled him, it saturated every fiber of his being and allowed him the safety and security of not addressing other problems.

"Dad, I don't know where I'm going. I just know I can't be here. I can't be anywhere close to her," he said, cocking his head in the general direction of Rose's hospital room."

"Come home, son. Please. Come home. Have dinner with us."

Eli looked away, grinding his teeth, and fighting back the tears.

"No," he said. "Not tonight. But soon. I promise."

Monty watched as his oldest son walked out of the hospital into the bright sunlight and past the hovering photographers snapping pictures for the next day's edition. Conquering hero or circus sideshow.

* * *

Monty spent the rest of the day with Rose. Walker and Isabelle left, and Walker said he'd come back and pick Monty up later in the day when he was ready to come home. Rose slept most of the time. When she was awake, they talked of the future, dinners together, and having the boys home for Thanksgiving and Christmas. They ignored the elephant in the room, though—all the questions surrounding Eli. What had he been up to? How had he escaped? Returned? And the big one—why he ran in the first place. And they didn't discuss his hostility earlier in the day. Monty figured Rose would share with him the conversation she had with Eli in her own good time. No, now was the time for rest.

As she slept, Monty had an orderly find a football game on the TV for him. The TV was mounted high up on the wall and Monty couldn't reach it from his wheelchair. The Atlanta Falcons were playing the Pittsburgh Steelers. Monty pulled for the Falcons but didn't think they had much of a chance that year against Terry Bradshaw. Monty liked Bradshaw; he had a blue-collar, working man approach to the game. Bartkowski, the Falcons' quarterback and hope for the future, had a cannon for an arm but was a bit too flashy for Monty's liking.

The football game played in the background as Monty read the *Post & Courier* Sports section. The LA Dodgers had beaten the Philadelphia Phillies the night before in game four and the Yankees had done the same to the Kansas City Royals. *So, here we go again,* thought Monty. *Another Dodgers-Yankees World Series.* Monty was pulling for the Dodgers. He was a National League man, all the way. But more importantly, he hated the Yankees. Anybody but the Yankees.

Rose was asleep and Monty's attention was broken when the room door slowly opened. Reverend Coker stuck his head in the door and Monty waved for him to enter. Monty wheeled his chair around the end of the bed to greet Reverend Coker and his wife, Mildred.

"Thank y'all for coming," said Monty.

"But of course, Monty. How is she?"

"Well, she's alive, that's about the best I can say right now. Let's step outside where we don't have to whisper."

Monty wheeled his chair into the hallway and gave Reverend Coker and his wife the gruesome details. They both listened intently. Monty's tone wavered, filled with a vile hatred when he spoke of Rath, and anguish when he talked of all the damage Rose suffered.

"Reverend, it may not be Christian, but I'm glad Rath is dead, and I hope he's burning in Hell."

"Monty, give your soul and conscience a break. You're worried because you're drawing some joy or satisfaction from the idea that that awful man is suffering in Hell? Don't. And don't fret over whether it's Christian or not. It's human, as are you. The Lord knows we're human. That's why his Son did all the heavy lifting for us. You don't have to think about that man, that psychopath, anymore. His fate is in the Lord's hands, and the Lord is more than up to the task."

"Thank you, Reverend. I Swany, I don't know how you folks do what you do. Never a day off it seems in your line of work. But thank you."

Reverend Coker smiled as if to bashfully say "thank you," but he agreed silently with Monty. There were days he wished he could be someone other than a reverend.

"Say, Monty, you look pretty tired. How about Mildred and I give you a break? Let us sit with Rose for a while. I'll keep an eye on the game in there while she sleeps."

"And I have some needlepointing in my bag here," said Mildred. "I can occupy my time, and when Rose wakes, she might appreciate having a woman to confide in."

"I don't know. When she wakes, I'd like to be here."

"Monty, you risked your life to rescue her. Don't you think she knows you're here for her?" asked the reverend.

Monty bit his upper lip. Nothing more needed to be said.

"You know, I could use a little rest. Let me just check in on her before I go. I'll stop at the nurses' station and ask them to call me if her condition changes. Just give me a minute."

"Of course, Monty. Mildred and I will be right out here."

* * *

Monty wheeled back into the room alongside her bed. He took Rose's hand in hers. She was still asleep. He looked at her and for a moment she looked like the same scared girl he'd met back in college. He'd been tending to chores around the church when he came into the chapel and saw a beautiful young woman sitting toward the back alone, bruised and distraught. Rath had been the culprit then as well. And Monty had been her savior then too.

"Rose, I don't 'spect you can hear me right now, but I've got some things I want to say. So here goes. I think I knew it from the first time I met you. The Lord brought me into this world for His good pleasure but also to be here to love you. And I do. And I did the first time I met you. I loved you then and I love you now. I know I'm not perfect. But I've done my best to protect you and to help you know that you are both loved and loveable. Forgive me for those times I was selfish and didn't pay enough attention to you. For those times when I was short with you or didn't listen to you or didn't notice when you had gone out of your way to do something nice for me or the boys."

Rose turned her head toward Monty and opened her eyes and smiled.

"It's about time you apologized," she said, smiling and crying.

Rose and Monty laughed, but doing so was painful for Rose, given her broken ribs, which caused her to laugh all the more. Rose and Monty talked for a few more minutes and then Monty told her the Cokers were waiting outside.

"Monty, yes, please go. You need your rest too."

"Okay, I think I will."

As he turned and started toward the door, Rose called out to him.

"Monty?"

"Yes, dear."

"I love you."

Chapter 45

Loose Ends

After Eli left the hospital, he hopped into the pickup truck Quaid Dawson had loaned him and started driving. He didn't know where he was heading; he just knew he had to get out of there. He had to escape.

Just two days ago, he'd learned that his biological father was a serial killer and the monster who killed his Kimberly, and on top of that, his parents, Monty and Rose, knew. Eli wanted to know for how long. How long had they known? Did they know all along? In other words, did they know who the real killer was back when Eli was arrested and before he ran? It was inconceivable and Quaid's explanation made sense, that Monty had learned all this from a private investigator he hired to find the real killer.

Then why didn't they just go straight to the police with the news? Why did they mail the proof anonymously from Savannah just a week ago? Why didn't they want people to know they had learned the truth? Was it because no one would believe them because they were his parents? But what about Rose? Was she in on sending the news anonymously? She had wanted Eli gone to begin with, wanting to save her the embarrassment of a trial. Had she had a change of heart? Too many questions spinning around and not enough answers. In fact, no answers at all.

Before he knew it, he was driving north on Highway 17, and he wasn't too far from Anglers, the bait and tackle shop Mrs. Babcock's family owned. From there, he was just a boat ride away from the shack where the day before he had gunned down Rath. Feeling drawn to the place where the shootout had occurred, he drove on until he was sitting in the parking lot of the bait and tackle shop. As a young boy, he spent plenty of time helping the Babcock family at this shop and at others they owned, and as Mr. Babcock's health began to fail, they gave him more responsibility. Some of his best memories growing up were associated with this place.

Being Sunday, the store was closed. He quickly found the hide-a-key, let himself in, and found the keys to one of the skiffs. Five minutes later, Eli was back on the water and heading for the shack.

* * *

MEANWHILE, BACK AT THE CHARLESTON POLICE DEPARTMENT

Officers Pearlman and Tyrell found the chief of police sitting at Mrs. Babcock's desk outside his office, rummaging through the drawers.

"Lookin for somethin', boss?" asked Will Tyrell.

"A BC Powder. Mrs. Babcock always fetches them for me when I have a headache. I have a doozy of one now," said Chief Crandall. "Ah, here they are. Hallelujah. Let me grab a Coke from the breakroom and I'll meet you in my office."

Chief Crandall returned to his office and took a seat at his desk. Officers Pearlman and Tyrell sat patiently in chairs on the other side and watched Chief Crandall pour the powder from the packet directly into his mouth and wash it down with a swig of Coke.

"Don't know what I'd do without these. Now, let's get down to business so we can get home and enjoy the game. So, what's the latest?" asked the chief.

"Well, as you predicted, it's all over town. We had breakfast this morning at the Waffle House."

"The one over on the Savannah Highway next to the Holiday Inn?"

"Yes, sir."

"Was Darla working the morning shift?"

"She was and she knew all about it. Kept pressing us for more."

"What'd ya tell her?

"Just what we talked about last night. We confirmed that the Atkins family was safe and doing well, that we had shot and killed the man who murdered Kimberly Prestwick, and that all charges against Eli Atkins had been dropped."

"So, that's all you told her."

"Well, not exactly," said Officer Pearlman. "She knew that the killer was actually Rose Atkin's first husband and Eli's real dad."

"Sorry, Chief," said Officer Tyrell.

"It ain't your fault. There was no way to keep that under wraps."

"So, boss, where do we go from here?" asked Officer Pearlman.

"I want you two to secure the crime scene. What with all the commotion Friday night and the hunt for Rose Atkins Saturday, we didn't get a chance to go through that cabin."

"What do you expect to find? We know Rath killed Kimberly and we killed him," said Officer Tyrell.

"That's all true, but you can bet the FBI will be all over that place and I don't want them finding anything we should have."

"Got it. We'll head out there first thing tomorrow morning."

"Do y'all think you can find it again?" asked the chief.

"Doubtful," answered Pearlman. "We can always ask Eli or Mrs. Babcock's son-in-law Francesco to show us the way."

"Leave Eli out of it. He's been through enough. If you need help, ask Francesco."

"Right, boss. Now, is there anything else or do you want to talk about the press conference this afternoon? The newspaper folks are gonna have a heap of questions."

"If that ain't the truth," said the chief. "The heavy lifting will fall on the FBI from this point on. We've solved the murder in our jurisdiction. If in fact this Rath is a serial killer responsible for other murders in the Southeast, they'll take it from here. I plan on letting Agent Morose from the FBI field the questions. He'll be here in an hour to review likely questions."

"But I tell ya, I got questions myself," continued Chief Crandall. "For the life of me, somethin' just don't add up. That press conference Monty and Rose Atkins were so hellbent on havin', for one. What was that all about? Lookin' back on it, it's as if they were sending a message to that madman Rath. Almost like they knew all along he was the killer."

"Okay," said Officer Tyrell. "But what message were they sending?"

"I ain't got the foggiest notion. All I know is that we have that press conference and here comes Rath. He showed up at Monty's house a few weeks later and kidnapped his wife Rose and his son Walker."

"I got to admit, it does strain credulity," said Officer Pearlman.

"Strain *credulity*! Ester finally make you turn off the TV and pick up a book?" asked Officer Tyrell.

"Kiss my ass, Einstein. She got me a set of cards with words on one side and definitions on the other."

"You sure it ain't pictures on one side and words on the other?"

"Knock it off, you two," said the chief.

"Well, all I know is that if Eli hadn't shown up when he did, we likely wouldn't have found them in time," said Officer Pearlman.

"And that's another thing!" said Chief Riddle "How in the hell does Eli just show up, five years later, just as we uncover evidence proving his innocence? And is it true he's been in the Bahamas this whole time?"

"That's what I heard," said Officer Tyrell. "Makes you wonder how he got there."

"And how he got back," said Officer Pearlman.

"And the first person he calls is Quaid Dawson. Quaid goes to the Bahamas quite a bit from what I hear. Has a big boat down there. Loves to marlin fish," said Chief Crandall. "Maybe I need to talk with him."

"I'd sure like to catch me a billfish someday," said Officer Tyrell.

"The chief said Quaid goes down there to catch marlin, not billfish."

"Same thing."

"No, they ain't."

"Yeah, they are. They both have them big fins on their back."

"You mean dorsal fins."

"Yeah. That's what I meant. They both have dorsal fins."

"So? That makes them billfish?"

"Yep."

"Well, then what's a sailfish?"

"What do I look like? An encyclopedia?"

"Really, would you two just knock it off," said Chief Crandall. "Sailfish and marlin are both types of billfish."

"Sure, would like to catch me a marlin someday?" said Officer Pearlman.

Officers Pearlman and Tyrell exchanged a glance and barely suppressed laughter as Chief Crandall stood up from his chair and walked toward the window.

"And then there's Monty and Eli," said Chief Crandall. "Monty knew all along his son was innocent and he was right."

"Monty's a good man. A good father," said Officer Pearlman.

"I don't doubt that," said Chief Crandall. "But what I don't understand then is ... why did Eli run?"

* * *

Monty wheeled himself out onto the porch and maneuvered himself into the rocking chair. The house was quiet. Walker was at Isabelle's house, and he had no idea where Eli was. Exhaustion was setting in. The neighbors across the street had brought dinner over for him. In fact, neighbors and folks from church had been bringing food by all day. From the looks of the refrigerator, he and Walker would be eating casseroles for the next month.

Monty was at peace. Well, not entirely. But for the first time in five years, his family was back. Well, almost. Eli was no longer wanted for murder but wasn't ready to come home and sleep in his old room. Rose was alive, but she was in the hospital and looked as if she might stay a while. But he was hopeful for Walker. Yes, Walker just kept plugging along. Monty knew he'd be losing him to college in a year. Georgetown University, most likely. But he'd be home for holidays and during the summer.

As he sat in the rocking chair, settling in for the night and enjoying the relative calm, a nagging feeling climbed from the back of his mind to the forefront. There was something still left to deal with. But what? It couldn't be Rath. He was dead. So, what was it? *What was gnawing at him*? Monty wondered.

* * *

Eli took his time in the boat. He knew where he was going and was in no hurry. Besides, it was a beautiful fall afternoon on the water. But why was he returning to the rundown cabin? What did he expect to find? What was the point? Maybe he needed to put it behind him? He thought of his mother and his father. No, not Rath. He thought of Monty. Monty had hired a private detective to find the killer. Monty never gave up on him. Maybe Mrs. Babcock was right. She talked about the power of forgiveness. He'd been pretty harsh with his mother in the hospital. To what end? But he wasn't ready to forgive her, and he had no idea how to do it anyway.

No, he wasn't ready to forgive her, but he was ready to be done with it all. He was ready to move on and start living again, as Eli. He was more relaxed than he had been in a while. When he first got on the water, he thought about turning around. No, he'd come this far, he'd forge ahead, toward the shack, to where he had killed the man who raped and murdered Kimberly, to where he had killed his father. Maybe then he could put this all behind him.

* * *

The letters!

Monty was almost asleep, his head bouncing on his left shoulder as he sat slumped in the rocking chair. And then it hit him.

The letters.

They were in his satchel. He'd seen Rath place the satchel behind the stack of logs next to the fireplace in the shack. What had happened to them? Had the police found them? Were they sitting in an evidence locker at the police department?

Oh, good Lord. Had anyone read them? Those letters were written by Rath and addressed to Rose, and they provided clear proof that she had known all along who had killed not only Kimberly but dozens of other girls.

He had to find the letters. If they fell into the wrong hands ... oh, good Lord.

* * *

Eli knew he was close, and then he saw it, the shack, decorated with yellow crime scene tape, hidden behind the drooping branches of a bald cypress tree. Surreal out there in the middle of the marsh, miles from anyone, the yellow tape was an invitation to come closer.

Eli slowly motored the skiff up onto the shore. He hopped out and pulled the boat another foot or two onto dry land. He stood motionless for a moment. It already seemed like a lifetime ago that he was running up the bank and kicking the door in. *Well, I've come this far,* he thought to himself as he walked toward the broken-down front door.

* * *

Chester would know what to do, thought Monty.

Monty crawled from the rocking chair back into the wheelchair and headed inside to the phone in the living room.

On the fourth ring: "Chester Baslin here."

"Chester, it's me. Monty."

"Monty! How's things? I was going to give you a call tomorrow. Figured you had enough going on today. But I want you to know I been thinking about you and your family."

"Chester, thank you. All is well, I guess, all things considered. But look, I need your help again."

"Of course. What's on your mind."

"It's about the letters."

"The ones I was holding for you?"

"Yes. Well, as you remember, I came and got them last Friday and took them with me to find Rath and my family. I placed them in a satchel and Rath took it from me when I got there. What I'm trying to say is that ... well ... I'm wondering where the satchel is."

"What do you mean?"

"I mean ... I don't know where the satchel is, and the letters are in the satchel."

"And you're afraid of who may read those letters and what they will do."

"You got it."

"Oh dear. I'm beginning to understand. You'd rather those letters just disappear at this point."

"In the worst way. Chester, if folks find out that Rose knew all along that Eli was innocent and hid the truth, can you imagine what her life will be like? And then there's the fact that Rath told her in those letters about other girls he'd killed and how he planned to keep on killing."

"But you told me she never got those other letters and that she'd only read the first letter."

"That's true, but do you think anyone would believe us? People would know I was returning the letters to Rath, for Pete's sake."

There was silence on the phone.

"Chester? *Chester*? Are you still there?"

"Yep. I'm trying to think this through. Can you tell me what you remember?"

"It's all kind of a blur. I've been trying to remember every little detail. Rath clocked me pretty good as I was getting out of the boat, and I must have dropped the satchel going down to the ground. The next thing I remember is seeing Walker tied to a chair and I ran into the cabin. I seem to remember Rath walking in after me carrying the satchel. But that's about it. So, the satchel and the letters must still be in the cabin, or they're ..."

"Or, the police have them. The police or maybe the FBI. They will have gone over that crime scene very carefully, especially the FBI—that is, if they are serious about investigating Rath for the other murders," said Chester.

"Chester, what are we going to do? I was thinking tonight that all this was behind us. That we could start rebuilding our family. And now this."

"Monty, our best hope is that our police department has it. If that's the case, I can claim attorney-client privilege and try get the satchel back. Of course, there's no guarantee that someone hasn't read the letters yet. But if the FBI has them, then I'm afraid we're out of luck. Are you sure the satchel made it into the shack? Is there a chance Rath could have destroyed the letters?"

"Don't think so. I'm pretty darn sure I saw him bring the satchel inside. Besides, that sick bastard probably wanted to read his own letters."

"I tell you what. I'll snoop around the police department and see what I can find out. Look, Monty, the worst is behind you. Rath is dead. Eli is back and all charges have been dropped. Rose is alive and receiving good care. This too will pass."

"Thank you, Chester. Thank you again."

"Don't mention it. Now try to get some rest."

"Will do."

Monty hung up the phone, too keyed up to even think about sleeping anymore. The game was starting soon. Maybe watching the game would help him take his mind off matters. But he kept coming back to the fact that someone may have the letters. Someone may have read them. Someone may know. But who?

"Oh, good Lord! What if Eli were to ever read those letters?" Monty said to the empty living room. Things had been bad enough between him and Rose before Eli left. But if Eli ever knew that Rose could have set him free five years ago ... Monty couldn't imagine the pain that would cause Eli.

* * *

Eli ducked under the yellow tape, entered the shack, and looked around. When Eli and Chief Crandall burst into the room Friday night, they both fired their pistols at Rath as he was rearing back to bash Monty with a bat.

Walker was lying on the ground tied to a toppled chair. The chair was now sitting upright and off to the side of the room. A stack of wood was piled against the wall next to the fireplace. A small square table was pushed up against the opposite wall, and the floor was littered with empty beer bottles, a few cans of beans, and some crumpled potato chip bags.

Eli took a seat in the chair and looked about. Nothing more to see or do. He slumped forward, placing his forehead onto the palms of his hands, and stared blankly at the floor. He'd come here and found the remnants of a wasted life, Rath's life. His mother had married the man. What had she seen in him? He loathed his mother, but he knew in his heart that she knew nothing of his murderous dark side when they met and conceived him. He knew he was a bastard child and that the wedding was a shotgun wedding. He'd done the math when he found the newspaper clipping in the attic that day announcing his mother's marriage to Rathbone Cummings. Was his mother a victim too? Should he feel a bit of remorse for her as well? Her life had also been turned upside down by this evil man.

Minutes passed. Eli sat back in the chair and gave the room one last glance. *Maybe it was time to let go. Time to start over again as Eli and to leave Aaron in the past, and leave all of this in the past,* he thought. *Maybe it was time to forgive.*

Then he heard a rustling noise coming from the stack of wood. He walked over and nudged the pile with his foot and a mouse skirted away. A log fell and that's when Eli saw it—a brown leather satchel shoved behind the woodpile. He picked it up and, seeing the initials MJA, immediately recognized it as his father's.

He opened it and found a stack of opened letters inside bound together with a rubber band. He dragged the chair over to the table, sat down, and removed the rubber band. The letters were all addressed to Mrs. Rose Atkins, but none had a return address. He removed the letter from the envelope on the top of the stack, dated November 3rd, 1973, and began to read:

> Rose, it's been awhile. But don't think I don't know you've been thinking about me. I've been in the news, and I suspect you put two and two together and figured it was me. I told you I wasn't going to stop. Kimberly was just the first, well the first I told you about, that is. And just think—you may have been able to put a stop to all of it. Many of those girls would be alive today, and who knows where I'd be ... probably strapped to old sparky by now. But I knew

> you was proud … too proud to go to the police. And now you're knee-deep in pig shit. You got too much invested, don't you? And just think what people would say all these years later if you was to go to the police? Oh my. No sir, that ain't happenin', is it? Well, I'll be signing off now. Just remember—every time I rape and kill, you deserve some of the credit.

Eli stared at the letter in disbelief. He pulled out another letter and read it. And then another. And another. There was no denying it. Eli stood from the table, grabbed the satchel and the stack of letters, and walked out of the cabin hellbent on righting a great wrong, hellbent on revenge, and as he fired up the motor on the back of the boat, one thought was coursing through his brain: *They knew. They both knew.*

Chapter 46

Unanswered Questions

Charleston Police Department, October 9th, Monday afternoon

"Charleston Police Department. May I help you?" answered Rebecca, the new girl at the reception desk.

"Well, I hope so. Is Mrs. Babcock in?"

"Why yes. Who should I say is calling?"

"Chester Baslin."

"One minute please."

"Mrs. Babcock's office. How can I help you?"

Chester smiled knowing that Chief Crandall, if he was in hearing distance, was shaking his head in bewilderment. For years, he'd asked Mrs. Babcock to answer the phone as "Chief Crandall's office."

"Mrs. Babcock, this is Chester Baslin. I bet you're looking as lovely as ever."

"That's so sweet of you to say, Chester. And how is your dear wife, Nancy?"

"Well. Quite well. And enjoying a slower pace. Two of the boys are in college, so we just have the one at home now."

"Please tell her I asked about her. Now, what can I do for you?"

"I just called to see how things were around the department today. I imagine the office is still pretty hectic given what happened over the weekend."

"You could say that. The phone won't stop ringing."

"And how is Chief Crandall doing?"

"Feeling like a prize-winnin' hog." Mrs. Babcock then looked left and then right and cupped her hand over the phone. "Seems to be takin' an inordinate amount of credit for catching the killer, if you ask me, but he was the one who shot the man—him and Eli, that is. So, I guess he has a right."

"There are rumors floating around, Mrs. B, that you are responsible for Eli's safe-keeping these past five years."

"Now don't go believing everything you hear. Is there anything else, Chester?"

"No, just wondering if there were any more developments."

"Don't think so. The FBI is takin' over from here. This morning the chief sent a couple of officers back to the cabin to tidy up before the FBI moves in. Just trying to close the file."

"I'll bet he sent Officers Pearlman and Tyrell, didn't he?"

"That's right. Had my son-in-law Francesco take them back out. Only fitting. They were the ones investigating Kimberly's murder when all this madness began."

"Yes, it is. Well, Mrs. Babcock, you have a fine day."

"You too and say hello to Nancy for me."

* * *

Francesco was standing in the parking lot waving goodbye to Officers Pearlman and Tyrell when he heard the phone ringing. He jogged back into the shop and scooted back behind the counter. He reached for the phone on the fifth or so ring and hurriedly answered: "Angler's Bait and Tackle."

"Am I speaking with Francesco, the owner?"

"Yes, sir. Can I help you?"

"Francesco, I'm Chester Baslin. I don't believe we've met. I'm a friend of Monty Atkins."

"Yes, sir. Oh, I know who you are. You're the lawyer who helped Eli."

"That's right."

"Well, isn't it great? Eli being back and safe? He's a hero for sure."

"Yes, he is. I was hoping I could ask you some questions about what happened over the weekend. I know you helped guide the boats in search of the killer."

"I sure did. 'Bout the most exciting thing that's ever happened to me. In fact, I was just going over the whole ordeal with two police officers from Charleston who wanted to do the same thing."

"Oh really? Who would that be?"

"Officers Pearlman and Tyrell. Do you know them?

"I sure do. Know them well."

"Yeah? I just guided them back out to the cabin where everything happened and then to the cabin where we found Monty's wife, Rose. They said they had to secure the crime scenes."

"Sounds exciting. Did they find anything to secure?"

Francesco shuffled his feet and looked out the front door after the police officers who were just pulling out of the parking lot. "Mr. Baslin, they asked me not to tell anyone about what they found or learned. They said it was confidential. I'm sorry."

"No problem. I understand perfectly. I'll go through the normal legal channels and follow up with them. Thank you for your time."

"Of course. Have a nice day."

"And you too."

* * *

Chester hung up the phone, checked his watch, noting that it was close to five in the afternoon, and calculated his next move. He wanted to talk with Officers Bruce Pearlman and Will Tyrell alone, away from the office, and figured he knew where he could find them. It was worth a try. He'd spend a few minutes straightening up his desk and then head home with a quick stop for dinner, where he expected to find two of Charleston's finest.

* * *

The rain picked up as Chester pulled into the parking lot. He grabbed the newspaper from the passenger seat and held it over his head and walked quickly, head down, toward the entrance. He stepped inside and out of the way of the door as it shut behind him.

"Welcome to Waffle House."

"Sit anywhere you like."

Chester acknowledged a few familiar faces with a quick wave of his hand and a nod of his head, and as suspected, he saw Officers Pearlman and Tyrell sitting in a booth next to the counter separating the kitchen from the dining area.

"Officers? How are ya?"

"Chester. Good to see you," said Bruce.

"Mind if I join y'all for a minute or two?"

"We don't usually dine with one of Satan's minions, you being a defense attorney and all," said Will Tyrell as he took a sip of his coffee and winked at Bruce.

After the briefest of moments, Will slid over and patted the seat next to him, inviting Chester to have a seat. Chester sat down and Darla walked over with a cup of coffee without asking, noted the three of them together, and walked away with a quick backwards glance that told Bruce she expected to be told the nature of their meeting.

Chester took a sip of his coffee, trying to decide how to proceed. He needed to know if the satchel had been recovered but he couldn't come out and ask the question directly. The longer the silence went on, however, the more he feared that they would suspect he had an agenda. It was Officer Pearlman who rescued him.

"Chester, between the three of us, we want you to know we never believed Eli was guilty, and we couldn't be happier he's back."

Chester looked sideways at Will Tyrell, who was looking straight ahead holding his cup of coffee between his two hands. Will quickly nodded his head up and down and muttered "Absolutely."

"We were doing our job. He ran from the gathering at Kimberly's house and our training kicked in. We gave chase and arrested him," continued Officer Pearlman.

Chester held up both his hands. "I know. You did your job, and you did it well. I have no beef with either of you. I did mine too. And here we are, and Eli is a free man."

"And we got the bad guy," said a smiling Will Tyrell.

The three men clinked their coffee mugs together in mutual celebration that justice was done.

"So, what happens now?" asked Chester. "I assume the FBI will try to tie the killer to other unsolved murders in the Southeast."

Darla appeared quick as a flash with her notepad in hand, waiting to take their orders and accidently overhear something she shouldn't.

The gentlemen stopped talking and all just looked at her.

"What is it, Darla?" asked Officer Tyrell.

"What'll ya have?"

The three answered in unison: "The usual" And then they stared at her until she walked away in frustration.

"Yep. They'll run the show from here. They owe us the courtesy of letting us know when they are in town and will likely ask for our assistance from time to time, but we pretty much finished up our work today," said Bruce.

"Oh, yeah? What do you mean?"

"Mrs. Babcock's son-in-law, Francesco, ran us back out to the cabin where Rath was holding Monty and Walker and then over to the cabin where Rose was found," said Bruce. "The chief wanted to make sure there was nothing in either cabin for the Feds to find that we should have found ourselves. We don't need anything to wrap up the case on Kimberly's murder, but since they'll be going after this guy Rath for other murders it's reasonable to assume they'll be looking for any of his personal possessions that may link him to other murders."

"Makes sense," said Chester.

Darla returned holding one plate in each hand and a third balanced on her left forearm. As quick as a flash, she placed a plate on the table in front of each of them and was gone as fast as she appeared. They each began their routine of applying salt, pepper, ketchup, what-have-you, to their plates and silently dug in.

After a bite or two, Chester spoke up: "Well, what'd ya find?"

The two officers shared a glance. Bruce put his fork down and reached for a napkin from the steel container resting at the end of the table between the salt and pepper and wiped his mouth before speaking.

"Well, Counselor, there's a train of thought down at the department that you and your client's mom and dad, Monty and Rose that is, knew who the killer was all along," said Bruce. "So, maybe we should be asking you: What do you think we found?"

"You've got to be kidding! There are folks who believe that?"

Chester was treading on thin ice. While he was protected by the attorney-client privilege and couldn't be forced to say what he knew or didn't know, he also knew that lying to the police or concealing evidence could get him disbarred or arrested. At a minimum, he could see his good reputation with the department sullied, and he had worked too hard building it up to lose it so quickly.

"Look, the Atkins family has been through hell and back. If there are going to be any more surprises, they'd like to know before everyone is reading and talking about it," said Chester.

Bruce and Tyrell had returned to the task of eating while Chester went on about his clients. They both liked Chester even if he was a defense attorney and had each, on more than one occasion, suggested that friends in need of a lawyer call Chester. And besides, they had no desire to make things any tougher on the Atkins family. They exchanged glances that communicated, between the two of them, an agreement of sorts.

"Chester, we don't think the Atkins family has anything to worry about. We found the boat Rath stole. There was a backpack in it with some dirty old clothes and a few personal items but nothing out of the ordinary."

"Anything in either of the cabins?" asked Chester.

Will spoke up. "No, nothing inside."

Chester didn't know whether to be relieved or not. If Officers Pearlman and Tyrell were to be believed, and he had no reason not to, they had not found Monty's satchel with the letters. But if they didn't find them, where were they?

"There was one thing, though," said Will. "In the cabin where we found and shot Rath, we got the distinct feeling someone had been there after the shootout Friday but before we returned."

"How do you mean?" asked Chester.

"When we got there, the chair Walker had been tied to was sitting upright next to the table. I was the one that helped Walker up when we arrived, and I remember setting the chair back upright, but on the other side of the room," explained Will.

"And not only was the chair now sitting next to the table, but there were lines on the floor you could see, lines through the dust on the floor, lines that indicated the chair had been drug across the room to the spot on the floor next to the table," said Bruce.

"You wouldn't know anything about that would you, Counselor?" asked Will. "The way we figure it, the only person other than Francesco that could have found their way back to the cabin would have been Eli."

Officers Pearlman and Tyrell both turned toward Chester, looking for a reaction, and a reaction is what they got.

"Chester? Chester? Hey, you okay?" asked Officer Pearlman.

Chapter 47

Tables Turned

Sunday evening, October 8th, back at the hospital

"Sir, visiting hours are over."

"I'm not visiting," said Eli as he stormed past the check-in desk at the hospital front entrance.

Eli bypassed the elevator and went straight for the stairwell. Taking two steps at a time, he arrived at the third floor before anyone figured out where he was headed. As he passed the nurses' station, again he was advised that visiting hours were over. He didn't knock; he barged in, grabbed a chair, and wedged it under the door handle, preventing anyone else from entering.

"Wake up."

She didn't stir.

He kicked the bed. "I said wake up."

Earlier in the day, after Reverend Coker and his wife had left, the attendant nurse had summoned the doctor to her bed. Her vitals had slipped, and her heartbeat had fallen to fifty-five beats per minute. Rose, struggling with the line between consciousness and unconsciousness, stirred and slowly turned her head.

"Eli?" she managed.

"Yep."

Rose looked confused, lost, not sure where she was.

"You're wondering what I'm doing here, I'll bet?" Eli said.

Rose answered yes with a barely perceptible nod of her head.

"Whatever I damn well please," answered Eli. "Now you listen to me."

Rose's breathing was heavy, and it took all her strength to keep her eyes on Eli.

"I know. I know all about it. You see, today I found the letters. The letters my dad, your first husband, wrote to you."

Rose lifted her left hand ever so slightly and tried to speak.

"SHUT UP."

Rose glanced at the door when the banging began. Eli never blinked.

"Open up immediately. Open this door right now," shouted a nurse. "The police are on the way."

"Well, Rose, we don't have much time, so I'll be quick about it. I own you. You're mine. Know this—that at some point, I don't know when yet, but I'll know when the time is right, I'm going to release all the letters to the newspapers."

Eli looked for a reaction and got none.

"Did you hear me?"

Rose's lips were dry and cracked and spittle was clinging to the left corner of her mouth. She nodded her head that, yes, she'd heard him.

"I'm going to ruin you. You and dear old Monty. Seems he was in on it. You could have gone to the police. You could have cleared my name. But you didn't. You sent me running and now my life will never be the same. I'll always be talked about behind my back as the coward, the innocent kid that ran anyway. And I've lost five years of my life. All because of you two, and now I'm going to get my revenge. Every last ounce of it. So, if you try to restore any normalcy to your life, just know that I'll be there ready to pounce, ready to destroy you. Let's see how you like living in a cage."

And with that, he stepped away from the bed and ripped the chair out from under the door handle, sending it flying across the room. He then barreled down the hall and into the stairwell before anyone could stop him.

Chapter 48

Turn for the Worse

Monty was woken from a painkiller-induced stupor by a phone call early the next morning. The night before, Walker found him asleep in front of the TV when he came home from dinner with Isabelle's family. Walker had declined their offer at first, figuring his dad needed and wanted the company, but Monty insisted Walker go.

"Son, you've been great. Just great. But you need a break from this too. Go and have a good time," he'd said.

Walker tried to wake Monty but to no avail, so Monty spent the evening asleep in the La-Z-boy and woke with a stiff neck to prove it.

"Hello," Monty managed as he gradually figured out where he was.

"Mr. Atkins?"

"Yes, this is Monty Atkins. Can I help you?"

"Mr. Atkins, this is Nurse Compton at the hospital. Can you come by this morning? Your wife took a turn for the worse last night."

* * *

Just shy of an hour later, Walker dropped Monty off at the hospital.

"Thanks, son. Now look. I'm sure everything's going to be fine. You head to school."

"But how will you get around?"

"I'll manage. I'll get a taxi and then Abigail can give me a ride home from the office."

"You're going to work?"

"I gotta be somewhere, might as well be the office. Now go."

Walker reluctantly pulled away and headed for school, and Monty entered the hospital praying all would be okay.

* * *

The elevator door opened on the third floor and Monty wheeled himself out and toward the nurses' station.

"Well, Monty, it looks like you're getting the hang of it," said Dr. Spelman.

"How is she?" Monty asked, ignoring the wheelchair comment.

"Monty, Rose slipped into a coma sometime during the night. I've been conferring with Nurse Compton about her condition.

"A coma? But how? She was doing pretty well yesterday when I left."

"Yes, she was, but after Reverend Coker and his wife left, the attendant nurse checked her vitals and became concerned," explained Nurse Compton.

Nurse Compton was a fixture at the hospital and a calming presence. She had grown up in South Carolina. Her parents were sharecroppers and slave descendants and worked hard to put her through college, and now she was able to support them. She took pride in her appearance and demanded it of the other nurses on the floor. She preferred the white uniform and matching hat to the blue scrubs.

"It seems her heartbeat had fallen and that's always a reason for concern," added Dr. Spelman.

"So, what did you do and why wasn't I called?"

"Now, Monty, there's no reason to get upset," said the doctor. "We have protocols for these situations, and they were followed. I was called and approved of the steps that were taken. An hour later her resting heart rate had risen out of the danger zone, so all seemed good."

Monty ran his right hand through his hair and gathered himself.

"Okay. But you said she's in a coma now. When did that happen?"

"That's what we're trying to determine. The night shift turned over and the morning round of nurses came on the floor at 5:45. When we turn over staff, we make our rounds and note any changes. That's when we noticed."

"Okay. Well, you keep records of every status check," Monty said as he waved his hand toward the clipboard Nurse Compton was holding. "So, we should know exactly when the last scheduled check was. Right?"

Dr. Spelman looked at Nurse Compton, who was trying her hardest to not look at anyone.

"Mr. Atkins, the night nurses skipped the last regularly scheduled check-up because they had taken her vitals thirty minutes earlier because ..."

Nurse Compton looked to Dr. Spelman.

"What?" said Monty.

"Monty, it seems your wife had a visitor late last night that may have traumatized her."

"A visitor? Who?"

"We don't know for sure," said Dr. Spelman.

"Then check the Visitor Log, dammit."

"Monty, this visitor didn't sign in."

Monty stared at the doctor and then at Nurse Compton.

"What aren't you telling me?" demanded Monty.

"We think the visitor was your son, Eli," said Dr. Spelman.

* * *

Monty tried to absorb that news, but he didn't want to go where his mind might take him.

"Can I see her?" asked Monty.

"Of course, go right in," said Dr. Spelman.

He wheeled himself into the room, and Dr. Spelman and Nurse Compton followed behind. After making a show of checking on things, Nurse Compton left the room.

"Monty, we'll watch her closely. Don't you worry," said the doctor. "Is there anything I can do for you?"

Monty had wheeled himself alongside Rose and was holding her hand.

"I'll need a bed," he said without turning to look at him. "I'll be sleeping here until she comes out of it."

"Monty, we don't know how long she'll be in this state. I would advise ..."

Monty whipped his head around and stared at the man.

"You asked me what you could do for me, and I'm telling you. I need a bed."

"There's no reason to raise your voice."

"There's no reason not to, Doc! Now am I gonna get that bed?"

"I'll see to it."

The doctor left the room and Monty turned back to Rose.

"I'm right here, honey, and I'm not going anywhere."

And then he wept.

* * *

"You two have a visitor," announced the young Candy Striper.

The young girl, couldn't have been more than sixteen, stepped to the side and Chester's full six-feet-six-inch frame filled the door.

"Chester, it's good to see you. Come on in."

Chester stepped aside so the young girl could pass, and then he walked in and gave his good friend a pat on the shoulder.

"Any change?"

"No. No change."

Chester and Monty exchanged small talk about this and that. They talked about the upcoming World Series. Monty asked about Chester's boys and their football careers. Chester said he was taking the boat out the next weekend and wanted to know if Monty would join him.

"Maybe some other time, Chester. I think I'll be here for a while."

"Monty, I've had clients before with a loved one in a similar situation. I understand your desire to be here. I do, really. But you're going to find that you need a break too. So, just know that when you do, I'm here. We can grab a beer or dinner together, or maybe I'll let you teach me how to play golf."

Monty smiled at the thought of Chester trying to swing a club around his massive chest. Chester had been a college football sensation and turned down a career in the NFL to attend law school instead, but he hadn't lost the size and shape that had made him so devastating on the field, but the thought of him swinging a club was a stretch.

"Thanks, Ches. I appreciate it. That day may come, but until it does, I'll be here. Besides, who's to say she won't come out of this in a day or two? No one I ask seems to know a damn thing about these types of things."

"Let's hope so."

After a moment of silence, Monty spoke up.

"Is there something else on your mind?"

"Yes, it's about Eli. The police are looking for him again."

"I'm not surprised." Monty was holding Rose's hand and watching her sleep.

"They think Eli may have busted in here last night."

"Looks that way."

"The police have asked if I can bring him in for questioning. They'd rather not issue a warrant for his arrest."

"Chester, I'm not for pressing charges if my opinion counts for anything. Just make it go away. Can you do that?"

"I'll do my best," said Chester, and then he quietly exited the room, leaving his good friend behind with his wife.

* * *

And that's exactly what Chester did. He made it go away. He later shared with Monty what he had learned over the last few days. Monty learned that Officers Pearlman and Tyrell had not found anything in the shack, but they felt sure someone else had been there. Chester interviewed the night nurses and learned that they'd identified the intruder as Eli from looking at pictures. They also told him that before they started banging on the door to Rose's room, they'd overheard the intruder shouting "I know, I know all about it."

Chester convinced the police to drop the matter when he told them that Rose had taken a turn for the worse before Eli had even arrived Sunday night. And frankly, given what the family had been through, no one from Chief Randall on down had the heart to add to the family's troubles. So, the matter was dropped.

Monty kept up his vigil, only leaving Rose's room to eat a meal in the hospital cafeteria or stretch his legs by walking the corridors of the third floor on his new crutches. Walker came by each afternoon to visit and bring him any mail and a change of clothes. Abigail dropped by every morning to talk about matters at the office. His business partners told him not to worry about the office, that they'd take care of things until he was ready. Rose's condition remained unchanged.

So, all was accounted for—that is, except for Eli. Monty and Chester figured Eli must have found the letters and that reading them had fueled his outrage on Sunday night. *But what to do now?* wondered Monty, for no one had seen Eli since he had barged in on Rose in her hospital room.

Chapter 49

The Conquering Hero

Friday, October 20TH, 1978

Eli turned up. It had been two weeks since he appeared on the scene as a hero, leading the police on a manhunt for a serial killer and saving Monty and his brother, Walker, in the process. But no one other than the night shift at the county hospital the previous Sunday night had seen him since. In the week that followed, hardly a conversation around town failed to bring up what everyone was calling the "shootout in the swamp." But over the last week, the conversations changed from "Did you hear what happened last Friday?" to "If he was guilty, then why did he run?" to "Where's Eli now?"

Monty was cleaning up after dinner and putting away the dishes when he learned that Eli had surfaced. Chester had been right—Monty needed a break from sitting with Rose. Her condition remained unchanged, which was both good news and bad. Monty still slept most nights in the roll-away bed next to Rose but going forward planned on spending every third night at home, where he could get a good night's sleep and a proper shower. Each day he spent a few hours at the office, and he vowed he would exercise at least one day a week even if that simply meant time on the practice putting green. Monty had graduated to crutches, no longer needing a wheelchair, but he still couldn't swing a club beyond a putter.

Monty picked up the phone on the third ring.

"Monty Atkins here."

"Mr. Atkins, it's Charles Dansby, from Wappoo Country Club. I'm so sorry to bother you at home."

"Why, that's no problem, Charles," said Monty wondering why in the world the club general manager was calling him on a Friday night. Maybe he hadn't paid his bill. Wouldn't surprise him. He'd been rather unfocused of late.

"How can I help you?"

* * *

EARLIER THAT DAY AT THE WAPPOO COUNTRY CLUB

"Hey, Curtis? Another round of drinks. On me."

The small group witnessing the goings-on kept growing as word spread. Eli was in the bar and buying round after round for anyone who'd join him. The younger crowd of men that had taken the afternoon off to play golf celebrated each time he cried out for another round while the older crowd playing gin in the corner looked on with disdain at Eli's brash behavior.

Every Friday afternoon at Wappoo Country Club, a group ranging in size from half a dozen to a dozen foursomes would show up to play golf in what had come to be known as the Train Game. Wives would show up in time for cocktails as the men were coming off the course, and many of the young socialites would stay for dinner on the veranda.

The Train Game was a simple game, and while handicaps were used, thus giving everyone a chance, it was a game that rewarded steady play. The entry fee was forty dollars. Half the pot would be paid out in skins and the other half was paid out to the winners of the Train. To win the Train Game, you accumulated points—one for bogey, two for par, three for birdie, six for an eagle, and eight for a double-eagle or hole-in-one. But you couldn't collect points until you got on the Train, which you did by getting a birdie or two pars in a row. The real twist to the game, though, was that you lost all your points, and would have to start over, if you scored a double-bogey or two bogies in a row.

The turnout this fall afternoon was strong, meaning the total pot available for skins was $960, and the pot to be split among first, second, and third place in the Train game would also be $960. Wappoo Country Club boasted a membership of strong players. While the average handicap at the club was fourteen, out of a membership of four hundred active golfers, 20 percent carried a single-digit handicap, and of that group, twenty-five were scratch or better. The competition each week was good-natured but intense. Given the high quality of golf and the large turnout each week, typically only a few skins were awarded, meaning anyone who won a skin won big.

No one knew how Eli heard about the game, but he had. Around eleven that morning he strolled into the pro shop and introduced himself to the head pro, Jay Swain, and asked if he could rent clubs and get in on the game that afternoon. Jay was shocked when he saw that none other than Eli Atkins was standing in front of him but was also wondering if he was even a member. He called the GM to ask for guidance, and Charles explained that since he had not yet turned twenty-six, he could still play under his father's membership. But Eli was wearing ratty old blue jeans and a dingy white T-shirt, and Jay struggled awkwardly to explain the dress code.

"Mr. Swain, not a problem. What do you say you set me up with a new wardrobe? You own this pro shop, right?"

"Yes, sir, I do."

"Then this is your lucky day."

That afternoon, Eli and the head pro bought Eli a full wardrobe for any man-about-town: slacks, shorts, golf shirts, sweaters, sweater vests, belts, golf shoes, rain gear, hats, golf gloves, golf balls. And why waste time renting clubs when you can own them? Jay was in a fine mood. Eli walked out of the pro shop decked out in the latest golf fashion, and after purchasing a hot dog and a beer at the snack bar, he walked onto the driving range to test out his brand-new set of Wilson irons and MacGregor persimmon woods.

Word spread quickly and before too long, folks who had been enjoying lunch were leaving their table to see if in fact Eli was back. Eli was aware of his notoriety and decided to bask in it and put on a show. He started off hitting wedges and moved methodically through each club in his bag, showing off a variety of shots, both high and low trajectories, some fades, some draws, some punch shots, etc. ... When he pulled out his driver, a murmur of anticipation spread through the small crowd gathered outside the pro shop, and the other golfers on the range stopped to watch as well. Eli did not disappoint.

By the time he finished on the range, most of the other golfers scheduled to play that afternoon had arrived. Eli knew many of the other young golfers who were playing that afternoon, having grown up with them. The mood was electric, and everyone was looking forward to a great time. The head pro ordered a second cart girl to follow along, ensuring that the good mood wouldn't wear off anytime soon.

On the 1st tee, Eli suggested bets with each of the other three players in his foursome, bets that were substantially larger than they were comfortable with, but not wanting to ruin a good time, each knuckled under and made the bet. Eli went out in the first group and picked up where he left off on the range by knocking his approach stiff and sinking a five-foot putt for birdie. He accepted the good-natured high-fives and headed to the next tee box.

Over the next several holes, the group walked down the fairway side-by-side, the other three feeling like celebrities in their own right, for they were playing golf with their old friend, Eli, who'd come back from the dead to slay a killer. On top of that, they were the first to hear what he'd been up to for the last five years, and the stories he was sharing would no doubt be retold many times over, not only by Eli, but by them as well.

Eli kept striping the ball, long and straight, and frankly, by the 8th hole, he was enjoying himself a bit too much. On the 1st tee, he'd cajoled each of them into a $25 Nassau with automatic presses once two holes down and $5 for all the junk—longest drive on par-fives, closest to the pin in regulation on par-threes and par-fives, putts made longer than the flagstick, sandy-pars, and $5 owed to the others if you three-putted or left a ball in a trap. The others were all good players, but none had the experience Eli did playing for this kind of money, and the stakes combined with Eli's game and obnoxious celebrations put them off their own game. The net result: They'd each have to explain to their wives how they'd blown a couple hundred bucks on the course. By the time they made the turn, Eli was walking down the fairway alone and the other three were holding back.

Eli walked off the 18th hole having carded another birdie and told the guys that drinks were on him. Since they were the first off, they were the first in the bar, and by the time the last foursome joined them, Eli was three sheets to the wind and getting louder and louder by the minute. Eli won three of the four skins that day and ran away with first place in the Train Game, pocketing $1,200 plus over $600 he took off his three playing partners, three men who left shortly after finishing one drink and then telling their wives, who had just arrived, that they no longer felt like eating at the club. But the other players that afternoon who had not been in Eli's foursome were still in the mood for a grand old time.

At some point, one of the older gentlemen in the corner, trying to enjoy his meal with his wife and another couple, asked Eli and his buddies to take it down a notch, and Eli responded by buying them a round of drinks and delivering them himself. When Eli wouldn't leave well enough alone and walk away, the elderly, and now very annoyed, gentleman, stepped away from the table and sought out the general manager. Hence the call to Monty at home.

* * *

"Mr. Atkins, it's about your son, Eli."

"What about him?" asked Monty warily.

"Well, he's here, in the club bar, and he's making quite a scene. He's been here all day and he's run up a sizeable tab. I suppose you knew he was heading out here?" asked Charles Dansby.

Monty hadn't seen hide nor hair of Eli in nearly two weeks, and the last place he expected Eli to show up unannounced was the club. He hadn't been a big fan of club life when he was growing up at home since he associated it so closely with Rose's social ladder climbing.

"Why yes, Eli asked if it would be okay," Monty lied. "He's still a member, right, Charles?"

"Oh, yes, sir. It's just that it had been so long since anyone here had seen him."

"I get that. I should have called ahead and let y'all know he'd be coming out," said Monty. "But you said something about him creating a scene—what do you mean?"

"Mr. Atkins, he shouldn't be driving but he wouldn't turn over his keys when we asked him. He became rather belligerent when I told the bartender to cut him off. I told him I'd call a taxi to take him anywhere he pleased, but he would have no part of it."

"Oh, dear."

"Mr. Atkins, under normal circumstances, in these situations I would call the police and have him removed, but given all that has happened, I decided to call you first."

"Thank you, Charles. Don't let him leave. I'm on my way."

Five minutes later he was on his way to the club.

"What now, Lord?" he said to the inside of his car.

* * *

Charles Dansby was waiting at the entrance when Monty arrived.

"Mr. Atkins, thank you for coming."

"Don't mention it. I'm just sorry you had to call. What can you tell me?"

Charles filled him on what he knew as he walked with Monty back toward the bar.

"And in addition to all of that, it appears Eli won nearly $2,000 on the course today," said Mr. Dansby.

"He did what?" asked Monty in a bit of shock.

"Yep, you heard me, nearly $2,000. He became quite the golfer while he was away, and he offended a few folks with his less than humble reaction to taking everyone's money. We have no beef with gambling, but the drinking is a problem. He was very loud and belligerent and physically threatened a member who asked him to quiet down. As I said on the phone, if it hadn't been for what you and your family have been through, I would have called the police."

"No, Charles, I understand, and thank you," said Monty as the two of them were standing just outside the bar. "I'll take it from here. Do you know if he's alone in there?"

"Curtis, the bartender, is still inside making sure Eli doesn't help himself, but other than that he's alone. All the other members have gone home for the evening. I told him you were on your way, and he seemed happy to hear that."

"Very well, Charles. Hopefully we'll be out of here in just a few minutes and you can lock up and go home yourself."

"Thank you, sir, and good luck," said Charles, and then after a brief pause, he added: "I'm a father too."

Monty smiled at Charles and shook his hand, and then steeled himself for what he feared would be a confrontation. Monty walked into the bar and saw Eli in the corner, slouched in his chair with his feet up on the table, eyes closed. Monty gently shook Eli's shoulder.

"Eli. Eli, wake up."

"Monty, old boy," said Eli as he removed his feet from the tabletop, sat up, and rubbed his face. "Did you forget to pay your bill? Curtis here won't pour me a drink."

"Eli, you've had enough for the night. Let's you and me go home and talk about this in the morning." Monty looked to Curtis, waved, and communicated that he'd take it from here. Curtis nodded, finished drying the glass in his hand, and left out the back.

"Nah, not necessary. There's nothin' to talk about, Monty. There's just you listenin'."

"Go ahead," said Monty as he took a seat across from Eli.

"I know about the letters. I know Rath told you and Rose that he killed Kimberly, and others."

At the mention of Kimberly's name, Eli seemed to sober up a bit. He sat up straighter in his chair and leaned over the table toward Monty.

"I know you and Rose could have ended all this years ago and that I would have been free to come home. But you didn't, did you?"

"Oh, Eli. It's not what you think."

"Bullshit. Don't lie to me."

"I'm not lying, son. Just let me explain."

"Nope, not gonna happen," said Eli as he bolted up from his chair. He staggered around a bit, rubbing his chin with his left hand. "You see, this is how it's gonna be. I own you. I own you both, you, and Rose. I have the letters and I'll release them if it suits my purposes."

"And what are your purposes?" asked Monty, still seated, and looking down at a spot on the floor between his two feet.

"Ah, good question, Counselor. My purposes are very simple. My purposes is *me*."

"You?" asked Monty.

"Yep. Me. I'll be here, at the club, every day, running up your tab, a tab you'll pay. Beginning tomorrow, I'm going to look for a house that you're gonna buy me. I'll rent in the meantime, and you'll sign that lease. I'll let you know how much cash I'll be needing on a weekly basis but plan on a lot."

"I see. So, this is how you're going to get your revenge."

"For starters, but I'll think of something else. And don't forget, if you try to rectify matters or rise above yourself in some way, I'll release the letters and both you and Rose could be looking at jail time for obstruction. I figure at a minimum you'll be disbarred, and by then I will have bled you dry of all your cash. So, Monty, old boy, looks like your future belongs to me, if you can call it a future."

Eli turned and headed toward the exit, stopped, and turned back to Monty.

"Tell me, Monty, how does it feel? Having your freedom taken from you?"

And then he walked out of the bar, leaving Monty all alone, again.

Chapter 50

A Kernel of Hope

Eli was true to his word. He was at the club nearly every day looking for high stakes matches and running up a big bill. Eli learned his craft well in the Bahamas. The trick was sizing up your opponent psychologically. If you were good at that, then it was a matter of roping them into agreeing with the number of strokes you would give them. Some golfers simply liked the action; win or lose, they enjoyed telling tales of their big bets. Others fancied themselves hustlers themselves and feared they would scare Eli away if they asked for too many strokes. But most golfers rarely play to their potential when money is on the line, so Eli didn't mind giving an opponent a stroke or two more than their handicap called for knowing they'd fall short of their potential. Eli, on the other hand, didn't crumble under the pressure and played his excellent game regardless of the size of the bet. Still, Eli was never short of folks who thought they could take him down. None did.

Eli followed through with his threat about the rent and made Monty sign the lease for a home in Folly Beach right on the beach. The folks who call Folly Beach their home like to think they put the "folly" in "beach," and if you've spent any time there, you'd agree. As added humiliation, Eli insisted that they meet at the club each week so Monty could pass him an envelope of cash.

When Monty and Eli were alone, Eli treated him like dirt, always reminding Monty of Rath's letters and the power they gave him. But to the outside world, as far as Monty could tell, Eli was the perfect gentleman, the humble conquering hero. Eli apologized to Charles Dansby, the Wappoo Club General Manager, and he bought dinner for the older couple he had so offended. Everyone chalked up his behavior that afternoon to the fact he was just overjoyed with being back. Yes, Eli had become a perfect gentleman. Folks loved him, even those he regularly fleeced, for Eli beating you on the course was worth something in and of itself.

Even though Rose was still in a coma and Eli was blackmailing him, Monty was doing okay, he was holding up. As for his feelings about Eli, Monty was confused and scared. He hated being blackmailed. But at the same time, he was scared for Eli. The way he was behaving was just wrong. Wrong in every sense of the word, and in Monty's mind, Eli's behavior was proof Eli was suffering and lost.

And Monty didn't know what to do. If he told Eli he had not known about the letters from Rath, would Eli believe him? And wouldn't Monty just be throwing all the blame on Rose? What if Monty told Eli he'd hired a private detective to find the real killer. Would he also have to tell Eli that he kept it a secret from Rose because he didn't trust her? No, he couldn't do that. Monty saw no way to repair relations with his son without abandoning his wife at the same time. So Monty did the only thing he knew to do—he loved them both, the best he could. And he prayed.

Monty's sunny disposition through it all drove Eli crazy. He'd hoped making Monty and Rose suffer would have brought him more joy, but it didn't. He wasn't even sure either of them was suffering. Rose was in a coma; he hadn't planned on that and tried to ignore feeling responsible for her condition since she slipped into the coma after he barged into her room. And then there was Monty. He kept paying, never objecting. He invited Eli for dinner and was always asking if they could play golf together. Frankly, Monty's good-natured response was killing him.

Eli, on the other hand, was miserable. Around Monty, he put on a show as if all was wonderful in his world, but just the opposite was true. All was not good. While a perfect gentleman at the club, in the early morning hours past midnight, he could be seen at Folly Beach bars causing trouble. His feelings of extreme loneliness returned.

He was lonely again because he missed Rachel. Yes, he had recovered his name, he was Eli Atkins again. But what good was that without Rachel by his side? Even when he was with others, playing golf, or carousing at night with old high school friends, Eli felt alone, utterly alone. The loneliness was eating him up. His father, on the other hand, though he really was alone, spending most of his time sitting at Rose's bedside, seemed content.

At night, as he tried to fall asleep, the tears returned. He hadn't cried since he walked off the boat in the Bahamas over five years ago, vowing he would never again let anyone hurt him, never let anyone get that close again. He'd failed. Rachel got that close, and he'd lost her. Was it possible? Was it possible to insulate yourself from ever being hurt again, from feeling anything, anything at all? Or would the loneliness always return? Yes, Monty had reason to fear for Eli. Eli was indeed lost, but Eli knew it too and in this knowledge rested a kernel of hope.

Chapter 51

A Thanksgiving to Remember

Sunday, November 19th, 1978, County Hospital, Room 312

"Reverend, can I pour you some more champagne?" asked Monty.

"Well, I don't think the good Lord would object to me havin' one more glass. It is a celebration."

"A celebration, indeed."

Monty had received a phone call earlier that morning around 7:00 a.m. from Nurse Turner, the night shift head nurse. Rose woke up sometime in the early hours of the morning. While ecstatic, the nurses on staff muted their excitement because they had seen patients come out of a coma before only to fall right back into one. No reason to falsely raise anyone's hopes. But by 6:00 a.m. there was no denying it—Rose was awake. Dr. Spelman was called and after his evaluation, he asked Nurse Turner to give Monty a call.

By early afternoon, the room was full of people coming by to wish the Atkins family the best. Chester was there, Walker and his girlfriend Isabelle were there, and friends from church were coming and going. Reverend

Coker had delivered the good news at the pulpit during morning services, resulting in a nonstop flow of well-wishers.

Everyone was there but Eli. Monty had called Eli's house on Folly Beach a couple of times earlier in the day, but the phone just rang. Having no other way of getting ahold of him, he let it go for now.

* * *

Monty spent Sunday night in Rose's room and was reluctant to leave her side Monday morning, but Dr. Spelman assured Monty that Rose was out of the woods. She had a long road ahead of her and would need to regain her strength, but there was every reason to believe she would make a full recovery. Monty headed to the office to wrap things up before the upcoming long weekend. Thanksgiving was in just a few days and oh what a Thanksgiving it would be. There was nothing that could ruin his fine mood now. Nothing at all.

* * *

TUESDAY NIGHT AT THE ATKINS HOUSE

Monty had spent Tuesday afternoon organizing the Thanksgiving dinner. The hospital was going to let him use a corner of the cafeteria for the big meal. Since it was Thanksgiving, the hospital would run a skeleton crew, only cooking for patients who couldn't leave the hospital and they couldn't accommodate a large group. So Monty would plan the Thanksgiving meal himself. He contacted the church and they lined up some of Rose's friends, who were happy to make extra dishes of what they were already cooking for their own family. That left only the bird. *Henry's* on Market Street agreed to cook Monty a turkey Wednesday afternoon and Walker could pick it up.

All was well—except for matters with Eli, of course. Monty had been in constant prayer about what to do. Monday, when his calls to Eli's house went unanswered, he drove out to Folly Beach. The club was closed on Mondays and Monty had no idea where else Eli spent his time. He'd heard that he'd become a fixture on the Folly Beach bar circuit.

Monty knocked on Eli's door but there was no answer. Eli was still driving a truck Quaid Dawson had loaned him and the truck was in the driveway, but no sign of Eli. Monty peered into the windows and past the curtains.

Yep, someone was living here, thought Monty. Monty anticipated finding Eli's house empty and had written Eli a letter before heading over. The letter explained that Rose had come out of the coma and was going to be okay. And in the letter, Monty invited Eli to join them for a Thanksgiving meal at the hospital. He left the letter in an envelope under the windshield wiper of the truck and walked back to his car.

As Monty sat on the back porch on Tuesday night, he assumed Eli had read the letter by now. Monty was miffed that he hadn't even gotten a call from Eli. Monty knew Eli was angry, and since Eli still thought that he and Rose had conspired to keep Rath's identity a secret, he could certainly understand why. And Monty was lost. If he told Eli the complete story, he might stop being angry at him, but he'd still be angry with Rose. Monty needed a way to tell Eli that Rose had changed and that she was sorry. Monty figured that if Eli could hear Rose apologize and ask for forgiveness, the healing process could begin. But until that time, Eli would continue to stew. How then to get Eli's attention?

Monty had been trying to kill him with kindness, hoping Eli would eventually let up and stop threatening to release Rath's letters to the press. He could not let that happen. Yes, the truth will set you free, but that was too much truth. No, this was a delicate situation Monty would have to manage. He needed to get the letters back.

And Monty was tired of it all. Rose was back and he was looking forward to rebuilding a life with her. He knew that for her to be truly happy, she'd want her children around, healthy and prospering. He'd been unwilling to do anything to further upset Eli. Yes, he needed to manage the situation until Eli calmed down and was willing to turn over the letters, then he could use tough love to get Eli back into shape.

* * *

Wednesday, November 22nd, the day before Thanksgiving

Monty walked into Room 312 with fresh flowers and placed them on the table by the window.

"Good mornin', Sweetheart. And how are you this fine day?"

"Oh, Monty, flowers again. I appreciate it, but really, you don't have to," said Rose.

"I know. That's what makes it fun. Now about tomorrow, Doc said we can wheel you down to the cafeteria and have Thanksgiving. How does that sound?"

"Who will be there?" asked Rose.

"Well, I've invited Mrs. Babcock and the Dawsons. Mrs. B said she would make it but would have to leave in time to go to her daughter's house and help with their meal."

"Anyone else we can count on?" asked Rose.

Monty knew she was hoping Eli would make it. She began asking about Eli Sunday afternoon and Monty had brushed the topic aside, casually remarking that he'd get word to Eli. Since then, Monty had remained silent.

"Monty, what's going on? I know you're hiding something from me. Now out with it. I'm his mother and I have a right to know."

Monty busied himself straightening up magazines on the table with his back to Rose, trying to figure out what to say.

"Monty, I'm getting the distinct feeling that you're trying to manage other people's lives again. Now, please, tell me what's going on."

And so he did, beginning with the evening five weeks earlier when Eli showed up at the club and made a scene.

"So, we're being blackmailed."

"No, honey, that's not it. Eli is lost and angry right now. I didn't want to push him away until you were better. You're his mother and I wanted him here by your side when you came out of it."

"Well, where is he? He's not by my side, is he, Monty?"

Monty had been leaning against the table with the stack of magazines in his hands. He placed them on the bed and walked over and sat down and took one of Rose's hands in his.

"No, he's not. Rose, and I don't know what to do."

"There's nothing you can do, Monty. I was a terrible mother, and I did a terrible thing, darn near unforgiveable. But I know this much, I can't force him to forgive me. I've received forgiveness from the Lord for what I did, and though I'm liberated, I know that for the rest of my life I will struggle with the horrible pain of guilt because of what I did to him. But if you keep trying to manage or manipulate the situation, your efforts will backfire. Eli must learn to deal with the facts of his life."

"But don't you want to see him?"

"More than anything. I want to see him. More than you can possibly imagine. I want him to hear me apologize. I want him to hear me ask for forgiveness, but I can't force him to accept anything I have to say. He's going to have to forgive me in his own time, and only the Holy Spirit can move that mountain."

"So what should I do?"

"Nothing. If he wants to release the letters, don't try to stop him. We can handle it."

* * *

Wednesday Evening, Back at the Atkins House

Monty was at home. He surveyed the kitchen and the food brought over by the church ladies. Laid out before him were dishes of green beans, squash casserole, mashed potatoes, sweet potatoes, stuffing, creamed corn, and pumpkin pie, as well as a twenty-pound turkey, enough food for a small army. That was all right because, in addition to their own family, Monty had invited the entire Quaid family and Mrs. Babcock.

After putting all the food away, Monty grabbed a beer and retreated to the porch. It was a wonderful evening. They were experiencing an extended fall, and winter was still somewhere on the distant horizon. Walker was with Isabelle and friends, leaving Monty alone. Frankly, he was happy for the solitude. It had been a fantastic week, what with Rose coming out of her coma, but a hectic one, nonetheless.

The solitude was interrupted by the phone calling out to be answered.

"Monty Atkins here."

"Mr. Atkins, this is Officer Tyrell at the police station. Can you come down here? We have Eli in custody."

A half-hour later, Monty was talking to Officer Tyrell in the lobby of the police station.

"Mr. Atkins, I'm sorry I had to call tonight, but we just can't keep covering for him."

"What do you mean?" asked Monty.

"For the last few weeks, we'd get calls about Eli causing trouble in a bar. Typically, he'd drink too much and would start fighting. I swear that boy of yours has a mean streak, and when he unloads on someone, it's downright scary. We'd haul his ass down here, but we've been letting him go each time. We'd pump coffee in him and send him home with a patrolman, who would drop him off at his house. But tonight was a bridge too far. He put a man in the hospital."

"Oh dear."

"Yep. But I think Eli will skate. The man ain't going to press charges. He has a record, and we found a lot of weed in his car, and he said he wouldn't press charges against Eli if we'd overlook the drugs. But Mr. Atkins, this is the last time."

"Officer, I had no idea."

"We figured you didn't. We arrested him. He will need to appear before the judge. He took a swing at my partner, Officer Jenkins. He's new on the job and doesn't know all your son's been through."

"I thought you and Officer Pearlman were partners."

"We are, but sometimes the boss has us take out younger cops and show them the ropes."

"Got it."

"Well, as I was saying, we arrested Eli. Just post bail and he'll be out in time for Thanksgiving dinner tomorrow."

"Okay. Understood. And Officer, you have a great Thanksgiving."

"You too."

* * *

Monty explained who he was and asked to see Eli. He was led back to a small room where lawyers met with their clients and was told to wait. Five minutes later, Eli was led into the room. The officer removed his handcuffs and Eli took a seat. He looked scared when he entered, but seeing Monty, he put on a tough veneer.

The two of them sat there, waiting for the other to speak. Eli broke first.

"How long is this going to take?"

"How long is what going to take?" asked Monty.

"You posting bail, what else. I need to get out of here."

"Oh, I'm not posting bail."

"Then what the hell are you doing here?"

"It's time we had a talk."

Eli sat across the table and listened as Monty told him about when he first met Rose, who Rath was back in college, about Rose's horrible father and brother, about the private detective he'd hired, and about everything he'd done on his own and what he'd done with Rose to clear Eli's name and bring him home. Eli was stoic, never responding to a word Monty said. After over a half-hour, Monty stood from his chair to stretch his legs.

"You know, I still have the letters. If I release them to the press, y'all will be done in this town," said Eli.

"Son, you do what you have to do. Your mother and I will be just fine," said Monty as he met his son's gaze. "Eli, nothing I've told you today excuses what your mother did, and she knows that. But I hope maybe now you'll have a different perspective."

Eli looked away.

"Son, you have a choice to make."

"What choice do I have?"

"Where you go from here."

Monty stood and slid the chair back under the table and began putting his coat on.

"I imagine you used your one phone call to get ahold of me. I'll let Chester know you'll be needing his services again. I'll be seeing you, son."

And then Monty did one of the hardest things he'd ever had to do—he left his son in jail and walked out.

Chapter 52

It's Not Too Late

The hospital, Saturday after Thanksgiving

"I'm here to see my mother. Is she still in Room 312?"

"The nurse looked up from her charts, visibly alarmed to see Eli standing before her."

"It's okay. I'm not here to cause trouble."

The nurse removed her glasses and pointed them at Eli.

"You'd better not." And then, smiling, told him she was still in Room 312, and that his father and brother were with her.

Eli walked down the hall, came to the room, and lightly tapped on the door jamb. Walker turned and smiled when he saw Eli.

"May I come in?" he asked.

Monty nodded and waved him in.

"How is she?" asked Eli.

"She's resting. The last two days have been hectic—well, hectic by her standards. She had a bad night, but she seems to be okay now."

Monty turned back to look at Rose and took her left hand in his. Eli was touched by the simple sign of affection. Eli had spent the last few days in jail, and while there he took a full accounting of his life, what had happened to him, but also what had befallen his mother and his father, Monty.

Despite all that had happened, Monty still loved Rose. Eli knew that now, and he knew what he wanted. He wanted what his father had, what his parents had. He wanted someone to love and a love so strong that nothing, absolutely nothing, could tear it apart. And if there were ever a marriage that had experienced events that could tear it apart, it was his parents. But here they were. Together. And here he was. And Walker too. A family. They were a family. Through thick and through thin. Eli had never felt such a sense of loss and hope at the same time. Loss, for what could have been. And hope, for what he wanted more than anything—a family.

"Dad?"

"Yes, Eli."

"Can I have a moment alone with Mom?"

Monty looked up at Eli and saw a young man at peace.

"Absolutely, son."

"Come on, Walker. Let's you and me head to the cafeteria. Eli, take all the time you need. Will you drop by the cafeteria when you're done?"

"Yes, Dad."

Monty and Walker left and shut the door behind them. Eli stared at his mother lying in bed and then he slowly approached and took a seat where Monty had been sitting. Eli just sat there, staring at his mother and thought about everything Monty had told him just a few nights earlier in jail.

"Why didn't you tell me about him? Maybe I could have understood."

His tears started slowly.

"But you just always pushed me so hard. I'm sorry I couldn't be what you needed me to be. But if you had just let me live my life, maybe you could have learned to love me."

Eli sat quietly.

"I needed a mom."

Eli leaned forward slowly and then his head collapsed against Rose's side. The tears came freely now, and Eli struggled to speak through them.

"I needed you to be my mom. I understand now why that was so hard for you, but it doesn't change the fact that I needed a mom."

And then Eli slowly raised his head and wiped his nose with the back of his hand and looked at Rose.

"But maybe it's not too late because I still need a mom and I want one."

Eli leaned back in his chair. Rose's head was tilted toward his, but she was still asleep. Eli looked at the array of monitors on the other side of the bed.

"Mom, I wish you could hear me."

Eli waited to see if there was any reaction from Rose. Seeing nothing, he continued.

"Mrs. Babcock tells me that this is as much for my benefit as yours."

Eli leaned forward and took his mother's hand in his.

"Mom, I forgive you."

And the tears returned, unabated.

* * *

HOSPITAL CAFETERIA

Walker and Monty were eating lunch at a table by the window when Eli joined them.

"Surprisingly, the meatloaf here ain't too bad," said Monty.

"Don't believe him, Eli. The food here is bogus."

Eli sat down next to his little brother across from Monty. He picked up Monty's spoon and helped himself to a bite of the meatloaf."

"Gotta go with Walker on this one, Dad. That's pretty awful."

"Fine. Just means more for me."

The three of them were smiling as Monty scooped a spoonful of meatloaf and a helping of mashed potatoes into his mouth. The silence around the table was the most beautiful thing he had heard in some time.

"Hey, Walker," Eli said. "I was thinking. Do you want to go deer hunting next weekend? That is if you don't have a debate tournament or cross-country meet."

"Yeah, that sounds great. Hey, Dad. Can I?"

"Absolutely."

"Hey, Pops? Do you want to join us?"

"Well, I'm not much of a shot but count me in."

The three of them slipped into an easy banter and spent the next half-hour just talking when Walker broached the six-hundred-pound gorilla.

"Hey, Eli. Are you gonna stay here or what? I hear talk from some you might go back to the Bahamas.

"Walker, that's a tough question. I did live there for five years, and I built a life there, or at least I tried to."

"But you have a life here," said Walker.

"That's true. I do. But ... you know how you love Isabelle?"

Eli didn't get a chance to finish his train of thought, because about that time Quaid came walking into the cafeteria at a furious pace.

"There you are. I'd heard you were in jail but when I went by this morning, they said all charges had been dropped. I've been looking everywhere for you."

"Well, ya found me. What's up?"

"It's about Rachel."

"What? What's wrong?" asked Eli with a look of obvious concern.

"Lasko kidnapped her, and he won't talk about releasing her until you're back on the Island."

Chapter 53

Like Father, Like Son

"Son, tell us about Rachel," said Monty.

Eli was pacing back and forth in the cafeteria kitchen. Quaid was standing where he was when he delivered the news.

"Son!"

Eli stopped and looked at Walker and then his father.

"She's my Isabelle."

"And who is this Lasko character?" asked Monty.

"He's a certified bad guy," said Quaid. "He's wanted in this country for all sorts of crimes he's committed, financial mainly. But he's also caught up in drug trafficking and worse."

"And worse, huh. Eli, how did you get wrapped up with this guy?"

"Monty, Eli is blameless in all this. Trust me," said Quaid. "But the 'and worse' is a real problem."

"What do you mean?" asked Monty.

"Bernard Lasko buys and sells women, Dad. It's called the sex trade."

"What? That stuff goes on?"

"I'm afraid so," said Quaid.

* * *

BERNARD LASKO'S HOME ON THE WESTERN COAST OF LYFORD CAY

"Is there anything I can do to make you feel more comfortable?" asked Bernard.

Rachel was sitting in a straight-backed chair in a room with a fantastic view of the Atlantic. Sixty miles away was the coast of Florida, but six feet away stood an armed thug whom Bernard called Juan when he used his name at all.

"You could let me at least sit on the patio."

"I'm afraid not, my dear. You see, someone may see you and we can't have that."

"Well bloody hell. In that case, bugger off."

Bernard poured himself a drink and then took a seat across from her.

"Such language, and from such a beautiful young woman. You might want to reassess your opinion of me if you know what's good for you. I give the word and Juan here and his comrades will be enjoying you for the rest of the weekend."

* * *

"Quaid, can you help me get back to Nassau?"

"Yes. We can leave in an hour."

"All right. Then let's go."

"Walker, Dad, we're going to have to postpone our deer hunting."

"Son, what are you going to do?"

"I'm going to do what you would do, Dad. I'm going to rescue Rachel."

And with that, Eli hugged his little brother and his father, and left with Quaid.

* * *

ROOM 312

"You're awake," said Monty.

"Yes, for a few minutes now. Did everyone leave? Where's Walker."

"Walker went home. Honey, I need to tell you something."

"Can it wait? What about Eli? He was here, wasn't he?

"Yes, he was, but you were asleep the whole time."

"Maybe but maybe not. I'm not sure but I sensed him here. It was good."

"Yes, it was, but..."

"But what, Monty?"

"It's Eli. He needs our prayers."

"Oh, Monty. Then let's pray for him. And for Walker, too. Yes, Monty, let's pray for our boys."

Monty shut the door and got down on his knees next to Rose's bed and she led them in a prayer for their family.

End of Part Six

PART SEVEN

Rescue

Chapter 54

The Highest of Stakes

An hour later, Eli and Quaid were airborne.

"Eli, get some rest if you can. We should touch down in Nassau in a little over an hour. I've alerted Nigel that you're returning. He knows how to get ahold of Lasko. By the time we land, we'll know what our next steps are."

"I don't know what Lasko expects of me, but I've got an idea. Can you let Nash know what's going on?"

"Sure can."

"Then do. We may need his resources."

* * *

Saturday evening, November 25th

Quaid and Eli landed at a private airstrip where Nigel and Lach were waiting.

"Welcome back, Quaid. Welcome back, Aaron."

"Good to see you again, Nigel. But it's Eli now. Aaron's been retired."

"Ah, very well. Then it's a pleasure to make your acquaintance, Eli. Right this way."

Eli shook Nigel's hand and then Lach's, but Lach wouldn't let go.

"Thank you for coming back."

"I'm sorry I left the way I did, without saying anything to anyone, but I'm back, and we're going to find Rachel. You have my word on it."

Lach pulled Eli in for a hug. "You must. I can't stand losing her too."

Quaid and Eli threw their bags into the back of Nigel's Land Rover, and they headed off toward Quaid's place while Nigel and Lach brought them up to speed.

"It happened sometime Tuesday," said Lach. "Rachel was alone in the house. I was at the course giving a lesson. They must have seen her leave and followed her. She'd told me that she was heading to town that afternoon to meet some girlfriends for dinner."

Turning to Eli, Lach continued. "You know, you broke her heart when you left without saying a word. That man she was engaged to, Chad Tillingston was his name, he was never right for her, and I believe deep down she knew it."

"Has this Chad Tillingston been alerted?" Eli asked.

"Oh, yes. He was in London when I called him with the news. Real arse, that one. Once he understood that it was you Lasko was demanding in exchange for her return, he washed his hands of the matter. Haven't heard from him since," explained Lach.

"Well, I'm here," said Eli, "and I intend to make it up to her—how I left, that is."

"So, Lach, Tuesday then, was that the last time you saw Rachel?" asked Quaid.

"Yes. She never made it to town. Her car was found along the side of the road by the police, but there was no sign of her anywhere. The police observed other tire tracks and believe she may have swerved to avoid being hit."

"So the police know?" asked Eli.

"No, they don't. They suspect but don't know anything for sure. You see, I received a note at my office Wednesday. It was mixed in with all my mail. When I returned from lunch I found it," said Nigel.

"And what did the note say?" asked Eli.

"What I received was an envelope containing a letter and another envelope. The letter inside directed me to deliver the enclosed envelope to Mr. Lach McGregor forthwith. Which I, of course, did."

"I wasn't worried at the time," said Lach. "The police hadn't contacted me yet about her car on the side of the road and it wasn't unusual—as you know, Eli—for her to stay in town with one of her girlfriends. But then Nigel shows up with this envelope and everything changed. I found this Polaroid of her inside tied to a chair and gagged. She was holding up the day's newspaper. Proof I guess that she was alive."

"Anything else?" asked Eli as he looked at the Polaroid.

Eli was sitting in the front seat of the car while Nigel was driving and Lach and Quaid were in the back. Eli was turned in his seat as Lach struggled to answer Eli's question.

"Yes. The note said that if we didn't find you within a week Rachel would be sold to the highest bidder."

The four men in the car were silent as that set in.

Nigel broke the silence. "I let them know earlier today you were on your way back. I'm to drop you off in town tomorrow morning around 10:00 a.m., and you will pick up a bus at Bay Street and Parliament Street and take it to Cable Beach. Someone will approach you on the bus and tell you what to do next."

"Simple enough," Eli said.

"One more thing," Nigel added. "The note said you should wear a swimsuit."

"You realize this could all be a trap," said Quaid.

"What choice does he have?" said Lach.

"I have a choice and I've made it," said Eli, and then turning to Nigel, "Set it up."

The men drove in silence to Quaid's place.

* * *

The next morning, Eli was dressed for a day at the beach when he boarded the bus. It didn't take long for someone to approach him. A young kid, couldn't have been more than thirteen, sat down next to him and asked if he preferred to be called Aaron or Eli. He doubted the answer meant anything and figured it was more likely a way the kid would know he was talking to the right guy. When Eli answered "Eli," the kid placed an envelope in his hand and hopped off at the next stop. The note told him to get off at Cable Beach and walk to the west end of the beach, where he would be approached by a man in a small boat. The author of the note also warned Eli that if he was followed he'd never see Rachel again.

Eli thought all this misdirection was unnecessary. He knew who had kidnapped Rachel. Lasko had. He knew where Lasko lived. So why all the theatrics? Eli surmised it was Lasko's way of showing everyone he was in charge.

When he reached the west end of Cable Beach, an old man was waiting for him. After the exchange of only a few words, enough to ensure the old man was talking to the right guy, they were off. Three miles out to sea, Eli found out why he was told to wear a swimsuit. The old man pulled up alongside a yacht and Eli was told to swim the rest of the way. Before he leaped into the ocean, he saw Lasko standing on deck wearing dark glasses and holding a drink in his hand.

The same bodyguard who'd held a gun to Eli's head at Lasko's home on Lyford Cay lowered a ladder for Eli as he swam up alongside Lasko's small yacht. Lasko offered Eli a towel and a reptilian smile as he boarded.

"Eli, it's so good to see you again. And I guess all the world can call you Eli now. I read all about it in the paper. You're a hero. You helped the FBI capture a madman and you saved your family in the process."

"Where is she?"

"I presume you mean Rachel."

"We have nothing to talk about until I know she's alive."

Lasko put his drink down and pulled a package of cigarettes from his breast pocket.

"And if she's dead, what are you going to do about it?" Lasko asked as his bodyguard pointed a pistol at Eli. "I could have you shot and thrown overboard, and no one would know or care."

"That's true, but you wouldn't have gone to this trouble if you didn't need something from me. So, I'll ask again: Where is she?"

Lasko smiled. "I have to admit, I'm a bit proud, kind of like a father. I've taught you well. Something for something. And from what I read, you could use a new father."

Eli's expression didn't change.

"Very well," Lasko said. Turning to his bodyguard, he motioned down below with a nod of his head. The lackey went down below and returned with Rachel in tow, her hands handcuffed behind her back.

Eli ran to her but was stopped by a pistol in his face until Lasko motioned to his bodyguard that it was okay. Eli hugged her and she leaned her head on his shoulder.

"That's enough," said Lasko.

"Should I take her back down below, boss?"

"No. Not just yet. I want her to hear what I have to say too. Eli, Rachel, have a seat. And you, keep your pistol pointed at her."

Rachel and Eli sat side by side across from the armed guard while Lasko remained standing.

"Tell me, do either of you know much about the sex trade?"

Silence.

"I didn't think so," Lasko remarked. "Let me tell you, I encounter a most interesting clientele. Now, typically I'm not involved with the merchandise. I leave that to others. But I've made an exception for Rachel here. No, typically my role is finding the buyers and brokering the transactions. My buyers are a most peculiar lot. Some are in the United States, but I won't be going to one of them. Our dear Rachel will bring top dollar in the Mideast where all that oil money funds perversions the likes of which you've never seen. And oh, how they love girls from the West. You may be asking yourself why the girls don't run. Where would they run? It's desert as far as they can see. And armed guards at every turn ensure they wouldn't get far. But from what I understand, once the girls are hooked on heroin, they'll beg their masters to fuck them if they can just get another hit."

Eli was fuming inside and calculating the odds that he could take out the bodyguard before he got off a shot. Lasko, knowing Eli well, sized up the situation and lifted his shirt to reveal his own pistol.

"Eli, don't even think it. Even if you could get to one of us, the other would drop you like a bad habit. Now, where was I? Oh, right, potential buyers for Rachel. So, yes, I'd have plenty of bidders in the Mideast and there's a bazaar next month where this sort of thing happens, but I may not want to wait that long. I could always just turn you over to some of my friends in Central America. They're a rough lot, living in the jungle as they do. But they are principled—yes indeed, hellbent communist. True believers, they are. No private property with these boys. Not at all. They share everything and that would include you, Rachel, my dear. So, you see, I have options, but you, Eli, do not. You have one choice."

"I'm listening," said Eli.

"Do as I say or seal Rachel's fate."

Seeing as he had everyone's attention, Lasko continued.

"So, this is how it's going to go down. In two weeks, my big charity golf tournament will begin. Don't let the word 'charity' fool you. Millions will be bet on the outcome of the matches, and as I said the first time I met you, Eli, you're going to make me millions. You're going to play, of course, and you will make it to the finals and lose."

"I've promoted this event far and wide and 128 players have signed up. Most of them are gamblers but I've secured the attendance of a few pros and plenty of others trying to earn their card. The PGA got word of the tournament and discouraged its top players from playing. Seems they're worried about their wholesome, family-friendly product being stained by the taint of big-time gambling. But I digress."

"The tournament will be played over seven days. On day one, there will be sixty-four matches and we will have sixty-four winners and sixty-four losers. You will lose and fall into the losers' bracket. On day two, we will host thirty-two matches among the winners and thirty-two matches among the losers. From this point on, if you lose, you are done. Over the next several days, and concluding on Wednesday, November 13th, matches will take place until we have a winner of the winners' bracket and a winner of the losers' bracket. These two players will play a final match on Friday, the 15th."

"So, if I am to lose in round one and enter the losers' bracket, I assume you expect me to win that bracket and make it to the final championship match."

"Correct, and you will lose that match and I'll walk away with millions."

"How can you be so sure? How do you know who folks will bet on or what the odds will be?"

"Because I'm running the whole show. I'm the bookie. I set the odds. I guarantee you everyone will be betting on you, except for me and a few friends, and when you lose, we'll pocket every dollar bet."

"Why will people bet with a bookie who is setting the odds and who is also placing bets on the outcome? Too easy to rig."

"Two reasons. First, I'm not holding the money. The casino is. Secondly, no one will know I'm placing bets. I have intermediaries who will do my betting for me. So, I can set the odds, and no one will suspect. Finally, Eli, people love me. I've already announced that I'm donating my bookie fee, my vig, to the children's foundation. I'm known on the island as a 'man of the people.' No one will suspect. Due to my standing in the community, I've persuaded every participant to donate a portion of their winnings to the foundation. The bank holding the money will deduct the donation off the top before dispersing any winnings and hold it for the charity. Don't you see? It's for the children!"

"And I suspect that you're running this charity."

"Right again, Eli."

"This will never work. Golf is a crazy game. There's no way you can control the outcome of every match."

"I don't need to. I just need you in the final match. I have a hunch who'll you be up against. Our friend Travis McCoy is made for this event, but you're right—anything can happen."

"So, you see, I could play my best and still lose."

"That's why you're going to lose on day one. It will be easier for you to come up through the losers bracket."

"Okay. So, I lose the final match and you'll release Rachel."

"Correct. After you walk off the 18th hole, I'll hand you a note with coordinates. You follow those and you'll find her waiting in a boat, unharmed. Now, between now and then, don't waste time looking for her. She'll be moved from boat to boat, from boat to land, and back again. And if you don't make it to the final match or if you do and win, well ... you'll have the rest of your life to dwell on how hers turned out."

"Lasko, this makes no sense. You're asking me to deliver something outside my control. If I make it to the final match, then sure, I can guarantee you I'll lose. But there's no way I can guarantee I'll make it that far. I gotta win, what, six matches? So, you can't be guaranteed you'll win the money. There must be another way we can resolve this."

"Resolve this? You don't get it. That ship has sailed, and you sailed it when you bolted for Charleston and wouldn't play ball. No one fucks with me. We had a good thing going but you wanted out. Well, I wasn't going to allow that, so to keep you playing for me I threatened to tell the world that Aaron Westfield was really Eli Atkins, known fugitive wanted for murder. But when I lost that leverage, I needed something else, and Rachel is excellent leverage.

"As for the money I stand to win, don't you fret. I've got several backup plans if you don't come through. But as for Rachel, there is no backup plan. I'm going to enjoy her demise if that's what it comes to, and enjoy her I will before I sell her ass.

"Eli, you crossed me and now you don't have a choice. Win those six matches or else."

Chapter 55

Suitably Incentivized

Lasko was back at his estate on Lyford Cay after having dealt with Eli and was waiting for a phone call. Rachel was safe. He'd keep his end of the bargain but wouldn't hesitate to dispose of her if Eli didn't deliver.

He lied to Eli when he told him why he wasn't going to hold on to the money people would gamble at the tournament. He had wanted to hold all the money but some of his less trusting investors wouldn't allow it. Over the last two years, as it became harder and harder to land new investors to keep the Ponzi scheme afloat, Lasko began accepting direct investments from criminals, like himself, but criminals with a taste for violence. The mob, for one.

Lasko was already washing the money of numerous nefarious characters by investing their cash in his fund, but accepting direct investments from the mob was another thing altogether. For one, when he washed money for weapons traders and drug dealers, he not only controlled the investment in his fund, but he took a 30 percent fee off the top. He kept this money aside and would draw on it to help make quarterly distributions to investors if necessary. But when the mob made direct investments into his fund, he couldn't take the fee and lost control over the investment.

One group in particular, an outfit from Chicago, was getting greedy and said that the ten percent returns were nice, but they felt Lasko could do better. They were happy to help him find new revenue sources and investors if it meant Lasko could generate larger returns. Several unions over which they held sway had sizeable pension funds and were always looking for good money managers. Lasko was intrigued and made keeping the Chicago outfit happy a top priority.

So, when they complained about Lasko holding the purse strings to the tournament wagers, he paid attention. They simply didn't trust Lasko, and they offered to hold the money. Well, lack of trust ran both ways, and Lasko convinced them that a local, neutral party would be a nice compromise. The Paradise Island Casino agreed to take the bets and hold the money. All parties were satisfied.

The anticipated phone call came through and Lasko took a seat at his desk.

"Lasko here."

"Boss, how's it going on your end?"

"The pieces are in place. All looks good. Stephen, do you have any good news for me?"

Stephen Drake was Lasko's chief accountant and the person most familiar with Lasko's investment funds. He knew the investors and understood the fund's legal obligations. What Lasko lacked in pedigree, the kind that Wall Street types favored, Stephen more than made up for. He oozed privilege beginning with the tony prep school he attended. Along with a degree in finance from the University of Pennsylvania, he carried a law degree from Harvard, and somewhere along the way, he picked up a degree in amorality. When others spoke of right and wrong, his eyes glassed over. To him, it was all background noise. He was the perfect partner for Lasko. He never questioned anything and remained focused on completing his assigned tasks, a job for which he was well compensated.

"My news is the same. We're running out of time. December 15th is the last day to make the third quarter distribution. We've been over this. The Offering Memorandum every fund investor received clearly states that quarterly distributions will be made on or before the seventy-fifth day following the end of each calendar quarter," Stephen explained. "That means Friday, December 15th is the last day. Period. No way around it."

"Yeah. Well, that damn Offering Memo you're always waving in my face also says that every investor in the fund acknowledges the risk and that a total loss of their investment is a possibility."

"And if you would like to remind them of that paragraph, be my guest."

"Okay. Okay. How are we doing with the pension funds? Are they ready to invest yet?"

"Close, but not yet. They want to see how the fund performs over one more rolling twelve-month period."

"So, you're telling me they've seen us dish out 10 percent annual returns every year since year one, but they won't move until we finish up December of this year?" Lasko fumed.

"That's what I'm telling you. Their hands are tied by federal law, ERISA to be exact. In the good old days, pension fund managers had wide discretion, but they got caught abusing it in the minds of some and are now heavily scrutinized by outside regulators. So, no money from them until next year, at the earliest."

"Okay, okay. So how short are we?" Lasko asked.

"If we don't come up with another $10 million by December 15th, we'll fall short of our projected payout for the first time ever."

"We'll fall short, but we'll still be able to make some kind of payment, right?"

"Yes, we'll be able to send out a payment, but it will be a crack in a dam holding back a tidal wave of trouble, and this crack will splinter very quickly. Once we fall short on one payment, the petal will be off the rose and everyone who suspects we've been cooking the books will stand up and scream, 'See, I told you so.' Raising money from new investors will become more difficult, and then we'll fall short on our next payment and do so by an even larger margin. So, let me make this perfectly clear. You've built a machine that is running hot and without any margin for error. Miss one payment and that's the beginning of the end—and an end that will come crashing down at record speed with the weight of a ton of bricks behind it."

Chapter 56

Drama in the Bahamas

The talk everywhere was of the tournament. Folks were calling it "Drama in the Bahamas." Lasko broadcast the tournament coast to coast and beyond. The tournament attracted golfers who gambled and gamblers who brought golfers with them. The entrance fee was $10,000 a man, so with a field of 128 players, the initial pot totaled $1,280,000. Only the last standing sixteen players who made it past the fourth round qualified to win a portion of the pot. At the end of each day, gamblers could put more money on a given player, and the minimum bet was $5,000.

The scourge of any golf tournament is the sandbagger—the player who lies about their handicap claiming to be a worse player than they are so they will get more strokes against their opponent. To prevent these scoundrels from perverting the integrity of the tournament, no one was allowed to play who wasn't a two handicap or better. Nevertheless, the Paradise Island Casino took their job seriously and contacted the home club of every golfer playing and verified his handicap. Going one stop further, the casino looked to Lasko to do a deep dive into each golfer to discern whether any of the entrants were known cheats. Lasko asked his friends with the Chicago outfit to lend a hand with this work, which they were happy to do.

In addition to the money wagered on a particular player to win it all, there were bets on individual matches. It was at this point that Lasko could influence and interfere with the gambling. Lasko could not change a player's handicap and he didn't have leverage on the other players as he did with Eli, but he could set the odds to encourage gamblers to place a bet on one golfer over another. For instance, if Player A was heavily favored to beat Player B, then people wouldn't bet on Player B unless they had an incentive to do so. Lasko might set the odds at two-and-a-half to one so that for every dollar you bet on Player B, if Player B won, you would win $1.50 plus the dollar you bet. But if you bet on Player A to win and Player A won, for every dollar you bet, you would win fifty cents plus your dollar bet.

In some matches, if Lasko felt strongly that a certain player would win, he would set the odds to encourage everyone to bet on the other player. When his favored player won, the house, and that was Lasko, won big.

As far as Eli was concerned, he wasn't. Quaid fronted Eli the money he needed to place bets on himself for appearances only because every player was expected to bet on himself. One of the wonderful curiosities about golf is that it is the only sport where gambling on oneself is allowed instead of outlawed, as it is with baseball and the other major sports.

Eli spent the next week and half practicing. He could be seen with Lach on the driving range or the golf course every day. He played the occasional match to keep his instincts sharp. But he was not concerned about winning the money. He needed to come up through the losers' bracket, win six matches, and then lose.

After Eli met with Lasko, he'd briefed Quaid, Lach, and Nash on everything. While Eli and Lach were busy focusing on Plan A, making it to the final championship match, Nigel and Nash were working on Plan B. When Eli returned from his meeting with Lasko, he gave Nigel the name of the boat on which Lasko was holding Rachel. Nigel researched public records and learned the boat, named *Let It Ride*, was registered to an LLC organized in the Cayman Islands. The managing partner was a law firm with a PO box address in the Cayman Islands. Nash, through channels of his own, was able to get a list of every limited liability company for which this law firm was the managing member. Next, Nash assembled a list of every boat owned by these LLCs and their whereabouts. Three of the boats on the list were docked in Nassau. It was a long shot, but Nash assigned three agents to watch these boats for any sign of Rachel.

While Nash would do what he could to find Rachel, he was still primarily focused on bringing Lasko down and stopping his financing of communist rebels. Eli and Lach made it clear there would be no attempt to rescue Rachel unless they were confident they would succeed and that no harm would come to her.

Eli was adamant. "I'll win my matches. Plan A is still our best bet."

Lach, the teacher, and Eli, the student, were in sync, on and off the course. The betting on Eli was heavy and on the last day before the tournament was to start, he beat a kid who had placed first in the PGA qualifying school and of whom great things were expected on the tour. So, it came as a great surprise to all when Eli lost the first round of the tournament and was relegated to the losers' bracket. But for Eli, the tournament was about to begin and he was ready. He was swinging the club and striking the ball better than ever. Eli was confident; despite throwing the opening match, the momentum was all his.

Chapter 57

Under Way

Momentum is a fickle beast. In the next round, the second of the tournament and the first match in the losers' bracket, Eli was matched against a notorious hustler from Nevada who regularly played golf for six figures. If Eli was counting on the pressure getting to him, he would be disappointed. The man couldn't hit the ball nearly as far as Eli, but he hit it straight and had the touch of a surgeon around the green. He opened the day with three straight pars and was never in trouble. Eli, on the other hand, bogeyed the first two holes and would have been three holes down after the third if his wedge shot from off the green hadn't struck the center of the flagstick and dropped straight down to save par.

Eli laughed out loud when the shot dropped, and that bit of luck calmed Eli's nerves. When they made the turn, Eli was one down and his game was coming around. His opponent never faltered and continued to record par after par, but Eli got hot with his putter and one-putted four holes on the back nine to ultimately win the match on the 17th hole, going two holes up with one to go.

* * *

That night, Nash and Quaid joined Eli for dinner at the Bastian home in Adelaide Village. The Bastians were excited to see Eli and he was welcomed as a hero since everyone had heard some version of his daring rescue in the swamps north of Charleston. Eli was embarrassed by the attention and Quaid gladly retold the tale.

After dinner, Nash and Quaid walked back to Eli's hut on the beach. Nash had never seen where Eli lived while on the island. Eli grabbed three beers from his small refrigerator, and they walked back out onto the beach. Eli sat in the hammock while Quaid and Nash marveled at the serenity of the surroundings.

"Not bad, Eli. Not bad," said Nash. "A guy could get used to this."

"Not to be disrespectful, Nash, but it came at a high price."

"I know, and I don't mean to diminish what you've been through with such a cavalier remark. Consider the comment an ice-breaker for what I really want to talk about," said Nash.

"Which is what?" asked Eli.

"What happens next? What do you see in your future? Have you thought about it?"

"There was a time when that was all I thought about, and what I thought about was how my future had been stolen from me. I'm still resentful, but to a lesser extent. But right now, for the next week, I'm thinking about one thing—Rachel."

"I understand, and we're going to get her back. And that's the other thing I wanted to tell you tonight. You focus on Plan A, and I'll continue working Plan B. We'll get Rachel back safely and catch Lasko at the same time."

"Sounds like a plan," Eli said as he tilted his beer toward Nash with a confident smile.

"And then will you talk to me about your future?"

"We'll see, Nash. We'll see."

Chapter 58

Collateral Damage

Wednesday, December 13th, Lyford Cay Golf Club

Lasko was sitting in the bar and in a fine mood. The seventh round had been played that morning and the championship match was set. Travis McCoy would play local legend Eli Atkins in the final match to take place two days later. He couldn't have handpicked a better opponent for Eli, the smiling, smooth-swinging Texas assassin. Before Eli returned to Charleston, he played Travis on a half dozen or so occasions and Travis routinely got the better of him. The matches were always close, but Eli's emotions and willingness to go for broke when a safe shot would do were his undoing. Eli won on occasion, but Travis was the safer bet. Travis knew when to press for birdie, and it wasn't on every hole. Perfect for Lasko. He set the odds such that, if you bet on Travis and Travis won, you'd win your money back and a bit more, but if you bet on Eli and Eli won, well, you'd win big.

So yes, Travis was the favorite, but since his shaky start in round one, Eli had played magnificently. Truly inspired golf. Plenty of people would bet on Eli even if the odds were straight up. By making Travis the favorite, and rewarding a bet on Eli with favorable odds, Lasko was all but ensuring that most of the money would be bet on Eli. Lasko, of course, operating through associates, would bet on Travis. Over the last week, after each round, more and more people were betting on Travis and Eli to win their matches and make it to the final championship match. Once all the new bets came in, Lasko would walk away with enough money to make the quarterly distribution due Friday and a nice profit for himself.

As Lasko was ordering another round for his entourage, the club general manager approached Lasko and asked to see him in private. Mr. Bradford Bishop, the club's GM for the last ten years, loathed Lasko and was looking forward to their meeting.

When Lasko entered the General Manager's office, he saw that another man was in the room and waiting for him.

"Please, Mr. Lasko, have a seat," said Mr. Bishop.

"What's all this about?"

"It's about the stakes that have been waged on the match this Friday. I'm afraid I don't understand it all, so I'm going to allow Mr. Pendergrass, from the casino, to explain matters to you."

"Mr. Lasko, the betting so far has been heavy, and we still have all day tomorrow for people to place their bets, but I need to alert you to a risk that has developed."

"What risk are you talking about?" asked Lasko.

"You have an unbalanced book. We anticipate that close to twenty million dollars will be bet on the match to take place Friday, and because of the large payout you've set on a bet were Mr. Atkins to win, close to 80 percent of all the bets that have been placed have been placed on Mr. Atkins."

This wasn't news to Lasko, and it was what he wanted, but he needed to feign ignorance over the implications.

"I don't understand your concern," said Lasko.

"Mr. Lasko, according to our calculations, if Travis McCoy wins, you will have to pay out about $6 million, leaving you with a handsome profit of $14 million."

"It's for the children," Lasko exclaimed.

"Yes, yes, of course. The children. But if Eli Atkins wins, you'll owe $40 million but will only have taken in $20 million. You'll lose $20 million dollars. If the betting was more equally divided between the two players, the imbalance would not be so severe, but the crowd clearly likes the odds and is betting heavily on Mr. Atkins. I can't help but wonder if you know what you're doing!" said Mr. Pendergrass.

"Know what I'm doing! Look pal, I know what I'm doing. Hey, Bradford, I don't have to sit here and be insulted."

"Mr. Lasko, please. Have a seat," said Mr. Bishop. "Mr. Pendergrass means no offense and he has a solution."

Mr. Bishop nodded for Mr. Pendergrass to continue.

"Yes, quite a simple solution really. You just need to post some collateral. If you could wire $20 million to our account, then we'll have nothing to worry about, will we?"

"You want me to wire you $20 million?"

"Yes, to cover the imbalance."

"Yeah, you said that. Well, it's like this. I can't get my hands on that kind of cash by tomorrow, so I guess you're going to have to trust me."

"Mr. Lasko, we're not in the trusting business. We're a casino. Unless you come up with some collateral, we're going to stop taking bets and then begin the difficult process of unrolling the bets that have already been placed and returning the money already wagered."

Mr. Bishop had a difficult time hiding how much he was enjoying the difficult spot Lasko was in.

"What are you laughing at, Bradford?"

"Oh, I'm not laughing," he said as tried to suppress a smile. "I was just thinking of the children."

"If I may be so bold," said Mr. Pendergrass.

"Please," said Mr. Bishop.

"Mr. Lasko, the house you purchased, on the west end of Lyford Cay, I believe you paid $10 million cash for the home. It was in all the papers. If you could give the casino a lien on that home, an additional $5 million in cash, and turn over your passport, I believe we could call it a day. Can you do that?" asked Mr. Pendergrass.

Lasko had Eli in his pocket, so Travis was going to win. There was no risk of him losing $20 million, but he needed to play the role for appearances.

"Yes, Mr. Pendergrass, that I can do. I'll have my attorney take care of the details tomorrow."

"Bravo, sir. Bravo," said Mr. Pendergrass.

Lasko stood up and showed himself out the door, leaving the two men behind to share a private smile.

CHAPTER 59

Match Play

FRIDAY MORNING, DECEMBER 15TH, THE DAY OF THE FINAL CHAMPIONSHIP MATCH

A large gallery was predicted, but the size of the crowd exceeded all expectations. Lasko was in his element. Holding a megaphone in his hand, he signaled for the crowd to quiet down. Once he had their attention, he directed it to the young girl in a wheelchair beside him.

"It's been a wonderful week, and I want to thank you all for your generosity. The betting has been stupendous, and I almost hate to walk away from the sizeable fee I'm donating to the foundation, but then I look at the face of such a beautiful young girl like that of Tisha here and I remember why we're all here. For the children!" he said.

Murmurs of "It's for the children" were repeated throughout the gallery.

"And now for the main event," Lasko continued. "Travis McCoy versus Eli Atkins."

The match would be eighteen holes of match play. The two men walked up to the 1st tee but were not alone. Following throughout the round would be the marker, who would keep a separate scorecard for each player. A familiar figure to all, and a man afforded his privacy in this exclusive club, the marker would also serve as the last word on any rule infractions.

"Gentlemen, we will draw straws to determine honors on the 1st tee. Mr. McCoy, please select a straw."

Travis walked up and picked one of the three straws protruding from behind the man's right hand. As he stepped to the side, Eli approached and selected one of the other two straws. Eli had selected the longer straw and would tee off first.

"Gentlemen, good luck."

Travis and Eli shook hands but said nothing. Travis was the picture of calm. He was tall and lanky and had a smooth, buttery swing. Eli, on the other hand, had a shorter swing, very compact but graced with quick, powerful hands. He was the longer off the tee and, frankly, with every club in the bag. The question with Eli had been and always was: Could he keep his emotions in check? His fiery temper had propelled him to some huge victories but had also fueled more than one meltdown.

As they made the turn, the match was even. Travis held a lead, one-up, after Eli bogeyed the third hole, a par-three. Eli's tee shot was buried in the side of the trap just under the lip, making an up and down to save par an impossibility. He got on in two, but two-putted for a four, which was one too many. Travis had hit the green with his tee shot and easily parred the hole to go one-up. His lead did not last long. On the next hole, a long par-four, Eli hit a low draw that ran another forty yards after hitting the ground, leaving him a short wedge into the green. Travis's drive was down the middle but thirty yards shorter than Eli's, thus necessitating a longer iron into the green. The green was elevated, and when his approach shot came in low, it bounced to the back of the green. Eli, with just an eight-iron in his hand, lofted a high fade toward the pin. It landed, bounced twice, and settled six feet from the hole. He made his putt, and the match was all tied, and it stayed that way until the 12th hole.

To the eye of anyone in the gallery, both men were a picture of steely nerves, each player fully focused on the task at hand. Hardly a word was exchanged between the two men beyond the occasional acknowledgment when the other hit a truly great shot. What the gallery could not have known and did not know was what Eli was concentrating on. He had to lose, but in fashion. An hour before the match had begun, both Travis and Eli were warming up on the driving range. Lasko was making his rounds, receiving praise for the marvelous spectacle he had put together. Lasko approached Travis and Eli separately to offer them his gratitude and to wish them all the best.

However, for Eli, he had an additional message. Holding Eli's right hand in both his hands, and smiling the entire time, Lasko spoke in a hushed tone that only Eli could hear.

"You're almost there. Lose this and Rachel is yours, safe and sound. But let me make one thing perfectly clear. If you lay down too early and too obviously so that the integrity of this match is called into question, the bet's off, and Rachel will be stripped naked and on her knees by the end of the day. Make it look good. Are we clear?"

"Crystal. And let me make one thing perfectly clear to you. If any harm comes to her, I'll hunt you down and kill you slowly. Are we clear?"

Lasko laughed for all to see as if he and Eli were old friends. He leaned in and whispered, "We could have been a beautiful team, you and me."

As Travis and Eli walked up to the 12th tee, Eli began looking for the right opportunity to lose a hole. As much as he hated Lasko, he was right. He had to make losing look legit. In part, Eli trusted Travis to birdie a hole down the stretch and that might be all that was necessary. But Eli was in complete control of his swing. He could fire at pins at will, but he could also just miss his target, and no one would be the wiser. Importantly, he had to remember that the crowd would expect him to celebrate when he won a hole and grimace at a poorly hit shot or at a case of bad luck.

The 12th hole was a short par-five that both players could reach in two. Eli had honors and laced a drive down the middle. Travis followed with a drive down the right side of the fairway that bounced into the first cut of rough. With his ball settled down in the rough, Travis chose to safely hit an iron short of the green instead of risk going for the green in two. Eli's drive was twenty yards past Travis', allowing him to easily fire at the green with a four-iron. Eli hit a towering iron shot and it appeared to be right online. But golf is a cruel game. The wind picked up slightly, causing his ball to rise even higher but lose distance in the process. The ball landed short of the green, hit a sprinkler head, and careened sideways into the thick rough. Eli stood motionless. In an instant, his shot went from one that was most certainly going to end up on the green, leaving him with a putt for eagle, to a difficult shot from a tough lie. The crowd groaned and Eli did too, but he also recognized that this bit of bad luck was the cover he needed.

Eli kept looking for his ball long past the allotted five minutes, but Travis asked the marker to ignore the time constraints as he helped Eli find his ball, which they did, in deep rough thirty yards left of the green. Eli would have to hack at the ball to get the clubhead through the thick rough, which meant controlling distance would be difficult. Eli selected his sand wedge, opened the clubface, and chopped down on the ball. It popped up, but without much forward motion, and landed five yards short of the green. He walked slowly, numbly, up to the ball, settled in, closed the clubface slightly, and chipped the ball, but he caught it a bit thin, and it rolled ten feet past the hole. Eli took his time lining up the putt, knowing he had to make it to have any chance. He missed and told Travis to pick up his ball, conceding the putt and the hole. Travis had waited patiently on the hole as Eli's struggles continued, but he didn't have to finish out, and as they walked off the 12th green, Travis was one-up.

Travis and Eli matched pars on the next five holes and came to the 18th hole with Travis still holding a one-up lead and with honors on the last tee box. The 18th hole was when Travis first became aware of Eli's skill as a golfer, the day he was caddying for Lasko and embarrassed Travis with his towering drive over the trees. Travis knew Eli had to win the hole to tie the match and send it into extra holes, which meant Eli would certainly try to cut the corner again. Travis was in command and played it safe with a three-wood down the middle, leaving him an easy second shot.

When Eli saw that Travis hit his drive safely, he was confident Travis would get on the green in three, making birdie a possibility but par a near certainty. Eli knew what he had to do: lose. But he'd do it on his terms, executing shots that only he knew were exactly what he intended. He took several practice swings with his driver, and the gallery was eerily quiet knowing the importance of the shot. It was perfect: a huge, towering drive over the trees that landed on the right side of the fairway, leaving Eli with a realistic chance of getting home in two. The gallery erupted and even Travis joined in. He had seen few shots better over his years of playing competitive golf.

They came to Travis' ball first and he hit a simple four-iron up to the left side of the fairway, fifteen yards short of the green. He was looking at a simple chip shot onto the green. Everyone knew what Eli had to do next. He had to get on in two and make birdie or better.

Standing in the fairway, Eli surveyed his shot. He had 275 yards to the pin and was holding his driver. He had the length, but he would have to hit the shot perfectly to get enough loft to have a chance at stopping the ball on the green. The three-wood gave him the loft he needed, but he didn't think he could carry the small trap protecting the right side of the green. He swung each club, weighing his options but doing it all for the gallery, for the show of it all, and for Lasko. Eli took the man at his word and knew he needed to make his loss look legitimate.

He selected the driver; it was what was expected. Standing on the inside of the dogleg and with a line of trees protecting the gallery from the breeze blowing in from the ocean, only a few people would know that wind would affect the shot. Eli was one of those people and was counting on it. A hush again fell over the gallery as Eli, standing behind the ball, walked up and took his stance over the ball. He took the club away slowly and with the slightest of pause at the top, his club dropped down into the slot effortlessly. His loose but powerful hands lagged and then caught up with blistering speed as they powered through the ball. The ball was on a perfect trajectory, drawing just slightly, and it looked to have enough height to carry the sand trap. But Eli had put a tad more whip in his hands, so as the ball rose and cleared the tree line, the wind grabbed it and it began to draw more, too much. The ball fell off its perfect trajectory and landed short of the elevated green and bounced and skidded into the thick grass. He was short-sided.

Advantage Travis. Although Eli was closer to the hole, Travis had the much easier shot. Travis didn't take much time over his shot, having hit thousands just like it. Taking his wedge, he hit a perfect shot; it popped up and landed just on the top shelf and rolled out to within five feet of the hole. Eli wasn't ready to concede the putt just yet though, so Travis marked his ball. Eli would need to get up and down for birdie and then hope Travis missed his short putt.

Eli stood over his ball. He would have to pop the ball up and land it on the putting surface; but without much green to work with, he would need the ball to sit and not roll out. Making matters worse, his ball was sitting up in the rough, which meant his clubhead could easily slip underneath the ball and it would never make it to the green. He would have to perfectly pick the ball from the rough.

It would have been very easy for Eli to flub this shot. To the casual observer, it didn't look difficult, but to anyone who has played the game, it was as difficult a shot to execute as any. The pin was on a small knoll, and if Eli's ball rolled past the cup, it would catch the hill and roll twenty feet away. Eli was in complete control, and for his own benefit, he hit an almost perfect shot. The ball gently rose from the rough and landed on the green, hole-high to the right with hardly any rotation at all but enough so that it rolled out. As it approached the edge of the swell in the green, it accelerated oh so slightly, catching the hill and rolling twenty feet away.

Neither Travis nor Eli expressed any emotions, though to the gallery, one that had bet heavily on Eli, the end was near, and their collective moan was audible. Eli would have to sink a twenty-foot putt that rose and broke right to left. He surveyed it carefully from all sides and, once confident of the line and the speed required, hit it right online but just a bit too hard and he missed on the high side. A hush fell over the crowd as Eli dropped his putter and bent over at the waist with his hands on his knees. Travis stood there and waited for Eli to compose himself, which he did. Eli conceded Travis' putt and then they each removed their hat, shook hands, signed their cards, and handed them to the marker.

As Travis received congratulations, Eli kept his eye out for Lasko. They spotted each other and Lasko made his way through the gallery. He walked up to Eli and placed his left hand around Eli's right elbow and whispered to him as he shook Eli's hand. Eli recoiled but then felt Lasko slip a piece of paper in his hand. *The coordinates,* he thought.

For all to see, Eli kicked his bag and stormed off the course, leaving folks to remark that his short fuse had finally gotten the better of him.

Chapter 60

Strict Rules of Golf

Eli walked quickly away from the crowds and around the backside of the clubhouse, with his head down, maintaining a good show for anyone watching. As he circled the club, he hurried back through the front entrance. Mr. Bishop, the General Manager, was waiting for him.

"Right this way, Mr. Atkins."

Mr. Bishop ushered Eli into his office and Eli picked up the phone to dial a number he had memorized twenty times over.

"Nash, are you ready?" Eli asked.

"Ready."

Eli read the coordinates over the phone and Nash, who had four boats and a helicopter waiting in the wings, was on his way. Eli shook hands with Mr. Bishop and was out the door before Mr. Bishop could say more.

Twenty minutes later, Eli was waiting at the cove behind his hut at Adelaide Village. He sat in the hammock and tried to relax, but his adrenaline was running too hot, so he paced. He didn't have to wait long. Lasko kept his word. One of Nash's men found Rachel, sitting alone on a boat with a bottle of water, and all things considered, in fine shape. Nash had circulated government-issue walkie-talkies the week before, so the team all heard the good news with a single radio burst. Eli was jumping up and down. He'd done it. Rachel was alive. He didn't care what happened to Lasko. He knew Nash did and that was fine. He wished him luck, but for Eli, Rachel's safety was all that mattered.

Within a half-hour, Rachel was sitting with Eli in his hammock, as they celebrated along with Nash, Quaid, and Lach.

* * *

BACK AT THE CLUBHOUSE

Shortly after Eli left the general manager's office, Lasko came barging in.

"Bishop. I need your office. Vamoose."

"But of course, Mr. Lasko. Anything for you."

Lasko knew the GM hated him and couldn't have cared less.

"And shut the door on your way out," Lasko said.

Lasko dialed Stephen Drake's number and the man picked up on the second ring.

"Well, did the boy come through for us?" Stephen asked.

"In spades. He played it perfectly. I saw that ass Pendergrass from the casino, and he said the wire would go out this afternoon, so we're good to go."

"Do you want me to wait for it to hit our account?" Stephen asked.

"No. Most of our investors still wait on the mail. Wire the quarterly distributions to those expecting wires and mail the rest. Those checks won't be received and presented for payment until late next week at the earliest, but I want them in the mail today. There's no Saturday delivery on this island, and if I wait till Monday to mail them, people will talk. You said so yourself."

"All right. You the boss."

"Oh, Stephen, it was a thing of beauty. Wish you could have seen the kid take the fall. No one was the wiser. Making these quarterly payments should be the last bit of proof we need to convince those union pension funds to invest with us. Think about it. Every payday, money taken from those saps' paychecks will be funneled to me."

"It's a beautiful thing."

"Now, unless we got more business, I'm heading back to the bar to celebrate."

* * *

The bar was not as crowded as it would have been had Eli won, but the Lasko sycophants in attendance were drinking heavily and on Lasko's tab. Lasko was in his element. A true man of the people. As rumor had it, a rumor he was responsible for, his fee for organizing the event, the fee he announced was his donation to the foundation, was well into the millions.

Off to the side of the bar sipping a beer stood Mr. Pendergrass, the casino's representative, present to certify the results and waiting on the marker to conclude his business. The marker had not joined them yet and was sitting off by himself at a table with the players' scorecards and his own, intently going over each card, hole by hole, with his finger comparing the scores. Suddenly, a waiter appeared and placed a drink in front of him, the likes of which one would never see this man hoist—colorful, filled with fruit and a tiny umbrella.

"Compliments of the house," the waiter said.

Smiling, the marker set his pencil down and leaned back in his chair. He reached for the beer he had been drinking and finished it with a last swig, then gathered up the cards and walked up to the men standing around the bar.

"Gentlemen, it seems we have a problem."

A hush came over the crowd as every head turned toward the marker.

"I've gone over the cards carefully, and I'll encourage anyone here who doubts me to double-check my work, but it's quite clear."

"What is? What's quite clear?" asked a chuckling Lasko, ignoring the man as he poured himself a fresh flute from a 1957 bottle of Dom Perignon.

"Travis, old boy, I'm afraid you signed an incorrect scorecard," said the marker.

"That can't be," said Travis.

"I'm afraid so. On the 12th hole, the hole Eli bogeyed, you must have been distracted by Eli's peril. When he conceded your putt, you marked down a five for par instead of a four."

"Then that means he's disqualified," yelled one of the men at the bar.

The import of what the marker had said descended on the crowd, and all at once everyone began to scream, a few for joy and others from outrage.

The marker handed Travis his card and the one Travis had kept. "You see, I kept your score quite accurately."

Travis was dumfounded, but Lasko was panicked.

"Strict rules of golf," uttered the marker.

* * *

Word spread quickly around the club. Many who had bet on Eli had not left the premises but were eating lunch on the veranda. When they heard the news, they returned to the bar where Lasko, in his haste to find a phone, had left without closing his tab. A good time, at his expense, was had by all. Lasko bolted from the bar toward the general manager's office, desperate to stop Stephen Drake from sending the wires and mailing the checks. He found Mr. Bishop's office locked and with a note on the door stating he had left for the day. He ran from the clubhouse for his car hoping to get back to his house as quickly as possible when he was met by Mr. Pendergrass from the casino and three large gentlemen.

"Mr. Lasko, we have a problem. Please, come with us."

* * *

Eli and his crowd didn't have any Dom Perignon to celebrate with, but the Kalik beers never tasted so good. Mrs. Bastion had invited them to her house for a dinner that night. Everyone was in a fine mood and was looking forward to a day of rest followed by a wonderful meal.

"Eli, son, your golf this last week was inspired," said Lach with tears in his eyes. "I couldn't have been happier or prouder, both as your instructor and, if I may be so bold, I hope as your future uncle-in-law. You are going to make an honest woman out of our dear Rachel here, now aren't you?"

"Uncle Lach!" said Rachel.

"Well, I wish I could have seen the look on Lasko's face when he found out he really lost the match," said Nash.

"What do you mean, lost the match?" asked Eli.

"Eli, Travis McCoy—well, actually his father—is one of our associates, one of our friends, and Travis has been helping us since the day he approached you on the driving range last spring and told you he'd heard you were looking for a match," explained Nash.

"Okay, but what do you mean Lasko lost?" Eli asked again.

"It was all Travis' idea. He figured out how we could rescue Rachel and bury Lasko at the same time. He signed an incorrect scorecard. The marker, also in our service from time to time, played his role. He waited for a signal. Once we safely had Rachel, I radioed the club GM and asked him to send our friend a fruity little drink, and that was his signal that all was safe. He then announced to all at the bar, including Lasko, that Travis had signed an incorrect scorecard."

"Which of course means Travis lost and Eli won," said Lach.

"So instead of making millions, Lasko lost millions," said Quaid.

"You idiot," screamed Eli.

"What?" asked a rather incredulous Nash.

"Mrs. Babcock. She's in danger. When I walked off the course this afternoon, Lasko handed me the coordinates, but he also whispered to me that he'd send one of his men to Mrs. Babcock's house as insurance in case we tried anything," said Eli.

"Oh, good Lord," muttered Quaid.

"Who is Mrs. Babcock and what exactly did Lasko say?" asked Nash.

"Mrs. Babcock is a very true friend, and it wouldn't have been hard for Lasko to learn that. News of how she helped me escape to the Bahamas five years ago was in all the papers after I killed that guy Rath."

"And what did Lasko say?" Nash asked again.

"He said, 'I know who your friend Nash is, and if you try anything, and my associates stateside don't hear from me, they'll send a man to kill Mrs. Babcock.'"

* * *

The prayer meeting had run long. So many people needing the good Lord's help, but praying for others was a profound privilege and pleasure as Mrs. Babcock saw it. She just hoped to get home before the real rainfall started; it had been raining most of the day as it was. But about a mile from home, her front left tire blew out. She pulled off the road and surveyed the damage. It was too muddy to risk raising the car on a jack, so she decided to walk the last mile. Tomorrow, she'd call her son-in-law Francesco and ask for help. Grabbing her giant purse out of the front seat and her umbrella out of the back, she set off for home.

She walked along the riverbank as it was the shortest route, and before too long arrived at her dock.

* * *

Nash contacted an officer stateside who was able to deliver a message to one of Quaid's boys. Quaid had given Nash a list of his seven boys and the phone numbers he would need and told Nash that as soon as they reached one of the boys that boy would reach the others.

"Seven? I thought you had six boys," said Nash.

"I get confused myself. What difference does it make? Just call them."

"Shouldn't we be calling the police?" Lach asked.

"If we call the police, they'll show up with sirens blaring, and Lasko's people will know it for sure," said Eli. "Our best bet of catching them by surprise is if we send Quaid's boys.

* * *

Mrs. Babcock opened the sliding door on her back porch—she never locked it—and moved to open the curtains as she entered.

"Leave the curtains shut, lady," he said. "And have a seat right over there."

Mrs. Babcock stifled a scream when she saw the man holding a gun on her.

"I said take a seat."

She moved slowly toward the chair and did what he said.

"What do you want?" she asked.

"Nothin'. I'm just waiting for a call on my radio. You sit there quiet, and if all goes well, I'll be gone, and you'll never see me again."

"If what goes well?"

"How in the hell am I supposed to know? Now shut up and just sit there."

Mrs. Babcock did as she was told, but she couldn't stop her eyes from glancing around the room.

"I see you lookin' around. And you can forget about the phone. I cut the line. So don't go gettin' any ideas. I got no problem shootin' a little old lady."

"I'm not surprised. You look mean. What? Did your mama not love you?"

"Shut up, lady."

She did, and he took a seat on the sofa across from her, his pistol resting on his leg. The dimwitted man was content sitting there doing nothing until he was told to do something, until someone told him to either leave or kill her. After what seemed like an hour, Mrs. Babcock heard a small outboard motor in the distance. Someone was on the water. The brute heard it too. What the brute didn't know was that four young men, well-armed and comfortable with the task ahead of them, had surrounded the house, the sound of their steps hidden by the steady rainfall. The noise from the boat provided the distraction they hoped it would.

The brute rose and walked to the window, pulled the curtains back, and saw two men on the boat paying close attention to the house he was standing in.

Without looking back over his shoulder, he called out to Mrs. Babcock.

"Now listen to me. You're going to poke your head out this sliding door and yell down to your friends that if they don't leave then I'm going to kill ya. You got that?"

And then he heard the unmistakable sound of a pistol being cocked.

"I don't think so, buster. Now slowly, very slowly, put down your gun and lie on the floor," said Mrs. Annabelle Babcock.

The brute looked over his shoulder and saw her pointing a gun at his head and he did as he was told.

"And people wonder why I carry such a large purse."

Chapter 61

Freedom

Sometime after Thanksgiving and after Eli had returned to the Bahamas to rescue Rachel, Rose Atkins slipped back into a coma. She never came out of it. A week before Christmas, Monty and their two boys, Eli and Walker, said their goodbyes at her bedside. It was their decision to hold a small memorial service for her.

In the weeks preceding her death, an interview Monty gave appeared in the *Post & Courier* in which he told the story of Rose's first husband, the letters she had received, the awful decision she made to scare her son Eli into running, and the forgiveness from the Lord she knew was her birthright and the peace she had found. It had been her decision to go public. Before doing so, Rose and Monty told Walker everything and asked him how he felt about it all, since no doubt his life would be impacted too. He was on board.

Lasko slipped Nash's noose, but Nash wasn't concerned. Lasko was no longer a source of communist rebel funding or money laundering for drug lords and other nefarious sorts. And according to Nash, the impact of his absence had already paid positive dividends. As for whether Lasko would resurface, only time would tell, but again, Nash wasn't concerned. In addition to the CIA being on his trail, so was the mob outfit from Chicago.

The Chicago outfit wasn't happy about Lasko's fund going under because they enjoyed the returns, but they made a tidy profit betting on Eli. They had applied the pressure that forced Lasko to utilize the casino's services, which meant that people who bet on Eli were paid and that Lasko never saw a dime. The Chicago outfit was happy to help Nash nail Lasko once they learned he was aiding communists and trafficking in young girls. According to a kingpin within the outfit, "I'm no saint, but I hate commies and pedophiles." It didn't hurt when Nash told him he could arrange to have the Department of Justice drop an investigation into an allegedly rigged union election.

* * *

Three weeks later, January 5th, 1979, at the Charleston County Hospital

The elevator door opened, and Eli and Rachel walked out and onto the third floor. At the nurses' station, Eli was greeted with a warm smile.

"Eli, it's so good to see you," said Nurse Turner.

"Thank you, ma'am. How is she?" Eli asked.

"She's doing fine. Just a little scare. Should be released in a couple of days. She's in Room 312."

"Thank you."

They walked to the end of the hallway and knocked lightly on the open door. Seeing a light on, Eli stepped into the room and saw Mrs. Babcock sitting up with a book in her lap.

"Eli, dear, come in, come in."

Eli and Rachel entered the room, hand in hand.

"Oh, you must be Rachel. The young girl I've been hearing all about."

"Yes, and you're Mrs. Babcock—I've heard so much about you! I can't tell you how happy I am to meet you."

"Oh. Enough of that. Now come closer so I can get a better look at the two of you."

"Mrs. B, what are you doing here? A hospital is no place for you," said Eli.

"Don't I know it, but just try telling these doctors anything."

The three of them conversed for a while. Mrs. B told Rachel stories of Eli hanging out at her bait and tackle store as a young boy, and Rachel told Mrs. B about the first time she'd laid eyes on him. Eli sat quietly at peace with these two women making a fuss over him, and who wouldn't? After a while, Eli wanted to know how she was doing. According to the doctors, Mrs. Babcock had suffered a small heart attack but would pull through and be good as new in no time. Eli and Rachel told her the good news, that they were to be married and they expected her in attendance.

"You can count on it," she said, punching her small right fist in the air.

Eli then turned to Rachel and asked if she could wait outside; he wanted a few words alone with Mrs. B. Rachel kissed Mrs. Babcock on the forehead and Eli gently on the lips and let herself out, closing the door behind her. Eli sat in the chair against the wall and waited for the words to come to him.

"What is it, child?"

"You were right. You were right."

Mrs. B said nothing, and with the silence implored him to go on.

"I didn't want any of this to happen, but it did. I could have stayed angry and grieved and felt sorry for myself, which I certainly did for a while, but to what end? But this is my life, and as you said to me, 'So what are you going to about it?' Well, I did something about it. I stopped feeling sorry for myself and started thinking of others, and somehow, through it all, Rachel entered my life."

Mrs. B smiled and tears filled her eyes.

"Of all the people in my life that could have stepped up to help me, it was you. How did you know? How did you know that everything would turn out okay, and how did you know what to say to me?"

"You've heard it said that the Lord works in mysterious ways?" she asked.

"Yes."

A calm descended upon the room and Mrs. Babcock pulled the covers back, turned her legs off to the side of the bed, stood, and walked over to Eli's chair. Standing before him with her arms outstretched, inviting him in for a hug, she told him. "Well, sometimes, you just need your mama."

* * *

Mrs. Babcock didn't make it to Eli and Rachel's wedding. In fact, she didn't make it out of the hospital. She had another heart attack later that day, a much larger one the second time, and died instantly. The attending doctor reported that it was painless. Her funeral was the largest her church had ever hosted. The police department manned the motorcade as if a president was being laid to rest, and Quaid was allowed to drive the hearse, carrying her coffin from the church to her burial site.

When Eli left the hospital that day, he left a free man, free to make a life for himself and start a family, and free to build a home. When Mrs. Babcock left the hospital that day, she went home.

THE END

For when the One Great Scorer comes to write against your name,
He marks, not that you won or lost, but how you played the game.

Grantland Rice

Afterword

Lach McGregor. The character Lach McGregor is inspired by the life story of Ernest Jones. Ernest Jones was born In Manchester, England in 1887 and was on his way to a promising career as a professional golfer when World War 1 broke out. He enlisted in 1914, and in 1916 he lost his leg below his right knee due to a grenade blast. He was determined though to make his way in the golf industry and did so as a teacher.

While standing on one leg, Ernest Jones was still able to shoot par and did so by concentrating on moving the clubhead instead of the body; he had to compensate for his missing leg. He refined his teaching methods in the United States where he taught from 1924 to 1960 and was renowned for giving up to 3,000 lessons a year to amateurs and professionals alike. He died in 1965 and he was inducted into the World Golf Teachers Hall of Fame in 1977.

In the teaching sessions between Lach McGregor and Aaron Westfield, I tried to convey Mr. Jones' teaching methods. If you are interested in learning more, I suggest you read his book entitled *Ernest Jones' Swing the Clubhead Method* which was originally titled *Swinging Into Golf.*

Bernard Lasko. The character Bernard Lasko was inspired by the real lives of Bernie Madoff and Robert Lee Vesco. Bernie Madoff was sentenced in 2009 to 150 years in prison for his financial crimes which amounted to the largest Ponzi scheme on record. He died in prison on April 14, 2021.

Robert Lee Vesco was called the "undisputed king of the fugitive financiers" by Slate magazine. At one point, Forbes magazine included him on the list of the richest 400 Americans and identified his occupation as "thief". He fled the United States for Costa Rica in 1973 while the SEC was investigating him for embezzling $220 million from several investment funds he managed. In 1978, he moved to Nassau, Bahamas where he evaded extradition to the United States.

His life was defined by one financial fraud after another. The CIA kept a close watch on him because of his relationship with Castro, drug lords such as Carlos Lehder, the co-founder of the Medellin Cartel, and other leaders of Caribbean nations which our CIA and State Department feared could become communist hotspots. Vesco was able to evade the authorities in the United States but not Cuba, and when he attempted to defraud Fidel Castro's brother, Raul, he ended up in a Cuban prison where he died in 2007.

Dick Wilson. Dick Wilson lived from 1904 to 1965 and designed over sixty golf courses in the United States. In the UK where the game of golf emerged, it was more typical to run your approach shot up onto a green. In the United States, and at the time Dick Wilson was designing courses, it became more accepted to approach greens with an airborne shot. Many of his golf courses feature elevated greens well protected by sand traps and configured at an angle to a direct approach shot from the fairway. In *Eli's Redemption,* Dick comments to Lach McGregor that Ben Hogan liked the course he designed at Pine Tree Golf Club in Boynton Beach, Florida. The conversation in the book occurs in 1956 but Dick Wilson did not design this course until 1960-61. According to the historical record, Ben Hogan called it the greatest flat course in America.

Acknowledgements

I would like to thank my wife, Lyn. Not only was she my first reader but she continued to critique and edit drafts throughout the process, and patiently listened to me talk out loud as I strategized storylines, twists, and turns. I wouldn't want to write a book without her support and encouragement. Excellent editorial services provided by David Aretha and Jonah Dorris helped turn my story into a book. I want to thank them for their professionalism. The cover was designed by Jerry Dorris. His work and creativity make the cover pop. I also want to thank those of you who read an Advanced Reader Copy and found all the mistakes I missed. You know who you are. Thank you!

Finally, I want to thank Justin Klemballa. Justin is a wonderful teacher (check out his YouTube channel) and an all-around good guy. He has very patiently been teaching me to swing the clubhead.

Paul was born and raised in the Atlanta, Georgia area. Paul and his wife, Lyn, met in college at Georgetown University and were married after Paul graduated from the University of Georgia School of Law. They moved to Phoenix, Arizona in 1988 where Paul embarked on a thirty-year business career before retiring so he could write fiction. Paul and Lyn raised three children together in Phoenix and now live in Charleston, South Carolina.

Eli's Redemption is Paul Attaway's second novel and is a follow-up to *Blood in the Low Country*. Writing, along with the move to Charleston, is a coming home of sorts, a return to the South. The history and culture of America's South is rich, complicated, at times comical, sad, tragic, uplifting, and inspiring. Paul hopes that his novels capture even a small bit of this tapestry.

You can learn more about Paul, his upcoming appearances, and his next novel at

www.paulattaway.com.

CPSIA information can be obtained
at www.ICGtesting.com
Printed in the USA
LVHW111646130622
721148LV00017B/584/J